Firestick
Once upon a
Time in Texas

FIRESTICK
ONCE UPON A
TIME IN TEXAS

WILLIAM W. JOHNSTONE
with J. A. Johnstone

PINNACLE BOOKS
Kensington Publishing Corp.
www.kensingtonbooks.com

PINNACLE BOOKS are published by

Kensington Publishing Corp.
119 West 40th Street
New York, NY 10018

PUBLISHER'S NOTE
Following the death of William W. Johnstone, the Johnstone family is working with a carefully selected writer to organize and complete Mr. Johnstone's outlines and many unfinished manuscripts to create additional novels in all of his series like The Last Gunfighter, Mountain Man, and Eagles, among others. This novel was inspired by Mr. Johnstone's superb storytelling.

All Kensington titles, imprints, and distributed lines are available at special quantity discounts for bulk purchases for sales promotions, premiums, fund-raising, educational, or institutional use. Special book excerpts or customized printings can also be created to fit specific needs. For details, write or phone the office of the Kensington sales manager: Kensington Publishing Corp., 119 West 40th Street, New York, NY 10018, attn: Sales Department; phone 1-800-221-2647.

PINNACLE BOOKS, the Pinnacle logo, and the WWJ steer head logo are Reg. U.S. Pat. & TM Off.

ISBN-13: 978-0-7860-4408-5
ISBN-10: 0-7860-4408-X

First printing: April 2019

10 9 8 7 6 5 4 3 2 1

Printed in the United States of America

Chapter 1

Later on, there would be those who claimed that the sight of Daisy Rawling in a dress was the first indicator of the trouble soon to follow. There was a natural order to things, these folks maintained, and if certain components started falling out of place then calamity was sure to result.

Be that as it may, on the day in question—the late summer afternoon when Daisy and Jim "Moosejaw" Hendricks came strolling arm in arm down the boardwalk of Trail Street—there definitely were no indications of calamity visible to anyone looking on, and particularly not to Daisy or Moosejaw. The pair and their romantic involvement were well known throughout the West Texas town of Buffalo Peak. Moosejaw was one of the town's deputy marshals; Daisy ran the local blacksmith shop. Despite this being a rather unusual role for a woman to fill, she was quite good at it and everyone had grown to recognize and accept the fact. This meant they also had grown to accept and expect the sight of her in work boots and bib overalls, not a frilly dress.

To the adoring eyes of Moosejaw, of course, Daisy looked perfectly fetching no matter what her attire, which wasn't to say that he didn't appreciate her added finery this day. Complemented by her butter yellow curls being specially arranged and even a touch of rouge applied to the already ruddy cheeks of her pretty face, the overall effect was cause for a bit of extra pride in his step as he walked beside her.

In fact, Moosejaw himself was also decked out a little finer than usual. A bright polish to his boots, a new pair of britches, a lightweight suit jacket and string tie to go with his starched white shirt, and a fresh shave to his broad face.

Though in sharp physical contrast to each other—he at six-feet-six and thick and stout as a post, she at five-two and also somewhat stout due to the physical demands of her trade yet still possessing a very full set of womanly curves—they made quite an imposing pair. And anyone taking note could plainly tell that today marked some special occasion for the two of them.

A demonstration of this was quickly evidenced by chief teller Oscar Holman when he greeted the pair as they entered the West Texas Cattlemen's Association Bank of Buffalo Peak. Holman, a spindly individual well under six feet in height, first craned his neck to look up at Moosejaw and then brought his eyes level to meet those of Daisy. Smiling earnestly, he said, "My, my! Deputy Hendricks and Miss Daisy. What a striking couple you make—as always. But, if you don't mind my saying, especially so today."

"We don't mind at all," Daisy replied. "But all the flattery you can roll off that silver tongue of yours, Oscar, still won't get you no better price on the set of new shoes you're needin' for that hayburner you ride."

Holman's smile stayed in place. "I never figured it would, Miss Daisy. You drive a firm but fair bargain . . . But never mind that. Since today appears to be something of a special occasion, may I ask what it is?"

"Today is Daisy's birthday," Moosejaw told him.

"But what you can't ask," Daisy was quick to add, "is how old I am. Especially not in front of my boyfriend and especially not when the gal in question swings a hammer for a livin'."

Holman held up his hands in a sign of surrender. "Such a question would never cross my lips."

"Smart man," Moosejaw said. "But not askin' certain questions still don't mean a celebration can't take place. So, soon as we're finished here, we're headed out to the Double M for a little whoop-de-doo of a birthday party that Firestick and Beartooth and some others are puttin' on."

"Well, now. That sounds like something not to be delayed any longer than necessary," said Holman. "So what business can I help you folks take care of so you can be on your way?"

"Like to spend a few minutes in the security room with my safe-deposit box," Daisy told him.

"The both of you?"

"Uh-huh. That a problem?"

"Of course not," Holman assured her. He came out from behind his teller's window and escorted them through a closed door and into a small room off one side of the bank's main lobby. There, he motioned them to thinly padded chairs hitched up before a bare wooden table. "Please have seats. I'll be right back with your lockbox. Would you like some water or perhaps coffee while you're here?"

Moosejaw wagged his head. "No, that's okay. We ain't gonna be long."

It was somewhat stuffy in the room, even though the thick adobe walls of the bank building kept it considerably cooler than the heat of the day outside.

Holman returned promptly with a square metal box that he placed on the table. "Here you are," he announced. "I'll latch the door for your privacy when I leave, but I'll be right outside. Just knock when you're ready. Then we'll get the box returned to the vault and you two can be on your way."

When Holman had again departed, Daisy produced a key and opened the box. Moosejaw tried not to, but he couldn't help but peek a little bit. The box was in Daisy's name, and had been since back before Moosejaw met her or had even arrived in the area. He knew that, in addition to a couple of items they had recently placed there together, the box's contents included many things deeply personal to Daisy. Among them, ones she had mentioned to him in the past, was the marriage certificate for her and her late husband, the deed to the blacksmith shop left in her name after he passed away, and some jewelry and other keepsakes that once belonged to her mother.

Of interest today, however, was one of the recently added items. A very special one.

Daisy reached in and from the larger box delicately withdrew a small, velvet-covered jewelry case. Her mouth curved into a wide, happy smile as she held it up for both of them to look at. Then, eyes dancing to Moosejaw, she said, "Can I open it up and have another look?"

"O' course you can. It's yours, ain't it?" said Moosejaw. "You just can't put it on yet."

Daisy opened the velvet case and took out a simple yet nicely crafted engagement ring. She held it between thumb and forefinger and gazed on it adoringly. "It's beautiful. I'll never get tired of looking at it," she said in a breathy voice. "And I'll never, ever take it off!"

"You'd better not."

Daisy's brows pinched together. "Well, if it's so blamed important to you that I keep it on, you big lug, you shoulda rattled your hocks a lot sooner and got it for me way before this!"

"Now let's not get started on that," Moosejaw said defensively. "The main thing is that now you've got it. Ain't that right?"

Daisy relented, though still harboring a faint pout. "I've got it, but I still can't wear it."

"That's comin' soon enough. Been our plan for a while now for me to slip it on you and then us announce our engagement as part of the birthday doin's. And that time is practically on us." Moosejaw grinned. "This was never meant to be a surprise birthday party, but we'll sure make it's a birthday party with a surprise as part of it."

Now Daisy was grinning, too. "I don't know how many times I thought I was going to bust these past few weeks, once the ring finally got here. Me, you, and Mr. Greeble from the general store, all holdin' back the secret. He's going to be there at the party today, too, isn't he?"

"Said he wouldn't miss it."

Daisy abruptly slipped the ring back into its holder slot and snapped the little box closed. Handing it to Moosejaw, she said, "Then I reckon *we* had better not be the ones to miss the shindig. Put that deep in a pocket and make sure not to lose it. Let's get ourselves gone from here and off to the party that's waitin' for us out at the Double M!"

While Daisy was closing and resecuring the lockbox, Moosejaw got up and went to the door. He gave it a rap with his knuckles, signaling Holman they were ready to be let out.

Chapter 2

Holman was slow to respond. By the time Moosejaw knocked a second time, Daisy had also gotten up from the table and carried the resecured lockbox over to stand beside him.

"Is something wrong?" she asked.

"Probably didn't expect us to be ready quite so soon. Likely got busy with another customer," Moosejaw said.

It wasn't much longer, though, before an impatient crease formed across his broad forehead and he was reaching to knock a third time. Before his knuckles made contact, though, he heard the sound of the latch shooting back on the other side and then the door swung open wide.

The neatly dressed Oscar Holman wasn't standing there to usher them out, however. Instead it was a tall, rawboned *hombre* decked out in dusty, hard-worn trail clothes and sporting several days' worth of whiskers on a weathered, sneering face.

But even more surprising and attention-grabbing was the long-barreled Remington revolver in his fist and the threatening way he waved the gaping hole of its muzzle under Moosejaw's nose.

"That's right, big man," the *hombre* growled. "Come ahead on out. Just step slow and easy and keep those hands up where I can see 'em plain. Same for the gal, too—elsewise that string tie of yours is gonna be danglin' from a neck with its head blowed off, you understand?"

Daisy drew in a sharp breath. Moosejaw clenched his teeth and said nothing. But he lifted his hands to shoulder height and took a slow step forward, just as he'd been told.

"You got it. Keep comin', just like that," the stranger said, backing up with his gun never wavering from Moosejaw's face. "Out to the middle of the room where you can join the others."

Moosejaw and Daisy exited the secure room. She kept close behind him. He could hear her breaths coming in quick little gasps and feel a sharp corner of the lockbox poking him in the back. But what he was more interested in was the scene being revealed to them as they eased into the bank's main lobby.

Obviously, a robbery was in progress. Holman, two other tellers, and two bank customers, one of them a woman, lay facedown on the floor. All appeared to be alive and unharmed. Over beside the front door, Hefty Shallihan, the bank guard, was slumped half-in, half-out of the chair he occupied while on duty. His shotgun lay on the floor beside his chair, and one side of his loosely hanging head bore a bloody gash from having been struck viciously by a hard object. Clearly, he hadn't kept a close enough eye on somebody who was able to walk up and bash him into unconsciousness.

Across the room, behind the teller windows and the waist-high counter that separated the lobby from the desks and workstations of bank personnel, two other men dressed similar to the first, complete with guns prominently displayed on their hips, were frantically rummaging through cash drawers and working their way toward the vault and its wide-open door. Bank president Jason Trugood and a bespectacled, well-dressed elderly man Moosejaw had never seen before sat ashen-faced and frozen at Trugood's spacious desk, obviously under threat not to move or try anything nervy in an attempt to halt what was under way.

Moosejaw took all of this in with a quick, thorough sweep of his eyes. It didn't look good. The bank robbers clearly knew what they were doing . . . had done this before. And any doubt as to how ruthless they were capable of being could be answered with one glance at the condition of Hefty Shallihan. Had the deputy's badge Moosejaw was wearing pinned to his shirt not been hidden by the lapel of the suit jacket he happened to have on and buttoned, he had a hunch that such ruthlessness might have been dished out to him as well.

What was more, the timing couldn't have been worse for the town or better for the robbers. Moosejaw's partners and fellow lawmen were already out at the Double M, preparing for the birthday party. Also invited and therefore likely already present were close friends from town and a few surrounding ranches—in other words, almost every man who'd proven in the past competent enough and trustworthy enough to be counted on for backup in a time of trouble.

Which meant that, for this moment that had suddenly turned very troublesome, Buffalo Peak was left quite vulnerable.

Except for Moosejaw.

Any attempt to stop these skunks in their tracks or, at the very least, give chase in the crucial minutes immediately on the heels of their flight, was resting solely on him. It was a heavy weight, even for his broad shoulders.

"Got two more here, Tuscarora," the first robber called to one of the men rifling for cash. "Came out of some room off to the side—where we heard that knocking."

"You know what to do. Keep 'em quiet and get 'em down on the floor with the others," said the man addressed as Tuscarora.

"You want me to strip 'em of their valuables first?"

Tuscarora glanced around, appearing somewhat annoyed. He was a big man, thick through the middle but thicker still through the shoulders. He had heavy-lidded, almost sleepy-looking eyes, but one glimpse of them told Moosejaw that anybody misreading that sleepy look and not seeing the danger simmering behind it would be making a big mistake.

"What the hell do you think, Hank?" he snarled in response to the latter's question. "Of course you should strip them of any valuables they got."

Hank's eyes bored into Moosejaw and Daisy with renewed intensity. He made a stabbing motion with the Remington.

"You heard the man. Fork over your wallet, watch, any jewelry you got, and lay it all on that counter over there. Be quick about it and don't make me have to come diggin' or else . . ." He paused, suddenly spotting the lockbox Daisy had inadvertently revealed after previously keeping it out of sight behind Moosejaw. "Say, what's in the box there, sweetheart?"

"Nothing of any value to you," Daisy was quick to say. "Just some personal papers and family keepsakes."

"Uh-huh. Keepsakes like fancy broaches and such handed down from your ma and grandmaw. Is that it?"

"No. Nothing like that," Daisy insisted. "Just paperwork, I tell you. Things with value—sentimental value—only to me."

"We'll be the judge of what we think is valuable," Hank told her. "So get that box open and spill it out on the counter over there, like I told you!"

Inwardly, Moosejaw bristled at Daisy being the subject of Hank's demands. But, on the strictly practical side, the robber's attention was momentarily diverted from him. This meant that the gun riding in a hip holster under Moosejaw's suit jacket—a .45-caliber Schofield—was going unnoticed, same as his badge. The fact his jacket was buttoned over the Schofield while Hank's gun was already drawn hardly gave the big deputy any kind of edge, but nevertheless it was something: a chance, no matter how slight. All Moosejaw had to do was prolong this bit of oversight on Hank's part and try to find a way to take advantage of it.

"Best do like he says," Moosejaw said over his shoulder to Daisy. "Go ahead and give him the box."

"I will not!"

"You will, one way or the other," Hank told her.

"It ain't worth takin' a bullet over," Moosejaw urged.

Hank chuckled nastily. "You oughta listen to your boyfriend, gal. Big ox is smarter than he looks. Maybe a little yellow, too, on account of he's worried about catchin' a bullet of his own. But it all shakes out the same for you. Now open up that damn box."

Seeing the glimmer of an opening, the one whisker of a chance he might have to turn this situation around, Moosejaw gritted his teeth and said again, "Just go ahead and do it, Daisy—give him the box!"

And so that's what Daisy did. Leaning away from Moosejaw, she abruptly and unexpectedly thrust out her arms and tossed the box in Hank's direction. The move so startled the latter that he reacted out of pure instinct and reached quickly, awkwardly, to try and catch what was pitched toward him.

This resulted in two failures. First, Hank fumbled the box, failing to get a good grip on it because of the gun he was already clutching in one hand. Second, the attempt caused him to momentarily jerk his gun hand down, failing to keep Moosejaw covered as he did so.

This was the opening the big deputy was hoping for.

Chapter 3

Moving with impressive speed, especially for a man his size, Moosejaw immediately yanked his suit coat open and swept his right hand down to grab for the .45 on his hip. As part of the same movement, he stepped back slightly, giving Daisy a sharp shoulder bump that sent her staggering out of the way.

And then the .45 was streaking out of its holster and his arm was a blur as it extended out in Hank's direction.

Realizing almost instantly that he'd made the mistake of allowing his attention to be diverted, Hank's gun arm was also in motion as he tried to swing the Remington back up so it was once again aimed at Moosejaw. He almost made it . . . Almost.

But Moosejaw's .45 spoke first, the sound a deafening roar that filled the bank lobby and sent a slug slamming into Hank, splitting his sternum like a wishbone. The robber spun away from the impact, yelping in pain as he pitched to the floor while simultaneously triggering a round from his Remington that smacked hollowly against the base of the service counter.

The woman on the floor clapped her hands over her ears and screamed shrilly in concert with the gun blasts.

With Hank out of the way, Moosejaw knew all too well that he'd taken care of only one-third of the problem that needed dealing with. At the first inkling of the disturbance initiated by Daisy tossing her lock-box, the remaining two men on the other side of the partition were alerted and had begun to react. And their reactions were swift and deadly intentioned.

Moosejaw hadn't forgotten the undercurrent of extreme danger he'd sensed from just one glimpse into the sleepy eyes of the one called Tuscarora, the apparent leader of the outlaw trio. Moosejaw had known from that moment that, if any kind of action broke out and he was given a choice, Tuscarora would be the main one to try and take out.

With that still in mind, Moosejaw immediately swung his gun hand toward the spot where he'd fixed Tuscarora's position from the corner of his eye, right before firing on Hank.

Trouble was, the outlaw boss's quick reflexes already had him on the move. Palming a sleek, black-handled Colt, he'd wheeled partway around and was dropping into a half crouch as he edged in behind the corner of a desk. Moosejaw tracked the movement, continuing to swing his arm. This ended with him over-correcting by several inches and then hurrying his shot. The bullet tore into the desktop Tuscarora was trying to get behind, gouging under a stack of papers and sending them fluttering through the air.

Instead of dropping to the floor, Tuscarora thrust his gun hand over the top of the desk and triggered a return round. But Moosejaw was in motion himself by then. He followed his shot by lunging forward and going into his own half crouch, meaning to drop in behind the counter for cover. Tuscarora's bullet sailed close above him as he rushed ahead. Before reaching the counter and dropping too low, Moosejaw had time for a second shot. He made it count. Tuscarora's slight pause to get off his own shot presented, just for an instant, a perfectly still head-and-shoulders target. And this time Moosejaw's bullet found the bull's-eye—right in the center of the outlaw boss's forehead.

Tuscarora flew backward, a red-rimmed black hole like a third eye appearing in wide-open contrast to the droopy-lidded pair just under it. Moosejaw had no time to savor the view, however, before he hit the floor and skidded in close to the front side of the counter that separated the lobby from the vault and employee area on the other side. He made it just in time, too, before a rapid-fire blast of three shots skimmed across the top of the counter and sizzled through the air above his head. The remaining would-be robber—a whip-thin individual with a face like a hatchet blade, that was the impression left by Moosejaw's brief glimpse of him earlier—clearly wasn't ready to go down without a fight.

Moosejaw pressed tighter against the face of the counter. Powder smoke stung his nose as he drew in some quick breaths. He made a scan of the lobby, assuring himself that everything there was still the same—no one had caught an errant slug or ricochet. Holman and the others were still hugging the floor, the woman customer done screaming for now, reduced to whimpering and trembling in terror.

Daisy, after the shove Moosejaw had given her to get her out of the line of fire, had shown the sense to drop to the floor, too. They made eye contact now. Moosejaw could see a trace of fear on her face. Typical of Daisy, he also saw anger and determination. And one more thing: Shining in the eyes of the woman he loved, he saw confidence in him.

Moosejaw's mind raced. What did he do next to earn that confidence? He'd opened up the ball on this, so it was up to him to see it through and make it come out right for the sake of Daisy and the others. It crossed his thoughts to shout out to the hatchet-faced remaining robber—identify himself as an officer of the law and implore the man to throw down his gun and surrender.

But that was no good. Any time wasted talking would only give Hatchet Face a chance to realize he had an ace up his sleeve. He still had bank president Trugood and the other elderly businessman over there with him. All he'd have to do was put a gun to one of their heads, declare them a hostage, and he'd have a bargaining chip to force Moosejaw to throw down his gun.

No, talking was no good. Moosejaw had to act and act fast before the momentum he'd gained fell apart and turned against him.

All these things coursed through the big deputy's mind in only a second or two. The three shots Hatchet Face had blasted his way were still ringing in the air.

Suddenly, Moosejaw had a plan and without hesitation he put it in motion. It was one of the oldest tricks in the book, but it was the best he could come up with. And in the raw, heightened tension of the moment, he reckoned it had at least even odds of working.

With his left hand, he seized a brass cuspidor—one

of three spaced out along the front of the service counter near where he crouched. Gathering his feet under him, gripping the Schofield tight in his right hand, Moosejaw caught a quick breath and then launched into action. First he flung the cuspidor up and over the counter, aiming it toward the opposite side of the room from where he figured Hatchet Face to be. As the brass vessel whistled through the air before landing with a loud clatter, Moosejaw's powerful legs uncoiled and thrust him to a standing position. He pivoted as part of this motion, so that he came up facing across the counter and extending his gun arm over its top.

Hatchet Face was a dozen feet away, poised at the edge of the desk where Trugood and the elderly businessman were cowering. Hatchet Face had a Colt Navy in his fist, and it appeared he'd been in the act of threatening the two men with it. But right about then was when the thrown cuspidor served its purpose, jerking away the would-be robber's attention so that his face turned toward the clattering brass and his gun started to swing in that direction also.

Moosejaw caught him in mid-turn. He triggered his Schofield twice. The slugs punched into Hatchet Face, lifted him up on his toes, and bent his upper body over backward at an impossible angle before his feet and legs kicked out from under him and he went toppling to the floor like a bundle of sticks.

Chapter 4

The departure of Moosejaw and Daisy for Daisy's birthday party out at the Double M had to be postponed.

Once the shooting was over inside the bank, people began to gather cautiously in the street out front. After determining that all three of the men he'd shot were dead and no longer a threat, Moosejaw hurried outside to check and make sure they had no accomplices. The fact that three horses remained tied at the hitchrail and there were no signs or reports of anyone riding away suddenly made it evident that the bodies inside represented the only ones in on the robbery.

Having satisfied himself of that, Moosejaw began barking orders at some of the townsmen who were now milling around. He sent men after the doctor and the undertaker, then told a third man to ride out to the Double M and report to those assembled there what had happened.

Back in the bank lobby, Moosejaw assisted Holman and one of the other tellers in gently lifting the injured Hefty Shallihan down off his chair and laying him out on the floor, making him as comfortable as possible until the doctor arrived.

While they were doing that, Daisy did her best to calm down the still-terrified woman customer, a middle-aged widow named Hester Mead. Moosejaw went over and knelt beside them to see if he could somehow lend a hand. On the way, he paused long enough to say to Holman, "Have somebody get a glass of water for this woman. And then, since there's gonna be a whole herd of folks stompin' through here in a minute, you and Trugood and your tellers had better gather up the contents of those cash drawers and whatever else the robbers tore apart. Lock it all in the vault. You can sort through it and put it back in order later on, after things have calmed down a mite."

As Moosejaw predicted, the next hour saw a flurry of activity inside the bank. The undertaker and his assistants removed the bodies of the three slain men, leaving bank employees the slightly less distasteful job of cleaning up the blood and starting to put things back in order. Nelson Greaves, the town's young and relatively new doctor, arrived to take care of Hefty Shallihan's head wound—announcing, in the end, that the tough old bank guard would live but would require some substantial healing time. By the time the doctor got to Hester Mead, Daisy had her mostly calmed down and her teenaged daughter had also shown up to help. Greaves nevertheless gave the woman a mild sedative and suggested the daughter take her on home for some additional rest.

While all this was going on, Moosejaw prowled the scene, making sure others did what was expected of them in order to return things to normal as soon as possible, tossing an order now and then when he saw something not to his liking, a suggestion here and there to help move things along.

During this, surprisingly little was spoken about the details of the attempted robbery. Simply that it had occurred but had been unsuccessful. But then, as her daughter was ushering Hester Mead toward the front door, the widow turned suddenly and said to Moosejaw, "Thank you, Deputy. Thank God for you and your bravery—only he knows what dreadful fate might been in store for all of us if you hadn't been here to act on our behalf."

Those few words were like the crack in a dike that suddenly released a flood of further comments and questions. All at once everybody present was clamoring to hear more. And though Moosejaw was clearly ill at ease and reluctant to have words like "bravery" and "hero" tossed his way, someone who was eager to take the lead in heaping on that kind of praise was none other than the elderly businessman who'd been seated with bank president Trugood all during the holdup attempt.

After first announcing himself, rather pompously, as one Rupert Oswald, a senior examiner for the Cattlemen's Association chain of banks, the bespectacled little man went on to proclaim, "Never in all my days—and I was present in Abilene, I'll have you know, during the time none other than Wild Bill Hickok was at his most prominent—have I ever seen a more impressive demonstration of bravery and gunmanship than I witnessed here today! This amazingly fearless deputy of yours went up against not one, not two, but *three* of the toughest hardcases ever to ride into any town. Leading them was the notorious shootist and villain, Tuscarora Billings. Seconding him, of only slightly less renown, was Needles Whitney. The third scoundrel, alas, I did not recognize. But here's the thing . . . he had his gun *already drawn* on your brave deputy. Yet, heroically and with lightning-like speed in his hand, this man"—here he made a dramatic sweep of his arm, indicating Moosejaw—"was able to draw his own weapon and shoot down the cur like the mangy dog he was!"

Gasps of amazement and appreciation rippled through the crowd.

Bank president Trugood was quick to join in. "It's absolutely true, every word of it. That first robber was outgunned even though the lowdown snake already had the drop on Moosejaw. Then, in a split second, Moosejaw wheeled and outdrew Tuscarora Billings."

"Now wait a minute," Moosejaw protested. "That ain't quite all there was to it. Tuscarora got off a shot, too, remember. And before that—"

"All the more to the point!" insisted Oswald. "With guns drawn against him and bullets flying all around, this brave man stood his ground and dispatched one after another of the bloodthirsty devils. Like the lady said a minute ago—all of our lives were in danger from those cutthroats. There's little doubt, at least in my mind, that they would have gunned down each and every one of us before they rode away. Would have, that is, if not for the fearless action of this un-deniable hero." Oswald marched up to stand before Moosejaw and thrust out his hand. "Please allow me the honor of shaking your hand, sir. I have no doubt that I owe you my very life!"

Somewhat tentatively, still bewildered and ill at ease under this wash of lofty praise, Moosejaw took the man's small, dainty hand in his big paw, saying, "I'm pleased to shake hands with you, mister, but I just did what needed doin' and came out of it lucky. You're makin' a lot more of it than it really was and I'd just as soon—"

"More of it than it was?" said Oswald, cutting him off again. "How can you say such a thing? You risked your life to save all the rest of us. Not to mention the bank money—deposits and savings belonging to good citizens throughout this community. And by dispatching the likes of Tuscarora Billings and Needles Whitney, who knows how many others you saved by stopping them from continuing on with their villainy and terrorizing ways?"

More and more people were crowding in from the street and now even Holman joined in.

"For heaven's sake, Deputy Hendricks," he said, "there's no call for false modesty. You're a hero deserving of all the accolades that can be bestowed on you."

"And I fully intend to see that such accolades come from far and wide," proclaimed Oswald. "I will be wiring Association headquarters at my very first opportunity and advising them what has occurred here. I further aim to see to it that newspapers all across Texas are notified and encouraged to carry reports of same. The days of lawlessness and pillaging by the likes of Billings and Whitney are coming to an end in our great state, ground out even in small towns like Buffalo Peak by decent, dedicated men who want to see peace and progress. Men like Deputy Moosejaw Hendricks, whose name should be repeated and held in esteem by all who hear it."

"Now hold on a minute!" This time Moosejaw's voice had a genuinely annoyed boom to it. "I'm real pleased to hear all these kind words aimed my way. Any man would be. But let's not get carried away. Maybe I don't *want* my name blabbed all over creation. I did what I done because . . . well, it was the right thing to do. It was my job to stop those varmints from robbin' the bank. But that don't make me nothing special. I figure there's plenty of other men around town who would have acted the same if they'd been in my place." He swept his gaze over the faces crowded in around him. "So let's just leave it at that, okay? Let's just be thankful that no innocent folks got hurt any worse than they did."

Chapter 5

Elwood "Firestick" McQueen, the marshal of Buffalo Peak, and Malachi "Beartooth" Skinner, his other deputy, came riding in to answer Moosejaw's summons just as the big fellow was getting the crowd dispersed. In addition to representing the law in Buffalo Peak, the three men—friends of long standing dating back to their days as mountain men in the high reaches of the distant Rockies—were partners in a horse-ranching operation, the Double M.

During those mountain man days, the trio had not only forged their lasting friendship but had also earned from the Indians they skirmished against the colorful nicknames that continued to endure. "Firestick" because of his unerring accuracy with a long gun—a Hawken in the early days, repeating rifles later on; "Beartooth" due to the knife he wielded so savagely and kept as sharp and deadly as a grizzly fang; and "Moosejaw" as the result of an occasion when the big man seized the jawbone of a moose skeleton and used it to beat back some attacking braves.

"'Bout time you two slowpokes showed up,"

Moosejaw drawled now, gazing up at his two friends from where he stood leaning against an awning post in front of the bank. Daisy stood close at his side.

Firestick cocked one eyebrow. "*Us* slowpokes? You're the ones runnin' late for your own party . . . well, Daisy's party, that is." The marshal was a solid six-footer in his middle fifties, still ruggedly built, with ice blue eyes and an air of quiet confidence that made him a natural leader.

"And it's a good thing we were runnin' a little late," replied Daisy. "A good thing for the bank and everybody who has money in it."

"Wes Peavey said something about a robbery?" Beartooth asked. He was a whisker under six feet, somewhat leaner than his two close comrades though packed with deceptive, sinewy musculature. Also deceptive was the dimpled chin and roguish grin that frequently split his narrow face—a grin that, if he was sufficiently provoked, could turn into a feral snarl that was no deception at all.

Wes Peavey, the man Beartooth had mentioned, was the townsman Moosejaw had sent to fetch him and Firestick. They'd left him in the dust as they hurried to Buffalo Peak.

"An *attempted* robbery," Moosejaw corrected. He slipped his arm around Daisy and added, "Too bad for them, we were on hand when the varmints made their try. With some help from my gal here, I got lucky and managed to foul things up for 'em."

"Fouled it up for 'em, permanent-like," Daisy said. "But all I did was toss a little ol' box to distract one of 'em."

Beartooth leaned forward in his saddle and rested a forearm on the pommel. "Aw, I got a hunch there was more to it than that. I bet you was such a dazzlin' sight, all prettied up in that dress and all, that those owlhoots couldn't keep their eyes off you. *That's* what musta really distracted 'em so Moosejaw could make his play."

Daisy blushed furiously but couldn't hold back a smile. "Beartooth, you golden-throated rascal. You can keep complimentin' me all day long and I won't mind a bit. But no matter what you say, it was my big, brave lug of a man here who was the hero of the day."

"Now don't start that hero stuff again," Moosejaw was quick to say, doing some blushing of his own in front of his pals. He looked around, not wanting to draw renewed attention from Oswald or Trugood. "Tell you what. Things are under control here now. Let's go on down to the jail where nobody will come around to bother us, and I'll fill you in on everything."

The lengthening shadows of early evening were reaching in through the windows of the marshal's office at the front of the jail building. Moosejaw had finished giving Firestick and Beartooth a thorough rundown of how the attempted robbery had gone. They were all settled into chairs hitched up around the marshal's desk. Daisy was seated beside Moosejaw, her hand resting on his arm as he talked.

When his big pal was done relating everything, Beartooth leaned back in his chair and gave a low whistle.

"Well, I gotta tell you, old pard, you have had yourself one eventful afternoon. Any time you can trim the wicks on a couple of hard burners like Tuscarora

Billings and Needles Whitney, that's a mighty tough chore to get on the other side of."

"Not to mention the other fella—Hank Scorp," added Firestick. "He didn't have himself a rep as big as the other two, but he was an up-and-comer in their world. The owlhoot world, that is."

Beartooth grunted. "The only direction he's goin' now is down. Six feet for starters. Then a little lower yet, I reckon, before he's done."

Moosejaw blew out a breath. "I never recognized none of 'em at the start. After Tuscarora got called by name, I figured out who he was. Then, after I went to check on him once he was down, I placed Needles. I never would have recognized that Hank fella, though. Never even heard the name before."

Before coming to the jail, they had stopped by the undertaker's so Firestick and Beartooth could have their own looks at the slain men. Firestick said now, "I was only able to identify him based on a wanted dodger that came through a while back. Something it wouldn't be a bad idea for you two to get more in the habit of payin' attention to when they show up."

Straightening in his chair, Beartooth said, "For cryin' out loud, Firestick. Moosejaw just blazed down three of the toughest *hombres* ridin' the back trails and you're criticizin' him for not shufflin' regular enough through a pile of musty old wanted posters?"

"I wasn't criticizin'," Firestick said. "I was just pointin' out that sometimes it's better to have a little advance warnin' on who you're goin' up against. When it comes to how you handle a thing, there's a difference in how you might brace a desperate *hombre* who's takin' the wrong side for maybe the first time or a seasoned hardcase who's been at the game a long, hard while."

Still prodding, Beartooth said, "So you're sayin' Moosejaw could have played it better if he'd've recognized who it was he was goin' up against?"

"Ain't sayin' no such thing," Firestick growled, getting annoyed. "I don't see how anybody could have played it any better than he did today. I just want him—and all of us, as far as that goes—to go at things as smart and prepared as possible."

"There you go, Moosejaw," said Beartooth, suddenly showing a wry smile. "I got it out of him to say he can't see how you could've handled today any better than you did. That's about as close to a compliment as the ornery old cuss is likely to hand out."

"That's okay," Moosejaw said with a wave of his hand. "The way Jason Trugood and that bank examiner fella was carryin' on, I got about all the compliments I could stand. All I wanted was to try and stop that robbery and keep anybody—includin' me and Daisy—from gettin' hurt. I had a hunch those skunks was primed to do some shootin' before they was done, no matter what."

Firestick gave a grim nod. "That's exactly how they've played it in the past. Seemed like none of 'em—especially Needles Whitney—was happy with just takin' money. They seldom rode away without some innocent blood bein' left spilled behind 'em."

"Well, thank God—and my Moosejaw—it didn't go that way today," said Daisy, who'd kept uncharacteristically quiet up to that point. "So, now that you've covered the whole thing seven ways from Sunday, how about giving it a rest for a while? Surely there must be something less gruesome you can think of to talk about."

"As a matter of fact, there is," said Moosejaw. "I know exactly the right thing to talk about and we have exactly the right people present for it." Easing his arm out from under Daisy's hand, the big deputy rose up from his chair. All eyes followed his movements. He stepped around and stood in front of Daisy. He kept his eyes locked on hers, though his words were for Firestick and Beartooth as he reached into the inside breast pocket of his suit coat, saying, "This is something we were going to spring on everybody as part of the birthday party out at the ranch. But those plans got sorta knocked sideways. Well, I been bustin' with this secret long enough and I don't aim to wait no more."

Sinking to one knee, Moosejaw withdrew the little velvet-covered jewelry box and pried it open with a thumb. Taking the ring from inside, he held it up momentarily for his two pals to get a good look at, then extended it toward Daisy, who by now was shiny-eyed and wearing a huge smile of delight.

"She already gave me her answer once," Moosejaw said, "but I want to hear it again and I want you two fellas, my best friends, to hear it with me. Daisy Rawling, will you take me as your husband?"

The ring slipped smoothly over Daisy's finger. An instant after it was in place, she lunged forward out of her chair and threw her arms around Moosejaw with such force that she nearly bowled him over.

"Of course I will, you big lug!" she exclaimed. "You know how bad and for how long I've wanted to hear you say those words!"

Firestick and Beartooth came out of their chairs,

too, their faces split into wide smiles as they reached
to shake Moosejaw's hand and administer some hearty
slaps to his broad back. Next came a round of hugs
given to and then returned by—with bone-crunching
eagerness—a jubilant Daisy.

"So when's the big day?" Firestick wanted to know.
"That's the next question that needs to be answered."

Back on his feet again, Moosejaw said, "We don't
have an exact date set yet. We're thinkin' sometime
next spring. A week or so back I put a down payment
on the old Brennan place—you know, that little cabin
and piece of land that sits just west of town? We're
gonna live there. It's gonna take me a while to get it
fixed up the way we want it, but when it's ready it'll be
sorta halfway between the ranch and town for me, and
not too far out from her blacksmith shop for Daisy."

Firestick wagged his head. "You *have* been busy,
you sonofagun—I'm surprised you had time to fit
in a little detail like stoppin' a bank robbery cold in
its tracks."

"Ain't he wonderful?" gushed Daisy. She held out her
hand at arm's length, admiring the ring now in place.
"And ain't this just a wonderful day? Now, at last, I can
start showing off my ring and announcing to everybody
that we're engaged! The only thing that could make it
better is if we would've been able to do it at the party,
with everybody there, like we planned." She stopped
short, catching herself, and then quickly added, "Not
to say that you two—Firestick and Beartooth—ain't
still the most important ones to know about it."

"And it don't mean this is the end of you bein' important," said Moosejaw soberly. "Next up, I'll be
lookin' to the two of you to stand up with me at the
wedding as my best men."

Beartooth grinned. "Hell, that ain't no problem—we're the best men wherever we go!"

"And something more, as far as Daisy's hankerin' to show off that shiny bauble and make the big announcement in front of a bigger crowd," said Firestick. "It ain't quite the lost opportunity you seem to think."

Daisy looked puzzled. "How so?"

"Aw, come on. You don't think we'd let a little thing like a bank robbery stand in the way of a good party, do you?" said Beartooth.

"When we heard there was a robbery but nobody that mattered got hurt too bad," Firestick explained further, "we saw how me and Beartooth still had to hightail it on into town. And everybody else gathered out at the ranch saw how you and Moosejaw, since you was caught in the middle of the fracas, would be tied up here for a while longer. So that's when they decided that if you couldn't make it out there for your party, then they'd bring the party to you."

Daisy's eyes widened. "You mean . . . ?"

"I mean," said Firestick, "that unless my ears was playin' tricks on me a little while ago, I heard a bunch of horses and a couple wagons pass by in the street outside. Based on that, I calculate that if we was all to mosey over to the Mallory House dining room right about now, it'd be a pretty safe bet we'd find a whole passel of folks and a big ol' birthday cake waitin' for a certain birthday gal to finally show up so's they could commence celebratin'."

Daisy squealed with delight. "I can't believe it!"

"You'd better believe it, 'cause it's true," Beartooth told her. "And, I gotta warn you, I'm feelin' way past due for a piece of that cake. With or without you, I ain't gonna be able to hold myself back much longer."

"Well, it sure ain't gonna be without me!" Daisy told him. But then she stopped suddenly, frowning.

"What's the matter?" Moosejaw wanted to know.

Her expression remaining troubled, Daisy's eyes touched each of the three men surrounding her. "Wouldn't it be in dreadful bad taste," she said, "to go and celebrate a party only a few yards from where three men died such a short time ago?"

Nobody spoke right away. Until Firestick said, "Those weren't three men, Daise. They might've been critters who stood up on their hind legs, but all they really were was vermin who dragged their bellies through the lowest slime they could find. Part of what we'd be celebratin' is the fact that they've gone back to the slime, permanent-like, and you and all the other good folks who were in that bank earlier today are still alive."

Daisy considered a moment, then managed a tentative smile. Her eyes brightening again, she said, "You're right. Let's go celebrate being alive!"

Chapter 6

The stagecoach run from Presidio to Sierra Blanca passed through Buffalo Peak once a week. It so happened that, on the day after the attempted bank robbery, the coach was bound for Presidio when it made its scheduled stop and then rolled on with Rupert Oswald, the ebullient Cattlemen's Association bank examiner, as one of its passengers.

In the days following—except for a handful of rambunctious young boys armed with toy wooden guns who kept reenacting the event—the buzz around Buffalo Peak regarding the failed holdup died down relatively soon. Daisy's birthday—and engagement—party took place to the fun and enjoyment of all, the bodies of the would-be robbers were buried, the bloodstains in the bank got cleaned up, and Hefty Shallihan was on the road to recovery. Once the townspeople had heard the gory details for the second or third time, they moved on to daily grinds that were decidedly less exciting but also thankfully minus the danger.

In fact, the announced engagement of Moosejaw

and Daisy might even have kept tongues wagging longer and busier. Much of this, of course, was due to Daisy's habit of thrusting her bejeweled hand in front of everyone who ventured anywhere near her blacksmith shop and badgering admiring statements out of them.

It wasn't until the stage returned a week later, this time on its run *from* Presidio, that the matter of the attempted bank holdup and Moosejaw's role in stopping it once more leaped to prominence. This resulted from among the stack of newspapers that were a regular part of the mail drop-off. While the local telegraph office could be counted on for short bursts of breaking news, it was the weekly delivery of these publications that citizens looked forward to for detailed accounts of happenings around the country and indeed the world. Some papers came all the way from El Paso and Dallas, their delivery delayed to the point where the contents could hardly be called news, but the information they contained was still of interest to a number of folks.

The papers that appealed to most, however, were those from closer sources, namely the Presidio *Press* and the Fort Davis *Dispatch*. And it was in editions of both of these that front-page coverage of the recent holdup attempt and Moosejaw's related actions fanned a whole new wave of excitement and appreciation.

Somehow, merely *hearing* about it was one thing, but *reading* about it—and splashed all over the front page of two different papers no less—was quite another. Nor did it hurt that the events were so vividly rendered under headlines like DEATH-DEFYING DEPUTY PREVAILS OVER 3-TO-1 ODDS! and THE LONG, LIGHTNING-FAST GUN ARM OF THE LAW!

As was common, Firestick was enjoying a quiet lunch with Kate Mallory in the dining room of her hotel, the Mallory House, when the stage rolled in that day. It was well understood around town that Firestick and Kate were romantically involved, and had been for some time now. They did nothing to deny this relationship, nor did they flaunt it unduly. The way things were building between them, they recognized as well or better than anybody that they likely would marry one day.

But each also recognized that they were both mature adults set in their individual ways, and any attempted union of those ways wasn't something to be rushed into. So they were taking their time and letting what they felt for one another continue to build and strengthen at its own pace . . .

Although, truth be told, the recent announcement from close friends Moosejaw and Daisy might have served to nudge things along just a little bit faster. The newly engaged couple had become a frequent subject of discussion when the marshal and his lady were together, today being yet another example.

"Moosejaw's out at the cabin again this afternoon," Firestick was saying, "clearin' and burnin' brush like he had to have the place ready by next week instead of next year. He's been goin' at it steady, every spare minute he gets."

"Is he shirking his other duties?" Kate asked.

"Moosejaw?" Firestick shook his head. "No, he'd never do anything like that. He takes care of all his other obligations like always. Maybe even a mite prompter. Then, as soon as those are met, he's off to that cabin. He's even showed up late for supper out at the ranch a couple of times lately . . . and

Moosejaw bein' late for a meal just ain't something that ever happens."

Kate smiled. She was a raven-haired beauty with smoldering dark eyes and a contrastingly bright smile that could light up a room.

"Sounds like a sure sign of true love."

Firestick pushed a forkful of mashed potatoes into his mouth, then said, "Heck, he already *was* in love. For some time now. But it never made him act like this before."

"Apparently making it official—you know, the ring and putting money down on the cabin and him and Daisy making their announcement to everybody and all—lit some kind of fire under him. Maybe setting everything in motion caused him to realize he likes the idea of marriage even better than he thought he would."

Firestick cocked an eyebrow. "You sayin' you think the two of 'em might haul off and get hitched sooner?"

"Not necessarily. Though I wouldn't say it's impossible, either. You know how much Daisy adores him and how long she chased him—she'd take the vows in a heartbeat and live in a sod hut if Moosejaw asked her to."

"A week ago, I'd've said that would never happen." Firestick looked suddenly reflective. "But then, a week ago I'd've also said Moosejaw would never keep a secret like buyin' an engagement ring from me and Beartooth, either."

"People change. Especially when they fall in love," Kate said, putting her hand on his forearm. "But don't worry, you're not on the verge of losing one of your close friends. The bond between you, Moosejaw, and Beartooth is as solid as the granite of the Rocky

Mountains it was forged in. Trust me, those of us who love you understand that. Just like we understand that, no matter how much you love us back, the best we can hope for is merely to *share* in that bond."

Firestick met her gaze, surprised by the intensity in her eyes and not quite knowing how to respond.

Luckily, he didn't have to. Because, at that moment, Beartooth came striding in and made straight for their table.

"So this is how you handle your peacekeepin' duties when nobody else is around?" he said, giving the marshal a good-natured jab.

"And slippin' off to town is how you handle runnin' the ranch when nobody else is around?" Firestick countered.

Beartooth pulled out a chair, spun it around, and sat down with his arms folded atop the backrest.

"I'll have you know I'm on official ranch business— I'm here to pick up some spare harness gear for Miguel and Jesus."

Firestick nodded. "Fair enough. And I'm on official peacekeepin' business. I'm here fuelin' this old body of mine so's I got the energy to deal with any lawbreakin' varmint that comes down the pike."

Kate rolled her eyes but said nothing.

"Well, I can't argue with that 'old body' part of what you just said," Beartooth allowed. "But the good news is that you don't need to worry about that problem no more. Leastways not accordin' to what it says right here in black and white."

He withdrew a folded newspaper that he'd had tucked under one arm and reached out, handing it across the table.

After Firestick took the paper, unfolded it, and

began to scan what it opened to, Beartooth drawled, "A whole bundle of those just came in on the stage from Presidio. You'll spot quick enough where it says that the law hereabouts is pretty much all in the lightnin'-fast, gun-blazin' hands of our pal Moosejaw and any need for you and me comes across as bein' almighty close to none at all."

Firestick concentrated on the article spread before him, his brows pinching together slightly as he read. Kate leaned over and read along with him. After a couple of paragraphs, she said, "Oh my."

Firestick lowered the paper when he was done reading. Scowling, he said, "This didn't come from Moosejaw."

"Of course it didn't," agreed Beartooth. "I make it out to be mostly from that bank examiner fella who was there that day. Him, with maybe a little extra juice throwed in by the reporter who was writin' down what he had to say. No matter, though—it's *about* Moosejaw. That's the thing."

"Yeah," said Firestick sourly.

"What's more, that's just the Presidio paper." Beartooth jabbed a finger at the pages Firestick was still holding. "The quick glance I got of the Fort Davis *Dispatch* that also came in was enough to see—splashed all over the front page again—that it was trumpetin' the same tune, maybe even louder."

"That's just swell," Firestick muttered.

"Why the gloom and long faces?" asked Kate. "I mean, this is nothing new. Right? Everybody already knows all about it. And this article isn't disparaging to Moosejaw, it doesn't make him look bad or say he showed poor judgment or anything."

"That's just it," said Firestick. "It makes him look *too* good. It makes him look like a rip-snortin' version of Wild Bill Hickok, Wyatt Earp, and Davy Crockett all rolled into one."

Now Kate looked even more puzzled. "You don't mean the two of you are jealous?"

Firestick gave her a look. "Come on, Kate. You know better than that."

Beartooth was quick to add, "What I said a minute ago about me and Firestick no longer bein' needed on account of how great that newspaper painted Moosejaw—you gotta know I was only kiddin', just tryin' to get a rise outta Firestick."

"Nobody is prouder or happier than we are for Moosejaw gettin' praise on how he handled that robbery. He deserves every bit of it," Firestick said. Then, tossing the paper he'd been holding onto the table, he added, "Every bit, that is, except *this* kind of exaggerated, pumped-up crap!"

Kate shook her head. "I'm sorry if I'm being terribly wool-headed. But I still don't see what the big problem is."

"The problem ain't what any of us think," Firestick explained. "The problem is how far these news accounts and others like 'em are likely to reach and what kind of thoughts they might put in the heads of hardcases and gunslicks wherever they spread. Needles Whitney and, even more so, Tuscarora Billings were pretty big names in certain circles. Before he turned outlaw, Tuscarora was a peace officer in some mighty tough cattle towns. And he made a reputation for bein' not only tough himself but fast with a gun. Don't you see? Anybody takin' him down—and two others to boot, all detailed in the colorful way of these newspaper reports—is gonna take on a rep for bein' even faster and tougher."

"The way most folks reckon, Buffalo Peak ain't but a speck of a place not amountin' to much," Beartooth pointed out. "But if word spreads, like Firestick is sayin', that we got ourselves a double-tough, lightnin'-fast lawman primed to take on any steely-eyed varmint who thinks otherwise . . . well, it'd amount to a challenge for certain types. Types who are liable to come around just for the sake of growin' their own reps by showin' they're tougher and faster still."

Kate said, "But we've had our share of trouble here before—too much, many would say. And you three have always handled it; that's why the town asked you to put on badges. And Firestick, in particular, has been forced to draw against men who gave him no choice. That didn't seem to attract the kind of attention and added trouble you're worried about."

"That's because it mostly stayed local," Firestick told her. "Like you said, it didn't get a lot of attention, and like Beartooth pointed out, Buffalo Peak in general don't rate a lot of notice. But this damn thing"—he slapped the paper now lying on the table—"and more like it, can make all the difference. It's sorta like something else you said just a little bit ago, about how there's a difference between the way Moosejaw acted before when he was in love with Daisy in a quiet, personal way and how he's actin' now that they're engaged and have made it official by *announcin'* their marryin' intentions and all. These newspaper accounts make it official that Moosejaw is a tough so-and-so with greased lightnin' in his gun hand. Hearin' word drift around about some tough *hombre* off somewhere is one thing. But havin' it writ down with all the gory details spelled out, that's a whole lot bigger. Big enough, I'm afraid, to make it for certain types just like Beartooth said: a damn challenge they'll come flockin' to answer."

Chapter 7

In spite of their stated concerns, not even Firestick or Beartooth could have imagined how fast the kind of thing they were worried about actually started taking root. Even as they were explaining the possible repercussions of the newspaper articles to Kate, another related discussion was taking place right across the street from the Mallory House.

At a corner table in the Silver Spur Saloon, three cowboys sat talking over plates of cold-cut sandwiches and foamy steins of beer. In the middle of the table lay a copy of the Fort Davis *Dispatch*, the bold print of its front page detailing Moosejaw's heroics against the "notorious Tuscarora Billings gang."

"I'm about sick enough to puke from hearing about that big damn oaf of a deputy and how he broke up that bank robbery!" exclaimed Curly Roy Hutchins, the youngest member of the trio, a husky individual of average height in his early twenties. Most women would call him boyishly handsome, complete with tangled blond curls spilling out from under his hat. "Just when folks had finally quit yammerin' about it, now these stupid damn newspapers show up and everybody is yammerin' all over again."

Harvey Bell sat to Curly Roy's right. A slat-thin fellow pushing forty, with practically every minute of those hard years showing on a leathery, hawklike face deeply seamed by exposure to the sun and other elements, he shrugged a bony shoulder and replied, "Why be so hard on Moosejaw? He's a decent sort. Why not let him have the credit he's got comin' for doin' a good thing in stoppin' those owlhoots?"

"'Cause I don't believe he's got all that credit comin', that's why," Curly Roy snapped back.

"How so?" Bell asked.

"'Cause I can look at a man and tell certain things about him, that's how." Curly Roy paused with his sandwich raised partway to his mouth and scowled fiercely. "And what I can tell right off about Deputy Moosejaw is that he ain't no lightnin'-fast gunslick. I can tell that plain as the set of knockers on a top-dollar whore."

Still displaying a mild, innocent-seeming curiosity, Bell said, "I ain't questioning the eye for prime womanhood in a young buck like you, but how does that relate to sizin' up a man and decidin' how fast he is or ain't with a shootin' iron?"

"Come on, Bell, you're just egging the kid on," said Clay Halstead, the third man at the table, a sturdy hard worker halfway between the ages of the other two and a mild sort who didn't like to see tensions build up. "You know Curly Roy is damned handy with a shootin' iron his own self. The best on our spread for sure, and probably anywhere close around.

Fellas like him know what to look for in other gun packers, know whether or not they show signs of measurin' up."

"That's right," Curly Roy declared. He glared at Bell. "And you know damn well what he's talkin' about, Harvey. You've knocked around more than a few places in your time . . . you must have seen some top hands with a gun. And you've seen me shoot. Admit the truth, you ever seen anybody faster?"

Bell took his time answering, first finishing a bite of food he'd just taken.

"Ain't no doubt you're fast with that shiny Colt of yours, Curly Roy," he finally said. "Yeah, 'bout as fast as anybody I ever seen. And you're dead accurate when it comes to blastin' cans and bottles off the top of fence posts. But that still leaves a couple things to consider. Number one, none of them bottles or cans was shootin' back. Number two, I ain't never seen Moosejaw at work with a hogleg to judge how fast or accurate he is. Though, by accounts, not too shabby."

"By accounts—bah!" Curly Roy sneered. "Accounts by who? A bunch of pencil-pushin' bank nancies and some newspaperman scribblin' down what they heard thirdhand. None of 'em hardly knowin' which end of a gun does what. To them, anybody who could manage to yank a hogleg out of its holster would look fast."

"That may be," Bell allowed. "But there's other accounts to consider, too. Quite a few of 'em, in fact. I'm talking about accounts on Tuscarora Billings and Needles Whitney that scatter back over a lot of other places and shootings before they showed up here. And all of 'em paintin' a picture of those two, especially Billings, as bein' mighty fast and not to mention deadly when it came to gun work."

"He's got a point there, Curly Roy," said Halstead. "In order for Moosejaw—or anybody else, as far as that goes—to get the bulge on a pair like that makes a pretty strong statement. And there was even a third fella, too."

"I know there was a third fella. I know the whole doggone story. Didn't I just get done tellin' you I've heard it so often I want to puke?" Curly Roy scowled fiercely. "I don't know a way to explain how that big lumbering deputy managed to outshoot those varmints. I'll even admit that it sounds mighty impressive. But damn it, there's got to be something more to it. That's the whole point of why it sticks in my craw so bad and why I look at Moosejaw and can't make myself believe it."

Curly Roy paused to swallow some beer from his mug, then went on, "Yeah, he's big and strong and tough, and him and his two pals were rip-snortin', Indian-fightin' mountain men and all that. Blah, blah, blah. But I ain't talkin' a rough-and-tumble fistfight against him. He'd break most men in two. But all that size and bulk and muscle, that's exactly the problem. A big oaf like Moosejaw can't possibly move fast enough and smooth enough to be a bona fide gunslick. I don't buy it, not for a second."

A tall, thin, middle-aged man in a well-cut swallow-tail suit jacket and slightly wilted tie happened to be passing by the cowboys' table as Curly Roy was making this declaration. The man was carrying a metal tray piled with bread, cheese, and a small bowl of hard-boiled eggs that he'd gotten from the luncheon spread the saloon laid out each day, the same one the cowboys had built their sandwiches from. The tall man paused in mid-step and turned his head to look down at Curly Roy.

"Pardon me," he said. "I assure you I don't make a habit of eavesdropping or intruding, but I couldn't help overhear what you were just saying and I found it immensely intriguing. Would it be too impudent of me to ask if I could sit with you gentlemen so that I might hear more of your fascinating conversation? I'd be happy to buy a round of drinks as compensation for any inconvenience."

Gazing up at the man, Curly Roy's mouth was hanging half open, as if in awe, by the time the tall gent finished speaking.

"Mister," he said, after clapping his mouth closed in order to speak, "I barely understood half of that fancy lingo you just slung out. But I did catch the part about buyin' a round of drinks. So that's enough to say, yeah, pull up a chair and take a load off. Be worth chewin' the fat with you just to hear some more of that fancy lingo."

"Excellent," said the tall man. He placed his tray on the table and then pulled out a chair and settled his long, lanky form down. "I must warn you, however, that my goal is to limit my own voice in your conversation. I'd rather just to listen to more of what you were discussing. Oh, my manners!" Suddenly he thrust his long right arm across the table. "My name is Howard Blessingame. I arrived only a short time ago on the stage without knowing a soul in your town. I greatly appreciate this bit of hospitality you are extending, even though I somewhat forced the matter."

The three wranglers each shook hands with Blessingame and introduced themselves in return.

"We ride for the Ace Low outfit," Halstead explained.

"The three of us have been night-hawkin' for a spell so the boss gave us the day off to have a taste of daylight for a change and to come to town so's we could lubricate our innards some before he sends us out again."

"Lubricate your innards. Indeed." Blessingame smiled. His face was smooth-shaven and pleasant, though not handsome in the classic sense. His nose was too big and his eyes a bit too close together. But his smile was broad and friendly, displaying even, well-cared-for teeth. "It's phraseology like that, among much else, that I find so special and endearing about the West. It's what I seek so badly to try and capture in what I do."

"There's that fancy lingo," Curly Roy said, flashing his own grin. "You say you don't aim to join in the conversation but you're already holdin' up your end by slingin' words like fazee-logically or ever what it was you just said."

Blessingame chuckled. "Phraseology. You're right, it is fancy lingo simply referring to the different phrases folks use when they talk. Colloquialisms is an even fancier term for basically the same thing. Some common examples, ones used almost everywhere, might be something like 'madder than a wet hen' or 'gullywasher' for a hard rain. But different regions have their own, more distinctive sayings. For me, coming from back east—St. Louis, originally—I find the West has many such distinctive, very colorful phrases that are particularly fascinating."

Halstead, who was nodding along as Blessingame talked, said, "I think I get what you mean. But what was that part you said earlier about trying to 'capture' these kind of phrases?"

"Oh. For my writing, is what I meant," replied Blessingame. "That's what I do, you see. I'm a writer."

Curly Roy's eyes dropped momentarily to the newspaper on the table, then lifted again. "A writer? You mean like there—for newspapers and such?"

Before Blessingame could answer, a plump, somewhat harried-looking barmaid appeared at their table. "Can I get you gents anything? Drink refills maybe?"

"Yes, indeed you can," Blessingame told her. "I would very much like a beer, and three more for my comrades, as well." When the barmaid left, he turned his attention back to Curly Roy's question. "Yes, I have done some newspaper work on occasion. Strictly stringer work, nothing regular. But what I really meant when I referred to my writing, what I'm involved in at the moment, is turning out books, novels."

"Books about what?" Bell asked.

"Well, in time, if I'm able to continue making a career of it, any number of things. Serious dramas are my eventual goal," Blessingame said sternly. Then his expression opened up and he grinned and continued on. "But for the moment—in order to keep the wolf from my door, if I may resort to another common but popular phrase—I am having reasonable success with adventure yarns. You know, popular action thrillers with chases and damsels in distress and shootings and so forth. Dime novels, they're called. Sheer entertainment, nothing serious."

"Oh yeah. We got a few fellas around the bunkhouse who read those. I've passed time with a few myself," said Halstead.

"Something like this, right?" His smile widening, Blessingame reached in a coat pocket and withdrew a couple of slim volumes bound in yellow paper that displayed illustrated covers. He spread them on top of the newspaper. One was titled *The Owlhoot Kid*, the other *Ghost Rider of Half Moon Canyon*. Both carried the byline Hank Blake.

"Yeah, them's the thing," Halstead said.

"Sure, I've read some of those, too," said Bell.

Curly Roy picked up one of the books and turned it over in his hands, then stared at Blessingame and said, "I'll be dogged. You write this kind of thing, eh?"

Blessingame's head bobbed. "Indeed I do. Both of those are mine, in fact. If you're wondering about the 'Hank Blake' byline, that's merely a pseudonym, a pen name that my publisher came up with. He thought it sounded more authentic and rugged than my real name. It's a common practice and he was offering to pay me money, so who was I to argue? Sales have been decent and if, in the future, I turn to more serious work as I plan, my own name will better stand apart."

Curly Roy squinted. "You sound like you're sorta ashamed of these."

"Not at all," Blessingame assured him. "True, I recognize they are not the epitome of great literature. But I'm honing my craft as I produce them, doing my best to give readers what they want while at the same time trying to make each volume better than its predecessor. It is with that goal in mind, as a matter of fact, that I have traveled here to your fair city."

"What the hell is there in Buffalo Peak that's gonna help you make your writin' any better?" Curly Roy wanted to know.

"Not 'what,' but rather who," replied Blessingame with a smile. He reached out and tapped the newspaper underneath his books. "The gentleman featured very prominently right there on the front page—your fearless, fast-draw deputy, Moosejaw Hendricks. Up to now, you see, the tales I've spun have been purely fiction, with an alleged true event woven in here and there. But to capture a genuine, freshly emerging, real-life hero like this Moosejaw . . . if I can be the first to tell his tale with complete authenticity, though enhanced perhaps with flourishes of my dramatic skills . . . it could be a huge best seller! Maybe the biggest since Ned Buntline introduced the world to Buffalo Bill."

"I hate to bust your bubble, writer man," Curly Roy sneered. "But Moosejaw Hendricks ain't nothing but a big, overblown phony who couldn't outdraw a half-drunk sportin' gal with a six-gun stuffed in her bloomers."

"Ah, yes," said Blessingame, leaning back in his chair, the smile spreading wider. "It was that very implication from you that stopped me in my tracks when I was first starting to pass this table. By all means, sir, tell me more . . ."

Chapter 8

"I swear! I hack away at this stuff and get a pretty good-size patch cleared—then I come back a day or so later and it's half growed all over again." Moosejaw scowled disgustedly at the brushy growth surrounding the oval of cleared ground he was standing on the edge of. "Man, if this earth is fertile enough to grow anything decent, the way it does scrub brush, then me and Daisy are gonna have a vegetable garden that oughta feed half the county."

"Or," Firestick suggested, "maybe a passel of your own kids."

Moosejaw's sweat-beaded eyebrows shot up. "Whoa, now. Let's not jump too far ahead with things."

"Says the fella who's already jumpin' with both feet into marriage and a place of his own and the whole ball of wax."

"Yeah, but there ain't nobody said nothing about no passel of kids rolled up in that wax ball."

"Well, don't fret too much about it," drawled Bear-tooth. "If another kind of passel starts showin' up, the whole works might be goin' up in a puff of smoke . . . powder smoke, that is . . . before it hardly gets started."

"What in blazes is that supposed to mean?" Moose- jaw wanted to know.

The three men were talking under a high, hot sun that had drifted little more than an hour past its noon peak. Firestick and Beartooth, still on their horses, had ridden out from town, which lay about a quarter mile back to the east, to have this discussion with Moosejaw. The cabin Moosejaw had put money down on stood a dozen yards behind the big deputy. It was a single-story structure of well-fitted timbers, a little run-down from having sat empty for a while but still solid and only in need of some basic attention to bring it back to good condition. There was a small corral and horse shed off to one side, a covered well in front, a grove of trees close by to the rear, and rolling countryside all around. The place would make a nice home for Moosejaw and Daisy.

"What it means," replied Beartooth, swinging down from his saddle, "is that these things startin' to circu- late around"—pulling a pair of newspapers from his hip pocket as he took a step toward Moosejaw—"might cause that other kind of passel I mentioned to begin showin' up."

Moosejaw set aside the broad-curved scythe he'd been working with and took the papers Beartooth handed him. They were copies of both the Fort Davis *Dispatch* and the Presidio *Press*. As Moosejaw shook them open and began scanning what was plastered across their front pages, Firestick dismounted also and walked over to stand beside Beartooth.

Moosejaw pored over the Presidio edition first, his brows pinching steadily tighter together as he read.

Then, after barely glancing at the *Dispatch* and seeing more of the same, he suddenly crumpled the publication in his big fist and shook it. "That blabber-mouthed pipsqueak of a bank examiner. Doggone him!" he exclaimed. "I told him not to make such a big deal out of what he saw. I should have throwed the little runt in the clink for . . . for . . . I don't know what. But some charge that would have kept him there long enough for his over-busy tongue to have growed tired of flappin'!"

"That might've worked," Firestick allowed. "But more likely it would have just gave him something to flap about even louder."

Moosejaw shook the paper again. "You know what this is apt to mean, don't you? You know what kind of attention this might possibly attract from certain *hombres*."

"Of course we do. We thought the same thing," said Beartooth. "That's why we rode out here to give you a heads-up. Those papers arrived on the stage just a little while ago, so it ain't like anything's gonna pop in the next handful of minutes. But on the other hand, we got to remember that those editions first came out a few days ago. So it's worth keepin' in mind that any-body who might work up a notion based on what's reported there could already be stirrin'."

"Or, we also need to keep in mind," Firestick pointed out, "they might not stir up nothing or nobody. There's that chance, too. Generally speakin', there don't seem to be as many gunslicks on the prod as there used to be. More towns have sprung up, things are more settled down, a lot of the gunnies have bit the dust or plain growed old."

"A lot, maybe. But not all," Moosejaw said sourly.

"There's still plenty of 'em on the prowl. Tuscarora Billings and Needles Whitney not only fit the mold, but they managed to find their way right here to land in our laps . . . my lap, more's the lousy luck. And with luck like that, who's willin' to give me odds that more won't follow? Especially with printed hoopla like this to egg 'em on."

Firestick spread his hands. "Okay. So if they do, we'll be ready for 'em and we'll handle it. Ain't like we haven't handled our share of trouble in the past."

"That's right," agreed Beartooth. "Ain't like the years we spent in the Rockies scrappin' with Injuns and fur robbers and whatever else was a cakewalk. And since we came down to these West Texas flats and especially since pinnin' on badges, the three of us stickin' together have held up against rowdies and rustlers and every other kind of owlhoot. I reckon we're still good for a few more skirmishes."

Moosejaw cut his eyes back and forth between his two pals and said, "That's mighty encouragin' to hear, fellas. And I appreciate you sayin' it. But don't you see? This would be a whole different animal. If some hardcase comes gunnin' for me on account of what these newspaper articles have painted me to be—it would be just me. Just my fight. I'd have to stand up to him alone, not be sided by the two of you."

"Hold on now," Firestick was quick to say. "That's crazy talk. No offense, old friend, but you're no gunfighter. Not against any gunny who might have some polish to him. Besides, what you *are* is a lawman, a deputy marshal. Anybody threatenin' you is automatically goin' against the law, and that would give me and Beartooth every right to step in and—"

Moosejaw stopped him short. "No. That don't cut

it. I don't need nobody else to do my fightin' for me or to hide behind my badge, neither one. If some sonofabitch comes lookin' to brace me one-on-one, then that's the way it'll have to be. Just him and me. And as far as me not bein' a gunfighter, thank you, I seem to recall doin' a pretty damn good job at something along those lines a few days ago when it came to them bank robbers."

Nobody said anything for several seconds until Firestick abruptly puffed out his cheeks and expelled a breath.

"Okay. I don't like it much, but I guess you're right. I understand why you have to look at it that way."

"Was one of us," Beartooth said in a low voice, "we'd see it the same."

Moosejaw made a catchall gesture with one hand. "Look, fellas, I don't like this, neither. Hell, I know I ain't no gunslick. I never had call to be. Up in the mountains all of us used long guns. When we came down here, I was the last one to start wearin' a gunbelt. It just made sense for deputy work, rather than luggin' a long gun around town."

"Oh, I don't know," Beartooth said in a kind of wistful tone. "I seem to recall a few scattergun holes in the ceiling of the Silver Spur Saloon from when you waded in and saw fit to break up brawls the easy way."

"Yeah, and I wish I'd've stuck to that," Moosejaw said.

"So let's cut to it," Firestick said. "How fast *can* you draw that hogleg and go to work with it?"

"How the heck do I know?" wailed Moosejaw. "Ain't like I ever felt the need to do quick-draw practicin' or any such. When I needed to, I've always managed to get my Schofield out in time to do what I set out to. The only time speed ever mattered much was that time I shot Orval Retlock when he tried to get the drop on you at the jail a couple years back. Well, and the other day at the bank. But that was as much about takin' advantage of a couple diversions and then bein' lucky and accurate, as it was about bein' fast."

Firestick nodded. "Often as not, that's what matters the most—bein' steady and accurate. But a healthy dose of speed sure don't hurt none."

"So what do you reckon I oughta do? Figure on worst case, start practicin' some to work on tryin' to get faster?" Moosejaw asked. "You took to it about as good as anybody, Firestick, maybe you could . . ."

The big man's words trailed off as his attention was pulled away by something beyond his two pals. Turning, Firestick and Moosejaw saw what it was. A group of riders, coming from town at a pretty good clip, were headed their way.

Chapter 9

The three lawmen planted themselves to face the oncoming riders, fanning out slightly as they did so. As the horsemen drew nearer, they were revealed to be seven in number with faces passingly familiar to those watching their approach—men seen around town at various times, some more frequently than others. Only one—a tall, lanky sort dressed incongruously in a swallowtail suit jacket, bareheaded, and sitting his saddle with obvious discomfort, especially compared to those about him—was a complete stranger.

The riders reined up and came to a halt a half dozen yards short of the awaiting men. Some of them checked their horses and hung back a bit farther. One in particular, a youngish number dressed in well-worn wrangler's garb with a boyishly handsome face set in a stern expression, nudged his mount up the closest.

Since this was his property, Moosejaw took a step forward and squinted up at the young wrangler, saying, "Afternoon, gents. Something I can do for you?"

"Matter of fact, there is," said the wrangler. "I got me a hankerin' to conduct a piece of business with you,

Deputy Moosejaw, and these other fellas . . . well, they sorta tagged along to see how it plays out."

Moosejaw frowned. "I ain't sure I'm followin' what you got in mind, bub. But whatever it is, if it amounts to anything serious, I don't generally make a habit of conductin' my business in front of a crowd."

"Oh, this is serious alright. Damned serious," the young wrangler assured him. "And havin' a crowd lookin' on ain't gonna be no problem, leastways not for me. Do you even know who I am?"

Moosejaw eyed him closer. "Recollect I've seen you around town now and again. If I ain't mistook you go by the name of Ray, ain't that right? Curly Ray, I believe, but I don't know that I ever caught—"

"Roy! Curly *Roy* is what they call me. Curly Roy Hutchins."

Moosejaw nodded. "Okay, then. But I still ain't clear on what business you and me got between us, Curly Roy Hutchins."

"You're holdin' it right there in your hand," Curly Roy said, jabbing a finger to indicate the wadded-up newspaper Moosejaw still had clenched in one fist. "That hogslop printed there—bein' scattered from hell to breakfast for every fool who don't know no better to gobble up and believe—about how you're some kind of double-tough *hombre* with lightnin' in your gun hand. *That's* the business you and me got to settle. The business of it all bein' a pack of lies and me steppin' up to be the one to prove it ain't so."

Moosejaw's expression changed. Went from being open and measuredly curious to closed and hard-eyed. In a voice now with a raspy edge to it, he said, "Let me guess. You aim to settle everything by showin' you got faster lightnin' in your own gun hand. That it?"

"You're catchin' on, big man," Curly Roy said smugly. "You havin' any?"

Moosejaw's gaze drifted over the faces of the other riders, came back to Bell and Halstead. "You fellas ride for the Ace Low, too, don't you? Same as Curly Roy here. You in on this with him?"

"Just lookin' on, Deputy. That's all," replied Bell. "Curly Roy is whistlin' his own tune."

Firestick couldn't hold back anymore. "You just said a word—Deputy." He started with his gaze locked directly on Halstead, then swept his eyes over the others. "You all realize this young loudmouth is threatenin' a duly appointed officer of the law, don't you?"

"I beg to differ, sir . . . Marshal, is it?" This came from the dude in the swallowtail jacket. "But I hardly think anything Curly Roy said constitutes a threat. Rather a challenge, which is quite a different thing. Furthermore, while it may be true that Mr. Moosejaw is a duly appointed lawman—as well as you and the other gentleman standing there—that fact is hardly germane to the situation. That distinction is only meaningful for the jurisdiction lying within the city limits of Buffalo Peak. And as we all here can clearly see, we are well outside of those bounds."

"Who the hell are you?" Beartooth growled.

"His name's Blessingame," Curly Roy answered. "But a bigger question is, why do you care? You or Marshal Firestick, either one. Never mind all that crap about jusserdiction or whatever, what this boils down to in plain English is that I'm callin' out Moosejaw. That leaves the only real question bein' whether he's got guts enough to face me. Or is it gonna take all three of you throwin' in?"

"You piss-whiskered young pup," Firestick raked

out through gritted teeth, "if the three of us took a notion to throw in, you'd never know it because you'd be dead before your pitiful little brain ever had time to clue you in."

"Here now," huffed an old-timer from farther back in the pack, a bourbon-nosed saloon regular by the name of Weeks. "We didn't none of us come here looking to get caught up in a whole raft of gunplay. We thought this was supposed to go down strictly between Moosejaw and young Hutchins."

"Likewise for me," said Halstead, his horse dancing somewhat nervously under him, as if the critter sensed the trouble in the air and didn't like it, either. "I ride for the same brand as Curly Roy, but I don't fight his fights. Him and that writer fella are the ones who set this in motion, the rest of us just came to watch."

"Yeah, like that's news to anybody, Halstead," Curly Roy sneered. "That's all you and that yellow streak down your back are ever gonna be good for—just watchin'."

"Then him and all the rest are gonna be leavin' disappointed," said Moosejaw. "Because there ain't gonna be no show to watch, Curly Roy. I ain't gonna let you goad me into something stupid just because you got a snootful of liquor and you're feelin' frisky. Best get on back to the ranch and sober up. You might wake up tomorrow with a hangover, but at least you'll still be alive to wake up at all."

"You damn coward! You can't just turn your back on me!" Curly Roy bellowed, his face purpling with frustration.

"I ain't turnin' my back on you," Moosejaw told him. "I'm lookin' you straight in the eye and tellin' you this ain't gonna happen. You think you're fast with a gun? Good for you. Me, I never made no such claim and it ain't nothing I'm lookin' for. You want to impress your pards and your drinkin' pals? Go shoot up some bottles and tin cans, twirl your shootin' iron a few times before you slide it back in its holster. That'll give 'em a show and everybody will be happy."

"*I* won't be happy, you sonofabitch! I won't be happy until I blast your guts out. That'll show everybody who the real gunslick around these parts is. Then word-slingers like Blessingame here will start writin' about *me*! And the next time I ask somebody if they know me, you can by-God bet they'll say damn straight, you're Curly *Roy* Hutchins the famous gunman."

"Let 'em say and write whatever they want about you," Moosejaw said wearily. "Just leave me out of it because I can't be bothered. I may be out of my jurisdiction as a lawman, but this is my property and you're not welcome here, so that amounts to trespassin'. Now, the lot of you, clear on out, you hear? I got work needs doin' to get this place ready."

"Ready for what? Oh yeah, now I remember—I heard you're gettin' hitched. Married to that chubby little gal who runs the blacksmith shop in town, right? I also hear tell she can be a real spitfire." Curly Roy's mouth pulled into a lewd, lopsided grin. "What are you gonna do when *she* wants you to draw your shootin' iron, big man—you gonna call your two pals to back your play on that, too?"

Moosejaw had started to turn away, thinking he'd successfully dismissed the matter. He froze for a long moment, then slowly turned back. His eyes bored into Curly Roy like two white-hot coals.

"Moosejaw . . ." Firestick cautioned. But he held himself in check from saying more. He could see it was too late; it had gone too far. And in his gut, he knew that in Moosejaw's place he would respond the same.

"Alright, you foulmouthed bastard," Moosejaw grated. "You're in such a hurry to die young tryin' to be a big man. Get down off that horse . . . let's see how big you grow from six feet under."

For the next several moments, the scene was gripped in stark silence. The only sounds were the creak of leather as Curly Roy slipped from his saddle and the scrape of Moosejaw's boots as he tramped over to retrieve his gunbelt from where he'd stripped it off and hung it on a well post when he started work clearing brush.

The faces of the men looking on were a mix of expressions. A couple showed nervous tics; others appeared awed, apprehensive. Firestick and Beartooth wore masks as blank and unreadable as the stone slabs of the well housing. Howard Blessingame, for his part, appeared bright-eyed and focused with an intensity that seemed to border on delight.

After buckling his gunbelt around his waist and checking to make sure the .45-caliber Schofield moved freely in the holster, Moosejaw stepped off a dozen paces, then turned to face Curly Roy. He planted his feet wide. The white-hot fire in his eyes did not flicker.

Curly Roy, on the other hand, suddenly did not appear quite so cocksure. His face had paled somewhat from earlier and his lips seemed dry and in need of frequent licking. A hard swallow caused his neckerchief to bob up and down with the movement of his Adam's apple. Without taking his eyes off Moosejaw, he said out the side of his mouth, "You watch tight, Blessingame. This is gonna go quick. Make sure you get it straight for the story you're gonna write." His voice was reasonably steady, maybe just a hint of a quaver.

In response, Moosejaw said evenly, "I'll be furnishin' the ending of your story, Curly Roy. But this is your show, so set it off when you're ready."

Nothing happened for what seemed like several heartbeats, though in reality it was quite brief.

Then Curly Roy's shoulder dropped and in an instant two hands were streaking for iron and two arms were swinging up to firing level. Both guns roared at the same time. Moosejaw's body jerked ever so slightly, twisting to his left maybe a quarter of an inch, but he remained upright, his gun arm staying steady and straight, extended from the waist. Every inch of Curly Roy went very rigid and became as motionless as a statue. Then, slowly, his gun arm began to droop downward and his knees buckled, one at a time, until they both gave way completely and he toppled to the dusty, freshly cleared ground.

Chapter 10

"Dead. Clean through his ticker."

It didn't take long for Firestick to reach this conclusion after walking over and kneeling to examine the motionless heap that now was Curly Roy. Once he'd announced his findings, he straightened up and raked his gaze over those gathered around him. All the men who'd ridden up with Curly Roy had dismounted and moved in closer. A couple of them had respectfully removed their hats.

"Well? Are you happy now?" the marshal said, disgust in his voice. "You got the show you were all so anxious to see. Are you satisfied? Is Curly Roy satisfied?"

"He only wanted to be somebody . . . something more than just another wrangler," Bell said quietly. "He thought his gun was a way for him to accomplish that."

"But it wasn't. All it got him was dead," Firestick said flatly.

"And if he'd've got Moosejaw instead, it would have worked out the same—because then I would have gone ahead and killed him anyway," Beartooth added icily. "Y'all might want to remember that, in case any of you suck enough courage out of a bottle and think about tryin' something equally as stupid."

"You can hardly blame anyone else for the actions of a grown man," said Blessingame. "It was young Hutchins alone who questioned the veracity of Deputy Moosejaw's notoriety as a gunman. He was determined to test the deputy's mettle in that regard. Such pursuits, as a right of passage in many cultures and societies, are neither uncommon nor—"

Halstead cut him off, saying, "You're the one who egged him on. Curly Roy was just mutterin' empty beer talk until you came along and stuck your nose in, promisin' to make him famous with the stories you'd write about him."

"What an outrageous accusation!" Blessingame protested. "I promised no such thing. All I did was take an interest in the claims he was already making to you and Mr. Bell. It wasn't like I put any ideas in his head—they were already there long before I stopped by your table back at the saloon."

"Shut up, all of you!" Moosejaw suddenly exclaimed. "A man is dead, ain't that enough? There shouldn't be any doubt about who's to blame. It was me; I pulled the trigger on him. It's what you was all so eager to see, so what more do you want? Why the arguin' about it?" He glared at everyone, his chest rising and falling with heavy breaths. "You got what you came for. You saw your shoot-out and you got a dead man for the payoff. You're the ones who brought him here, so now you can haul him off. Do it! Get his body on a horse and the rest of you get on yours. All of you get the hell out of here!"

It didn't take long for those he was addressing to comply. They hoisted Curly Roy back onto his horse, belly down, then all save Firestick and Beartooth rode away. The townsmen returned toward Buffalo Peak. Bell and Halstead, leading the corpse-laden horse, swung in the direction of the Ace Low spread.

Blessingame lingered momentarily, as if he wished to say something more. But another look into Moosejaw's hard glare changed his mind. He wheeled his mount and spurred after the townsmen.

The three former mountain men stood watching silently until both clumps of riders had nearly faded from sight.

Turning his head to fix Moosejaw with a very direct look, Firestick said, "You gonna be okay?"

Not returning his gaze, continuing to look out across the prairie, Moosejaw replied, "I ain't the one shot dead. Reckon that oughta give me no complaints."

"You're bleedin', in case you didn't know it," Beartooth told him. "Expect you could grumble some about that, if you was of a mind to."

"Ain't nothing but a bullet burn clear out on the corner of my left shoulder. Had worse beestings."

"Everybody else is gone. You can quit workin' so hard at actin' tough any time you take a notion," suggested Firestick.

Moosejaw finally turned his head and looked at him. "Okay. Some beestings smart like hell, and so does this. That better?"

"It's a start. Let's step over to the well so we can flush that crease with some fresh water, then have a closer look."

As the three moved in that direction, Beartooth said, "I saw you jerk when Curly Roy took his shot, but I couldn't tell how bad you were hit. You know, you bein' broad as a damn barn and all, it might have been a good idea to twist your body a mite in order to make a narrower target."

"I figured if it was in the cards for that skunk to nail me, then cuttin' the deck wasn't gonna make much difference," replied Moosejaw. "So I played what got dealt and I guess I came out alright."

"This time," Firestick said. "I don't want to rub the shine off your winnin' streak, but the chances you're gonna need to keep ridin' it just hiked up considerable."

"What do you mean by that?"

Ignoring the question, Firestick scooped a dipper of water out of the wooden bucket that sat on the rim of the stone well housing. "Turn around some so's I can get at that shoulder."

Moosejaw turned to one side, hunching the damaged shoulder forward and slightly down, revealing a horizontal tear in his shirt just below the curve of his shoulder. Through the opening made by the tear could be seen a purplish red welt smeared with blood already beginning to coagulate.

Spreading the tear in the cloth and examining the welt closely, Firestick said, "The bleedin' ain't bad . . . it's mostly already stopped. The skin's barely broken."

Beartooth gave a low whistle. "Man, that's about as close as you want to get without takin' a serious hit."

"Tell me about it," Moosejaw muttered.

Firestick said, "I'll go ahead and pour a couple dippers of water over it, dab it some to clean it. I don't want to start it bleedin' again. Best thing would be to go into town and see Dr. Greaves, let him put some ointment on it and dress it proper."

"Ain't worth a special trip just for that. If it's still

smartin' when I get to the ranch this evenin', I'll get a spoonful of lard from Victoria and smear it on. Be just as good. In the meantime, go ahead and pour that water."

As Firestick poured, Moosejaw grimaced and said, "That torn sleeve is the worst of it, darn the luck. This shirt is only four or five years old."

"That shouldn't be a problem," Beartooth told him. "Your bride-to-be ought to be able to patch it up good as new. Daisy can sew, can't she?"

Moosejaw looked suddenly perplexed. "You know what? I don't know if she can or not. I know she can straighten horseshoes and hammer wagon rims into shape, but I don't know if she can sew a lick."

"Well, if she can't, you can teach her. Ain't like we didn't spend a lot of years up in the mountains sewin' our own clothes." Firestick removed his neckerchief and dipped it in a second dipper of water that he'd scooped out of the bucket. After he'd dabbed gently at the welt a few times, he said, "This is gonna keep seepin' blood. Give me your neckerchief, too, Beartooth, so I got enough cloth to tie around his shoulder and keep some pressure on to hold the bleedin'."

As Firestick knotted the two bandannas together, Moosejaw craned his neck and frowned down at his shoulder. "Great. Now, on top of the tear, I'll have to worry about gettin' the bloodstains out, too."

"Like I said, you should've turned your body more. Made yourself a narrower target," Beartooth told him.

Moosejaw's frown deepened. "Yeah, gettin' back to that . . . What did you mean a minute ago, Firestick, when you said something about the chances for me needin' to keep ridin' a winnin' streak havin' just took a hike up?"

"Should be plain enough," Firestick said, concentrating on getting a folded portion of the tied-together neckerchiefs pulled tight over the welt so he could then knot the dangling ends under the big man's armpit. "The very thing we was talkin' about before those riders showed up—the possibility of other gunnies comin' 'round to challenge you on account of your rep as a gunslick. Now you've had to shoot again, against Curly Roy. And especially with that fancy-talkin' writer fella on hand to fan the flames and spread the word even wider, I sure don't see the possibility lessenin' any when it comes to attractin' more challengers."

"That's the last thing I want. Ever wanted."

"You know that. Me and Beartooth know it, too . . . But I got a hunch it ain't gonna make much difference."

"What's the story on that writer dude, anyway?" Beartooth wanted to know. "Where did he come from?"

"You heard as much as I did," Firestick answered. "Reckon he came in on the stage from Presidio. I got the impression he came here lookin' to talk to Moosejaw but then heard Curly Roy blowin' loud in one of the saloons and took a notion to stick with him instead, see where it led."

"Halstead said he egged Curly Roy on."

Firestick nodded. "Uh-huh. I heard him say that, too. My hunch is that he's the type who wouldn't be above it."

"Can we do anything to stop him? From doin' his writin', I mean." Beartooth's brow pinched into a low, tight scowl. "If he didn't sling his words around and keep things stirred up, maybe more gunnies wouldn't be so apt to come flockin'."

"Shuttin' him down might help some, but I don't think it'd solve the whole of it," Firestick allowed. "Besides, there ain't nothing legally we can do about him. You saw what an arrogant cuss he is—if we tried to get in the way of his writin', he'd only put up a squawk likely to draw even more attention to the situation."

Moosejaw's massive shoulders sagged. "So what am I supposed to do? You saw how I tried every way I could to avoid drawin' against Curly Roy. But a man can be pushed only so far."

"Then that's the line you'll have to continue to hold . . . providin' more gunnies *do* come around," said Firestick. "Me and Beartooth will be around to back you as much as we can. As much as you'll allow."

Moosejaw's gaze drifted to the bloodstain on the ground where Curly Roy had fallen. In a quiet voice, he said, "A little while ago I was worried about this land bein' fertile enough to grow something else besides brush. Now it's startin' to look like that something else is only gonna be trouble. That sure ain't the crop I had in mind."

Chapter 11

"Damn that Tuscarora Billings and double-damn the whole stinkin' state of Texas! The last thing I tried to tell brother Hank was to warn him against gettin' mixed up with Tuscarora. But he just wouldn't listen."

Liam Scorp voiced this lament as he sat at a rough-hewn table in a dingy, dirt-floored cabin located deep in a remote canyon in the heart of Oklahoma Indian Territory.

"Still, even if he was set on payin' no mind to that part, you'd think he would have knowed better than cross the line into that heathen state what has proved a hex to the Scorp name ever since they hung Pap and Uncle Juniper there, back before the war. Then our other uncle Rafe and my older brother Leon met their ends on Texas soil, too. And now it's claimed still another . . . poor little brother Hank."

Liam was a wiry six-footer, fiftyish in age, with a full, thick beard that thrust out wildly in all directions. Like the tangle of unkempt hair on his head, his beard was coal black in color though both were shot with streaks of gray. A gnarled, smoldering cigar was clamped between the fingers of his left hand while his right was wrapped possessively around the base of a fat ceramic jug with a cork stuck in its spout.

"Harder and harder to keep young'uns in line these days," said Jebediah Scorp from where he sat on the opposite side of the table. "I swear I don't know what the country's comin' to."

"That's exactly why it ain't gonna be *our* country much longer," Liam grunted. "Leastways not mine."

Jedediah scowled at his cousin. "What do you mean by that?"

"I said it plain enough, didn't I? I been a long time thinkin' how things are workin' out and not much likin' it. Not much at all. If you ask me, we'd be better off crossin' the border into Mexico. We could sell our guns to one of them big ranchin' operations down there—*haciendas*, they call 'em—and walk around free and live like kings. Bein' holed up here in Injun Territory with nothing but lowlife scum in every direction you look, dodgin' the damn law dog marshals that keep sweepin' through . . . Hell, we ain't no part of this country no more, anyway."

"We ain't?" said Jebediah, looking somewhat disappointed.

"When Ma passed away last fall over in Arkansas," Liam went on, "that's when it first hit me and I about decided then. We couldn't even go to her funeral on account of law dogs hangin' around thick as fleas on an old hound, layin' for us to show. What kind of country is that, not even allowin' for a man to attend his own mother's funeral in peace?" Liam paused long enough for a haunted, pained expression to pass over his face. "She was your ma, too, in every way but givin' birth to you. She raised you from the time you was three or four, after you lost your own mama. Didn't it make you feel awful—havin' to stay hid away like a diseased animal—and not bein' there to pay last respects to the woman who was about the only decent thing in either one of our lives?"

A forlorn expression also touched Jebediah's face. "O' course it did. Hearin' she was gone plumb broke my heart. You know that. And thinkin' how we wasn't there to comfort her none in her final days was an ache almost as bad." He was roughly the same age as Liam, with the same coarse black hair though his showed very few signs of gray and he had no beard. The latter might have been of some service to him, though, for the purpose of obscuring the roll of fat that hung under his chin. The rest of Jebediah ran to fat, too, most prominently a swollen gut that pushed the front of his bib overalls nearly to bursting their seams. Nevertheless, his massive shoulders and thick forearms indicated still-powerful muscles buried in the layers of fat.

"Not only wasn't we there to offer her any comfort at the end, we did almighty little to furnish her any for a long stretch before that," Liam muttered. "You want to talk about bein' brokenhearted? What do you think we did to Ma—disappointin' her and breakin' little pieces of her heart, steady-like, practically from the time we was weaned. You realize, cousin Jeb, we been raisin' hell and dodgin' the law for over half of our lives. Stompin' in the same footsteps as both of our paps and Uncle Rafe and brother Leon, one right after t'other.

"And Ma sat by and watched it all. Watched and hoped—and likely prayed—that at least one of the brood would turn out better, decent. Brother Hank was her last chance. That's the last thing she said to me the last time I talked to her. 'Please keep Henry'— she always called him Henry, never Hank—'out of trouble.'"

"She never asked for much."

"No, she sure didn't. Just that one thing. And I let her down. Again. When brother Hank was bent on ridin' off with Tuscarora, instead of me findin' some way to reason him out of it—even if it meant killin' that skunk Billings, which might've been the only way—I instead lost my temper and told him to get the hell out of my sight." Liam's face again took on that haunted look and this time it lingered. "And so he did . . . forever. Another Scorp planted in that god-forsaken hellhole they call Texas."

"Aw, come on, cousin Liam," Jebediah said in a concerned tone. "You can't heap too much of the blame for that on yourself. Yeah, Hank was your baby brother, but he was still a man full-growed. He was powerful set in his ways, just like all us Scorps. And now his stubbornness has . . . well, it worked out bad for him. I feel sad for that. I liked young Hank, too. But I repeat, there ain't no call for you to heap his bad end on yourself. And not to sound cold, but neither is there any way for you to change how things turned out for him."

"You're right, I can't change it." Liam put his cigar in his mouth and took a long, slow drag. Then he exhaled, wrapping his next words in a thick cloud of noxious smoke. "But I can damn sure square some things with those who played a hand in it."

Jebediah's look of concern turned into a scowl.

"There you go talkin' in circles again. Cut to it, cousin. First you say we got no country no more and now you got something in mind about squarin' things for Hank. Say it out straight, whatever you're drivin' at."

Liam reached out and thumped the end of a blunt forefinger down on the newspaper that lay on the tabletop between them. It was a copy of the Fort Davis *Dispatch*, folded open to the front-page account of the attempted Buffalo Peak bank robbery that had been foiled by Moosejaw.

"Right there," Liam declared. "The start of what I got in mind begins right there in that miserable town where brother Hank got gunned down like a dog."

"But that's in Texas! You swore you'd never set foot in Texas."

"That was before one too many Scorps got put in the ground there. Sometimes a big enough reason can give a body the right to change his mind. So that's what I'm doin'." Liam's expression turned flat and hard. "I'm not only gonna set foot in Texas, but when I do I'm gonna leave behind—on my way passin' through to Mexico—a set of bloody footprints they're gonna remember for a long, long time . . . from the spilled blood of the lowdown vermin that gunned down brother Hank!"

Chapter 12

The morning following the shoot-out between Moosejaw and Curly Roy Hutchins, Howard Blessingame woke in his room at the Mallory House Hotel. He lay diagonally across the bed, still fully clothed except for having kicked off his shoes. The bedspread was bunched and rumpled underneath him and the pillow his head had been resting on was twisted and wadded, indicating a fair degree of restlessness during his slumber.

Blessingame swung his feet over the edge of the mattress and sat up with a groan. He felt almost as bad as if he were waking with a hangover. But no, it hadn't been an overindulgence of alcohol that had kept him up into the wee hours and left him in his present wrung-out condition.

Rather, it had been a writing frenzy that held him virtually chained to the small desk in one corner of the room, hunched over a lined yellow tablet, filling page after page with passages that he scribbled as fast as his aching hand was able to try and keep up with his imagination. He'd paused only long enough to repeatedly sharpen his pencil with the blade of a penknife, until his cramping arm and shoulders finally brought on a wave of exhaustion that led him to the bed where he'd collapsed into instant slumber. Even that, judging by the mangled bedspread and pillow, had not been without an ongoing churning in his mind that prevented truly peaceful sleep.

His bleary eyes cutting to where the open tablet and pencils still lay on the desk, Blessingame smiled wryly. It wasn't the first time his creative juices had interfered with a fully satisfying night's sleep, but he couldn't remember having ever been as excited as he was by this current project. Even now, barely woken to the new day, he felt the urge to go straight to the desk, sit down, and immediately begin writing some more.

Everything was *right there*, totally clear in his mind— the story he wanted to tell, the way he wanted to present it, the thrills and excitement he wanted to convey to readers. The chapters he'd already written had flowed from the tip of his pencil almost as if some force beyond himself was pulling out the words.

Yet Blessingame knew it was all his own energy driving him, the enthusiasm he felt for his subject matter and the reception he envisioned once he had the details down and publication was completed. He'd openly shown that enthusiasm in the wire he sent to his Chicago publisher yesterday as soon as he returned from witnessing the shoot-out west of town.

HAVE DISCOVERED THE GOLIATH OF
GUNFIGHTERS STOP REMEMBER THAT
TITLE STOP WILL SOON BE BIGGEST
SELLER EVER PUT IN PRINT STOP

And that was *before* he'd spent another few hours in the saloons, buying drinks and gleaning even more details on the remarkable background of Moosejaw Hendricks. Not only him, but his colorful companions as well. For this initial tale, they would of course be background characters; but if *The Goliath of Gunfighters* was even half as popular as Blessingame anticipated, there would certainly be sequels to follow. Hell, Goliath's comrades might even rate separate titles of their own.

As these thoughts passed through Blessingame's mind, his expression sobered. For all his eagerness and excitement, he couldn't help but reflect on how much more of an impact all of it might make if Hendricks would be cooperative, allow his true name to be used, and provide input of his own that Blessingame could use and embellish yet nevertheless promote as a *true* representation of actual events.

Alas, based on the reactions the writer had gotten yesterday there at the scene, he was fairly convinced that neither Moosejaw nor his comrades would consent to willingly participate in his portrayals of them and their deeds.

So, for the time being at least, in his work in progress, he was using the name "Mooseheart Mulligan" for his protagonist. If the reputation of the real Moosejaw spread, as Blessingame predicted it would, the resemblance would be close enough to attract an added readership yet at the same time be fictionalized adequately to protect him from any potential claims of slander or libel. Though he wasn't ready to entirely give up on possibly getting the big deputy to come around, neither did he intend to let the lack of that slow his momentum. By the time he'd be able to catch a stage back to Presidio and then continue on to Chicago, he fully intended to have a completed manuscript ready to place in the hands of his publisher.

Sighing, Blessingame got up from the bed and went over to the room's washstand. Once more he was tempted to stop and do some writing, or at least skim over some of what he already had down. But he resisted. He needed to wash up, refresh himself, take in a good meal and plenty of hot coffee.

Then he would be ready to return full tilt to chronicling the adventures of Mooseheart Mulligan.

The way Firestick, Beartooth, and Moosejaw worked it—an arrangement agreed to by the Buffalo Peak town council when the latter first asked them to pin on badges—was that they'd split their time between their ranch and their duties as lawmen. This meant that, except for the overnight hours and taking breakfast and supper together at the Double M, at least one of them was usually present in town; the other two floated back and forth, wherever needed the most.

This morning was a rare occasion when all three came riding into town together, first thing after breakfast. Though the shops and stores lining Trail Street were only just opening for business and there was hardly any activity yet in the street itself, the former mountain men made quite an imposing sight, riding three abreast with their badges winking in the early sunlight.

One of the earliest-rising business owners—for the sake of getting as much forge work as possible done in the cool of the morning, before the heat of another summer day built up—was Daisy Rawling. She stood in the broad, open doorway of her blacksmith shop and watched with hands planted on hips as the three rode in. And although her shop was a ways farther down the street than the jail building where they'd intended to stop, seeing her standing there caused the trio to continue on and rein up before her.

Smiling up at them, Daisy said, "Any gal who was honest with herself would have to say that the sight of three big, strong, handsome gents galloping down the street was a mighty fine way to start her morning. But me, since I got eyes only for the biggest, handsomest lug amongst you, I'm afraid I can't make such a sweepin' statement."

"Here now," said Beartooth. "You shouldn't talk about me that way right in front of Moosejaw. Not only might you hurt his feelin's, you need to keep in mind that you're engaged now so you'll have to give up pinin' for me."

"She said 'biggest, handsomest' . . . not biggest blowhard," Moosejaw was quick to respond. "Somebody better start scrubbin' his ears a little better when he does his mornin' ablutions. Too much prairie dust can build up otherwise, and affect a fella's hearin'."

"Maybe that's the trouble," said Beartooth, grinning. "I only scrub my ears when I take my Saturday-night bath."

"*If* you take a Saturday-night bath," Firestick amended.

They all had a bit of a chuckle over that. Then, squinting up anew, Daisy said, "Seriously, though— what brings you into town so early and all together? Some new trouble?"

"Nothing that we know of. At least not yet," replied Firestick. "I've got a meeting with the town council later this mornin'. That's never exactly a picnic, but I can't claim it rates as serious trouble."

"While Firestick's tied up with that," Moosejaw explained, "I figured to sort of hang around and keep an eye on things. Later, I'll be goin' back out to the cabin to do some more work."

"And me, I'm just playin' errand boy for the ranch again," said Beartooth. "I missed pickin' up the stuff I got sent after yesterday on account of that fracas those fools from the Silver Spur decided to stir up."

Daisy's expression showed concern. "I wish we could all believe that fracas yesterday was the end of any more such foolishness. But I'm afraid it might not be, not with all the talk still goin' around town about Moosejaw's growin' reputation as a gunslinger and the chance for more trouble that might bring. I gotta tell you, that writer fella stayin' in town, askin' questions and sayin' how excitin' it was to see you in action, sure don't help matters any. If his way of tellin' things spreads very far, it's bound to stir up the kind of interest we don't want or need. Rumor has it—though Clayburn, the telegraph operator, won't confirm it—Blessingame already sent a wire off to some big-city publisher, primin' 'em for the story he's gonna write about Moosejaw."

Moosejaw scowled. Looking over at Firestick, he said, "He can't do that, can he? He ain't able to use my name and write a bunch of stuff about me without me agreein' to it, is he?"

Firestick matched his scowl. "I ain't sure how that works. If he claims it's a true account, like for a newspaper or some such, I figure he maybe can. But for that other kind of stuff he writes, dime novels and the like, no, I don't think he can just take your name and spin yarns."

Beartooth didn't look quite so sure. "I hope that's the case. But there's dozens of those dime novels been writ over the years about the likes of Crockett, Cody, Hickok, Kit Carson, and on and on. Some of them are whopper yarns that no human coulda really done, so you know they can't be strictly true. Does that mean, then, that the fellas they was about agreed somehow to all of 'em? Seems to me that's kinda doubtful."

"This whole mess just ain't gonna let me be, is it?" groaned Moosejaw. "I'm almost beginnin' to wish I would've kept my hands in the air and let those varmints go ahead and rob the damn bank."

"You don't mean that!" snapped Daisy. "What you did was brave and wonderful and you had darn well better not regret it. You said yourself those robbers would have likely shot up the place before they rode off, hurtin' and killin' innocent folks, maybe even me. What if you'd failed to take action when you saw the chance but you somehow survived while others died— you think livin' with that would've been easier?"

Moosejaw averted his eyes. "No, of course not. I didn't mean it like that, I was just . . . Hell, I guess what I was doin' was feelin' sorry for myself." He lifted his eyes and swept them over all those around him. "Reckon I been doin' more than my share of that lately. Hopin' you all know me well enough to know that ain't my way, and I'm swearin' to you now—I'm finished with it. However this business plays out, I'll just have to deal with it as it comes."

"That's more like it," Daisy said.

"And you'd damn well better know you won't be dealin' with it alone," added Beartooth.

Firestick cleared his throat and said to Moosejaw and Daisy, "You two stay here and talk some more. I'm goin' on to the jail and start gettin' ready for my meeting with the council. You can catch up with me there, Moosejaw."

"And me, I need to go pick up that harness gear and get it back to the ranch," said Beartooth. "See y'all around later."

"What about that writer fella?" Daisy wanted to know. "Is anybody gonna have a talk with him and see if maybe you can pin his ears back a little? Get him to lay off some of his talk about Moosejaw that's practically like wavin' a red flag to attract more *hombres* who might come aimin' to try their luck?"

Firestick nodded. "I'll look him up after I get done with the council. See what I can do."

Chapter 13

It was close to noon when Firestick went looking for Howard Blessingame. He wasn't hard to find since he was perched on a bench right out front of the Mallory House, situated comfortably in the shade thrown by the shingled awning that extended out across the width of the building, forming a front porch of sorts where residents could relax and get some fresh air.

The writer sat with one long leg crossed over the other, the fat yellow tablet he was writing on propped across the bend of his knee. A curved pipe was clamped in his teeth and on the bench beside him sat a tall glass and a moisture-beaded pitcher of lemonade. He looked nearly as comfortable as a man settled into an easy chair in the comfort of his own parlor.

When the clump of Firestick's bootheels approached on the boardwalk, Blessingame looked up.

"Oh. Marshal. Good morning, sir."

"Yeah, it's mornin'," Firestick allowed.

"Ah, but a fine one. Though shaping up to be quite a hot day by the feel of it."

"You appear comfortable enough," Firestick observed.

"Indeed. I was working up in my room until a short time ago, when it began to grow rather too stuffy. Added to, I must admit, by this infernal habit." He took the pipe from his mouth and held it up as evidence. "It was then I decided to stretch my legs a bit and seek a change of locales. After leaving the window cracked slightly behind me, in order to air things out for my return, I repaired here to the shade and a most pleasant hint of breeze."

"And you can continue your work, your writin'"—Firestick gestured to the tablet—"even out here with the street activity goin' on all around you?"

"Oh, to be sure. A writer must strive to respond to his muse, no matter the circumstances." When Firestick looked somewhat puzzled by that answer, Blessingame added, "Pardon me, that was an overly dramatic reply—exactly the kind of thing I need to work on avoiding in the very writing we're talking about. What I meant is that when a story is really flowing and the right words are coming with relative ease—such as in this current work in progress—a writer must take advantage of that, no matter what or where. Trust me, there are too many other times when neither the flow nor the ability to capture adequate words can be achieved without agonizing difficulty."

"Tell me," said Firestick, "this story you're workin' on—this work in progress, you call it—is the reason it's comin' so easy for you because you're basin' it on my friend Moosejaw?"

Blessingame's tone turned cautious. "I'm not detailing his actions in any way that invades his privacy or is disparaging to his character, if that's what you're suggesting. Have I been inspired by the tales I've heard about him and what I saw with my own eyes yesterday? Yes, that is certainly true—inspired to capture, *fictionally*, the adventures of an individual with similar bravery and heroic accomplishments. But, I repeat, it is strictly a fictional representation."

"Uh-huh. Yet you led Curly Roy to believe that, if he'd been the one who won that gunfight yesterday, you would have written stories specifically about him. Ain't that right?"

"I don't recall promising or in any way agreeing to such a thing," Blessingame huffed. "That's what Curly Roy wanted, to be sure. To gain fame and notoriety via his gun. And if he *had* won against Moosejaw, I may have indeed taken further interest in him, learned more about his background and so forth, and perhaps I would have found him worth weaving a story around. But a single rather obscure gunfight hardly rates a lot of attention in and of itself."

"Yet, judgin' by the interest you seem to be takin' in Moosejaw and all the questions I hear you're askin' around town about him," said Firestick, "he sure appears to be ratin' a lot of interest from you. More than just as an inspiration, from the sound of it. And he was in that very same 'obscure' gunfight."

"Oh come now, Marshal," Blessingame responded in a condescending tone. "Deputy Moosejaw was in much more than just that one gunfight. What about the bank holdup where he blazed down three desperadoes, two of them with considerable reputations as fast guns in their own right? Yes, I find Moosejaw very interesting . . . fascinating, in fact. And the more I learn about him—not to mention you and your other deputy as well—that fascination only grows.

"Further, I'll admit I came here with my interest in Moosejaw already established. I would like nothing better than to do a factual account of his exploits. Of each of you three former mountain men, in fact. But the message was pretty clear following that shoot-out yesterday than none of you were open to the prominence I could give your names. At least not at this point in time."

"Not now, not at no point in time," Firestick assured him. "You see, none of us are like Curly Roy Hutchins. Especially not Moosejaw. We're not interested in fame or notoriety due to gun work or any of the other things we've done. For us it was all strictly about survival."

"Fame could bring monetary rewards you might find very beneficial to your survival, particularly in your later years when the hard lives you're living grow harder to maintain," suggested Blessingame.

"Uh-huh. Except the kind of fame you're tryin' to push," Firestick said dryly, "could make survival a hell of a lot tougher real quick-like. And don't pretend you don't know what I'm talkin' about. Like you just admitted, the newspaper reports about that bank robbery Moosejaw broke up is what interested you enough to bring you here to begin with. And it's what prodded Curly Roy—maybe with help from you, maybe all on his own—to take a different kind of interest. An interest to test his gun in the hope of gettin' folks to take a bigger notice of him."

Blessingame nodded. "I'm well aware of the pattern you're alluding to, Marshal. Someone who gets a reputation as a fast gun often becomes a magnet for others looking to prove they are faster and better."

"And it's scribblers like you, on top of the reports in legitimate newspapers, who crank out the exaggerated yarns that help build and spread those reputations like wildfire."

Blessingame cocked his head indignantly. "I take offense, sir, at the implication that the work I do, the words I 'crank out,' are not every bit as legitimate as newspaper accounts. I toil hard to provide my readership the color and excitement they seek as entertainment to offset the drudgery of their lives." The writer paused, his mouth puckering, his chin jutting out in an attempt at boldness. "Are you, perchance, *threatening* me to cease doing what I am involved in?"

"Mister," Firestick grated, "if I was threatenin' you, you'd know it plain enough without havin' to ask. All I'm sayin' is—for the reasons you rattled off a minute ago about how a man who gets a reputation as a fast gun runs the risk of havin' to defend that rep whether he wants to or not—I hope you use some care in what you write as far as anything that's 'inspired' by Moosejaw. He ain't no fast gun, not in the way that term gets used, and bein' painted that way is the second to the last thing he wants or needs. The very last is havin' hardcases show up lookin' to . . ."

Firestick let his words trail off as it became apparent that, right in the middle of what he was saying, Blessingame was no longer listening to him. Instead, the writer's attention was drawn away by something beyond the marshal, something out in the street.

Turning his head, the marshal swept his gaze up and down Trail Street. Nothing unusual jumped out at him. There seemed to be a normal amount of midday activity. Shoppers moving along the boardwalks on either side, a few pausing to visit in groups of two or three. A standard number of horsemen and wagons traveling back and forth out on the dusty street itself.

"You must have the power of premonition within you, Marshal," murmured Blessingame.

Firestick's head came back around. "What the hell's that supposed to mean?"

In a very calm voice, Blessingame replied, "Unless I'm mistaken—and I'm quite confident that I am not—the very words you were saying about the last thing Deputy Moosejaw needed was a hardcase showing up . . . Well, with absolutely no prompting by me or my writing, I believe that last thing has just manifested itself in spite of your fervent wishes otherwise."

"Can your fancy-ass talk and speak English!"

"Catty-cornered across the street"—Blessingame tilted his head to indicate where he meant—"see the tall man with longish red hair ducking under the hitchrail after tying his horse and getting ready to enter the Lone Star Palace Saloon? You probably can't recognize him from this angle, but trust me . . . that is one William Caskett, better known as 'Coffin Bill.'"

Firestick watched the back of the tall, red-haired man as he pushed open the batwings of the Lone Star Palace and then melted into the smoky gloom inside. Blessingame sounded so confident in his identification of the man that Firestick felt no doubt about his accuracy. Under his breath, the marshal muttered, "Damn."

Chapter 14

Hector Barlow peeled back one corner of his upper lip and sneered. "You got a lot of brass, comin' 'round beggin' us to help you out."

Liam Scorp paused with a shot of red-eye raised partway to his mouth. Slowly, he turned his head to lock eyes with Barlow, who was leaning on the scarred, cigarette-scorched bar top about three feet to his left.

"Well, now. Reckon I got me some brass. Always have had," Liam said measuredly. "As for the beggin' part, though, I don't rightly see what you're crowin' about. How do you figure invitin' you and your boys to join me and my cousin on a job rates as beggin'?"

"You said yourself that part of the job means gettin' revenge for your brother Hank, didn't you? That makes it a personal thing for you—one that you need the backin' of some extra guns to pull off." Barlow's lip curled a little higher. "I rate askin' help for something personal as needin' a favor."

"Whatever stake I got in it don't change the fact that what I'm throwin' down where you're concerned is a job offer—one that promises good money," Liam reminded him. "Where's any beggin' in that? Plus, I already told you that all me and Jebediah are lookin' for, other than the revenge part, is a small cut of the take, just enough to carry us on down into Mexico."

"That's another thing I don't like," said Barlow. "This job is clear down almost to the Tex-Mex border. That's a helluva long pull from here."

Liam shrugged. "I can't help that. It is where it is. Both the bank and the bastard who gunned down Hank."

Barlow screwed up his face. "What's the name of the town again? Buffalo Peak? I never even heard of it. I ain't sayin' I know every town in West Texas, but I reckon I've heard of any that amount to anything. So the bank in this piss-ant little town that nobody ever heard of—what's the likelihood of it havin' enough money, no matter how big the cut, to be worth such a long ride?"

"All I know," Liam replied, "is that there's a growin' number of cattle ranches in the area. That means businesses to supply 'em and money passin' back and forth to stock and buy those supplies. And accordin' to the newspaper, the bank is part of the West Texas Cattlemen's Association. They don't usually mess with small potatoes." Liam paused a moment, then added, "And it seems worth keepin' in mind it's a bank that was big enough to draw the attention of Tuscarora Billings and Needles Whitney. Me, I got no high feelin's for either one of those cold-blooded bastards who led my little brother to his death. But generally speakin', Tuscarora and Needles weren't exactly known for goin' after pickin's that wasn't worthwhile."

"He makes a good point, Hector," spoke up Silas Clapton, occupying a slice of the bar just past where

Barlow leaned. "The likes of Tuscarora and Needles wouldn't have messed with a bank if they didn't figure there was good pickin's to be had."

Barlow turned and glared at the speaker. Except for height, the two men were nearly mirror images of one another. Barlow was a couple inches short of six feet, beefy build, with a moon face dominated by bulging, expressive eyes under bushy brows and a wide mouth that flashed oversized teeth usually displayed in a snarl or fit of vulgar laughter. Clapton was four inches taller, also beefy in build, with a roundish though slightly elongated face possessing bushy brows over beadier eyes and an extended upper lip less given to displaying rows of teeth that were equally oversized when they did show. Each man had dark hair, thinning in front and badly in need of a trim around the ears and the backs of their necks. Their attire was rugged, hard-worn range clothes and each had a Colt six-shooter holstered on his hip. Even while leaning against the bar, both held their bodies positioned in such a way that their gun arms and Colts were never encumbered.

In response to Clapton's statement, Barlow said in a sharp tone, "Excuse me all to hell, but I thought *I* was the one havin' this discussion and decidin' what valuable points these two beggars might be capable of makin'."

Setting his jaw firmly and not backing away any from the sharp retort, Clapton replied, "Yeah, you're doin' the talkin' right enough. And it's true you've sorta took over things since Clemson got hisself killed. But it's also true we ain't done much of anything since then. And now, for whatever reason, you seem bent on turnin' a mighty cold shoulder to what Scorp's pitchin' without givin' him a reasonable hearin'-out."

"Oh, I do, do I? That's the way it seems to you?"

"To put it plain—yeah."

Barlow leaned out and looked past to the wiry, dark-skinned man on the other side of Clapton. "How about you, Grimes? You hearin' this? You want to jump in and help tell me how to run things, too?"

Mojave Grimes, a leathery-faced half-breed with unreadable eyes and a fluid, unhurried way of moving that belied the speed and power he possessed when required, said, "I'll only repeat what Clapton already said. We have done nothing of late except sit here and watch others come and go while our pockets have become lined with dust and our joints stiff from inactivity. What Scorp has to say sounds worth consideration."

The "here" Grimes referred to was a nameless, mud-walled saloon that sat on a high bluff overlooking the Ricksaw River, with open plains spreading across the low ground to the south and east and a ragged fringe of mountains to the north and west. In other words, it was a good vantage point from which to spot approaching riders and provided outlets to make a quick disappearance for those who didn't want company. Most of the men seeking out this off-the-beaten-path rat hole tended to be on the run from something. Occasionally, a posse showed up in pursuit. But since it was generally known that Ballou, the tight-mouthed Cajun who ran the joint, never seemed to notice or remember anything about his customers, most savvy lawmen considered it pointless to waste time coming around.

Still, there were exceptions—greenhorns who

didn't know any better or sometimes stubborn old law dogs who were desperate enough to think they might be able to squeeze something out of Ballou. For these rarities, Ballou's half-wit son held a steady lookout and had developed a reliable eye for spotting the approach of any potential trouble.

"Well, ain't this a fine howdy-do," declared Barlow in the wake of Grimes's answer to the question he was asked. "All of a sudden my judgment ain't good enough for the men I thought were my pards. All of a sudden I'm bein' unreasonable and cold-shouldered to the pitch from some beggar that's supposed to be worthy of my consideration!"

Finally tossing down the shot he'd been about to take earlier, Liam returned the emptied glass to the bar top with a loud clap. "Look, Barlow, I'm gettin' mighty sick of that 'beggar' shit," he said. "What the hell's your problem?"

Barlow spun back to face him. "You! You're my problem, Scorp. You think I'm just supposed to forget about last fall when it was Clemson and me who came to *you* with a job offer? Then you were the one who was unreasonable and decided you'd rather not get involved."

"There was nothing personal in it. I didn't like the sound of the job, that's all," responded Liam. "Robbin' the flyer out of Fayetteville was too damn risky. Was, and still is. It's too well guarded and Clemson wasn't figurin' near enough men."

"That's why we came to you and Jebediah. We recognized we needed more men."

"It still wasn't enough, not even with us. I could see that; that's why we turned it down." Liam's expression hardened. "Look, I don't want to speak ill of the dead. Clemson was a decent fella, usually planned pretty good. But he was in way over his head tryin' to take on the flyer. Had he been able to see that and not tried to bull through with it anyway, he'd still be alive today."

"Maybe so," Barlow allowed through gritted teeth. "And maybe I wouldn't have ended up with three busted ribs and an ache I wake up with every cold mornin', still to this day, from the bullet I took through my side. Yeah, you can say none of that would've happened if we hadn't tried to take the flyer . . . But you also could say maybe none of it might've happened if you and your fat-assed, lazy cousin had the stones to have joined in with us and provided some extra guns!"

Liam straightened up and took a step away from the bar. Behind him, Jebediah also straightened up. But instead of stepping away from the bar, he lifted his arm in an unhurried, leisurely movement and laid on the scarred surface a double-barreled shotgun with the twin muzzles aimed in the general direction of Barlow, Clapton, and Grimes.

From behind the bar, Ballou, who tended to shuffle around slow and droopy-eyed, appearing not to hear or notice anything except for a glass that needed re-filling, suddenly wailed, "Here now! No shooting in here. My walls already have too many holes and leaks, and my ears cannot stand the loud bangs. Plus, since my old wife died, I have no one to clean up the spilled blood."

"Rest your tongue and take it easy," advised Liam. His words were for Ballou but his eyes never left Barlow. "Ain't gonna be no shootin'. Ain't gonna be no need for none. That is, as long as Hector here shows the good sense to take back his insultin' words and do some real sincere beggin'-your-pardon."

"To hell with you. I ain't takin' nothing back," snarled Barlow. "Everything I said was the truth. If not for you two gutless slobs, Earl Clemson would still be alive today! He was worth ten of you two put together. And now you think we're gonna raise a hand to help you pull off some stupid act of revenge that you dangle as a money-payin' job? If there's any revenge owed, it's for Earl!"

From behind him, Clapton spoke softly, saying, "You need to cool down, Hector. We all miss Earl, but this ain't no good. It was those Pinkerton men, thick as flies on that flyer, who pumped the bullets into you and Earl. Not these two fellas."

"No, it for damn sure wasn't them. They were too gutless to be anywhere near!"

"You're pushin' this way too far, Barlow," warned Liam. "All you had to do was say you wasn't interested in the job. Would've been your right, just like it was mine to turn down that flyer job last fall. But now you've gone and made it personal with words we can't just leave go. If these feelin's have been festerin' in you all this time, you should've stepped forward before."

"Well, I'm steppin' forward now, damn you," Barlow hissed, his entire body starting to tremble with the rage he'd worked himself into. "I'm steppin' forward to—"

What he ended up stepping into was ten inches of razor-sharp Bowie blade that Liam lunged to slip into his gut just above the belt buckle. A single upward jerk sliced a diagonal slash to the tip of Barlow's sternum, releasing a gush of blood and bulging intestines that poured over Liam's wrist and forearm before he could pull away and let what was suddenly a corpse crumple to the floor.

It all happened very fast and unexpected. Clapton and Grimes, disconcerted by Barlow's behavior to begin with, were frozen in place by the silent threat of Jebediah's shotgun muzzles. Barlow, so incensed and apparently priming himself for gunplay, had failed to notice—like everyone else—the way Liam had covertly unsheathed his Bowie when he stepped away from the bar and then stood with it held at his side and angled out of sight behind his back. Until he decided there was no rational way to deal with the pent-up rage in Barlow. Having neither time to waste nor a willingness to ignore the insults that had been issued, Liam swung the Bowie around and brought the matter to a quick, vicious close.

Maybe.

Wiping the Bowie blade on his pantleg before re-sheathing it, he cut his eyes to Clapton and Grimes. "All he had to do was say no to the job and not resort to the insults. I would have walked away. But he pushed it to where I had no choice. What about you two? A minute ago you were makin' noises like you had some sense. Are you still interested in that Buffalo Peak bank job?"

The pair exchanged a lengthy look. Then Clapton turned back to Liam and said, "Earl Clemson was a good leader. Leastways he was up until he got that fool notion about the Fayetteville Flyer. Barlow was never fit to take his place, but I reckon me and Grimes let him think he was because we wasn't interested in tryin' it on for ourselves. Like you heard, it didn't really matter much on account of Barlow never came up with a direction to lead us anyway. Now it sounds like maybe you got one. A worthwhile direction, that is. The way you did Barlow was a mite sneaky, but like you said—he pushed you into it. We got no grudge over that. Point us in the direction of Buffalo Peak and tell us our part when we get there. We'll take the ride with you."

"Good," Liam said with a nod. "We'll start out right away. We can make a stop at Feeney's Tradin' Post to stock up on supplies."

Liam next swung his attention to Ballou, who was leaning over the bar and gazing with anguish at Barlow's dead body—not so much due to the death of a fellow human being, but rather at the mess his dying was making on the already filthy floor.

"Ballou, I did my best. I avoided gun noise to keep from hurtin' your ears, but I couldn't help Hector not bein' able to hold in his guts," Liam said. He took a handful of coins from his pocket and spread them on the bar. "Here's for the inconvenience. Try to bury him at least deep enough to keep the varmints from diggin' him back up the very first night."

"I'll do my best, but the ground is very dry and hard and my back ain't what it used to be," Ballou said, snatching up the coins.

As they were getting on their horses once outside, Jebediah said, "You know ol' Ballou's got some hogs in a pen out back. That's where Barlow's body is likely to end up. Hell, he'll probably bring in the hogs to lick up the saloon floor, too."

"Think what you want," Liam said, stone-faced. "Me, I choose to believe the Cajun will dig at least a few scratches in the ground for Hector. Either way, I don't plan on ever comin' back around to find out any different."

Chapter 15

"Coffin Bill," Kate said, echoing the name. "I've heard talk of him, but not for quite a while it seems. Actually, if asked, I probably would have guessed he was dead."

Firestick nodded. "Uh-huh. I would have thought so, too. Last I heard—and, like you said, it goes back a ways—he was somewhere in the Tombstone area. Before that, when his name was poppin' up more regular-like, it was up north, mostly in Kansas. Abilene. Dodge. He rubbed elbows with some pretty big names. Was a deputy for Bat Masterson at one point. Supposedly backed down Doc Holliday durin' that time, steppin' into a dustup when Masterson wanted to avoid bracin' Doc himself on account of their mutual friendship with Wyatt Earp."

"But eventually he became just a gunman and outlaw. Right?"

"A gunman, that's for sure," agreed Firestick. "Callin' him an outlaw might be stretchin' it some, though there's little doubt he hired his gun for causes that rubbed mighty close to crossin' the line."

"In any case, since he's still alive and has shown up here, you figure it's for the purpose of confronting Moosejaw?"

"Kinda hard to swallow it just bein' a coincidence."

They were having their customary lunch together in the Mallory House dining room. The only difference was that this time, instead of sitting at a table toward the rear for more privacy like they usually did, today they were seated at a table near the front where Firestick could look out the window and watch the activity up and down Trail Street. In particular, he was keeping an eye on the front of the Lone Star Palace, making sure there was no further sign of Coffin Bill and that the horse he'd ridden in on remained tied to the hitchrail.

"If he *is* here to challenge Moosejaw," Kate went on, "I'm not sure I see the point. I mean, what is there for him to gain? He already has a well-known name, a reputation. Why go out of his way to add to it?"

"Can't say, exactly," Firestick replied. "But if I had to guess, I reckon he might see it as a way to, well, sort of advertise. West Texas is new territory for him. If he figures on operatin' in these parts for a spell, rather than just driftin' through, maybe he figures tanglin' with Moosejaw—who's gettin' all this fresh notice— will spread word that he's on the scene and hasn't lost his touch. So if there's any cattlemen or whatever who might be in the market for a hired gun, they'll be aware he's around. Be especially useful if there's other folks like us, who haven't heard his name mentioned in a while and might even believe he's dead."

"Good Lord," said Kate. "Calling a man out, being willing to gun him down or risk taking a bullet yourself, just as a means to announce your availability—that's awfully barbaric, wouldn't you say?"

Firestick shrugged. "I didn't say it was a good idea. I was just explainin' what reason Coffin Bill might have for seekin' out Moosejaw—*if* that's what he's here for."

"So you're going to have to find out. You'll have to talk to him and see what he has in mind. Right?"

"Expect so. But what kind of answer he gives me and what he actually ends up doin' might be very different things."

Kate scowled. "At least it will give you the chance to make him aware you know who he is and to let him know that, in return, you won't stand for it if he's here gunning for Moosejaw."

"And you figure that's all it'll take to send him scurryin', is that it?" The corners of Firestick's mouth curved up in a tolerant smile. "I got a hunch Coffin Bill has heard words along those lines in a lot of the places he's been. And I got an even bigger hunch they've pretty much rolled off his back because he knows there ain't a doggone thing can be done, legally, about him just showin' up in a town. Not unless or until he does something against the law. And even if he ends up callin' somebody out—like Moosejaw, in this case—and that somebody draws against him, then there still wouldn't be no law broke because it'd be seen as a fair fight, self-defense for whoever was left standin'."

"How could it be called a fair fight if one of the participants is an individual like Coffin Bill—a well-known shootist, someone proven to be faster and more deadly with a gun than the average person?"

"That's a choice that falls to the fella on the other

end of the thing. He can walk away, refuse to meet the challenge, let it end without gunplay."

"But then such a man would be branded a coward. Called yellow." Kate's full lips pressed momentarily into a thin line. "Most men wouldn't allow that. Certainly not someone like Moosejaw."

"No, not Moosejaw. Never," Firestick said.

Kate's eyes bored into him. "And there's nothing you can do to intercede on his behalf if it turns out Coffin Bill *is* here for him?"

Firestick's head turned once to each side. "He'd see it as me tryin' to fight his battles for him. He'd hate that and never forgive me."

"And if the situations were reversed, you'd feel the same way, wouldn't you?"

"That's the way it works."

Kate let out an exasperated sigh. "You men and your foolish pride. Because of attitudes like that, I sometimes find it amazing there are enough of you left to keep this stupid planet populated, especially out here in the West."

"Well now," said Firestick, one corner of his mouth quirking upward. "Matters like that—leastways handlin' our end of the work that goes into keepin' things populated—is another area where a lot of us take a fair amount of pride."

Spots of color appeared on Kate's cheeks, though not because she was embarrassed. "Darn you, don't tease me or try to make light of what we're discussing. What if it does come down to Moosejaw having to face Coffin Bill and he ends up getting shot, maybe killed. Then will you still see it as a fair fight? Or will you or Beartooth feel obligated to respond in some way

for Moosejaw? One of you perhaps challenging Coffin
Bill as a result?"

Firestick didn't answer right away. These weren't
questions he wanted to think about. Yet at the same
time he couldn't keep from remembering Beartooth's
response yesterday, when, in the aftermath of the
shoot-out at Moosejaw's cabin, the notion of Curly
Roy having come out on top had been posed as an
alternative outcome: *"Then I would have gone ahead and
killed him anyway!"* And in that instant, though he
never spoke or even acknowledged the words, Firestick recognized them as exactly the same way he felt.

Now, with her insightful wisdom, Kate wanted him
to admit as much.

Thankfully, an interruption saved him.

"Excuse me, Marshal . . . Miss Kate . . . Don't mean
to barge in on your lunch, but I wonder if I could
have a quick word . . . with you, Marshal, that is."

Firestick and Kate looked up to see the speaker was
a lanky young cowboy standing at the edge of their
table, his approach gone unnoticed due to the intensity of their conversation. Both recognized the young
man as Andy Lowe, the middle son of Asa Lowe, who
ran the Ace Low spread southwest of town.

"Sure, Andy. What's on your mind?" said Firestick.

Andy looked a little uncertain. "Well, uh . . . it ain't
really what's on my mind. It's my pa. He wanted me to
get word to you. About the shootin' yesterday—you
know, Curly Roy and Deputy Moosejaw."

"What about the shootin'?" Firestick's expression
turned more sober. "I was there, I think I'm pretty
well up to speed on everything that happened."

"Yessir. I know that."

"Maybe Andy would like to sit down," Kate suggested.

"Perhaps he'd like a cup of coffee or a cold drink after his ride in from the ranch?"

Andy shook his head. "No thanks, ma'am. I just got to let the marshal know and then get on back."

"Let me know what, Andy?" said Firestick.

"Pa wanted to warn you that some of the wranglers out at our ranch are pretty worked up about what happened. To Curly Roy, I mean. Pa got 'em all in a bunch after we buried Curly Roy this mornin', told 'em they needed to cool down and not do anything foolish. But he ain't so sure they're gonna listen." Andy's forehead puckered. "Pa's thinkin' some of 'em might head into town tonight and cause trouble over it."

"Cause trouble with my deputies and me?"

Andy's eyes widened. "Oh no, sir. Not that. Everybody understands how Deputy Moosejaw got pushed into doin' what he had to do. But it's that writer fella that Harvey and Clay told us all about—how the troublemakin' skunk egged Curly Roy on, filled his head with notions of writin' about him and makin' him practically as famous as Wild Bill Hickok. Maybe he didn't pull the trigger, but him proddin' Curly Roy along with such highfalutin notions was sure a part of puttin' him in front of a bullet. It don't seem right that he ought to get away with doin' that and not havin' to answer for it somehow."

By the time the young man was finished, his eyes had narrowed and his chin was jutted out aggressively. It was clear that, even though he was faithfully carrying the warning from his father, his own feelings weren't too far apart from those of the agitated wranglers.

"You tell your pa I appreciate the heads-up," Firestick said to him. "And I appreciate you deliverin' it. I know how close a crew of wranglers get on a ranch, so

I'd also appreciate if you'll deliver something back to your pa and the rest of the boys out there. Tell 'em we regret what happened to Curly Roy—and that goes for nobody more than Moosejaw. I'm glad they seem to understand he had no choice.

"Tell 'em, too, that we don't care very much for Blessingame, the writer, either. But the problem is, while he might be a skunk hidin' behind fancy words, he ain't done nothing illegal. I'm hopin' to get rid of him on the next stage out of here. But, until then, he has as much right to talk and put pen to paper as anybody else. So if your Ace Low pards come 'round to rough him up or however they plan to make trouble for him, I'll have to stand in their way. It's my job. I may not like it, but I'll do what I have to. You understand, Andy?"

Andy nodded. "Yessir. I understand. I'll tell everybody what you said."

When the young cowboy had gone, Firestick turned back to face Kate. He took a sip of his coffee, which had grown cold and bitter.

Kate regarded him. She said, "Sometimes that badge weighs a lot, doesn't it?"

"Once in a while," Firestick allowed. "Mostly when it means I've got to walk light around critters I know damn well should be stepped on like bugs—yet I can't do anything until they make the first move to prove they're what I figured 'em for all along."

Chapter 16

Howard Blessingame was practically giddy. He couldn't believe his luck. He'd gambled on coming to Buffalo Peak, hoping it would gain him an exclusive on Moosejaw Hendricks, the sensational new hero filling the newspapers. And while it hadn't quite worked out as far as providing him the "real life/true story" angle he would have preferred, it nevertheless had inspired the Mooseheart Mulligan adventure he'd begun feverishly penning as an alternative.

But now . . . the arrival of none other than William Caskett. Coffin Bill! Not merely a new sensation, a possible flash-in-the-pan, but rather a rock-solid, bona fide legend! A man who'd stood shoulder to shoulder with the likes of Bat Masterson and Wyatt Earp. A shootist so renowned he had backed down Doc Holliday—the deadly consumptive who feared nobody because he didn't care if he lived or took a bullet that would save him from the inevitable racking death of tuberculosis.

Coffin Bill. Right here, nearly within arm's reach. Just across the street.

After the marshal had departed following their

discussion, Blessingame remained seated out front of the Mallory House. He sipped his lemonade and attempted to resume his writing. But it was no use. He couldn't concentrate. Not on the fictionalized adventures of Mooseheart Mulligan. Not when he had the real thing—a renowned gunman whose true adventures could fill a half dozen volumes, maybe more—only a couple hundred yards across the street.

Blessingame tried to think if he had ever seen or read any accounts of Coffin Bill's exploits. He couldn't remember any, not even any gaudily embellished dime novel publications. His pulse quickened at the thought of such fertile ground being as yet untapped. This could be his big chance, the break he needed to take that next step toward being a more seriously accepted author. What was more, since most of his previous work had been under the Hank Blake byline, he could continue that sort of thing as a means to pay the bills while he began the transition to more serious work under his own name.

His pulse quickened a bit more as his gaze came to rest on the batwing doors of the Lone Star Palace. A great opportunity, he told himself, might very well lay just on the other side of those doors.

All he had to do was work up the courage to walk over there and reach out to seize it . . .

Moosejaw wasn't clearing brush this afternoon. Instead he was working on repairing the shutters over the windows of the little cabin. Most of them only needed tightening and a few hinges replaced . . . a few required new slats being fitted in. All of them were also in need of a coat of paint, but the dust being whipped around by today's wind gusts—although a good reminder of why it was important for the shutters to be in good shape before the cold blasts of eventual winter—made painting them work for another time.

Moosejaw was aware of Firestick having ridden up, but he continued concentrating on the task he was involved in, trying to fit several new slats into the slotted frame of one of the shutters. The slats were proving difficult to slip into the existing grooves, and the wind buffeting the overall shutter wasn't helping any at all. This combination was causing the big deputy to try and assist his efforts with an increasingly steady string of curses.

Having dismounted, Firestick sauntered over and came to a halt at a safe distance, his arms folded over his chest. "My oh my," he said, "I don't think I ever heard anybody suggest to a few innocent pieces of wood that they could do something like that to one another."

"Stick around, I'm just gettin' warmed up," Moosejaw muttered through gritted teeth, not taking time to look back over his shoulder. "In about a minute, this devil-spawned pile of lumber is gonna end up in the kindlin' pile for the fireplace!"

"By 'pile of lumber,' do you mean just that particular shutter, or the whole cabin?"

"Smart remarks not only ain't helpful but they damn sure ain't appreciated," growled Moosejaw.

Firestick couldn't hold back a wry grin. "Tell you what. Sometimes the best thing for a frustration like that is to step away for a few minutes, cool down a mite, then go back at it fresh. To help with the coolin'-down part, I happen to have a couple bottles of beer in my saddlebags. They were good and cold when I packed them in there, so if we don't waste any more time gettin' to 'em, they should still be pretty good."

Moosejaw finally looked around. "Pearls of wisdom from the elderly, especially comin' with the promise of a cold beer," he said, "is something I reckon a body ought never turn down."

"Be a step toward growin' older and wiser your ownself."

A couple minutes later, after Moosejaw had secured the shutter with a leather thong so it wouldn't get caught by a wind gust and knock loose what little progress he'd made, the pair were carrying the bottles of beer around to the back side of the house, into a patch of shade and out of the wind. Moosejaw dragged two tree trunk sections over from the woodpile for them to sit on.

"Man, that tastes good," the big deputy declared, emitting a satisfied sigh after tipping up his bottle and guzzling down half the contents. "Not to sound ungrateful, but I wish you'd've packed those saddlebags a little fuller."

"Trouble with that is, it might've been a little too much of an interruption to your problem, not to mention your overall progress," Firestick said.

Moosejaw sighed again. "Maybe. But I don't think so, not really." He tipped his head back against the side of the cabin. "This whole thing, Firestick . . . the cabin, the engagement, and the upcomin' marriage . . . I feel really caught up in it. Excited by it all. After thinkin' for so long that I'd probably never get hitched and then meetin' Daisy and comin' to realize that I *wanted* to be married but at the same time feelin' kinda scared by the thought of it . . . Now that's all gone. I've never been more sure of anything in my whole life, and I can't hardly wait to go through with the rest of it."

Firestick smiled. "I'm happy for you, old friend. I can't tell you how much."

Moosejaw drank some more of his beer. Then, lowering the bottle, he looked over at Firestick. "Say. I don't reckon you left town and came out here just to bring me a beer. Something more on your mind?"

Firestick took a minute to answer. First he raised his own bottle for a long pull. Then: "Couple hours ago, a stranger rode into Buffalo Peak. A stranger to our neck of the woods, that is. But he's got a name I think you'll recognize quick enough. William Caskett, better known as Coffin Bill."

Moosejaw's expression didn't change, but there was a different edge to his voice when he said, "Coffin Bill . . . damn."

"That was pretty much my reaction."

"You don't hear his name much anymore. I kinda thought he might be dead."

"Didn't appear that way when he climbed down off his horse and walked into the Lone Star Palace."

Moosejaw gave it a beat, then said, "He here for me, you reckon?"

"Good possibility, I figure. No way to be sure until he says or shows what brings him our way."

"Ain't no rancher disputes goin' on anywhere close by. No reason for him to be called in as a hired gun."

"Nope. Though that don't mean he might not be just passin' through."

"So you ain't talked to him at all?"

"Thought I'd run it by you first. Otherwise I figured

you might take exception, see it as me interferin' in something that might be your business."

"Appreciate that," said Moosejaw. He rolled his beer bottle back and forth between his big palms. "Seein's how it would be a pretty big coincidence otherwise . . . Coffin Bill showin' up here most likely means he's bent on *makin'* it my business."

Firestick didn't say anything.

After he'd drained the last of his beer, Moosejaw said, "So how do you think I oughta play it?"

"For starters," Firestick replied, "I'd say somebody—me, you, whoever—oughta have that talk with Bill. He went straight to the Lone Star Palace when he hit town . . . I expect he's likely still there. I checked all the wanted dodgers in the jail office before I left—he ain't wanted for nothing. Not around here, not nowhere that I could find. But he's still got enough of a reputation that I don't think any lawman would be out of line inquirin' as to his intentions when he shows up in a town."

"You expect he'll flat-out say so, if he's here to have a go at me?"

"If that's his intent, he's gonna have to show it sooner or later. Havin' a talk with him would at least give us a chance to try and get some kind of read off him."

Moosejaw nodded. "That makes sense. Okay. Let's go do it, then. See what we can find out. No sense puttin' it off."

When he started to get up, Firestick put a hand on his arm. "Hold on a second. There's another matter sorta brewin' that we need to talk about, too."

"What's that?" Moosejaw wanted to know.

Firestick gave him a quick rundown on the visit

from Andy Lowe, relating the anger of the Ace Low riders as described by the boy and how they were planning a trip to town to confront Blessingame as a result.

Moosejaw was frowning thoughtfully by the time he was done. "I'm of two minds about such a situation," he said. "For starters, I'm glad the Ace Low riders understand how I was dragged into that shoot-out with Curly Roy and they don't harbor no hard feelin's against me over it. Secondly, I gotta admit that it'd be hard for me to work up much sympathy for Blessingame if they was to show up and pound some knots on him. I figure, same as they do, that Mr. Fancy Writer and Talker played a hand in proddin' Curly Roy out here yesterday."

"I don't necessarily dispute that," Firestick said. "But, unfortunately, it ain't the kind of thing, as lawmen, we can stand by and let happen. You know that as well as I do."

"Yeah. I know it, but I don't have to like it." Moosejaw regarded him. "I got a feelin' you have something particular in mind. What is it?"

"I can't help thinkin'," the marshal replied, "that it might work out better if we rode out to the Ace Low and faced those wranglers there. It'd not only catch 'em by surprise, I figure, but it'd also catch 'em before they rode clear into town and got their anger all worked up fresh and hot, feedin' off one another. Plus, at the ranch, we'd have Asa Lowe in our corner, helpin' to talk sense to 'em."

"Might work," Moosejaw allowed, though not looking entirely sold on the idea. "But what about Coffin Bill, back in town?"

"I reckon he'll keep. If his aim is to confront you, he'll still be around whenever we get there. If he's just passin' through, maybe he'll have moved on by the time we make it back."

"You didn't come up with this notion about goin' out to the Ace Low just to delay me havin' to face Coffin Bill, did you?"

"If that's what I was anglin' for, would I have ridden out here and told you about him in the first place?"

Moosejaw wagged his head. "No, I reckon not."

"Okay then. Let's swing by the Double M and pick up Beartooth, too. I figure a show of force wouldn't be a bad idea when we get to the Ace Low. Not to be threatenin', just to show 'em we mean business. After that, returnin' to town and tryin' to find out what Coffin Bill has in mind will come soon enough."

Chapter 17

"I been on the trail of Tuscarora Billings steady, for near six weeks. Hell, if you count the time I was hospitalized and recuperatin' from the slugs he put in me, you could say it was nigh on to a year." Coffin Bill's mouth turned down at the corners and his eyes seemed to glower at some faraway thing no one else could see. "Every minute of that time, even when I was fever-riddled and clawin' not to get pulled through death's door, inside my head I was trackin' that low-down snake. Plannin' what I was gonna do to him once I caught up."

"Revenge can be a powerful motivator for one to endure and prevail," Blessingame said agreeably.

Coffin Bill grunted. "I don't know about those fancy words. But revenge, yeah. Hate. Those are the things that saw me through. How can you not hate a scurvy bastard who's so dirt low that he pumps another slug in an *hombre* after he's already gunned him down? I never in my life resorted to anything like that. If I put a man down, that was the end of it. Usually when I put 'em down it was permanent-like anyway.

But on the rare occasions I planted a slug in 'em and they still had some life left, I sure as hell never saw fit to drill 'em again once they was on the ground.

"Yet that's the way Tuscarora done me. The cur never would've got the bulge on me in the first place if he hadn't slickered me with that damn saloon whore, Gabriella. She climbed all over me and threw on a hug that partly pinned my gun arm. I knew the second her fat ass landed in my lap that it was a setup, but I wasn't able to dump her and clear leather fast enough. Tuscarora's Colt was already spittin' lead. And after I hit the floor, the villainous bastard stood over me and shot me a second time."

"And this was in Galveston, you say?" asked Blessingame, writing furiously in his tablet, trying to keep up with the details of what Bill was saying.

Bill nodded. "That's right. Galveston. A place called the Lacey Garter Saloon."

"But even with two bullets in you, one of them fired at point-blank range, you managed to survive," said Blessingame in an awed tone.

"That's right. There was enough blood to make 'em think I was done for. So they dragged me into an alley out back and left me for the rats," Bill related. "But a different kind of rat found me there. A wharf rat. An old rummy who'd seen what they did to me and didn't like it. He'd done some doctorin' in the late war—the things he saw was what drove him to the rum, he claimed—and was somehow able to patch me up and pull me through. He had some kind of cockeyed notion he was evening the scales some for all the brave young lads he'd lost on the battlefields."

Blessingame shook his head in wonder. "What an

amazing tale. What became of him—the wharf rat, er, doctor, I mean?"

"He got knifed for his shoes one night when he went out late for a fresh bottle of hooch. Whoever did it slit his throat from ear to ear. For a broken-down pair of shoes. When I found him, even though he'd been able to save me," Bill said bitterly, "there wasn't a thing I could do for him."

The memory made him reach for the bottle of whiskey on the table between them and tip it up for a long gulp, not bothering with a glass. Blessingame watched, unsure what to say.

Bill was in his middle forties but looked older, the ravages of a hard life having added nearly a decade, appearance-wise. He had a flat, cleanly shaven face framed by gray-flecked reddish hair that fell unevenly past his collar on the sides and down the back of his neck. His eyes were sunk back in shadowy sockets, his cheeks hollowed, almost gaunt-looking, and the lines around his mouth cut deep, like cracks in water-starved ground.

His attire was of top quality: dark blue frock coat, striped trousers tucked into high boots that reached to just below the knee, pale blue vest with a gold watch chain on prominent display. A fedora-style hat was perched just-so atop his head, and the long-barreled Colt .45 riding on his hip was encased in a polished black holster and was made easily accessible by the careful manner in which he sat and the way his coat was unbuttoned and swept back. Like the man's physical features, the clothing showed no small amount of wear. Yet overriding everything, there remained about him—for anyone who knew what to look for—an air of alertness, a readiness, like a cagey old cougar poised for the hunt.

When Bill lowered the bottle, he said, "Once I was healed the rest of the way and lit out of there, I should've left that whole rotten wharf in ashes behind me. Especially the Lacey Garter. Got me in mind to go back there some day and take care of that little piece of unfinished business. One thing I did make sure to do, though, before I took out after Tuscarora, was to take time for a little visit to his slut Gabriella and pay her back for her part in the wrong was done me. She won't be flauntin' herself to distract anymore chumps, not after I was done with her. Way I left her face, man'd have to be stone blind to pay any attention to her these days."

Blessingame shuddered inwardly at the implication in Bill's words. He was appalled at the thought of such behavior, yet at the same time fascinated, mesmerized by the way Coffin Bill was opening up to him, the things he was revealing.

Once he'd screwed up his courage and marched into the Lone Star Palace, it had proven remarkably easy to strike up a conversation with the man. Blessingame had found him sitting alone at a rear table, back to the wall, facing out where he had a full view of the establishment's interior. He'd walked up boldly, introduced himself, and stated it would be an honor to buy a drink for the renowned Coffin Bill. Bill had given him a long, slow looking over and then told him to go fetch a bottle and come on back.

Blessingame had wasted no time complying and they'd been sitting together and talking ever since, well over two hours now. To the writer's surprise and delight, when he stated his trade and asked if he might jot down some notes on the exploits Bill was freely discussing, a generous go-ahead wave of the hand was his answer.

In the ensuing time, Blessingame had grown gradually aware that a recognition of who it was he was sitting with began to spread around the room. When he'd first entered, it seemed none of the other customers in the lunch-hour crowd had as yet realized they had the notorious Coffin Bill in their midst. Whether the change was triggered by someone else finally recognizing him or came as the result of an overheard snippet of their conversation, the writer didn't know.

But the muted buzz traveling from one mouth to another and the frequent guarded glances tossed their way left no doubt. Bill had been recognized, even though no one—not even Earl Sterling, the dandified owner of the place—had the courage to approach and say anything. The fact that *he* had made the move right off gave Blessingame cause to feel proud, and the fact he was now seated with such a celebrity made him feel a little special. Let the rabble keep their distance.

Bill continued to hold his hand wrapped around the whiskey bottle he'd drank directly from, as if considering doing it again. Then, staring balefully at its depleted contents, he said, "One thing I want to get straight, Burlingham—"

"Blessingame," the writer was quick to correct.

"Whatever," Bill grunted. "The thing is, I've done some harsh stuff in my time. Mostly I saw it as doin' what I had to in order to survive. So I make no apologies. All the same, some of it no man could be proud of. But it's done and can't be undone, so I won't crawfish and try to deny it. If you write about me and tell it straight, I won't be expectin' you to sugarcoat nothing I actually did. What I *do* demand is that you don't use any of the things I got blamed for that I never had a hand in."

"You have my word, sir. I won't do you wrong," Blessingame assured him.

"I thought about that kind of thing a lot while I was recoverin' from those bullets Tuscarora plunked in me," Bill said. "Bein' in such bad shape, I suppose, is what set my mind in that direction. What if I died, I kept thinkin'. Likely would have gone down that I was bested in a gunfight. The history of a thing is writ by the winners—ain't that what they always say? That would have meant, if I *had* died, my whole life would end on a lie. You can bet Tuscarora would have presented it like he flat beat me.

"And that's what got me to thinkin' about the rest, about all the other things from my life that could be twisted around and laid out with false turns here and there. Which is why I'm layin' it out straight for you here now. There've been other writers who flocked around me in the past, wantin' to hear about the things I'd done, the gun battles and such. But all they really wanted, I could tell, was a smidge of actual facts and bein' able to say they talked to me so they could fill the rest of what they wrote with a bunch of bloody shoot-outs and chases that never took place and claim it as the solid truth, straight from my tellin'.'"

"Unfortunately," Blessingame said somberly, "there are scoundrels on the fringes of my profession who operate exactly that way."

"But you ain't one of 'em. I took one look at you, Blithingdale—"

"Blessingame."

"Yeah, yeah . . . I took one look at you and could see right off you was different. For one thing, the timing of you comin' 'round after I'd had those thoughts and concerns while I was healin'. Hearin' you was a writer and everything, it was like . . . that thing . . . what's the word I'm lookin' for?"

"Fate?"

"Yeah! That's it—fate. You showin' up and me bein' in a mood to lay everything out and set the record straight, it's like it was meant to be." Bill nodded, as if agreeing with himself. "So as soon as I finish the business that brought me here to Buffalo Peak to begin with, we'll have another sit-down together. For as long as it takes you to scribble all the notes you need. Then I'll expect you to turn 'em into the straight story on me, once and for all."

"It's a genuine privilege to have you place that kind of faith in me, sir. And, once again, I assure you I will prove worthy of that trust," Blessingame said. Then, frowning, he added, "But what, if I may ask, is the other business you mean to tend to first?"

Bill looked at him as if he found the question rather foolish. "Why, I've got to settle the score with that local law dog—you know, the one in all the papers, the one who gunned down Tuscarora and those other fellas."

Blessingame's eyebrows lifted. "You mean Deputy Moosejaw?"

"If that's what he calls himself, yeah. I knew it

was something odd. What the hell kind of name is Moosejaw?"

"He got it from the Indians, back in the days when he was a hunter and trapper up in the Rocky Mountains," Blessingame explained. "The other two lawmen in town—friends of his dating back to that same period—also have rather colorful names bestowed on them by the Indians."

"Good for them. But it don't matter a damn to me," Bill growled. "If they like their Injun handles so much, then that's what can go on their tombstones."

Somewhat to his surprise, Blessingame found it rather disturbing to hear that Coffin Bill harbored ill feelings toward Moosejaw and apparently intended harm for him and possibly the other Buffalo Peak lawmen, too. While the three of them had shunned Blessingame and his writing, they nevertheless came across as decent, honest sorts who did a good job taking care of their town. And Moosejaw, in particular, was undeniably brave and inspiring.

"At the risk of sounding dense," said Blessingame, "I'm afraid I don't follow why you see the need for settling a score with Deputy Moosejaw. After all, he killed the man you so badly wanted to see punished for what he did to you."

"Yeah, wanted him punished by *me*. Havin' somebody else do it not only robs me of my chance to get even, but robs me of bein' able to show I could take Tuscarora in a fair face-off. If I leave it go as is, there'll still be those left believin' he bested me, even if I didn't die. Don't you see?" Bill's tone was demanding. "So the only way for me to square the whole works is for me to face the *hombre* who took down Tuscarora and I beat *him*. Then you write it up and everybody will know the straight of it."

Blessingame was once more left temporarily at a loss for words. Part of him was excited by the prospect of seeing the legendary Coffin Bill in action. But the convoluted logic behind the reason for that to be necessary and, again, the identity of who Bill meant to go against remained troubling.

Before Blessingame had time to grow overly concerned about this pending conflict, however, his attention was drawn away by activity at the front of the saloon. The lunch-hour crowd had long since thinned out and it was still too early for the after-work and evening drinkers to have started showing up. Except for some old-timers playing cards at one of the tables and a few drifters nursing drinks along the bar, the Lone Star Palace was in its afternoon slump.

But suddenly, with a loud clumping of bootheels on the boardwalk out front and then on the hardwood floor inside the saloon, six wranglers came slapping through the batwings. Behind the bar, Gunther, the beefy stick man, scowled at them briefly but otherwise remained attentive to the stack of glasses he was polishing.

Once all of them were inside, the newcomers bunched for a moment, eyes scanning the wide room. The ranged in age from twenty to forty and all appeared dusty and sweat-streaked from recent labor and hard riding. As one, their eyes settled on the table where Blessingame and Coffin Bill sat. They proceeded toward it.

"Well, well. What have we here," Bill muttered. There was no particular concern in his tone, yet at the same time Blessingame sensed a change, a coiled-spring preparedness taking hold of the gunman. Blessingame felt his own pulse quicken.

But then, as the group of wranglers drew close, the writer spotted a pair of familiar faces and his apprehension quickly eased.

"Well now. We meet again, gentlemen," he said, smiling. "Good afternoon to you."

His expression dour and his mouth set in a hard, straight line, Harvey Bell responded, "We ain't here to trade friendly greetings with the likes of you, Mr. Slick Talker. And by the time we're done with what we did come for, a good afternoon is the last thing you're gonna be havin'."

Chapter 18

A handful of miles outside of town, Firestick, Moosejaw, and Beartooth were pushing their horses hard, holding them to a steady gallop over the rolling hills and in and out of the grassy draws of the West Texas landscape. Their visit to the Ace Low ranch, after detouring to the Double M to pick up Beartooth, had not gone well. In fact, it turned out to be a complete waste of time—because the riled-up wranglers they had gone to try and settle down were nowhere to be found. A none-too-happy Asa Lowe was on hand to report that the bunch, six in number, had worked themselves into such a state that they'd knocked off early for the day and were already headed for Buffalo Peak.

Firestick knew immediately this wasn't good news. If the men in question had their hackles raised sharply enough to have ridden off not only in defiance of but right under the nose of their boss, then that marked them as being hell-bent for trouble. If Firestick and his deputies had come from town instead of angling in from the Double M, they would have encountered the men and still had a chance to turn them away. Instead, they'd missed them entirely, and by Lowe's estimation, the wranglers had nearly a half hour's start as far as reaching town.

All the three lawmen could do now was put the spurs to their horses and try to make up as much of that lost time as they could . . .

In the Lone Star Palace Saloon, the quiet and near emptiness that had settled in following the departure of the lunch crowd now had been disrupted by the loud entrance of the six cowboys. And Harvey Bell's surly response to Blessingame's friendly greeting only added an edge of tension.

Quickly adjusting his own tone and adopting a boldness he most surely would not have shown if he hadn't been in the very competent company of Coffin Bill, Blessingame said, "I know not the cause for such rude behavior on your part, Mr. Bell, but I assure you it is neither warranted nor welcome. You and your friends are interrupting a private conversation. A moment ago we might have tolerated that and been open to a friendly exchange. But that certainly is no longer the case. I therefore will thank you to take your insolent mouth and attitude elsewhere!"

Harvey Bell appeared caught off guard by this unexpectedly sharp retort. But it only took a second for his surprised look to pass and his lower lip to again curl disdainfully.

"What we're welcome to do or not do ain't in no way up to you, bub. You had your say when you goaded Curly Roy into goin' out to that cabin and bracin' Moosejaw. Now we're here to see that you get what you got comin' for that—for proddin' a simple young cowpoke with your fancy words and promises of fame and glory only to have him end up with a bullet in his heart. A heart that ain't never gonna beat no more on account of you."

"And look how tore up you are over it," added a surly voice from somewhere in the bunch behind Bell. "Sittin' here suckin' up liquor and havin' a high old time while poor Curly lays six feet down in the cold damn ground!"

"This is preposterous!" Blessingame exclaimed. "You're blaming *me* for what happened to Curly Roy?"

"You're the one we're lookin' at, ain't you?" demanded Bell.

"Look all you want. I can't help that. But your accusations are ridiculous," said Blessingame. "Yes, I listened to Curly Roy's claims about how good he was with a gun and how his skill with one was far superior to that of Deputy Moosejaw, who he thought was receiving undeserved praise. And it's also true that I revealed I was a writer who'd traveled here seeking a firsthand account of the deputy's recent shoot-out that I hoped to use in my work. But your friend's decision to challenge Moosejaw and perhaps take his place as a subject in my writing was entirely his assumption. I certainly made him no promises. Nor did I in any way encourage him to seek out Moosejaw for the shoot-out that subsequently took place."

"But you sure as hell went along to witness it, didn't you?" said Bell in an accusatory tone.

"Indeed I did," Blessingame admitted. "As did you and Mr. Halstead and several others from the saloon. I'll also point out that, long before I ever arrived on the scene, you and Halstead were already sitting with

Curly Roy and listening to him bragging about how good he was with a gun and how much better he was than Moosejaw."

"Curly Roy was always carryin' on about how good he was with his gun," Bell replied. "That was just his way."

"And he *was* pretty damn good," another anonymous voice interjected.

"But none of it ever led to him gettin' hisself killed," said Halstead, speaking up for the first time. "Not until you came along—wavin' around your flashy books and spewin' your slick words—causin' Curly Roy to believe you was gonna make him famous if he showed you something to back up his claims."

Blessingame slapped a palm down flat on the table. "I repeat. I made no such—"

"Now everybody just hold on a minute." Coffin Bill's voice wasn't overly loud yet it was enough to cut short Blessingame's statement and cause the eyes of all six cowboys—pointedly ignoring him up until then—to swing instantly in his direction. Continuing in the same low, steady tone, the gunfighter said, "Let me get this straight. How old was this Curly Roy everybody seems so het up about?"

Now the wranglers exchanged confused looks among themselves—confused first by the question itself and then, apparently, by what the answer was. Until Bell abruptly responded, "Twenty or thereabouts, I reckon. What difference does that make?"

"Twenty," Coffin Bill repeated, leaning back in his chair and gazing absently down at the tabletop. "In other words, just one more wet-behind-the-ears pup who thought twirlin' a gun was gonna make him a man."

"He never got to grow to a man. He died too young, thanks to that fancy-pants slickster you're spendin' your time with," said Halstead.

"Bein' a man is measured by more than years," said Coffin Bill. "He wrangled alongside you fellas, took his pay every month, didn't he? Or was he a slacker who didn't hold up his end?"

"He held up his end of things just fine."

"Okay. So there was enough to him for that. And enough for him to strap on a gun and blow about being good with it." A corner of Coffin Bill's mouth quirked up in a humorless half smile. "But now, since him and his mouth bit off more than they could chew, all of a sudden this man here"—he jabbed a thumb toward Blessingame—"who never saw your Curly Roy before in his life, was supposed to know he had to be coddled and his big talk wasn't to be taken seriously. Is that what you're saying?"

"What we're sayin' is that Blessingame should've kept his nose out of our business and his mouth shut," answered Bell. "If he'd done that, Curly Roy would still be alive. But, since he *did* stick his nose in and prod Curly the way he did, he needs to pay for it."

"And there's a lesson there for you to learn real quick," Halstead added, "since you also seem bent on stickin' your nose in where it's none of your concern."

"Speaking of lessons," Blessingame said, his mouth curving into a sly smile, "there's one you fellows would be advised to take time to learn before this goes any further."

"What the hell's that supposed to mean?" snarled Bell.

"It means that the lesson—and it comes in the form of a simple introduction—is this: Gentlemen,

allow me to introduce to you Mr. William Caskett."
Blessingame gestured with one hand. "Or, as he is
perhaps better known . . . Coffin Bill."

The expressions on the faces of the six wranglers
ran a gamut from disbelief to uncertainty to dismay.
No one, however, appeared not to recognize the name.

"I heard Coffin Bill was dead," somebody ventured,
but not with a lot of conviction.

"I heard that same thing myself a time or two,"
Coffin Bill allowed. "But then my bar tab came due
and I was still the one who had to pay it, so I decided
it must not be true."

"Okay, so that's real interestin', but it don't change
a doggone thing," Halstead said, scowling. "You've
heard by now, Mr. Caskett, how it went with our friend
Curly Roy and this smooth-talkin' writer fella. He
egged Curly on to a foolish act just so's he could see a
shoot-out firsthand and use it for his worthless damn
writin'. Well, Curly died as a result, and as his friends,
we can't let that stand. I can appreciate how he
probably bought you a drink and sidled up all
friendly-like—same as he did Curly—to get some
more fodder for his writin'. You couldn't've knowed
what came before. But now that you understand, I
trust you'll agree none of this is your affair and you'll
leave us go on about our business."

"No. As a matter of fact," Coffin Bill was quick to
reply, "there's hardly a single word of that I agree
with. For starters, you see, I have befriended Mr. Both-
ingham."

Blessingame automatically opened his mouth to
voice a correction, but then immediately thought
better of it in this instance and kept silent.

"And," Coffin Bill continued, "I'm hardly in the

habit of standing aside while a friend of mine is faced with six-to-one odds. Therefore, any quarrel you have with him you are advised to consider now includes me.

"Secondly, *your* friend, this Curly Roy, sounds to me like nothing more than a loudmouth whelp who happened to have some skill with a gun and allowed it to make him believe he was something more than he truly was. I've met a hundred of his kind in my day, and left a good number of them dead in my wake. In a manner of speaking, you might say each one of them insisted on it. Just like, from the sound of it, Curly Roy did. He was destined to meet a bullet in the end no matter what. And trying to blame it on anybody but him is wrong and stupid on y'all's part. And what else it is, is an effort by each of you to try and shrug off the guilt you're feeling over praising Curly Roy for being good with a gun yet not talking him out of going up against somebody who was better."

Coffin Bill slowly raked his gaze across the faces of the cowboys while he was talking. He continued doing this as he added, "There's one final thing you should consider, and it's this: If your friend Curly *had* been fast enough or lucky enough to've beaten that deputy, it wouldn't have done him a whole lot of good. Because I'd be standin' before you now on the prod for him—makin' it only a matter of one more day before he ended up where he already is."

Bell's face scrunched into a confused expression. "I don't understand. What beef did you have with Curly Roy?"

"None," Coffin Bill answered. "Did you listen to what I said, or have you got cowshit in your ears? I said *if* Curly Roy had beat the deputy, *then* I'd have had a beef with him—because he would've robbed me of settlin' a score of my own."

Bell looked around at the others standing with him, obviously still not quite understanding.

Observing this, Coffin Bill stood up. It was a smooth, seemingly unhurried movement, yet it was like he went from sitting to standing in the span of a heartbeat. Part of the motion was a backward sweep of his right arm, shifting the fall of his suit coat so that the Colt holstered on his hip was fully exposed and accessible.

"Alright, this dance has gone on long enough," Coffin Bill announced. "You pack of cow crowders are interruptin' our privacy, and the dribble runnin' out your mouths is startin' to annoy the hell out of me. If you came to make trouble, commence doin' it and we'll see how it plays out. Otherwise, clear on out of here and go back to lookin' up the ass ends of your cattle."

From behind the bar, Gunther, who had been paying closer attention than he'd outwardly appeared, called out, "Hey, over there! No fighting and for damn sure no gunplay in here. You got problems to settle, take it outside!"

Keeping his gaze locked on the cowboys yet monitoring the bartender in his peripheral vision, Coffin Bill said out the corner of his mouth, "What happens next is all up to these boys. Best you stay out of it, barkeep. And if you raise your hands above the top of that bar, you better hope one of 'em is fast enough to swat away the .45-caliber slug that'll be comin' your way."

The drifters who'd been leaning along the bar pushed away and went scrambling out the front door.

The old-timers at the card table got up and moved stiffly but hurriedly over against the far side of the room.

The six wranglers stood motionless, as if locked in place by Coffin Bill's hard glare.

"I ain't gonna tell you again," the gunfighter grated. "I'm sick of the look and smell of you. Clear on outta my sight before somebody gets hurt."

"You only got six rounds in your wheel—maybe only five," said Halstead, fighting hard to keep the quaver out of his voice. "No matter how fast you are, you ain't likely to get all of us without one of us plantin' a pill in you, too."

"If you got the stones to back up your mouth, go ahead and start the ball. Let's see how it works out." A wild glint now danced in Coffin Bill's eyes and his lips peeled back, exposing his teeth in a wolf-like grin.

Shoulders within the group of wranglers started to sag. A few bootheels scraped backward. Finally, somebody muttered, "This ain't no good. This ain't what we came for."

"More of us gettin' plugged ain't gonna do Curly Roy no good," somebody else added.

Then another: "There'll be another time."

As if on some unseen signal, the group started to shuffle backward. A couple near the back actually turned away. The rest remained facing Coffin Bill as they retreated.

Emboldened somewhat by the growing distance between them, Bell raised one arm and pointed a finger at Blessingame. "This ain't over. You better hope none of us ever catch up with you when your new pal ain't around, writer man."

Through clenched teeth, Coffin Bill responded,

"Say another word—any one of you—I'll consider it a threat that I need to take immediate action against."

The cowboys continued their departure. Bell and Halstead were positioned to be the last ones out the door. They remained facing Blessingame and Coffin Bill as they started easing out through the batwings. The others were already out on the boardwalk. Coffin Bill stood motionless, silently watching them back away. Blessingame remained seated in his chair, though leaned forward in an odd way, almost a crouch, as if prepared to throw himself to the floor.

Bell and Halstead were halfway out the door. It was almost over, even though the tension that gripped the scene was squeezing as tight as ever.

Suddenly, one of the cowboys already outside—a young man named Hanson, one of Curly Roy's closest friends—pivoted a hundred and eighty degrees and lunged back toward the entrance. As he did this, he pulled a six-shooter from the cross-draw holster on his left hip and thrust it out at arm's length, pushing it between Bell and Halstead. Shouting, "No! Somebody has to pay for Curly!" he began pulling the trigger.

Coffin Bill's response was instant, his gun hand streaking faster than the eye could follow. As bullets from Hanson's gun sizzled through the air less than a foot from one side of his head, Coffin Bill snapped off two return rounds in quick succession. His did not miss. The near simultaneous impacts punched Hanson backward, slammed him through the loose knot of his fellow wranglers, and sent him sprawling onto the dusty street.

There was a split second of stunned hesitation but then—almost as one—the remaining cowboys began clawing for their guns. Bell and Halstead ducked back around the doorframe on either side. The other men spread out and took positions along the edges of the saloon's front windows.

Curses were spat. "Kill that sonofabitch!" rang out more than once before any further words were lost in the thunderous eruption of gunfire that began pouring into the Lone Star Palace.

Chapter 19

As they reached the edge of town, Firestick, Moosejaw, and Beartooth heard the sound of the shooting above the rataplan of their horses' hooves. The source of this, Firestick instantly knew down low in his gut, was the very thing he'd been hoping so hard to head off. Grating a curse, he urged his mount faster. Moosejaw and Beartooth did likewise, keeping pace on either side.

They raced past the outlying buildings and went tearing down Trail Street. Ahead of them everything appeared empty—nobody on the boardwalks, no horses or wagons moving on the street. The gunfire had scattered whatever late-afternoon business might have otherwise been taking place.

Then Firestick's eyes locked on the only business that *was* being conducted. Bad business. The five Ace Low wranglers positioned outside the Lone Star Palace, vigorously trading lead through the doorway and broken-out windows with somebody on the inside. On the edge of the street, directly behind those who were crouched and blazing away on the boardwalk, lay the sprawled, motionless body of a sixth cowboy who'd been unlucky enough to stop a slug.

As the lawmen drew near and started to rein in their horses, another of the wranglers made the mistake of rising up to take a shot through a shattered saloon window and instead exposed himself to a round coming from the interior. The bullet caught him in the forehead, just under the brim of his hat. The man pitched backward, hat flying, a spray of blood and brains slung high in the air as he staggered back drunkenly until he came in contact with the railing on the outside edge of the boardwalk. Over he toppled in a kind of reverse somersault, limbs flopping loosely, hitting the ground in the street and collapsing into a lumpy, lifeless heap.

"Spread out!" Firestick barked to Moosejaw and Beartooth.

As they complied, he drew his Colt, raised it above his head, and triggered two rounds skyward. In conjunction with this, he bellowed, "Hold your fire! Hold your fire! Stop shootin', damn it!"

Despite the crack and roar of their own guns, this was enough to draw the attention of at least some of the cowboys crouched outside the saloon. It helped that their fire had already begun to falter somewhat. This was a result of seeing two of their number lying dead on the ground, combined with the fact that none of them had come here prepared to engage in a gun battle to begin with. Roughing up the tinhorn writer, running him out of town as a means of avenging Curly Roy, that was one thing. But more shooting and dying, that was never in the thoughts of any of the cowboys.

Given how it had turned out tragically otherwise, the arrival of Firestick and his demands for a cease-fire came as a welcome reprieve for the men of the Ace Low. They promptly dropped back lower in their cover and let their guns go silent. Shortly after they stopped shooting, the gunman inside the saloon halted as well.

Firestick walked his horse up to within a few yards of the Lone Star Palace, careful to keep back from the line of fire in case any shooting should start again from within. The men on the outside were all in his sight and all in the general sweep of his still drawn .45. To his left, on the opposite side of the street, Beartooth held his Winchester cocked and ready, its shoulder stock propped against his hip. To the marshal's right and slightly behind, Moosejaw struck a similar pose with his own Winchester.

Firestick nodded to the Ace Low men who'd stopped shooting. "Alright. That's a start. Now lay down your guns and step back away from 'em."

Harvey Bell balked at this. "What about those inside?"

"I'll deal with them, you just worry about your part. Which, judgin' by those two bodies sprawled in the dirt behind you," Firestick pointed out, "you ain't been doin' a very good job of up to now."

Bell's eyes flicked involuntarily to the two fallen men and his mouth pulled down at the corners. Slowly, he leaned over and placed his gun on the boardwalk at his feet.

As the others followed suit, Beartooth asked, "Who all's on the inside?"

"That book-writer dude," Halstead answered. Then, his voice shifting to a more somber tone, he added, "And Coffin Bill, the gunfighter—it was him doin' all the shootin'."

The answer hardly came as a surprise to Firestick, but it nevertheless made him grimace briefly. He nudged his horse forward a couple more steps, then drew back on the reins and called out, "Inside the saloon! Blessingame! William Caskett! Can you hear me?"

An unfamiliar voice, not Blessingame's, called back, "We hear you."

"This is Marshal Elwood McQueen. The men out here have laid down their guns. I'm callin' for you to do the same."

"That's a mighty tough biscuit to chew, Marshal. I don't cotton much to layin' down my gun, not for nobody," replied the same voice, obviously that of Coffin Bill.

"It's something I'm gonna have to hold to," Firestick told him. "I don't want no more shootin'. But if you refuse to cooperate and give us no choice, I've got two deputies out here with me and we'll be forced to accommodate you."

"I had six *hombres* out there accommodatin' me a few minutes ago. How'd that work out for them?"

"Me and my men ain't a handful of punchers fresh off the ranch. We've done our share of gun work, same as you. I think you'll find there's a difference."

"Those men of yours, those deputies—one of 'em a fella named Moosejaw?"

"What of it?"

"Might be I've got some particular business with him."

Firestick cast a quick glance over his shoulder at Moosejaw before saying, "No matter if you do, it'll have to wait its turn. We've got other business here to handle first."

"About this other business . . . Say I was to consider

layin' down my gun, do you in turn have a mind to try and arrest me?"

"I'm lookin' at two men layin' dead out here in the street and the bullets that killed 'em came from in there where you are. Anybody else in there doin' any shootin' besides you?"

"Nary a soul, Marshal."

"Then that oughta give you a pretty good idea on whether or not I mean to arrest you."

"That might be all well and good if not for a little thing called self-defense. There are plenty of witnesses—in here and out there, too, if there's an honest bone in any of those cowboys—who'll tell you the first shot came from out there and I only fired back to defend myself."

"He's telling true about that part, Marshal," called Gunther the bartender. "One of the cowboys fired the first shot, and then all hell broke loose—you should see how everything in here is shot to pieces!"

The glance Firestick cut toward Bell and Halstead and the way they averted their eyes from meeting his told him all he needed to know about the accuracy of Gunther's and Coffin Bill's claims. In a tight voice, he said, "If that's the way it was, then those are the details we need to work out. But I ain't gonna do it hollerin' back and forth through a damn wall!"

There was a hesitation before Coffin Bill called back. "Very well, Marshal. I'll holster my gun and come out with my hand held away from it, in plain sight. I'm not willing to make myself any more vulnerable than that."

Wordlessly demonstrating a willingness to go along with those terms, Firestick motioned to Beartooth. "Get those cowboys herded out in the middle of the street, get 'em well away from their guns. Watch 'em close, make sure they don't try anything."

As Beartooth skinned from his saddle then motioned with the muzzle of his rifle for the cowboys to do as directed, Firestick said over his shoulder to Moosejaw, "Stay where you are and stay sharp. Keep that Winchester trained on him as soon as he steps out the door." Once he'd gotten an affirmative nod from the big deputy, Firestick turned back to the saloon and called through the bullet-riddled batwings, "Alright. Come ahead on out, Caskett. You heard what I said about tryin' anything—it'll go hard on you if you do."

"First things first," responded Coffin Bill. "I'll be sendin' some other fellas out ahead of me. This ain't me tryin' anything funny, I just don't like nobody behind me in a tense situation."

Firestick said nothing, just waited.

Presently, the four old-timers who'd been forced to abandon their card game and find safety by remaining plastered against the side wall during the gun battle emerged. They appeared a little mussed and agitated, but not unduly traumatized; they were gristle-tough frontier veterans who'd endured as bad or worse in their day. Following them came Gunther, looking highly distraught; he also doubled as the bouncer for the Lone Star Palace, and his ire was likely due as much as anything to failing to handle this trouble himself. Next came Blessingame, ashen-faced and wild-eyed and stepping uncertainly on legs that trembled to the point of barely being able to hold him up.

As each came out, Firestick wagged his .45, motioning them to go over and stand with the cowboys out in the street.

Finally, it was Coffin Bill's turn. The cautious gunman appeared in the doorway, pushing the bat-wings open a couple feet and then pausing there, hands loosely gripping the inner frames of the two half-doors. His gaze slowly swept the scene before him, halting for a moment on the two sprawled bodies, then lifting and coming to rest on Firestick. Their eyes held for a long beat before Coffin Bill's shifted to touch on Moosejaw, just past the marshal's shoulder, then shifted back.

"A waste of lives," the gunman said, "is always a regrettable thing, Marshal. I share in that regret and assure you that something like this was never part of my purpose for coming to your town."

"Then what *was* your purpose for comin' here?" Firestick wanted to know.

Once more Coffin Bill's gaze shifted to Moosejaw, and a very faint smile touched his lips before he again addressed the marshal, saying, "I agree, as you suggested a minute ago, that this matter presently before us ought to be handled ahead of any other business."

Chapter 20

Now that the shooting had stopped and people could see the marshal and his deputies appeared to have the situation under control, faces began appearing in several of the shop windows on either side of the street. A few of the braver souls were emerging, somewhat tentatively, to determine what was going on.

One individual came forward more aggressively than any of the others, a fair-haired, well-dressed man in his early thirties, carrying a doctor's bag as he strode diagonally across the street. He brushed past those Firestick and Beartooth had ushered into a group and then came to a halt just short of the two dead men.

Having approached in time to hear Coffin Bill's remark about "this matter before us," Dr. Nelson Greaves responded to it ahead of whatever Firestick might have said.

"Whatever's going on here," he announced, "it's clear I'm too late to do these unfortunates any good. Given the amount of shooting that took place, however,

I can't help but suspect there may be other injuries. Is there someone in need of attention?"

"This whole bunch needs attention, Doc—the legal kind," Firestick replied, somewhat exasperated by Greaves's interruption. "Since I don't see nobody limpin' or gushin' blood, I'll have to ask you to stand aside until me and my deputies finish takin' care of our part of this. If we run across anybody who's wounded, we'll be sure and let you know."

"Bullet wounds aren't something to be addressed leisurely, you know," Greaves told him rather stiffly.

Firestick fought to stay patient as he said, "I'll keep that in mind, Doc. Now, I appreciate you bein' anxious to provide care and all, but if you'd just—"

"Hold it a minute, Firestick." Moosejaw's voice came loud and clear, his tone demanding. All eyes turned to him as he shoved his Winchester back into its scabbard and swung down from the saddle. Advancing forward, he said, "You might as well keep the doc close by for a while longer. The shootin' ain't necessarily over."

Greaves looked around, puzzled. "What do you mean?"

But Firestick knew full well what his friend and deputy meant. He said, "Moosejaw, now ain't the time."

"Why not?" Moosejaw said, again in a demanding tone. "Is there gonna be a better time? A *good* time? And am I supposed to stand patiently by and let *him* be the one to pick when?"

He continued to move forward, eyes locked on Firestick as he threw out the series of questions. Then, abruptly, he came to a halt and glared at Coffin Bill.

"My name is Jim Hendricks. Everybody calls me

Moosejaw. You said a minute ago that you came here because you had some particular business and made a glance toward me. Care to spell it out a little clearer? What have you got in mind?"

Coffin Bill suddenly looked a bit ill at ease. One side of his mouth lifted in an uncertain smile. "Really, Deputy, I think your friend the marshal is right. I think the business between you and me is best left for—"

Moosejaw cut him off. "And I think it's best gotten to and settled right now. Everybody knows who you are, Coffin Bill. Everybody knows your game. You show up announcin' you got business with somebody, ain't much doubt what kind of business you got in mind."

"He said as much inside, Moosejaw," spoke up Clay Halstead from the pack of men in the middle of the street. "He said he had a score to settle with you on account of you gunnin' down Curly Roy. Didn't make no sense, but that's what he said."

Beartooth took a step closer to Halstead and said, "Anybody wants to hear anything out of you—or any of the rest of you—you'll get asked. Otherwise keep your yaps shut and stay out of this."

Moosejaw's glare bored into the gunman. "How about it, Coffin Bill? You figure you got a score to settle with me?"

The uneasiness faded and Coffin Bill's expression hardened. "Most men ain't so anxious to find out the answer to that question. I expect you wouldn't be, either, if you weren't backed by your two armed friends and surrounded by a whole street full of sympathizers."

More and more people were drifting out of the shops and starting to line the boardwalks, looking on apprehensively from a safe distance.

"You make the call and none of that will matter. I give you my word on it," Moosejaw stated flatly. "It'll be strictly you and me."

Coffin Bill's mouth curved in a way that showed his teeth in a cold, humorless display no one would call a smile. "That's real decent of you, Deputy. But what good is *your* word going to do me after I blast you to hell? How about you, Marshal? You willing to let this play out as another case of self-defense for whoever's left standing? You heard your man say that's the way he wants it."

"I'm nobody's man but my own," Moosejaw said through clenched teeth. "Tell him, Firestick. I'm ex-pectin' you to back me on this. If these tinhorn gun-nies keep comin' to try me, there's no way I'm gonna dodge 'em all and no use in tryin'. If it ain't this blow-hard with a big rep, then next time it'll be another punk like Curly Roy. It ain't for you to try and stand in their way—nor Beartooth, nor anybody else. It's for me to handle, same as you damn well know you'd insist if you was in my place."

Firestick couldn't find the words. The look on his face showed both his anguish and his understanding of what Moosejaw was saying.

"He's right. I don't like it, either, but it's his call," Beartooth said in a low voice from where he stood out in the street.

Suddenly, Daisy was coming up the street behind him, hurrying from the direction of her blacksmith shop. She was clad in her work apron and trousers, and a streak of soot ran down her cheek. There was no way of knowing how much she'd heard on her approach, but she stopped short alongside Beartooth and called to her man in an anxious tone, "Moosejaw?"

He didn't dare look at her. "Stay back, Daisy. I told you before how it had to be if something like this came up. Nothing's changed."

Coffin Bill's cold smile didn't change, either, even as a hollow chuckle rolled up from his chest. "You got all kinds of complications tuggin' at you, don't you, Deputy? You sure you don't want to save this for another time, after you've had a chance to get rid of some of these distractions?"

"The main distraction I aim to get rid of is you," Moosejaw grated. "You lookin' for a reason to crawfish out?"

"That'll be the day," Coffin Bill snapped. "The only question I got is how many men am I facing? You got that answer for me, Marshal?"

This time, without hesitation, Firestick said, "You've only got to worry about one man . . . the last one you'll ever face."

Standing nearby, Dr. Greaves wailed, "You can't be serious! You can't possibly be condoning this!"

"It ain't for me to condone one way or the other," Firestick said, reaching out and grabbing a fistful of the doctor's coat. Dragging him along, out toward the middle of the street, he added, "They're bound to do it some time, someplace. Might as well let it get done with."

In a matter of minutes, all the onlookers had shifted to the north side of the street, either up on the boardwalks or along the edge of the street itself. Those who had previously emerged out onto the south boardwalk, the one running parallel with the front of the Lone Star Palace, had promptly scurried to the opposite side when it became clear what was going to take place.

Moosejaw shooed away the horses he and Firestick had rode in on, then edged a few steps out onto the street. His eyes never left Coffin Bill. The latter silently watched him take his spot before he came the rest of the way out through the batwings and also moved out onto the street. He had to step over the legs of one of the cowboys he'd shot earlier.

The two men faced each other at a dozen paces.

Those looking on were deathly quiet. A low, moaning breeze danced down Trail Street, stirring up a brief dust devil and fluttering the left side of Coffin Bill's frock coat. The other side was pulled back and tucked snugly behind his holstered Colt.

"It's your town," the gunman said. "Make your move whenever you're ready to say good-bye to it."

Moosejaw wagged his head slowly, one time in each direction. "You're a visitor. Our guest. Honors go to you."

To the onlookers it seemed like the pair stood motionless for an agonizingly long time. Then, quicker than it can be told, both were very much in motion. Knees bent into slight crouches, fingers curled frantically around pistol grips, hands blurred up and thrust forward.

Moosejaw's Schofield roared. Twice. In between, Coffin Bill got off a single shot. But Moosejaw's first bullet had already struck just under his right collarbone, jerking his body, causing his shot to go wide by more than a foot. The deputy's second slug punched into the side of Bill's heart and ripped on through, coming out his armpit on the opposite side. The famed gunman spun around a hundred and eighty degrees, performing a lonely, loose-limbed pirouette of death, and then collapsed to the ground.

Chapter 21

It was late. Firestick was sunk deep in an overstuffed easy chair in the parlor of Kate's apartment at the rear of the Mallory House Hotel. A globe lantern was burning low, filling the room with a soft golden glow. Kate sat facing Firestick in a high-backed, horsehide-covered chair. A tray containing a decanter of brandy rested on the low table between them, and each held in one hand a chunky glass partially filled with amber liquid poured from it.

At the close of most days, Firestick, Moosejaw, and Beartooth took supper together at the Double M along with Miguel and Jesus, the ranch *vaqueros*, and their cook-housekeeper Victoria Kingsley, whose presence had evolved into a romantic relationship with Beartooth. After the meal, the three lawmen had established a routine for one of them, on an alternating basis, to return to town and make late rounds to ensure things were locked up and peacefully settled down for the night. On the occasions when it was his turn for such duty, Firestick invariably concluded by stopping to spend some time with Kate before returning home to the ranch. These visits provided their most private and intimate moments together.

This particular instance was somewhat different in that Firestick had remained in town following the shootings at the Lone Star Palace and stayed into the late hours without ever going home. His final rounds now completed, he'd gone to Kate's place. His mood had grown to match that of the town— outwardly subdued, reflective, but with an undercurrent of restlessness running just below the surface. He didn't particularly feel like talking, and in spite of how lovely and sensuous Kate looked in the gold-tinted illumination of the moment, neither did he— amazingly—have the urge to take her in his arms. Yet he knew that here was exactly where he wanted to be, just to have her close by.

Kate recognized quickly enough how distracted her man was. After setting out the brandy and pouring some for each of them, she sat quietly and waited until he'd had the chance to center himself a bit.

At length, Firestick said, "I can't help feelin' like I handled that whole business this afternoon wrong . . . and yet, at the same time, I can't think how I could have done it much different."

"What part do you feel you did wrong? Allowing the shoot-out between Moosejaw and Coffin Bill to take place?" Kate asked.

"Seein's how that's the part comes to your mind," Firestick replied, "I take it as a sign you must be thinkin' the same."

Kate shook her head. "Being who you are—and who Moosejaw is, which is an important part of it—I understand how you couldn't have done anything else. It wasn't a choice between right or wrong, it was your *only* choice. Like you said, you couldn't have done it much different."

"But three men got left layin' dead in the street. It sure seems like there should have been a better way than that."

"For two of those men, the cowboys, some will call it a tragedy. But the harsh reality is that what happened to them was the result of their own actions. You made every effort to keep it from coming to that, but they were so eager to confront Blessingame that they left their ranch unexpectedly and gave you no chance to stop them."

Firestick lifted his glass and gazed into it for a long moment. Before taking a drink, he said, "And then two of them got stopped, permanent-like."

"Again, that came as the result of their own action," Kate reminded him. "With some very willing help from Coffin Bill."

Firestick went ahead and took his drink, didn't say anything more right away.

"Moosejaw seemed to disappear after the shootout. What became of him?" Kate asked.

"He went out to his cabin, said he wanted to be alone for a while. He's still there as far as I know. Though I think Daisy went out to be with him."

Kate took a sip of her drink and also went quiet for a moment.

Into the silence, Firestick said, "I think that's the thing botherin' me the most . . . what this is doin' to Moosejaw."

"I'm not sure I follow you," Kate said, frowning. "He wasn't wounded, was he?"

"Not by a bullet, no. Curly Roy scorched him a little the other day, but Coffin Bill never even came close."

Firestick's tone seemed to hold a curious mixture of pride for his big friend yet at the same time a touch of bitterness. "That ain't the kind of wound I'm talkin' about, though," he went on. "I'm talkin' about the kind on the inside. I can see it in Moosejaw's eyes. He's hatin' every minute of this—hatin' that he has to face a man and gun him down for no more reason than to show which one of 'em is the fastest.

"Hell, Moosejaw has killed before. Plenty of times. Injuns, back in our mountain man days; other trappers attackin' our camp, tryin' to steal our furs and leave us dead in our bedrolls; owlhoots showin' up here in Buffalo Peak, lookin' to rob and kill . . . But that was fightin' back to survive or to keep others from gettin' hurt. Not just to settle a stupid contest for the sake of some fool's pride and braggin' rights."

"But if Moosejaw *doesn't* gun down a man facing him under those circumstances, no matter how senseless," Kate said, "then that would end up his own fate. The only alternative is to turn away and not accept the challenge at all—and, as you explained to me the other day, that just isn't in the makeup of certain men."

"Not a man like Moosejaw, no."

"Nor one like you. Or Beartooth. That's why you couldn't bring yourself to interfere in the face-off against Coffin Bill."

Firestick took another drink and then sighed.

"If I thought what happened today was the end of it, I might be able to accept it as bein' that simple. But when word starts spreadin' that Moosejaw has now bested the likes of somebody with Bill's reputation, I can only see it gettin' worse."

"Especially with the writer Blessingame on hand

to make sure word gets spread as widely and garishly as possible."

Firestick's face took on a strange expression. "Funny thing about that. After all the shootin' today, Blessingame was left . . . I don't quite know how to describe it. Shook up, I guess, is one way of puttin' it. He was stumblin' around all pale and quaking like he just shook hands with a ghost. Or maybe the Devil. When I tried to ask him about the shootin' between Coffin Bill and the cowboys, aimin' to get some firsthand details out of him since he was right there beside Bill durin' the thick of it, he could barely put words together that made any sense. Kept mumblin' about all the noise and the bullets and the blood . . . almost as addled as somebody who'd got mule-kicked to the head."

"I guess that might explain why he went up to his room a short time afterward and nobody's seen him come down since."

"I guess maybe a close-up look at a gun battle, bein' practically in the line of fire," Firestick speculated, "taught him mighty quick-like how different the real thing is from the flowery ways he's used to describin' it in the stuff he writes."

"I walked across the street after the crowd had thinned out some, and took a peek inside the Lone Star Palace," Kate said. "I can understand how anybody who was caught inside there during the shooting could come out of it shook up. Lord, it's amazing any of them made it out alive."

"Coffin Bill was a crafty old dog, you have to give him that," Firestick said. "He drew the fire from the cowboys on the outside all to himself, but he kept on the move behind tipped-over tables and the pool table, while they stayed stationary in the doorway and windows. That's how he was able to pick off a couple of 'em, but they weren't able to pin him down in one spot long enough to plant any lead in him."

Kate said, "What became of the cowboys—the ones left alive, I mean? Did you arrest them?"

"Could have, certainly," Firestick replied. "They racked up plenty of charges against themselves. But in the end, I decided not to put 'em behind bars. Asa Lowe showed up and stood bail for all of 'em, made arrangements with Sterling, the owner of the Lone Star Palace, to pay for the repair of all damages. The two dead wranglers were taken back to the Ace Low for burial there, and the town will go the expense for plantin' Coffin Bill." The marshal shrugged. "Outside of that, there didn't seem much sense in lockin' up the four survivors just because I could. Asa Lowe is already short three men; he can't hardly afford to lose four more all in one whack. I figure the four will feel beholdin' enough to him to stick with the Ace Low for a while, at least until they earn out what he paid to cover the damage from their foolishness. If any of 'em do cut and run at some later date, he'll at least have time to line up some replacement hands."

Kate regarded him with adoring eyes. "Your sense of justice may not be strictly by the book, Marshal McQueen, but it certainly sounds fair and reasonable to me."

Firestick met her gaze and suddenly the urge to take her in his arms that had been absent before now engulfed him like a great wave. Setting aside his glass of brandy, he said, "Would it also seem fair and reasonable for this weary old marshal to do something else not strictly by the book—like takin' a certain lovely lady citizen into personal custody for a while?"

"That depends," said Kate, her normally somewhat husky voice dropping even a shade lower as she set aside her own glass. "As long as the lady in question is the right one, then I think it would be very reasonable . . ."

Up in his room, Harold Blessingame lay wide awake on the bed. He was stretched out flat on his back, fully clothed, arms folded behind his head, staring up at the ceiling. From time to time, he glanced fleetingly over to the writing table where two lined tablets lay folded open on its top. They were a pair of pale, murky blobs caught in the faint illumination—part streetlamp, part moonlight—that filtered in through the room's curtained window.

One tablet contained his work in progress, *The Goliath of Gunfighters*; the other held the notes he had been furiously scribbling during the time he'd spent with Coffin Bill. Two pieces of writing that earlier in the day had poured forth faster than his poor, cramping hand could keep up with.

But now both lay dormant. The magic that came when he took up a pencil and placed its tip on either set of pages was gone. Dead. Nothing happened when he went through those motions now. The words wouldn't come. Worse yet, the desire to try and find them, to attempt recapturing the magic . . . was gone. It no longer burned inside him. There'd been times in the past when he struggled to find the right words, he knew that feeling. But never before had the fire inside him flickered and gone totally cold.

Now he had experienced the real thing. Had experienced it to the point of thinking a hundred times in those moments at the Lone Star Palace that he was going to feel the impact of a bullet and die. The screaming lead, the stink of the powder smoke, the crack and crash of bullets striking all around, the scream of the cowboys getting hit and the sight of the one with the top of his head blown off . . . There was nothing exciting or dashing or romantic about it. It had been only one thing. Awful.

And the thought of continuing to present it as anything else, to make it *entertaining* as he'd strained to do so many times in the past and had planned to continue doing . . . No. With a resolve as solid and certain as forged steel, Blessingame knew he no longer had it in him. Neither the capability to do so, nor the willingness to even try.

He removed one hand from behind his head and brought the forearm to rest across his eyes, closing them. After a moment he fancied he could smell the stink of powder smoke caught in the hairs of the arm and he quickly yanked it away.

In the cabin they were preparing to be their home once married, Moosejaw and Daisy lay together on a spread of bedroll blankets.

"I've never been out here at night before," Daisy was saying. "It's so peaceful and quiet, it's almost unreal."

"It feels good. Especially now," Moosejaw said.

Daisy shifted her head where it rested on his arm.

"I guess it'd be even more peaceful if I wasn't here yammerin'. You told Firestick you wanted to be alone, but I followed you out anyway. You don't mind, do you?"

"'Course not. I plan on you bein' out here with me for a lot of nights to come."

They lay quiet for a minute or so. Then Daisy said, "It's the time to come that's weighing on your mind, ain't it? Not our time together, but . . . well, what else might happen."

"Like more gunslingers comin' 'round lookin' for me? You might as well say it out."

"Alright. It's been said. Ain't that what you're broodin' about?"

"I don't know if broodin' is the right word, but yeah. Kinda hard not to have it on my mind."

"And killing Coffin Bill today is only apt to make it worse, is that what you're thinking?"

"Hard to figure otherwise."

Daisy put her hand on his chest. "But you *did* kill him. You faced somebody who was supposed to be one of the fastest guns around and you beat him. Doesn't that count for anything? Ain't there a chance that might cause others to shy *away* from you rather than come lookin' for a taste of the same?"

"A chance maybe. But I'd say a mighty slim one."

"Still, you did beat him. That must make you pretty good, right? I don't mean make you *feel* good, I mean make you good with a gun. When I saw you standing there, getting ready to . . . All the fears in the world rushed in on me. I saw our future together hanging in the balance and, I'll admit, I was scared. Yet, at the same time, you looked so tall and strong and magnificent I somehow knew it was going to be okay. And it was. The guns went off and you were the one left standing. You were faster and you beat him."

"I don't know about fast. I was fast enough, I guess," said Moosejaw, placing his hand over hers. "Firestick told me at the start of all this that bein' fast ain't the only thing. You got to be steady and accurate and . . . well, in my case I think, determined."

"Determined?"

"Yeah. Determined not to let Coffin Bill or any other hardcase who might come along rob me of my future—*our* future. Now that I've found you, Daisy gal, I ain't aimin' to let nobody or nothing keep me from havin' a lot of years with you right here by my side."

Daisy tipped her face up, eyes glistening. "You big lug, that's the most romantic thing I could've ever dreamed you would say to me."

Leaning to kiss her, Moosejaw said, "In that case, let me tell you something else . . ."

Chapter 22

Jebediah Scorp straightened up after pouring himself a cup of coffee and then leaning over to place the bubbling pot back on the edge of the campfire. He held the cup under his nose for a moment, breathing deep the welcome aroma of the brew, before he turned and spoke to the man a few feet away who had just crawled out of his bedroll.

"Well, cousin Liam, you've now spent your first night in Texas. How was it?"

From where he sat, reaching to pull on the first of his boots, Liam Scorp grunted, "Just as rotten as I expected it to be. The ground was hard and cold, the night air stunk, and by the light of mornin' I can look in any direction and all I see is nothing but raw, rugged country as uninvitin' as an ugly whore you wake up layin' next to sober and hungover."

Jebediah's mouth spread in a wide, crooked grin. "Then it's a good thing you got my handsome mug around to help prettify things up a mite, ain't it?"

Liam groaned. "The only thing looks good about you is that cup of coffee you're holdin'. Find an empty cup and pour me some before I throw this other boot at you."

By the time Liam was on his feet, stomping more securely into both boots and getting his hat clamped properly onto his head, Jebediah was holding out a cup of coffee to him. The sun just climbing above the eastern horizon was a shimmering pale gold, promising to deliver a scorcher of a day, but for now the air was still crisp from the dark hours.

On the other side of the fire, Silas Clapton was kneeling close, holding the long handle of a frying pan with one gloved hand while he used the fork he had clamped in the other to poke at the slabs of bacon sizzling and crackling in the pan. He looked up as Liam stepped closer, taking a loud slurp of his coffee.

"This here bacon is about ready," Clapton announced. "I figured I'd divvy up some for each of us and then, to go with it, use the grease to soften up some chunks of hardtack. That suit you fellas, or do you want me to rustle up some beans, too?"

"No, the bacon and hardtack will do for now," Liam said. "We can noon on jerky while we're ridin' and then fix a bigger spread when we stop for the night, after we've got on the other side of a good stretch of miles."

Clapton nodded. "Figured you'd want to do it that way again, set to makin' tracks as soon as possible."

Liam looked around. "Where's Mojave?"

Clapton jerked his chin toward the south. "Took himself a mosey off onto that high ground over yonder. Said he wanted to have a look at the lay of the land, see what's out ahead of us for startin' off the day."

"Expect it won't be much different than what we can see from here or what we passed through the end of yesterday. No harm in lookin', though." Liam's tone had a measure of satisfaction in it. He was pleased with how Clapton and Mojave Grimes were working out as trail companions for this venture. They didn't talk overly much, unlike Jebediah at times, did as directed without question or complaint, and even saw to necessary tasks without being told to.

"How much farther you figure to Buffalo Peak?" Jebediah asked.

"I'm thinkin' probably another couple days after this one," Liam answered. "If we don't run into anything unexpected and the horses hold up, maybe a half day or so less."

Jebediah took a drink of his coffee. "That don't sound too bad. This time of year, the weather oughta hold, too, except for bein' blazin' hot."

"We'll just have to work with it. Like I said, we need our horses to hold up so we can't risk bakin' 'em, even if it means slowin' down some and takin' a little extra time." Liam's eyes narrowed. "I don't reckon either that bank nor that deputy I mean to kill are goin' nowhere—leastways not until we send 'em there."

"Supply-wise, long as we keep things simple," Clapton said, pulling the frying pan off the fire and straightening up with it balanced in his gloved hand, "I figure we're in good shape, even if it does take an extra day or so." Then he lifted his brows and added, "Though, if we happened to pass by a town or a ranch, I wouldn't mind tryin' for some fresh eggs or a few more canned goods—you know, just for a little variety."

Jebediah grinned. "I know the kind of variety I'm wantin'. Maybe we'll come across some local gal willin' to share a touch of honey."

"Knock off that crap," Liam was quick to say. "Some fresh eggs or canned goods would be one thing. But as for the other, we ain't gonna mess with no local gals or do anything else to draw undue attention—not till we get where we're goin'. Until then, the last thing we want is to end up with a posse or some pack of irritated ranchers on our tails."

Jebediah held up a hand, palm out. "I know, I know. I was just sayin', that's all."

"Well, *don't* say it. You can think all the dirty thoughts you want, I can't help that. But keep 'em to yourself and for damn sure don't figure on doin' anything about 'em. When we get across the border, you can commence goin' after all the honey—or tamale sauce or whatever it is those Mexican chicas dish out down there—you want."

"Don't think I won't," Jebediah said stubbornly.

"Here's Mojave comin' now," said Clapton, happy for something to break up the exchange between the two cousins. "Why don't y'all grab your plates so I can divvy up this bacon and then get the hardtack to soakin' before the grease starts hardenin' up."

A handful of minutes later, Mojave Grimes, the half-breed, had joined them. Clapton had prepared a plate for him.

As the four men ate, Liam asked of Grimes, "See anything of note out ahead?"

Grimes shook his head. "Not really. Mostly just more of the same. A couple miles out and just a twist to the west, though, I spotted a line of trees likely running along a creek. Unless I miss my guess, that'd be a good spot to top off our canteens and water skins and let our horses saturate themselves thoroughly for the hot day ahead. That should put us in good shape for quite a while and leave us not havin' to worry even if we don't run into any more water for a stretch."

Liam nodded. "Sounds good to me. Soon as we get saddled up and on our way, we'll make for those trees."

From the seat of a canopied, heavily laden wagon pulled by a pair of sturdy, broad-backed black horses, Milo Harper watched the lone rider approaching down a long, grassy slope. Upon reaching the wagon, the rider reined up sharply and halted his horse in a cloud of dust that swirled like a yellow mist in the early morning sunlight. The wagon rolled to a stop as well.

"Good news," announced Jack Davies from the saddle. "There's a town just ahead. Buffalo Peak, it must be. Shouldn't take no more than a couple of hours to reach it, even with the wagon."

"Thank God," Harper said with a relieved sigh. "Is there a doctor there?" He was a slender, somewhat frail-looking individual, middle thirties, with a long, pointed nose extending from between intelligent brown eyes. At the moment, the brow above those eyes was puckered with a degree of concern that hadn't lessened for some time now, matching the somber expression that gripped the rest of his otherwise handsome features.

"Don't know for sure," Davies replied to the question. "I didn't take the time to ride all the way on in. I wanted to get back and steer you the shortest, quickest way. But the town's got some size to it—lot bigger than the last time I came through these parts—so I reckon they almost surely got a sawbones of some kind."

"Lord, I hope so," Harper said.

Now it was Davies's turn for a question. "How's little Belle?"

"Pretty much the same. No worse thankfully, but at

the same time unfortunately no better." Harper looked over his shoulder, back into the wagon. "Would you mind going to the rear of the wagon and letting Mrs. Harper know the good news about the town being so close? I'd best keep rolling toward it, in order to get us there as soon as possible."

"Good idea," Davies agreed. "Just swing a little to your right, stay on a line with the way I came down that slope. Stick with that, it'll take us right straight in."

"Got it."

Harper gigged the team of horses into motion and the wagon started rolling again. Davies nudged his mount closer and leaned out of his saddle in order to scoop a dipperful of water out of the wooden barrel lashed to its side. He, too, was a man in his thirties, perhaps a year or two closer to the front end than Harper. He was of average height, though solidly enough built so that he appeared bigger. His facial features, presently more grizzled than usual due to needing a good shave and scrub, were even and not unpleasant; but a certain grimness about the mouth and the hint of a hardness around his eyes suggested he might at times show tendencies that weren't always pleasant.

After slaking his thirst, Davies returned the dipper to the water barrel and then dropped back and nosed his horse up close behind the rear of the rolling wagon. Through the open flap of the wagon canopy, a woman seated inside looked out at him as he set the pace of his horse to that of the pulling team.

"Did you hear the news, ma'am?" he said to her. "That the town of Buffalo Peak is ahead just a couple more hours?"

"Yes, Mr. Davies. I heard most of it as you reported

to my husband. It is good news indeed, and very thoughtful of you to ride ahead and confirm as much. You left so early, you barely took time for breakfast."

"I can always grab a bite of grub," Davies told her. "Far more important to get little Belle somewhere she can be comfortable and receive the doctoring she needs in order to get better. How's she doing so far this morning?"

As he made this inquiry, Davies craned his neck to look deeper into the wagon in order to better see the little girl nestled on some pillows close beside her mother. The child was four years of age, plump-faced and pretty, with a tangle of golden curls that matched the color of her mother's loosely pinned back tresses. Betty Harper herself was a very pretty woman, blue-eyed and full-figured, but, just as her husband's up on the wagon seat, her facial features were currently locked in an expression of deep concern.

"She sleeps mostly, but it's very unsettled," Betty answered. "Whenever she wakes I try to get her to drink, but she refuses because she says her throat hurts. All the while she's burning up with a fever. I keep sponging her face with water, but I can't seem to get it to break."

Davies's mouth turned down at the corners. Yet when he gazed in on the little girl, the hardness around his eyes softened and disappeared.

"Kids are tougher than we tend to give 'em credit for. Even delicate flowers like little Belle. You'll see, when we get her to town and she gets the right kind of medicine in her, she'll snap right out of this."

"I pray you're right," Betty said. She lifted her gaze

from her daughter and settled it on Davies. "Do you pray, Mr. Davies?"

Davies shifted uncomfortably in his saddle. "No, I can't say it's something I've spent a lot of time doing, ma'am. But I have full respect for those who do. I've seen it bring considerable comfort to a lot of good folks."

Betty smiled tolerantly. "I suspect there's more holiness in you than you may recognize, Mr. Davies. If nothing else, you certainly were an answer to *our* prayers when you came along and corrected our course when we were sadly misdirected. Had you not set us right and then stuck with us, we might be days away from Buffalo Peak rather than mere hours."

"I wouldn't attach too much holiness to me, ma'am," Davies said, flashing a shy grin that, for the brief moment it lasted, made him look innocent and boyish. "But if me showin' up when I did means little Belle endin' up quicker in the healing hands of a doc, then let's just agree on callin' it a good thing."

Chapter 23

Firestick and Beartooth rode into town together that morning. They'd eaten a rather hurried breakfast at the Double M and then left earlier than normal. The fact Firestick had risen at the same time as the others at the ranch was also a departure from standard practice. Usually whoever covered the late duty in town claimed the right to sleep in a little extra.

Yesterday's events in general, however, combined with the subsequent restless undercurrent the marshal had sensed while making those late rounds, resulted in fitful slumber for him and the feeling he ought not lose too much time getting back on duty today. And then, when he'd shown up at the breakfast table and learned that Moosejaw hadn't come home all night, it provided still another reason not to delay. Prompted by his own concerns, Beartooth, who often lagged behind as the partner who worked most closely with the day-to-day operations of the Double M, this morning decided to head out with Firestick.

Rather than proceed directly to town, the pair had first made a slight detour to Moosejaw's cabin. The big deputy had announced this as his destination when he'd struck out to be by himself for a while yesterday and hadn't shown up anywhere else since, so the hope was that he could still be found here. Such was not the case, however.

But a short time later, Firestick and Beartooth made it to town and noted wisps of smoke rising out of the jail building's stovepipe as they rode up. This time, after hitching their horses out front and stepping inside, they had better luck finding their absent friend.

From where he was seated behind the marshal's desk, with a steaming cup of coffee and a stack of wanted dodgers in front of him, Moosejaw looked up innocently as the pair entered.

"Hey. Mornin', fellas," he said.

Beartooth spread his hands and repeated, "Mornin'? That's all you got to say?"

Moosejaw looked puzzled. "Ain't that what folks usually say to each other this time of day?"

"Yeah," Firestick growled. "And the other usual part—leastways how the three of us work it—is that we say so over the breakfast table at the Double M. Which you wasn't at, in case it slipped your notice."

Moosejaw's forehead puckered. "Oh. About that . . . Listen, I told you I needed to be alone for a spell, didn't I?"

"You did," Firestick allowed. "But I didn't take it to mean you wasn't comin' back around for the whole night. Meant you missed supper and breakfast both— for you, you gotta admit, that ain't usual at all."

"Daisy brought me supper. Out to the cabin," Moosejaw explained. "Far as breakfast, well, I figured I'd grab me something here in town before long."

Beartooth frowned. "That's real thoughtful, how

you had it all figured out. All except for the part about givin' your two pards some clue what you was up to."

"I didn't necessarily set out to stay away all night. But after Daisy left to go home, it was so peaceful and quiet out there at the cabin . . . well, I kinda hated to leave. Pretty soon I realized how late it had got and it just seemed to make more sense for me to finish out the night there." The big deputy's brows pulled together and his eyes darted back and forth between his two friends. "Hold on a minute . . . you sayin' you two fellas was actually *worried* about me?"

"Why wouldn't we be, you big oaf?" grumbled Firestick. "You been drawin' gunslingers like flies to a manure pile. One after another lookin' to plant lead in you. How was we to know you didn't run into one who'd maybe decided it was easier to bushwhack you for braggin' rights rather than face you straight up?"

"I never thought of it that way," Moosejaw said. "Jeez, I'm really sorry if I caused you to—"

"Don't let it go to your head," Beartooth cut him off. "Wasn't like we was fussin' and frettin' and gettin' all *that* bothered over it. Speakin' for myself, I slept like a baby last night in spite of you not showin' up. And at breakfast, for once, it was kinda nice to reach for an extra flapjack and not risk gettin' my arm wrenched off by you makin' a grab ahead of me."

Moosejaw grinned faintly, recognizing that Beartooth's bluster was aimed at hiding how much he truly had been worried. The big deputy regretted having caused his friends any undue concern, though at the same time he was pleased to know they cared.

"Look," he said, "even if I caused you just a tiny amount of worry, I'm sorry. I wasn't thinkin'. I reckon

I was bein' a mite selfish and . . . well, maybe even feelin' sorry for myself too much over this whole business about bein' branded a fast gun and all."

"You got a right to feel weighed down by it, nobody can argue that," said Firestick. "The rest of us can all look on and think we have an idea how it is, but that still leaves you the one havin' to shoulder it."

"But that's the way it has to be. Same as it would for either one of you if you was standin' in my boots—or anybody else deservin' of bein' called a man." Moose-jaw stood up and came around one end of the desk. "The thing is, though, I've come to grips with it. That's what came out of my time alone at the cabin last night. Lots of time to ponder and grind on it . . . and to decide. Decide I might have this weight to carry but, damn it, I'm up to it. I by-God ain't gonna let it weigh me down. I told Daisy I was determined. For myself, for me and her together, for us three and the Double M—I'm determined to get through this and walk out the other side. And no more feelin' sorry for myself durin' the trip."

Firestick and Beartooth exchanged glances. "Hell, *we* knew all along you wasn't gonna let it weigh you down," said Firestick. "We've just been waitin' for you to come around to gettin' pissed off enough—and yeah, determined enough—to make up your own stubborn mind about it."

"Well, it's made up," Moosejaw stated. "I aim to quit frettin' over if or when the next tinhorn gunny might show up, and to go on about my business like always. Well, no, *not* like always—I got me a weddin' and a new bride on the horizon. Those are the things, the good things, that oughta be occupyin' my thoughts.

And if some skunk comes along aimin' to try and get in the way of that, then it'll be his hard luck."

"That's more like it," said Beartooth, making his way over to the coffeepot that sat simmering on the stove. He snared a tin cup off a nearby peg and paused, wagging it in Firestick's direction, inquiring if he wanted some. When the marshal shook his head no, Beartooth proceeded to pour a cup of mud for himself. Then, turning back and blowing a cooling breath across the smoking brew, he said to Moosejaw, "But now that we got that settled, here's something else where I think you got some answerin' to do. Just how long was Daisy out there with you at the cabin last night? For however long it was and considerin' what you said a minute ago about gettin' on with the business of your upcomin' wedding, well, I can't help wonderin' what kind of business might've been on somebody's mind last night well ahead of those weddin' bells goin' off."

Moosejaw blushed furiously. "Hey, come on now. Don't start in on that. You know doggone well Daisy made me promise to hold off on any of that stuff until after we're married. To think just because we was out there alone for a while last night—"

Beartooth cut him off with a chopping motion of his free hand. Grinning, he said, "Alright, alright. Calm down. I believe you. I just wanted to get a rise out of you and see how purple I could make you turn. Dish you some payback for stirrin' up me and Firestick by goin' off missin' the way you did."

"How many times do I have to say I'm sorry for that?" Moosejaw scowled. "And what you said, by the way, not only wasn't funny, it was in bad taste. What's more, I'd advise real strong against hintin' anything like that in front of Daisy. You do, she's apt to whop you over the head with an anvil or something."

"Come on, give me credit for bein' smarter than that."

Moosejaw's scowl turned into a slyly arched brow. "Wait a minute. Maybe I should be *encouragin'* you to go ahead and spout off in front of her. She might surprise us both by showin' a better sense of humor than we're givin' her credit for."

Beartooth waved him off again. "No thanks. I'll stick with your first piece of advice."

"How about the lot of us stickin' with doin' something to earn these badges we're wearin'," Firestick suggested wryly. When his two deputies turned to look at him, he gestured to the pile of wanted dodgers Moosejaw had been going through earlier. "You have a particular reason for diggin' those out?"

"Sure," Moosejaw said. "You told us the other day we needed to start payin' closer attention to 'em. Right? So I thought I'd do that with some of the more recent ones that have come in. Also, I especially wanted to see if there were any *hombres* reported as bein' handy with a gun as well as bein' a wanted outlaw . . . you know, on account of they might decide to go out of their way and swing by here due to the fuss over me. Bein' better prepared to spot 'em for both of those reasons—because they're outlaws and because they might come gunnin' for yours truly—seemed like a good idea."

"It is," agreed Firestick. "So why don't you go ahead and finish what you started? The ones that strike you as the strongest candidates for possibly showin' up here, for any reason, set their papers aside so me and Beartooth can familiarize ourselves with 'em, too."

"You got it. I'll give 'em a good porin' over," Moose-jaw said.

Firestick turned his gaze to Beartooth. "Now that we've tracked down our wanderin' partner, are you gonna head on back to the ranch or are you figurin' to hang around town for a while?"

"I can go either way," Beartooth replied. "Nothing on tap right away at the ranch that Miguel and Jesus can't handle. You got something in mind for me here?"

Firestick rubbed his jaw. "All that shootin' yesterday— not surprisin', I reckon, seein's how it was right out in the street with so many folks lookin' on—left the town sort of on edge. I could feel it all the time I was makin' rounds last night. Nothing in particular was said or done, but it was there, right under the surface. Like a raw nerve." His mouth pulled into a tight, straight line. "How about you take a stroll around this mornin' and see if you pick up the same feelin'? It's a little early, what with the shops and stores just openin' and the saloons still empty. But see if you get any sense of that mood still lingerin'."

"Sure," said Beartooth. "Let me finish my coffee . . . I'll see what I can sniff out. What are you gonna be doin'?"

"I'm gonna go look up that writer fella, Blessin-game," Firestick told him. "After gettin' caught in the middle of all that gunfire yesterday, he was singin' a little different tune the last I saw of him. He'd found out the real thing when it came to gun thunder and bullets and blood wasn't hardly the same as that dashin', excitin' stuff he paints it as bein' in his books and stories. I'm curious to see if he's still lookin' at it that way come the new day. If he is, then that oughta help the overall situation. Without him workin' to glorify and spread the word on the shoot-out with Coffin Bill and the rest, maybe we got a chance for things to start tamin' down instead of gettin' worse."

"Ain't nobody wantin' that more than me," Moose-jaw declared firmly.

Chapter 24

Milt Kruger ran the freight outfit supplying most of the goods that got distributed throughout the Buffalo Peak region. His mule-drawn wagons, arriving three or four at a time, rolled in from Presidio every few months loaded with products the local retailers had ordered for resale from their various businesses to the townsfolk and surrounding ranchers.

Kruger was a few years past fifty, stocky in build, with a barrel chest and muscle-corded forearms usually bared by shirtsleeves rolled up to just below his elbows. The bowler hat perched on his headful of bristly gray hair and the cigar stub poking out one corner of his mouth were fixtures that seemed to be as permanently a part of him as his arms and legs. And a surly disposition—except when addressing his beloved mules—could also be counted on as usually being present.

One look at the freighter boss as he came stomping down the boardwalk along the south side of Trail Street was enough to tell Firestick that the surliness clearly didn't appear to be lacking this morning. The marshal was coming down the north side of the street, on his way to the Mallory House in hopes of finding Blessingame in his room. Upon spotting him, Kruger immediately veered off the boardwalk on his side and crossed over.

"Marshal Firestick," he called out. "I was on my way to see you, hoping to catch you at the jail."

Firestick smiled pleasantly. "Well, you caught up with me without havin' to travel quite so far. Mornin', Milt."

"Yeah, it's morning right enough. No denying that," returned Kruger. "But I'm glad you didn't say '*good* morning'—because I don't think it's shaping up to be one." He stepped up on the boardwalk beside where Firestick had halted, puffing slightly from the briskness with which he'd crossed the street.

"Why do you say that? What's wrong?" Firestick wanted to know.

Kruger's expression soured. "It's a sorry boss who can't control his hired help, but that's what I'm running into."

Firestick knew that the freighter had arrived with a four-wagon supply train the previous afternoon, not too long before all the shooting had taken place. During the evening, he'd seen men from Kruger's crew circulating around town, mostly in the saloons. Kruger hadn't been among them, it now occurred to him. But there had been no trouble out of any of them, at least not he was aware of.

"My crew is in that big empty lot out back of Greeble's General Store," Kruger continued. "We got in too late yesterday to get everything unloaded. I let 'em knock off for the evening rather than push to try and hurry it all done. Wasn't like we were going to be heading out right away anyhow, and it's always a long, hot haul coming that last stretch across Jacinto Flats, so I figured they'd earned the right to a little relaxation. Me and a couple of the older fellas stuck with the wagons, guarding the goods still left until morning, while the younger bucks went out on the town and did some howling."

"Yeah, I saw 'em around," said Firestick. "A few of 'em hit the red-eye a little hard and made some noise, but nothing that got out of hand."

"Yeah, I know about that—how they behaved themselves okay. They've all returned to the wagon area by now, even though some of them hit their bedrolls plenty late. Trouble is, the ungrateful pups ain't exactly getting the unloading finished. Seems they got other things on their minds."

Firestick frowned. "I'm sorry to hear that you got a bunch of hungover slackers on your hands, Milt. But that ain't really a legal matter. I'm not sure why you're tellin' me."

Kruger switched his cigar stub from one side of his mouth to the other. "Well, I'm kind of afraid it is a matter that's going to involve you, Marshal. Leastways, that's what it's shaping up to be."

"Reckon you'd better get to it then," Firestick said, his frown deepening. "What is it you're dancin' around the edges of?"

Kruger moved farther onto the boardwalk, getting in under the shade thrown by the shingled overhang that ran along the front of the bakery where they were standing.

"Since that trouble with those renegade Apaches from south of the border a while back," he said, "you know I've added more guards when I bring a supply train here. Hasn't been no more Indian trouble, but there's still plenty of robbers and owlhoots of all stripes roaming around out there."

Firestick said nothing, waited for him to go on.

"I got this one young hotshot by the name of Cord Ellis who's been riding with my guard crew for a spell now. He's good with a gun. Maybe not quite as good as *he* thinks he is, but still awful good. You know the type." The freight boss paused, heaved a sigh. "Ellis has a habit of showing off every chance he gets—snap-firing to blow the head off a rattler along the rail, setting up empty cans on the edge of camp when we're stopped for the night and blasting 'em to hell and gone. All the while calling attention to himself, how fast and how good he is. Some of the fellas find it sort of entertaining; others get a mite annoyed by it. Especially Burt Lauson—you know him—my lead mule skinner. Every once in a while Ellis will take a notion to haul off and blaze away at something for no particular reason. Sometimes when he does that it spooks the hell out of the mules and, needless to say, riles Lauson to no end. They've had words about it more than once."

Firestick had a growing hunch, like a knot tightening in his gut, that he knew where this might be headed. He waited for Kruger to continue, hoping he was wrong.

"Most of my boys—including Ellis—heard the shooting that broke out in front of the Lone Star Palace yesterday afternoon. They naturally left their unloading chores long enough to try and get a gander from a safe distance at what was going on. They saw you tame things down and flush out Coffin Bill. By then I had joined in the looking right along with everybody else. And next we saw the face-off between Coffin Bill and Deputy Moosejaw. I was never more pleased—and surprised, I'll admit—than I was at seeing Moosejaw left standing."

"Let me guess the rest," Firestick grated, growing impatient for Kruger to get to his point. "Your boy Ellis came away thinkin' he's faster than either of the men he saw in action. And now he's makin' noise about it, itchin' for the chance to prove himself against Moosejaw. Is that right?"

"Pretty near," Kruger said dejectedly. "But it's even a little worse. Ellis has got men prodding him, encouraging him to go through with it. And there's others, like Lauson, looking to call what they think is his bluff. They're so sick of hearing him brag and carry on about it, they're putting up money. It's building to a pretty good-size pot. If Ellis goes through with it and wins, it's all his; if he bites the dust, those who bet against him split out their cut. I tried backing the crazy fools down, but I don't think there's any talking them out of it. Leastways not by me. That's why I came looking for you."

Kate Mallory was in the front lobby of her hotel, busying herself with little chores like tidying up behind the registration desk, making sure the inkwell was full and fresh quills were available for signing the guest book. She'd seen Firestick and Milt Kruger walk by a short time earlier, both of their expressions clouded by some matter. The fact Firestick hadn't bothered to take even a moment to peek in and say hello suggested it was something of consequence. Kate wondered what it was without worrying too much about it. She held her man in high regard and had confidence he would be able to handle whatever the problem was.

The sound of footfalls entering the lobby caused Kate to look up from dabbing a few spots of spilled ink. A slender, thirtyish man of average height approached the desk, holding his hat in his hands, worrying the curled edges of its brim. He wore a corduroy jacket over a shirt and trousers of good quality, though all had seen some wear and were presently coated with a fine layer of dust that spoke of recent time on the trail.

"Excuse me," the man said. "I'm looking for the town doctor, a Dr. Greaves I understand his name is. A fellow up the street directed us to his office and said if he wasn't there this early I could probably find him here, where he has a room. We tried the office but it was locked up so . . ."

"Yes, Dr. Greaves does keep a room here," Kate confirmed. "However, I fear he's not here, either. I understand he got called out late last night to one of the outlying ranches where a bull gored and stomped a couple of the ranch hands. The men were apparently injured too badly to bring into town, so the doctor went to treat them out there. I'm guessing it must have been so late by the time he got done that he decided to stay overnight before returning."

The man in the corduroy jacket looked forlorn. "That's regrettable news."

Kate peered out the front window to try and see by what means the man had arrived and—since he'd made references to "us" and "we"—if he was accompanied by someone. She could see a team of horses and only the front foot or so of a canopied wagon pulled up on the edge of the street.

"Is your need for medical care urgent?" Kate asked.

The man nodded woodenly. "Yes. Yes, it's our little girl. She's very listless, complaining of a sore throat, and running an awfully high fever."

"Are you new in town?"

"We just arrived. My name is Harper. Milo Harper. I'm planning to set up a law practice here in Buffalo Peak. Somewhere in town there's an empty house my wife and I arranged to rent through a Mister—"

"Trugood. Jason Trugood, our bank president," Kate interjected excitedly. "Yes, of course. I'm a colleague of Jason's on the town council and so many of us have been looking forward to your arrival." She paused then, dropping her excitement and returning to the matter of the ill child. "But first we must give full attention to your daughter."

"I hope that's possible. My wife and I are very distraught and we pushed so hard to make it here. But now, arriving only to find the doctor is out of town . . ."

"With any luck he'll be returning soon." The fine lines of Kate's eyebrows pinched together. "But until he does, there is an option I think you should consider."

Harper looked puzzled. "What do you mean?"

"Before Dr. Greaves settled in town," Kate explained, "we had a man who took care of our medical needs. He's not a full-fledged doctor but he had battlefield training during the war and developed skills that served the needs of folks around Buffalo Peak quite adequately for a long time."

"And he's still available?"

"Yes, he is. He runs the barbershop just up the street, and I'm sure he would be more than willing to look at your little girl and provide at least some measure of comfort until Dr. Greaves returns."

Harper looked uncertain.

"I assure you Frank Moorehouse—that's his name—won't do anything to jeopardize your child," Kate said. "If he can do something to aid her, he will. If her condition is beyond his skill, he will say so and not do anything that might put her at risk."

Harper gave an abrupt nod. "Very well. I think we should go see what Mr. Moorehouse has to say."

"I'll take you there," Kate said, coming around the end of the registration desk. She paused, turning back toward the rear of the lobby long enough to call, "Marilu! Thomas! I have to rush out—somebody keep an eye on the front, please."

Chapter 25

The large, rectangular lot behind Greeble's General Store stood empty most of the time. A few stubborn weeds thrust up around the edges, but the grass across the center was too exposed to the sun, leaving it stunted and baked to a sickly, brownish green fringe most of the year. Tumbleweeds danced unencumbered across its surface, and the young boys from around town gathered frequently to play baseball or other games, or to plot adventures that took them elsewhere.

But things were different when the supply train was in town. During these periods, the lot was congested with wagons, unloading activity, and a steady stream of merchants showing up and then departing with their wheelbarrows and pushcarts loaded with the goods they would take back to their various places of business to meet the needs of their customers.

The scene this morning presented a sort of in-between tableau. The wagons were there, as were the members of Kruger's freight-handling crew, and even a handful of impatiently waiting merchants, standing off to one side. But there was no unloading activity taking place. Instead, Kruger's men were bunched into two groups, facing each other over a three- or four-yard gap, busy only glaring and grumbling at each other.

"See there?" said Kruger as he and Firestick rounded the back end of Greeble's store and walked out onto the lot. "The lazy bums are still at it, jawing and jeering and not doing a lick of work."

"You can always fire 'em," suggested the marshal.

"Don't think I'm not tempted. And it might damn well come to that," growled the freighter boss. "But that would leave me a long way from home with four wagons and mule teams and not a lot of replacement prospects to be found in your little town . . . and these dirty rats know it. But don't worry; my turn to balance the scales will come. Right now, my main goal is to see this cockamamie flare-up put to rest without anybody getting killed."

"I'm with you on that," said Firestick.

They continued walking. The men in front of the wagons turned to watch their approach, faces wearing scowls and belligerent expressions.

As they drew nearer, one of the men, a tall, thick-bodied number with a broad, beefy face bracketed by gray-streaked sideburns, said, "What's the big idea of bringin' the law into this, Milt? We ain't up to nothing illegal."

Firestick recognized the speaker as Burt Lauson, Kruger's lead mule skinner. He'd been part of Kruger's crew for a long time, and the marshal had met him on a number of occasions. He'd always seemed a decent sort, a little boisterous in the saloons when he'd had too much to drink maybe, but never the cause of any trouble.

In response to Lauson's challenge, Kruger said, "The problem is, you ain't up to nothing. Sure as hell not getting those wagons unloaded and doing the work you were all hired to do!"

"Those wagons will get unloaded," Lauson told him. "You know me, I've made plenty of hauls with you and never shirked my job in all that time. But in this case, a little matter has come up that needs tendin' to first. Still, it wouldn't be any business for the law, either way."

The men in both groups were quick to grumble their agreement.

Until Firestick cut them short by saying, "I'm the law around here and I'll be the one who decides what is and ain't my business. Whether or not you honor the bargain you made when you signed up to work for Kruger is between you and him. The way you're all loafin' here, weaselin' on that bargain, I may be of the opinion you're a bunch of lowdown slackers—but you're right, there ain't nothing illegal about it. This other 'little matter,' though . . . If it's buildin' up to involve gunplay and shootin', then that's damn sure something that *is* my business."

"According to what all of us saw yesterday," drawled a clean-cut, good-looking young fellow from the group opposite Lauson's, "you didn't seem too quick to get in the way of gunplay that involved a couple *hombres* squaring off against each other, one-on-one.

Something all of a sudden change in the course of one lousy day?"

Firestick had no trouble deciding this specimen was Cord Ellis, the young hotshot who fancied himself a top hand with a gun. In addition to the mouth, he had the all too familiar look of a barely dry-behind-the-ears pup on the prod. His clothing was as simple and trail-worn as any of the rest of the crew, but the Colt riding low in the sleekly oiled, tied-down holster strapped to his hip was as gleaming and well-cared-for as a precious jewel. And in the young fool's eyes danced a wildness, a craving to show off the one thing in his otherwise drab life that he thought made him special. One look deep into those eyes told Firestick, with a sinking feeling, that this proddy's craving wasn't going to be easily satisfied. Not until it had been fed on the crash of gunfire and the stinging smell of powder smoke.

"Nothing changed to my way of lookin' at things," grated the marshal. "Ain't like we've ever had a standin' invitation for gun twirlers from all over creation to come here and try to make a name for themselves."

Ellis slowly lifted his left hand and pushed back the front brim of his hat. "That's a real interestin' state-ment, Marshal. Kinda curious, though, how it appears you never got around to makin' it to at least one of your deputies. You know, the big, shufflin' one they call Moosejaw? He not only burned down Coffin Bill yesterday, like we all saw, but talk all around town and even in the newspapers has it he's been gunnin' *hombres* on a regular basis lately. Practically right under your nose."

"It's true enough that Deputy Moosejaw has been involved in a string of shootin's lately." Firestick's words came out like they were scraped across sandpaper. "But he never went lookin' for a one of 'em. Sometimes things happen too quick for anybody to get in front of."

A dry chuckle escaped through the bared teeth of Ellis's smirk. "Now there's another curious thing about what you just said. Don't get me wrong; I got no call to dispute anything about those other times. But as for yesterday . . . Usin' the word 'quick' for any of what I saw? You got to be kiddin', right? One half-drunk old gunny who might have been something a long time past, and big ol' lumberin' Moosejaw—who looks more to me like his pa got too friendly with a buffalo cow than a moose bein' any part of the picture. Anyhow, they sure enough clawed out their hoglegs and blasted away at each other. But to use the word 'quick' for their fumblin' gun work? No way, says I. Not even close."

"It was quick enough for one of 'em to end up dead."

"Once the bullets hit, maybe. But the time it took for any triggers to be pulled is what I'm talkin' about."

"See how it is with him, Marshal?" said Lauson. "All mouth. Arguin', insultin', braggin' . . . that's what the rest of us have been listenin' to ever since he joined this outfit. Well, now that mouth has bit off more than it can chew and we've cornered him into backin' it up. It's put up or shut up time."

"Speakin' of talk and gut wind, you had plenty of chances to shut me up, Lauson. Any time you wanted to try," sneered Ellis. "All you ever had to do was step up and say the word."

"And all you ever had to do," Lauson returned, "was unbuckle that Colt and do some of the blowin' you can't seem to hold back. You know I ain't no gun-slick. But you got a pair of fists, don't you? If you had a set of stones to go with 'em, you could have shucked down and I'd've gladly settled things with you a long time ago. Like men."

"Little boys ball up their empty fists and scrap in schoolyards. Men do it with iron in their fists."

"Talk like that," interjected Firestick, "just adds to how big a fool you're makin' of yourself, son. Didn't the blood and the dyin' you saw in the street yesterday jar any sense into you? You think that was some kind of damn game that makes the winner a better man?"

The wildness in Ellis's eyes danced brighter. "Makes him better than who he drops in the dirt. Except maybe in the case of your deputy, considerin' how all he shot down was an old relic. All that makes him is somebody who put a has-been out of his misery."

"Yet you seem to be thinkin' if you challenge him and beat him, that'll still make you somebody?"

"It'll be a start," Ellis said through clenched teeth. "Hell, I already am somebody when it comes to bein' good with a gun. I know it, so does anybody who's ever seen me draw and shoot. Trouble is, I never had a chance to show it where it got any notice before. Now I got that chance. I do your deputy—since he's ridin' high on so much attention—then I take his place. They'll be writin' about me as the man who shot the man who beat the legendary Coffin Bill."

"An old relic, you called him a minute ago."

"My trained eyes saw him for that. Not everybody did. He still had the name and the rep. That's what

I'm figurin' to make work for me." One corner of Ellis's mouth lifted sarcastically. "Besides, in addition to all that we got this whole bunch of fellas behind me and those over there with Lauson havin' put up hard-earned money to see me go against Deputy Moosejaw. You wouldn't want to deprive 'em of a good show with one bunch or the other pocketin' a handsome bonus to boot, would you?"

"Yeah, as a matter of fact I would," said Firestick. "All bets are off, everybody put your money away. There's gonna be no shoot-out, so there's gonna be no loss or gain for anybody."

Ellis's grin faded. "And you're gonna put a stop to it all on your own?"

"If I have to." Firestick's tone was as hard as his eyes. "What's more, even though I said before I didn't see anything illegal, I've changed my mind. If you men are gathered here and not doing any work, then you're loiterin'. And that *is* against the law. So you've got one minute to get on about doin' the jobs you came here for or I'll run the lot of you in for vagrancy."

A few of the men in each group shifted apart somewhat nervously.

"Now hold on a damn minute," said Ellis. "Don't the big deputy have a right for some say in this? He spoke up pretty plain yesterday about not wantin' to duck when somebody was gunnin' for him. And he made it mighty clear he didn't appreciate you interferin' on his behalf. Does he know that's what you're tryin' to do here this mornin'?"

"He does now," came a familiar voice from the rear corner of Greeble's store building. "And once again he ain't appreciatin' it very much."

The second to the last thing Firestick had wanted was for Moosejaw to catch wind of what was going on here and make an appearance. Now, turning to see the big deputy tramping purposefully across the lot, it looked like the *very* last thing—his friend and partner being drawn into yet another shoot-out—was on the brink of happening once more.

Chapter 26

"The best thing I know to do," Frank Moorehouse was saying, his forehead deeply creased with concern, "is to make her as comfortable as possible on cool, fresh sheets—I've got a padded table in the back room for that—and keep sponging her with water. It will help to make the water as chilled as we can so I'll send for some ice from the Silver Spur Saloon just a couple doors down. It's also important to get some fluids and nourishment into her."

"I haven't been able to get her to drink hardly at all," said Betty Harper. "She complains of a sore throat, says it makes it too hard for her to swallow."

"I can appreciate that," Moorehouse allowed. "But we must be persistent, force her if necessary. The fever isn't just on the outside. It's burning up all her internal juices, too. She needs them and she needs some kind of nourishment in order for her body to keep up its strength for fighting the infection."

"Is there no medication that can help?" Betty asked.

Moorehouse shook his head. "None I know of. I doubt even Greaves has anything that's proven effective."

"What about bleeding?" Harper wanted to know. "Isn't that the common practice for diminishing the infection contained in the bad blood?"

Moorehouse gave the anxious father a sharp look. "Not by me, it isn't. I have neither the proper tools nor the skill. Especially not for a child. Plus, I'm not convinced that's a practical step nor ever has been. If Dr. Greaves chooses to pursue it, then it will be up to him. Let's hope he shows up very soon . . . the quicker the better."

"There was a gentleman accompanying the Harpers, a horseman by the name of Davies," Kate spoke up. "I gave him directions to the Wingate spread—that's where those two cowboys got hurt last night—and he rode out to get the doctor back here with all haste."

The four grim-faced adults were standing in Moorehouse's barbershop, all gathered around sick little Belle, who reclined in a bundle of blankets on one of the barber chairs. The focus of each of them was on the child, even as they exchanged words back and forth.

"That was good thinking," Moorehouse told Kate. "Let's hope your rider encounters the doctor already partway here."

"Jack Davies joined our party at a time when I fear I had gotten us somewhat lost," Harper explained. "He got our course corrected and stuck with us to make sure we made it all the way. He became very devoted to Belle along the way, especially after she got sick. You can rest assured he will see to it the doctor understands the urgency of getting here."

"That's fine," said Moorehouse. "But we still need to do everything we can until Greaves does get here. Give me a minute to get things ready in the other room; it's been a while since I've done any doctoring back there. While I'm doing that, Kate, could I trouble you to go get some ice? And flip that sign on the front door over to CLOSED."

While those gathered in the barbershop were focused intently on taking steps to care for and possibly save a precious life, the mood among the men in the sun-washed lot behind Greeble's store had once again shifted into a heightened anticipation for activity geared to very likely end someone's life.

As Moosejaw strode closer to Firestick, he jabbed a thumb over one shoulder, indicating a rumpled little man who hung back meekly at the edge of the building. The runt's name was Scobey. He was a ne'er-do-well who swamped saloons and did other menial work around town for meal scraps and beer money. "Somebody sent Scobey over to the jail to tell me there was some trouble brewin' back here and I oughta come check it out," Moosejaw announced. His eyes bored into Firestick's. "I take it that message didn't come from you, did it?"

"No, it sure as hell didn't."

"No, it wouldn't have come from you because you were too busy aimin' to try and save me. Is that right?" Moosejaw demanded.

"Yeah, I was busy. Busy tryin' to tame down a situation before it got out of hand." Firestick's words had some heat in them, and his glare was equal to that of the big deputy. "I got more than your big, ungrateful ass to worry about if gunfire keeps eruptin' in this town of ours. The more that kind of crap happens, the greater the odds of some innocent citizen gettin' hurt, maybe killed. If you stopped frettin' about yourself for a minute, maybe you'd realize that, too."

"I ain't got much choice but to fret about myself—not with every two-bit, gun-happy jackass in the territory showin' up to plant lead in me," Moosejaw said. "But that still don't mean I want you or Beartooth or anybody else fightin' my battles for me. How many times do I have to tell you that?"

"What am I supposed to do?" Firestick snapped back. "Every time I run into a spot of trouble ask your permission if I can handle it myself—just to make sure you won't think I'm hornin' in on something you might take personal?"

A shrill whistle out of Ellis stopped Moosejaw from making a reply. Both lawmen's heads swiveled to face the cocky young gunman.

Ellis spread his hands under a lopsided grin. "Hey, fellas. This is enjoyable as hell, watchin' two law dogs bark and snarl at each other. But if you don't mind . . . Number one, we're holdin' up work that could put a blight on the good name of Mr. Kruger's freight business. Number two, I—along with all these other gents who have a money interest in both keepin' their jobs and in the bets they've laid down—have got what you'd call prior dibs on Deputy Moosejaw's time and attention."

Moosejaw cocked one eyebrow. "Who the hell are you?"

"Cord Ellis, at your service. I would say I'm an

admirer of your work, but that would be a lie. As I've already explained to the marshal, I feel that, as a gunman, you're a joke. I am, however, an admirer of your reputation, especially now that you've bested Coffin Bill. That's why I intend to take it from you."

Moosejaw cut a quick glance back to Firestick. "Is this bawlin' calf for real?"

"As real as his gun." Firestick heaved a weary sigh. "I was hopin' to find some way to avoid this. But I can see that neither one of you are havin' any . . . unless you're fixin' to tell me I'm readin' you wrong."

"Sorry, I can't tell you that," Moosejaw said, maybe a trace of weariness also in his tone. "Just like the other times, I don't see any way around this. And if it has to be, the lot here is as good a place as any. Better than out on the street, especially before more of a crowd gathers. You know, to keep down that risk of any bystanders gettin' hurt."

"Alright, damn it. Go ahead and get it over with, then."

Moosejaw turned his full attention to Ellis. "You heard the man. The rest of you fellas better clear out of the way. Mr. Reputation Seeker, find yourself a spot and get planted. Make it comfortable, even though you ain't gonna be standin' there very long. Where you pretty soon *will* be spendin' a nice long stretch of time, though, is a toasty little place called hell. When you get there, you can look up Coffin Bill and the two of you can hash over what a big joke this ol' mountain man is as a gunman."

The freight crewmen gathered around Ellis, as well as Lauson's bunch, wasted no time scattering out of the way. Some scooted around behind the wagons . . . some came over and stood with Kruger and Firestick.

Moosejaw edged forward until he came to a spot in line with where Ellis had taken up a stance, feet planted wide. A little over five yards separated the two men. Everything went quiet except for the occasional chuff of one of the mules.

Firestick looked around, hoping to spot Beartooth, but there was no sign of him. He didn't know what difference it would make, really, having his other friend and deputy there. He only knew that it would somehow make him feel better. The three of them together had never faltered in the face of any adversity. Having Beartooth present to complete the strength of their bond, their unification, even with two of them as mere bystanders, might provide some mystical force to work in Moosejaw's favor.

And then, suddenly, hands were streaking with blurred speed and guns were blazing and mules were screaming and stamping their feet . . . For a long moment, after their guns went silent and coils of powder smoke rolled slowly in the air between them, the two men with drawn weapons still extended from their waists stood tense and motionless. At last, in agonizingly slow motion, the barrel of Ellis's Colt tipped down and slipped from his grasp. A second later, his body still totally rigid, the rest of him tipped forward until it was overbalanced to the point of crashing to the ground like a toppled tree.

Chapter 27

Having completed his examination of Belle Harper, Dr. Nelson Greaves stood wiping his hands on a towel.

"I concur with all of Mr. Moorehouse's advice and the steps he has taken so far," he said to those gathered around him in the back room of the barbershop. "I would add the suggestion that we change to a solution of rubbing alcohol for keeping her sponged down. It seems to have a deeper, more penetrating effect when it comes to helping break a fever—the main thing we need to stay focused on. As far as getting some fluid and nourishment in her, which is also very important, I recommend trying some warm honey at first. The taste will be appealing to her and it will help coat her throat. From there, we'll move on to broth and possibly, if she'll tolerate it, some willow bark tea. The latter will not only introduce fluid but in some cases it seems to carry a healing agent."

As he spoke, the doctor allowed his gaze to touch on the faces of those around him. The Harpers were present, of course, as were Kate and Moorehouse.

Standing back a ways, in the doorway that opened out to the barbershop, was Jack Davies, who had encountered Greaves a short distance out of town and had hastened him the rest of the way in. All looked on now with expressions of deep concern.

"What could have brought this on?" Betty Harper asked.

Greaves shook his head. "No way of knowing. Out on the trail, it could have been any number of things."

"Is there no medicine you can administer?"

"The best we can do is help her body fight the effects," said Greaves. "We do that by means of the things Mr. Moorehouse and I are both recommending. Fluids, nourishment, break the fever."

"What about bleeding? Draining off some of whatever ailment is inside her?" queried Milo Harper.

The negative shake of Greaves's head was very quick and firm. "No. That is becoming more and more a disputed practice. I not only don't recommend it, I refuse to perform it as a treatment."

"We need to gather the things you *have* prescribed," said Kate. "The honey, alcohol, broth, and willow bark tea. Where do you intend to administer them, to treat her?"

"Her own home would be best. We can get her settled and comfortable and not have to worry about moving her anymore," Greaves said. His eyes traveled back and forth between Milo and Betty. "I understand you just arrived in town. You do have a place to stay, though, don't you?"

"They've arranged through Banker Trugood to rent the Widow Dunphy's old place," Kate answered him. "But they haven't had time to even lay eyes on it yet."

"Your little girl can stay here while you go make ready a place for her," Moorehouse said to the Harpers.

Milo Harper looked thoughtful. "In our correspondence, Mr. Trugood said the house was partially furnished."

"It is," Kate confirmed. "And Widow Dunphy was a very tidy woman. Naturally you'll want to add your own touches over time, Mrs. Harper, but I think you'll find the conditions quite livable right from the beginning. If you'd like to go with your husband in order to start unloading your wagon and get Belle's room ready, I'll stay here with her. I'll keep sponging her and try to get her to take some honey."

"You're too kind," said Betty Harper gratefully.

"Think nothing of it," Kate told her. "Someone will just have to bring me the honey—and some alcohol, if you want me to get started on that."

"I'll see you get everything you need," said Moorehouse.

From the doorway, Jack Davies said, "And I'll go along to help unload the wagon so you can get the house ready as soon as possible."

Milo Harper looked around, clearly touched by the outpouring. "Everyone's being so helpful. In spite of the shooting we heard a few minutes ago, we've obviously come to a town with friendly, caring people. I can't express how appreciative Betty and I are to all of you."

"We'll get our thanks when little Belle is smiling up at us from a face no longer flushed by fever," said Moorehouse. "Now, let's all get a move on to do what has to be done so's she can get settled in her own bed and finish the healing she needs to do."

"By all means," agreed Dr. Greaves. "For myself,

however, since there's nothing more I can do right at the moment regarding Belle, I was told on the way in that the shooting you heard resulted in one of our town deputies receiving a bullet wound. I therefore should take my leave and go check on him. I'll come by the house as soon as I finish."

As the doctor began closing up his medical bag, Kate took a step closer to him and said, "You heard it was one of the deputies who got wounded, you say? But nothing too serious?"

"I understand it was Moosejaw," Greaves told her. "I was told the little girl was more urgent, so I gather from that the other isn't terribly serious, no. But I won't know for sure until I examine him."

Kate nodded silently in response, her bottom lip tucked between her teeth.

No one in the room noticed the expression that passed over Jack Davies's face—the momentary tightening of his mouth, the narrowing of his eyes—when Greaves said the name "Moosejaw."

"Lucky for you, you've got ribs as thick as chair legs," Doc Greaves proclaimed as he tied off the layers of foot-wide bandaging he'd just finished wrapping around Moosejaw's torso. "Even though that bullet hit a glancing blow, I'm judging by the gash and the bruising that it had enough force to have fractured a rib or two on an average-size man."

Moosejaw grunted. "I'll keep in mind how lucky I am when I'm tryin' to lay comfortable and get some sleep tonight. Or when I go to try to take a deep breath in this doggone corset you got cinched around me."

"That rib may not be fractured, but you can bet it's

still awfully tender," Greaves told him. "If you were to take a sudden, sharp breath without that wrap restraining you, it would hurt like blazes and you might finish the job of cracking the rib in its weakened condition."

From across the room, Beartooth drawled lazily, "I've been tryin' to tell him that when he's in a gunfight—like he seems to have taken up as a hobby here lately—he oughta turn sideways a little so's to make a narrower target."

Greaves made a sour face. "I only provide medical advice and treatment. What you're suggesting is outside my realm to comment upon. If I *were* to venture beyond the boundaries of strict medical talk, however, I might offer the opinion that the best way to minimize being a target would be to avoid getting into gunfights at all."

"Now there's *my* kind of talk!" spoke up Daisy from where she sat close to Moosejaw. "Nothing I'd like better than to see this big lug of mine stay outta the line of fire from now on."

"Well, that's a real dandy notion the two of you've come up with," returned Moosejaw. "And I'd be more than happy to follow it if you'd explain to the varmints who keep comin' around to plug me that they need to knock off their part of it."

"Kind of hard to explain anything to dead men— which is how you tend to leave such 'varmints,'" Greaves remarked somewhat acidly.

Firestick stood up from where he'd been parked in one of the straight-backed chairs in front of the marshal's desk. "Alright. Speakin' of knockin' it off, let's stick with that before anybody gets too far out of line."

The five of them were assembled in the front office

area of the jail building. Following the shoot-out in the freight lot, Firestick had brought the wounded Moosejaw here to await the doctor. Beartooth had joined them en route, and Daisy—catching wind of what had happened as word spread throughout town—had arrived shortly after they'd reached the jail.

"You make a good point about avoidin' this kind of thing, Doc," Firestick continued in a tone that started out geared to smooth any ruffled feathers. "Believe me, there ain't nobody here who don't want that as bad as you. Maybe more, considerin' we're the ones most at risk for catchin' a chunk of lead. But there's the thing, that's what makes Moosejaw's point valid, too.

"When the kind of *hombres* who've been comin' around lately show up, throwin' lead is the only thing they got in mind. I've seen the wildness in their eyes—like that young whelp this mornin'. I did my damnedest to tame him down before Moosejaw ever showed up. But he was hell-bent on goin' through with what he'd set in motion. Slappin' leather. Tryin' to make a name for himself. And it reached a point where anybody who knew what to look for could see there was no way to stop him short of droppin' him in the dirt."

As he talked, Firestick had taken steps closer to Greaves. And his voice had grown more intense, angrier. His eyes were penetrating as they bore into the doctor's.

"So you tell me, Doc. What's a man—a *man*—in Moosejaw's position supposed to do? Walk away? Suffer the taunts of bein' called yellow and then still have to go around with an itch between his shoulders on account of wonderin' if he'll be bushwhacked, shot in the back out of some dark alley because he didn't finish the job when he had the snake right in front of him?"

Now it was Beartooth who stepped closer. "Hey, take it easy," he said. "No gettin' out of hand, remember?"

It took a moment, but then Firestick's breathing leveled off and the heat in his eyes started to cool. He eased back a half step and made a catchall gesture with one hand. "Sorry, Doc. I guess all these doggone shootings are workin' on everybody's nerves."

"That's understandable. And you have nothing to apologize for," Greaves said earnestly. "I had no right to take the tone I did. I'm used to dealing with death thirdhand, encountering it only when it claims others I have been unable to help. But facing it firsthand, staring at it down the barrel of a gun . . . That's something I've never experienced and have no right to make judgment on."

"Trust me, it ain't nothing you want to know firsthand. Nor are the choices you have to make when you're put in that position," said Moosejaw solemnly.

"I'm quite sure," Greaves conceded. Then: "And something else I'm fairly sure of, even though I've never experienced it firsthand, either, is that having one's middle bound up like I've now done yours will be annoying and uncomfortable, as you indicated. But if you can stand it for just three or four days, then I believe that rib will be strengthened enough to leave you unwrapped. I'll check it tomorrow when I change the dressing on the gash underneath and we'll go from there."

"Whatever you think is best, Doc," said Daisy. "He

may grumble and complain, but I'll see to it he does what he's supposed to."

Greaves smiled. "The good news, judging by that burn on his shoulder where he appears to have had another recent close call, is that he appears to heal quickly."

Rolling his shoulder and glancing down at the scabbed-over welt left by Curly Roy's slug, Moosejaw said, "Aw, that's just a bullet crease. I larded it up a couple times and now I hardly even notice it. The worst part was the torn shirt that came with it. And now, blamed if I don't have another shirt with an even worse tear!"

"Lard, eh?" said Greaves. "Maybe I ought to start packing a jar of that in with the rest of my medical equipment. Speaking of which . . . Since there's really not anything more I can do here, I'd best button up my bag and get back to the side of a sick little girl."

Firestick frowned. "Yeah, I heard somethin' about that as we were comin' down the street. She's with a new family just arrived in town?"

"That's right. The Harpers." As he spoke, Greaves continued returning items to his bag. "The father, Milo Harper, is going to be starting up a law practice here."

Beartooth's eyebrows pushed up. "I'll be danged. Buffalo Peak's first lawyer, eh?"

"Kind of ironic, don't you think?" said Greaves. "On the one hand, we seem to be suffering a plague of ruffians who only answer to the law of the gun. On the other, we'll have someone seeking to resolve disputes and other trouble with a set of lawbooks."

Beartooth's eyebrows stayed up. "I don't know how

much sway a set of lawbooks will ever have over them used to speakin' the language of hot lead . . . not unless one of those books is thick enough to stop a bullet and this lawyer fella has some spares he's willin' to use to clunk over a few heads."

Chapter 28

Jack Davies hoped a shot of red-eye would soothe the raw, scratchy feeling inside his throat. But it didn't. Instead it ignited a fit of coughing that he tried to drown with a quick gulp of beer. That was better. The foamy brew slid down cool and comforting.

"Take it easy, honey," said the red-haired dove seated at the table with him. She placed a warm hand on his forearm and moved it back and forth with a practiced motion that hinted at intimacy or at the very least implied a familiarity well beyond the few minutes they'd been together.

"Just comin' off several days on the hot, dusty trail," Davies said. "Appears not all that dust settled back onto the ground. I need to get it washed out of my pipes, that's all."

The dove—her name was Holly, she'd said—smiled invitingly. "Well, you come to the right place for that. Here at the Lone Star Palace we got the coldest beer and the smoothest whiskey anywhere around." She leaned forward, placing her plump, powdered face closer to Davies's and, at the same time, allowing the daringly scooped front of her spangled dress to slip a little lower still and cause the tops of her generous breasts to bulge nearly to the point of escaping all confinement. "And, if you're lookin' for other ways to relax and get comfortable after that hard ol' trail . . . well, I'm sure we got something to satisfy those needs, too."

Davies grinned. "I'm sure you do, darlin'."

"You can find out for certain, if you want. All it takes is a little money and a trip up those stairs over yonder. I got me a room up there where everything is nice and private and quiet, and I can show you ways to get real comfortable. We'll get that trail dust cleaned out of your pipes and a whole lot more."

"I'm sure you can." Davies took a hurried sip of beer to quell another cough he felt coming on. Then he continued, "But before we get to that, let's just sit here and talk a bit."

The smile left Holly's mouth and instead she looked suddenly impatient and annoyed. "Talkin' ain't something I'm nearly as good at as . . . other things. If talk is all you want, look around. There's enough leftovers from the lunch crowd so that strikin' up a conversation oughta be easy. Some of those old-timers will talk your ear off, if that's all you want. In the meantime, this gal has got to find payin' ways to occupy her time."

The day had worked itself into midafternoon. After helping the Harpers unload their wagon and get partially settled into their rented house, Davies had stuck around long enough to also aid in transferring Belle from the barbershop to what was now her new bedroom.

It troubled him more than he ever would have

expected to see the little girl so sick. Having been on the drift since leaving home at seventeen, Davies never developed a particular attachment to anything or anybody. Yet, somehow, in the handful of days he had traveled with her and her parents, the child had melted his heart. The hard shell he had developed as a shield against all the hardship he had seen and endured— and, truth be told, caused in some instances—had cracked and fallen away when Belle smiled at him and clearly showed a fondness for him in return.

But then the illness had set in. The damned fever. Davies tried not to think about it, but few on the frontier were unaware of how serious a bad fever could be, especially for the very young. The remotest possibility that Belle might succumb to the one gripping her now made Davies question how he would handle such a devastating turn. He even considered climbing back on his horse and riding off, riding away, so he would never know if that was the outcome.

But no, that would be the coward's way. And Davies had never run from trouble in his life. In fact, his whole purpose in coming to Buffalo Peak—before encountering the Harpers, at least—amounted to riding *toward* trouble. Settling a long-overdue debt. And no matter what happened to Belle, he had to follow through with squaring that account.

When Holly went to stand up, it was Davies's turn to place his hand on her arm. "Hold on. Don't be in such a hurry," he said. Then, digging into a vest pocket with his other hand, he pulled out a wad of money, paper and coins mixed, and spread it on the table. "There. If gettin' paid is what you're worried about, you got it right there. Sit right there. We *will* be takin' that trip upstairs—but first we'll talk."

Holly settled back down on her chair and her smile returned. Scooping up a few of the coins and dropping them down the front of her dress, she said, "You certainly are speakin' my language now, honey. Commence to chattin' away. I'm all ears."

Davies's gaze dropped to her ample bosom and lingered there rather blatantly. "No, not completely, you're not. But we'll get to that in due time."

"This here is just talkin' money, remember," Holly said, patting the front of her dress and creating a muted jingle. "We head for those stairs, we'll have to negotiate for some extra."

"We'll deal with that when the time comes." Davies turned his head and emitted a short series of hacking coughs.

Holly frowned. "You sure you're up to a trip up those stairs, honey? Sounds to me like you might oughta be spendin' your money on seeing a doc or something."

"I told you. Just coughing out some trail dust. Don't worry about it."

Holly shrugged. "Whatever you say."

Davies took a long pull of his beer. Then: "How long have you worked in this town?"

"Too long."

"Come on. I'm payin' for a straighter answer than that."

After a moment's consideration, Holly said, "Two years about. Maybe a month one way or the other. It was in the spring when I first came here, I remember that much."

"The law in this town. Those three old mountain men. They been here all that time?"

"Oh yeah. Longer. I think I heard they first came to these parts six or so years ago. They didn't start out as lawmen. That horse ranch they've still got west of town is what caused 'em to settle here in the beginning. Before too long, though, after they helped tame down some rowdiness that kept bustin' out in town, the town council hired them as marshal and deputies."

Davies cleared his throat, stifling another cough. "The one they call Firestick, he's the marshal, right?"

"Uh-huh. And Beartooth and Moosejaw are his deputies."

"Bunch of funny-soundin' names, wouldn't you say?"

"I guess. When you first hear them, anyway. Reckon most folks hereabouts have got used to 'em and hardly even notice. And it ain't like those are their real names, not their Christian ones, I mean. Those are what the Indians up in the Rockies took to calling them during their mountain man days. Guess the three fellas didn't mind too much, so they stuck. By the time they came down to settle here on the flats, it's what they were calling each other."

"So hardly anybody uses their real names?"

"Not that I ever hear."

Davies drained his beer. Holly took some money off the table, went to the bar, and brought him back a fresh one. She also brought a shot of whiskey for herself. She returned to her seat somewhat tentatively, watching to see if he objected. He gave no indication that he did.

As if their conversation had never been interrupted,

Davies said, "You ever have any dealin's with those three . . . in your line of work, that is?"

Holly shook her head. "Nope. By the time I showed up, they each had a steady town gal. Even before that, from everything I've heard, none of them ever came around for any upstairs business."

Davies stifled another cough, took a hurried drink of beer. "The one called Moosejaw—his real name is Jim Hendricks. That's accordin' to all the newspaper reports that have been poppin' up about him. That sound right to you?"

"I guess so." Holly suddenly looked uncomfortable. "I wouldn't know what it says in the newspapers. I ain't ever had the learnin' to be able to read. But he's sure been in a lot of shoot-outs lately, so I reckon it wouldn't be surprising if he *is* in the papers."

"I heard he was in another shoot-out just today."

"Uh-huh. Earlier this morning. Some freighter guard who thought he was something special with a gun. Moosejaw had no choice but to drop him in the dirt, just like Coffin Bill yesterday. You must have heard of Coffin Bill, right? I was lookin' out the window and saw that one happen. Moosejaw planted two slugs in him, one right through his heart."

Davies scowled. "You say Hendricks 'had no choice.' It sounds to me like he's a cold-blooded bastard who relishes makin' the choice to kill other men."

"Oh no. You're wrong about that," Holly protested. "These shootings are only recent things. All brought on by men challenging him, forcing his hand. Before that, Moosejaw was always . . . well, kinda gentle. Tough and strong as a bull, but gentle whenever he was able to be."

"The hell he is!" Davies said in a loud voice, bringing

his fist down hard on the tabletop. His face became flushed to a bright red, and beads of sweat suddenly popped out across his forehead. "Jim Hendricks is a dirty, cowardly killer reachin' all the way back to his early mountain days. It's time you fools around here woke up to that fact, and I'm gonna be the one who proves to you how . . . how . . ."

Davies's words trailed off as his anger and the rawness in his throat combined to throw him into a furious coughing fit. His face turned an even more brilliant red and he fought to catch his breath. He rose to his feet, clutching at his throat. Gargling, gasping sounds escaped from him as he struggled to breathe or cough or do both. Until, desperately starved for air, he collapsed onto the table and slid off onto the floor.

Chapter 29

Frank Moorehouse stepped into Belle Harper's bedroom and pressed the door quietly closed behind him. The room's curtains were drawn, leaving an oil lamp on the bedside stand to fill the space with a soft, shadow-edged glow. Belle lay sleeping on a crisp white pillow and sheets. No one else was present in the room except Dr. Greaves, who stood close over the little girl with his head hung forward and down but not quite far enough to hide the grim expression on his face.

"You sent for me, Doctor?" said Moorehouse.

Greaves looked up. In a tone as grave as his expression, he said, "Yes. Yes, I did. Come over here, please. I want you to witness something."

As Moorehouse stepped closer to the side of the bed, Greaves reached over and turned up the wick of the lamp. In the brighter wash of light, Belle's face, especially her plump cheeks, was shown to be considerably more flushed than Moorehouse remembered. The child appeared to be resting comfortably, but it was obvious that she was still burning up with fever.

After getting the lamp adjusted the way he wanted, Greaves next reached down and pulled back a portion of the sheet that had been drawn up and smoothed across the girl. With the sheet tugged away, the doctor gently lifted one of Belle's shoulders and rolled it slightly. "Look closer, Mr. Moorehouse. Tell me what you see."

It only took a second for Moorehouse to spot what it was Greaves wanted him to see. In contrast to her fever-tinted face, the rest of the little girl's body was very pale. But speckled across the back of her shoulder and reaching up toward the side of her neck was a tight pattern of pinkish bumps forming the early stages of a rash.

"It spreads high across her back and, as you can see, is reaching up to her throat," Greaves said. "And if we examined the inside of her mouth—which I don't want to do again at the moment, for the sake of allowing her to rest—you would see the rest . . . the infamous and dreaded 'strawberry tongue.'"

"Oh my God," Moorehouse murmured.

"One would hope this isn't his work," Greaves said, releasing Belle's shoulder and smoothing the sheet back into place. "But at the same time, we certainly could use a little help from him going forward."

"Do the parents know?" Moorehouse asked.

Greaves shook his head. "No. I wanted to discuss it with you first. Discuss not only my diagnosis, but then what steps will be need to be taken from there—both medically speaking and as a town . . ."

The doctor's words trailed off and both men stood silent for a long moment, gazing down at the patient as if she might have a response.

Until Greaves spoke again, saying, "I haven't even said the words out loud yet. But it's scarlet fever, there can be no doubt. The parents will have to be informed, naturally. That falls to me. After that is when I'm asking advice from you and whoever else you recommend as far as how to proceed next. We both know what kind of panic could result, but at the same time, there is unfortunately no way we can contain it to just this room."

"Let me get this straight," Firestick said. "You're blamin' Moosejaw for all these shootin's and suggestin' he be run out of town in order to get them to stop?"

"Come now, Marshal," replied Jason Trugood, making an appealing gesture with his hands. "It sounds harsh to say 'blame' in regard to Moosejaw, as if he's the one who's done something wrong. We realize, of course, that in each of these cases he has merely defended himself."

"And nobody's saying he should be run out of town, either. Not in the way you make it sound," added Hans Greeble. "But no matter where the exact blame lies, you can't deny that all the recent shootings have been centered around Moosejaw. And with one gunslinger after another showing up—from well-known ones like Tuscarora Billings and Coffin Bill to young hotheads like that freight guard this morning—there don't seem to be any end in sight."

"That's why," Trugood picked up again, "it crossed our minds that perhaps a way it *could* be brought to a halt might be if Moosejaw took a trip somewhere long enough to let things calm down around here. Surely you and Deputy Beartooth, as law officers—and that would, of course, include Moosejaw as well—can see how a continuation of this sort of thing is bad for our town as far as our reputation and chances for continued growth. Not to mention the risk, if these almost daily shootings continue to take place, of some innocent citizen possibly being hurt."

Firestick rocked back in his chair behind the marshal's desk and regarded the two men occupying chairs on the other side of the desk. Off to one side, leaning against an internal support beam with a cup of coffee in one hand, Beartooth stood looking on. Trugood, bank president of the local branch of the West Texas Cattlemen's Association, and Greeble, owner-proprietor of the area's largest general store, were both members of the town council. Although they hadn't announced themselves as representing those positions in any official way, it was clear this was a factor they counted on being considered when presenting their proposal.

"Mighty curious thing how the passin' of only a few days can change the way a person looks at things, ain't it?" Firestick's gaze settled directly on Trugood as he posed this question. "Wasn't but a week or so back, Mr. Trugood—when Moosejaw shot it out with those *hombres* who were robbin' your bank and threatenin' the lives of you and everybody else inside—that you praised him to high heaven for his bravery and gun skills. But now, when he acts the very same way but it's only his own neck he's savin', you don't seem to think that's reason enough to keep him around."

Trugood's bristly brows pinched together. "Here now. None of this is to say that I don't still remain immensely grateful for Moosejaw's actions that day, nor any of the other times he has acted in the service of our town. But this is something that goes beyond gratitude or my personal feelings."

"Come to think of it," spoke up Beartooth, "that 'immense gratitude' of you and the bank examiner fella who was on hand that day when Tuscarora and his gang showed up, sort of led to this whole mess."

"What kind of preposterous statement is that?" Trugood wanted to know. "How did either myself or Mr. Oswald do anything to contribute to this wave of shootings and gunfights that has washed over our town?"

"With your mouths, that's how," Beartooth answered. "The two of you were so worked up that day outside the bank, after Moosejaw had cut down the robbers, you started paintin' him right there on the spot as the next Wild Bill Hickok and Wyatt Earp all rolled into one. You think word wasn't gonna spread based on the way you was carryin' on? And then, by the time he got back to where the newspapers was, in Presidio and the like, Oswald must have really had his spiel polished, probably pumpin' himself up for bein' part of it. So what we're seein' now, this parade of gunslingers all comin' around wantin' a piece of Moosejaw . . . you can thank yourself and Mr. Oswald for blowin' your trumpets and helpin' to lead the charge."

"That's preposterous," Trugood said again. "All we did was heap deserved praise on Deputy Moosejaw. That hardly makes us worthy of blame."

"We're already past layin' blame," Firestick reminded everybody. "It ain't like anybody *wanted* what's been happening. Not any of us here, and certainly not Moosejaw. But we're in the middle of it, regardless. That's the thing."

"It sure is," agreed Greeble. "I had customers in my

store this morning when the shooting in that lot out back took place. I had a woman faint dead away and fall at my feet. And my wife and children were upstairs in our apartment over the store—what if a stray bullet had come through the window?"

Firestick heaved a frustrated sigh. "Look, you think we haven't already fretted over all of this? Tryin' to figure some way to stop it? For the sake of the town, yeah, but also so our best friend ain't facin' a parade of gun swifts and havin' the odds build against him with each one who shows up, until it's just a matter of time before it's him who gets left layin' in the dirt."

The marshal stood up and paced around the end of the desk. "Hell, before you two ever came up with the idea, we even tossed around the same notion—the possibility of gettin' Moosejaw out of town for a spell."

"What did he say to that?" Greeble wanted to know.

"Nothing. He never had a chance. He wasn't part of the conversation," Firestick said tersely. He glanced over toward Beartooth. Ironically, the two of them had been discussing that very thing just prior to the two councilmen showing up. They'd discussed it but had reached the conclusion it was an unworkable solution not worth pursuing any further.

"For starters," said Beartooth, "unless he traveled a considerable distance away and went to the bother of goin' by another name or some foolery, what good would it do Moosejaw himself? Yeah, it might take the shootin' trouble away from *here*, but a gun-happy varmint lookin' to make a name for himself would still have the chance to recognize him, no matter where he was. All that would accomplish would mean takin' Moosejaw away from his home ground and his friends and puttin' him even more at risk. You'll have to excuse me if I don't see that as any kind of improvement."

"Plus," Firestick added, "no matter how the idea got dressed up, I can pretty much guarantee Moosejaw would see leavin' here as runnin'. And I can double-damn guarantee that ain't in his nature."

"Where is Deputy Moosejaw now?" Trugood asked. "Doesn't he at least deserve to have the idea presented to him so he can have his own say?"

"Right now he's back home at our ranch," Firestick said. "He took a bullet crease in that shindig this mornin', so he's goin' a little easy for the rest of the day. As far as runnin' your idea by him the next time you see him, be my guest. But I'd advise bein' careful how you present it. And like I already told you, I can pretty much guarantee he won't want nothing to do with it."

Trugood made a chuffing noise. "So, in the meantime, the best you can offer is that all we can do is wait for the next gunfighter to come riding into town. Is that it?"

"You got any other recommendations? Any sensible ones?" Firestick said, scowling, clearly growing annoyed. "Maybe you think we should post sharpshooters all around the city limits and have 'em shoot anybody headed this way—you know, just *in case* they might be gunfighters?"

"Or," Beartooth drawled, "how about one of those old-timey things they used to build for castles and such. You know, what do they call 'em . . . a moat? Yeah, that's it. A moat! We could dig one all around the town with only one bridge in. Any scoundrel who showed up lookin' like a narrow-eyed gunslick, we'd just toss 'em into the drink."

Trugood thrust to his feet. "I hardly came here to be ridiculed and made light of! I have a very prominent standing in this town, you seem to forget, and I assure you this isn't the last of—"

He was cut short by the front door being suddenly thrust open to allow the entrance of three somber-faced people. Leading them was Kate Mallory and pressing close behind her came Frank Moorehouse and Dr. Greaves. Once they were inside, Moorehouse shut the door again with a backward swat of his hand and then took an added step forward.

"Sorry to barge in, but I think you'll agree this is something you need to hear right away. And the fact that council members Trugood and Greeble are already present is all for the better."

The five-person town council consisted of Kate, Moorehouse, Trugood, Greeble, and—the only missing member—Pete Roeback, who owned and operated the town livery.

Reading the tense expressions on each of the new arrivals, Firestick was quick to respond, "What is it, Frank? What's so urgent?"

"I regret to report," said Greaves, taking over, "that Buffalo Peak may be standing on the brink of a scarlet fever outbreak."

Chapter 30

Scarlet. Fever. Hearing the two words in combination hit like a punch low to the gut.

Trugood emitted a moan and plopped back down onto his chair. Greeble, normally possessing a certain ruddiness to his cheeks, turned notably pale.

Firestick gritted his teeth. "Are you certain? There's no chance of it being anything else?"

"None. I'm positive," said Greaves. "The first case has presented itself in the daughter of the Harpers, who arrived in town early this morning. He's planning on starting a law practice here. The little girl, her name is Belle, arrived already burning up with a fever that could have been anything. The actual identifying features didn't show up right away. Not until just a short time ago."

"What steps have you taken?" Trugood asked.

"We confined the Harpers to their house, for starters. Quarantined them, though in a very quiet way for now. Informed them of their daughter's disease, told them not to go out or allow anybody in." Greaves's gaze swept the room. "The worst thing we can do, especially at this early stage, is start a panic."

"Yet, at the same time," Moorehouse said, "we need to alert folks, put them on the lookout for symptoms that might start showing up elsewhere."

"But if this little girl only arrived this morning and was already sick and has now been quarantined," said Greeble, "doesn't that leave little chance for her infection to have spread?"

Greaves shook his head. "Not necessarily. She's been in town long enough to have come in contact with several people. Luckily, most of them have been adults."

"That's right, scarlet fever usually hits kids the hardest, don't it?" said Beartooth.

"As a general rule, yes," confirmed Greaves. "But it certainly can—and does—strike adults, too."

"Belle spent two or three hours in my shop. First out in front, then in the back room," said Moorehouse. "Afterwards, after she'd been taken to the Harper home, I had several customers in my barber chair. The same one Belle had occupied for a while. Most of them were men, but there were a couple of boys, too."

Trugood looked horrified. "Can the disease be spread that way—by merely being in the same space as someone who's come down with it?"

"There's differing theories on that," answered Greaves. "But it is extremely virulent, that much is for certain. At the height of some of the larger outbreaks, all clothing and possessions of the ill were removed and burned. I'm not saying I advocate anything that extreme, but precautions must be taken nevertheless."

His expression flinty, Firestick said, "Startin' with,

I'd reckon, those who came in direct contact with the girl. That what you're thinkin'?"

Greaves nodded. "At the very least. Like you say, for starters. I recommend those individuals also be quarantined and kept under observation."

"I guess that means me," said Kate, speaking for the first time. "I spent at least two hours with Belle, sitting with her and sponging her while her parents were getting their house ready."

"Since they came to me first, it includes me, too," said Moorehouse. "Plus Charley Hurt and Virgil Mantz—they helped the Harpers unload their wagon and also transport the little girl from my shop to the house. The neighbors on either side, the Rudasills and Clevengers, crowded plenty close during the unloading as well. And there's young kids in the mix of both families."

"Sounds to me like we might want to consider quarantinin' all three houses—the one the Harpers moved into and the ones on each side," suggested Firestick. "Or would that be bitin' off too much, Doc?"

"No. At this stage, it's better to err on the side of caution," agreed Greaves. "That means the same for myself, Mr. Moorehouse, Miss Mallory, and those two other fellows Frank mentioned. We'll also require quarantine accommodations, though I will have to float back and forth among all so identified in order to monitor for signs of the fever possibly taking additional hold."

"What about the rest of the town?" Beartooth wanted to know. "What if the fever pops up somewhere outside the quarantined places?"

"Individuals will have to keep a sharp watch for early signs," Greaves replied, his brow puckering into deep seams. "I'll issue a list of what to look for. It will fall to you law officers to distribute copies and help monitor for any eventualities."

"God help us if it turns into a widespread outbreak," murmured Greeble.

"Wait a minute," Kate said abruptly. "There's one more person we almost forgot. There was another man who rode in with the Harpers, a drifter who joined them somewhere on the trail. Duncan . . . no, Davies, that was his name. He helped all through this morning and spent days with Belle and her family during the time she first grew sick. He surely should be quarantined, too, shouldn't he?"

"Definitely," said Greaves. "Does anybody know where he got to?"

Blank looks were exchanged all around. Until Beartooth said, "Well, if he's a drifter fresh in off the trail, I think I can make a pretty good guess where he can be found. Davies, you say? Leave it to me and Firestick . . . we'll root him out and bring him 'round."

Chapter 31

Jack Davies opened his eyes and immediately felt the urge to cough. He tried to suppress it but was unsuccessful. What resulted was an eruption of growling, raspy hacking that burned like fire inside his throat and left him once again gasping for breath. Arms flailing, he lunged from a prone position to a sitting one.

Vision blurred by watering eyes brought on as a result of the coughing, Davies looked around somewhat frantically, trying to get his bearings. He saw that he was on a rumpled bed in a narrow, cramped room lighted dimly by the glow of a lamp past the foot of the bed. He swung his feet over the edge of the mattress and rubbed at his eyes, blinking, trying to clear his vision. His face felt hot to the touch, almost as hot as the burning in his throat, and was beaded with fat drops of sweat. His hands came away slick and wet.

As the coughing finally began to subside and he could start to see better through the blur, a shape moved before him, stepping closer. The blur became a face. He recognized Holly, the dove he had been sitting with in the saloon. She was holding out a glass of water.

"Here, try to drink some of this when you catch your breath," she said softly.

Davies took the glass. His hands were trembling slightly and it was a moment before he brought it to his lips. He hesitated, remembering how the shot of red-eye had scalded his throat earlier. But he badly wanted a drink, his throat already aflame and feeling as raw and scratchy as if a mountain lion had clawed it from the inside.

He took a cautious swallow of the water, then gulped some more. It felt cool and soothing, even though he emitted another short cough as he lowered the glass. Looking around again, seeing more clearly this time, he said, "W-where are we? How did I get here?"

"This is my room," Holly told him. "I had Gunther, the bartender, help me get you up here after you had that bad coughing spell downstairs. I took the money you'd spread out on the table and told him you paid for all night . . . with me. I figured after you felt better, it would be okay . . . that maybe you'd want . . . but that was before I realized how sick you are. You're burnin' up with a fever. You really need to see a doctor."

"I told you before, I don't need a damn doctor," Davies snapped. He tipped up the glass again and drained it.

"Would you like a drink of something stronger?" Holly asked.

"No. I'll take some more water, though."

She went to a pitcher and basin at the far end of the room, on the table where the lantern was burning. She filled the glass and brought it back.

After taking another drink, Davies said, "Thank you.

Look, I'm sorry I barked at you a minute ago. It's kind of you to pay me so much attention and show concern. But this is just one of those summer colds or something. It'll pass."

Holly shrugged. "If you say so. But I think it's more serious than that."

Davies passed a hand over his face, his palm once more slick with sweat when he pulled it away. "What time is it?" he wanted to know.

"Well into evening, almost full dark outside. You slept quite a while after we got you onto the bed."

"Jesus," Davies muttered. "I'd better get a move on. I've already taken up too much of your time."

"Didn't you hear me? I told you . . . I took your money," Holly reminded him. "You're welcome to stay here and get some more rest for that 'cold,' if you want. Hell, you're owed even more than that, if you've a mind . . ."

Davies regarded her for a long moment. As doves went, she certainly wasn't hard to look at. Not even when sober. A little plump, a little worn and tired looking around the eyes, but otherwise rather fetching. And although she'd taken money for it, she had gone out of her way to be kind to him. Under almost any other circumstances, he very likely would have remained and taken her up on her offer. But not now, not this time. He had too much else on his mind.

"That's mighty temptin', darlin'," he assured her. "And, like I said, I'm more than grateful for your concern and all you've already done. But there's things I gotta get on with, so let's leave it at that and call things square between us."

When Davies stood up, his knees felt a little weak and spongy, and a momentary wave of light-headedness washed over him. He took another drink of water, finding it still more soothing than the coughing and hacking it seemed to help prevent, yet at the same time he couldn't help wondering why it caused its own burning sensation when he swallowed. A vision of little Belle resisting sips of water and murmuring how they hurt her throat flashed through his mind.

"Thanks again. I've got to be goin'," he said, handing the half-emptied glass back to Holly and then turning to snag his hat and gunbelt off the bedpost.

She stood watching as he buckled the gunbelt around his waist and shifted it a little until its holster was hanging just the way he wanted. Then she said, "You're not going after him, too, are you?"

Davies looked at her. "What do you mean? Goin' after who?"

"Deputy Moosejaw. Jim Hendricks, you call him. Down in the saloon, right before you had that coughin' fit, you was talkin' awful mean and angry about him. You're not another gunfighter come here to challenge him, are you?"

For a moment, Davies looked on the verge of anger. But then his expression changed, took on a hint of smugness. "No, Holly. I'm not a gunfighter. You're right, though, that I damn sure got no love for Jim Hendricks. What's more, I have some long-overdue business to settle with him. But it's got nothing to do with me bein' a gunfighter."

Holly looked confused. "But I don't understand. You still make it sound like . . . like . . ."

"Like what, Holly?"

Before the girl could answer, there was a sharp knock on the door. When a response was slow in coming, a second, more insistent knock sounded.

"Who is it? What do you want?" Holly asked.

A deep, firm voice called through the flimsy wooden slab. "It's Marshal McQueen. I'm lookin' for a man by the name of Jack Davies, who I have reason to believe is in there with you . . ."

Chapter 32

As he stepped back after removing the tongue depressor from Jack Davies's mouth, Dr. Greaves spoke in a tone as somber as his expression. "To my great regret, sir, I must inform you that you are infected with scarlet fever."

If Davies's mouth had had the chance to close completely upon the conclusion of the doctor's examination, it likely would have dropped open all over again. As it was, it simply stayed gaping while, above it, his eyes widened under brows suddenly knitted by great anguish.

"W-what did you say? Scarlet fever? That can't be!"

"Unfortunately, it can," Greaves said, his own mouth pulled into a tight, straight line. "And in your case, it very much is. I haven't a shred of doubt."

"But that's a kid's disease. Like mumps or measles," Davies protested.

"All of those are more common in children, true," Greaves conceded. "But they also occur in adults, far more often than generally believed."

Davies remained seated in the patient chair of Greaves's examining room. Only the two of them were present. The expression on Davies's flushed, sweat-beaded face was one of stunned disbelief. A racking cough suddenly seized him. He pressed a hand against his chest and fought to control it. When it was sub-dued, he said between puffs of breath, "So what now? What becomes of me? What can you do to help?"

"You heard what I prescribed for Belle Harper," Greaves told him. "The treatment doesn't vary based on age."

Davies's frown deepened. "Little Belle? What does she . . . oh Lord! You don't mean . . . ?"

"Sorry, I forgot you were no longer present when I made that diagnosis earlier this afternoon." The doctor nodded sadly. "Yes, I'm afraid Belle has scarlet fever, too. The same identifying features as yours—the rash, the blistered tongue—manifested themselves when I did a follow-up exam after she was settled in her new home."

"So, you mean I caught it from her?"

"Or her from you. One of the many frustrating things about this infernal disease," Greaves explained, "is the varying pace at which its symptoms reveal themselves. In some, it lies almost dormant for a time and then suddenly flares. In others, it strikes imme-diately."

Davies groaned. "Oh God. If I thought that I was in any way the cause of Belle gettin' sick . . . How is she? How's she doing?"

Greaves shook his head. "No change really, other than the symptoms I described finally revealing them-selves more clearly. She's holding her own, but the fever still persists. As long as that continues to be the case, she'll be in danger. As is the case for you. You, too, have a raging fever, and adults, generally speaking, can't tolerate long periods of high fever as well as youngsters."

Davies's shoulders sagged and he rocked his head back as if his neck suddenly had trouble supporting it. "I don't know what to think . . . let alone what to do."

Greaves didn't beat around the bush. He put it to him straight, saying, "I can't give any guarantees. But if you want your best chance for making it through this, you'll let me do the thinking and you do exactly as I tell you."

A handful of minutes later, Greaves emerged out into the reception area of his small office where Firestick and Beartooth awaited after bringing Davies here from the Lone Star Palace. The two lawmen sat in straight-backed wooden chairs against one wall. Pacing restlessly in the middle of the room, trailing smoke like a locomotive from a fat cigar clamped between his teeth, was Frank Moorehouse. The eyes of all three men immediately locked on Greaves.

Pressing the door to the examining room closed behind him, the doctor announced glumly, "Another confirmed case. He's got it, same as the little girl."

"Damn," muttered Moorehouse. "As soon as I saw the flushed face and the sweat when Firestick and Beartooth were bringing him in, I was afraid . . . Did you tell him?"

"Had to. No choice."

"Yes, of course."

Firestick stood up. "So now what? This changes everything, don't it?"

Greaves gazed forlornly out the office's front window for a moment, as if a better response might be lurking somewhere out there on the shadowy street. Then, expelling a ragged breath, he said, "Tremendously. I think we have to consider the possibility of a town-wide quarantine, structured with a few varying degrees of containment."

"I'm not saying I disagree with the quarantine part," replied Moorehouse. "But I'm not exactly clear on what you mean about the different degrees."

"Same goes for me," said Firestick.

Greaves ran a hand back over his forehead, pushing back the spill of wheat blond hair that never seemed to stay in place. "First things first. We've got to get Mr. Davies settled in somewhere where he's more isolated and can start receiving what limited treatment we can provide to help combat his fever. I've got what I think is the best idea for that, though I could use some assistance from you, Frank." His gaze turned to Firestick and Beartooth, who had also risen to his feet. "While we take care of that, I suggest you two might want to gather the other members of the town council and bring them to the jail office. Frank and I will meet you there. To make what I've got in mind work as smoothly as possible, it will be critical to get the council's support. So I might as well explain it to everybody all at once and get any differences ironed out right up front."

"Sounds like reasonable thinkin'," Firestick said. "We'll get the others gathered up for you, Doc."

"By the way, where's Moosejaw?" asked Greaves.

"He went back to the ranch earlier, to let his wound heal up some. Most likely he's wonderin' by now why me and Beartooth haven't made it home for supper yet," said Firestick.

"Wouldn't be surprised if he shows up before long to see what's keepin' us," spoke up Beartooth. "And if he's held off eatin' his own self, it's a safe bet he won't be in a good mood."

"Well, I don't know about that," Greaves admitted. "But I suspect you'll appreciate having him on hand. And along those same lines, while you're out summoning the council members, you might want to consider being on the lookout for some additional men you can trust as temporary deputies. I have a hunch you may be needing them before this is all over."

Chapter 33

By the time he was ready to address the men assembled around him in the marshal's office, Nelson Greaves was showing signs of stress and exhaustion. His limp hair was again spilling down over his forehead, and his posture appeared nearly as wilted as the clothes he'd been in since the previous day. When he spoke, however, his voice was firm and confident.

"For those of you who haven't already caught wind of what this is about, I'll get right to it. Our town suddenly finds itself on a very treacherous brink. We have an outbreak of scarlet fever on our hands."

The room filled with sharp intakes of breath, a few muttered curses, and grumbles of alarm. Eyes snapped this way and that, exchanging looks of concern.

"At the moment," Greaves continued, his voice increasing in volume until the rest quieted back down, "we only have two confirmed cases. One child, one adult. That's the next thing I want to make clear— although this is a disease that more commonly strikes children, adults must *not* consider themselves free of risk. That's important to remember. If we want to get ahead of this outbreak and minimize its spread, then for the next several days it is crucial that everyone of all ages carefully monitors their own condition and that of those around them for any sign of early symptoms."

"Signs like what?" somebody wanted to know.

Greaves held up a hand. "I'll get to that. Just let me finish."

Another voice: "What do you mean by 'several days'? How long and what else is gonna be happening during that time?"

"Again. Let me finish," said the doctor, "and I'll try to cover all your questions and present what I think is a suitable plan for best dealing with the problem."

"In other words, shut up and let the doc say his piece," boomed the distinctive voice of Firestick. "Those of us in this room are who the other folks in town are gonna be countin' on to keep cool heads and get everybody through this without panic or allowin' things to get out of hand. The best way for us to do that is to listen to what the doc is gonna lay out and then stick to seein' it gets followed."

Everybody quieted down again, though the faces remained an array of uncertain, deeply troubled expressions. In addition to Greaves, Firestick, Beartooth, and Moorehouse, the others present consisted of banker Jason Trugood, store owner/proprietor Hans Greeble, and livery owner/proprietor Pete Roeback. These three, along with Moorehouse and Kate Mallory, who remained at the Harper residence where she declared there was a greater need for her, made up the town council.

Also on hand was Sam Duvall, a retired New York City constable who often served as jailer for the marshal; Irish Dan Coswick, owner-proprietor of the Silver Spur Saloon; Big Thomas Rivers, who was Kate's all-around right-hand man when it came to running the Mallory House; and Pastor Bartholomew Rich of the First Baptist Church. Trugood and Greeble were there strictly as representatives of the town council. Duvall, Coswick, Big Thomas, and Roeback, in addition to his spot on the council, were there as the result of Greaves's suggestion for Firestick to have on hand some men who could serve as backup deputies. Pastor Bart was there for his general input as well as the obvious reason of being the community's spiritual leader.

When Greaves had the floor again, he laid out his proposal quickly and succinctly. It would have an impact on the entire town by means of a three-pronged approach meant to address the confirmed cases of the fever, those known to have been in close contact with the stricken, and then those on the periphery yet still not outside possible risk.

This meant that Belle and Jack Davies would be completely quarantined and isolated to the Harper home, along with Kate and Mr. and Mrs. Harper to provide immediate ongoing care. Everyone who had come in direct contact with the two victims, even though showing no signs so far of contracting the disease, would be quarantined separately in Pastor Bart's church. The rest of Buffalo Peak would be quarantined as far as no one being allowed to leave or enter, but otherwise those not confined to either of the two more strictly controlled facilities could go about their daily routines as normally as feasible.

When the necessity for closing off the whole town

was questioned, mostly by Jason Trugood, it was Moorehouse who stepped forward with a response.

"Only this morning," he said, "was when this dreaded disease came within our city limits. It was just a little girl with a fever, not yet showing fully recognizable symptoms. Now, only a handful of hours later, both the child and a grown man who'd been in her company for a few days are suffering the full effects. Which of them contracted the disease first—or where—we can't know. That's one of the greatest difficulties in dealing with scarlet fever. It can spread quickly in ways we don't fully understand, and then it doesn't necessarily show itself right away in someone who *has* been infected.

"In the handful of hours since the Harper wagon arrived in town, the two known victims each came in contact with several of our citizens. The fever may show up in all or some or none of those individuals. That's why we need to isolate them until we know for sure. If any of them *are* infected, it might become evident right away or it might take several days. In the meantime, we must also consider who they came in contact with before being isolated, and the possibility— albeit remote—that they in turn could have passed on a trace of the disease. That's why everybody currently in town needs to remain here. We don't want to risk in any way being responsible for spreading the disease wider. And the reasons for not welcoming anyone *in* to town, until this is over, should be obvious enough to require no further explanation."

Once the plan had been presented and accepted, the next step was to implement it. This fell to Firestick and those he'd solicited to be acting deputies in addition to Beartooth and Moosejaw. The latter, in a double stroke of good fortune and good timing, showed up just as the marshal started handing out assignments for what had to be done. It took only a couple of minutes to inform Moosejaw what the situation was and then Firestick returned to assigning duties.

"I've already wired some of the surroundin' towns about our situation, warnin' 'em to advise any travelers that might be headed our way to hold off," he started out. "Occurs to me, in addition to that, it's only proper we also give the outlyin' ranchers some notice of what's goin' on here. Not only for the sake of lettin' 'em know they'll be turned away if they come to town, but also to warn 'em to be on the lookout in case any sign of the fever shows up in any of their people.

"Doc Greaves has written up a list of warning signs to look for. We'll be postin' copies of that around town for our citizens to get familiar with. But I'm thinkin' that a rider—and I'm lookin' at you, Moosejaw, since you're fresh in, still saddled up, and the least exposed as far as carryin' out any of the bad that's here in town—could make a sweep of the ranches with that same list, and also with the news that Buffalo Peak is under quarantine. You up for that, considerin' your taped ribs and all?"

The big deputy's head was quick to give a positive nod. "I'm your man."

"Good. Get a list of those signs from the doc, then head on out. Hit some of the bigger ranches first, ask them to help pass the word to nearby smaller spreads."

As Moosejaw turned to go, Beartooth said to him, "Once you're in the clear, you might want to consider stayin' that way. Returnin' to town once you've notified those ranchers means returnin' to a higher risk of runnin' up against the fever yourself if you come back. Nobody knows how bad this thing is gonna get."

Moosejaw met his eyes. "However bad it gets, reckon facin' it here with the rest of you is where I'll be."

A corner of Beartooth's mouth quirked up. "Figured you'd say that, you stubborn jerk. When you swing by the Double M, tell Victoria for me . . . well, tell her I'll be seein' her again before long."

Chapter 34

"We covered a powerful chunk of distance today. Don't you agree, cousin Liam?" Jebediah Scorp posed this question on the heels of a loud belch he issued upon lowering the ceramic jug of moonshine from his lips.

"We did for a fact," said Liam. Then added, "Pass that jug back here."

From where he sat on the warped, badly weathered boards of a sagging porch, leaning back against the rough outer wall of the cabin that the porch accessed, Jebediah held out the jug so his cousin could reach over and take hold of it. Liam was seated beside him on a split-log chair covered over with animal skins, also tipped back against the front of the cabin.

The latter was built near one edge of a flat, grassy clearing surrounded by a fringe of trees. It was dark, though lantern light pouring out of the cabin's open door and windows cast the porch in a soft glow. Across the clearing, a spray of stars and a rising, nearly full moon bathed things beyond the lantern glow in a contrasting silver-blue illumination.

A dozen yards out from the porch, murkily visible in a mixture of the two light sources, lay the body of a man. He was sprawled on his back, shirtless, spare in build, clad in trousers held up by a single strap and covered by numerous patches. A pair of cracked work shoes with the soles worn paper-thin covered his feet. He lay on his back, arms and legs flung wide, staring up at the night sky with lusterless eyes. Above those dead, unblinking eyes, in the center of his forehead, was a round black bullet hole.

Scratching his prominent belly, Jebediah said, "A good stretch of miles put behind us and then, just as the sun was settin', this here homestead poppin' up to give us shelter for the night . . . I'd say Texas is treatin' us pretty good so far."

"I wouldn't get too carried away with that kind of thinkin'," Liam cautioned. "There's still time for this treacherous bitch of a place to play a trick or two on us. So don't go lettin' your guard down."

"Yeah, I guess you're right," Jebediah said with a sigh. "Reckon that dirt scratcher layin' out there with a hole in his head is a good reminder about not lettin' your guard down. Damn fool shouldn't of been so open and friendly, steppin' right up and welcomin' four hard-lookin' *hombres* like us the way he did. If he'd had the sense to clear outta the way and let us root around and help ourselves for the night, he could've had the place to himself again tomorrow after we rode off—instead of wakin' up dead come mornin'."

Liam lowered the jug after taking a long, gurgling drink. "Him livin' out here all alone the way he was, I reckon it might not have done too much harm to've left him alive. But after we do what we're aimin' to do down in Buffalo Peak, the safest thing is to leave no sign or description of ourselves ever passin' in that direction. Besides, I could tell right off by the way he was smilin' and actin' hungry for company that he was gonna be annoyin' as hell with a lot of questions and such. So I just went ahead and got it over with."

"Yeah. He ain't gonna be askin' no annoyin' questions now, that's for sure."

"Hell, in a way I probably did the poor bastard a favor," said Liam. "Look at this sorry place he's livin' in, way out here in the middle of nowhere. Likely was many a time he thought about puttin' a bullet in his own head."

"Could be," Jebediah allowed. "But other than bein' alone, it looks like he had himself set up pretty good. A cow and some chickens out there in the barn, a nice little still out back, and a well-stocked pantry and root cellar here at the house. Just the smell of the supper Clapton is in there cookin' up tells me it's gonna be made from some mighty tasty vittles."

Liam gave him a look. "Well, hell. Maybe you just want to stay behind and take over runnin' this little piece of paradise then." He jabbed a thumb in the direction of the dead man. "I guarantee he ain't gonna put up no argument."

"Aw, come on, Liam. I was just sayin', that's all." Jebediah held out his hand. "Give me another swig from that jug."

After Jebediah had taken his swig, the two cousins' attention was drawn to a shadowy form gliding through the moonlight from the direction of the small barn that lay off to one side and slightly behind the barn. The dark, somber face of Mojave Grimes became discernible as he grew closer.

"The horses are all bedded down," he announced. "There was some not too moldy hay and even a little grain out there in the barn. They'll eat good and rest good tonight."

"From the smell of whatever Clapton's cookin', it seems like that's gonna be the case for all of us," Jebediah said.

"More important for the horses than us," Liam grunted. "They've got to hold up for another hard push tomorrow, just like today. They do, I figure by this time tomorrow night we'll only be about half a day out of Buffalo Peak."

Grimes nodded. "Sounds good to me."

Jebediah's eyebrows lifted. "Me too. You really think we're that close, eh?"

"What I said, ain't it? It all hinges on another miles-eatin' day," Liam stated.

The light pouring out of the cabin was suddenly broken up by the shape of Silas Clapton filling the doorway. "Hey, you hungry hounds. You ready to put yourselves on the other side of a mess of ham, sweet taters, and fresh-baked biscuits?" he wanted to know.

His answer was three bodies swarming eagerly to crowd either past or through him.

Only the man lying out in the grass failed to show any interest.

Smiling somewhat wistfully, Kate Mallory said, "This makes me feel sort of like we're young lovers having a secret rendezvous."

"Well, that ain't too far off the mark, is it?" replied Firestick. "I mean, I am sorta slippin' around on the sly.

And we are lovers. It's just the not bein' particularly young part that—"

"Watch it, buster. Speak for yourself," Kate cut him off. "You ought to know better than to remind a lady she's not particularly young anymore."

Firestick held up his hands, palms forward, in a sign of surrender. "I stand corrected. Forgive me."

It was past midnight. The town around them was quiet and mostly asleep, awash in star- and moonlight cut by deep, sharp-angled shadows filling the spaces between the darkened houses in this residential section. The newly occupied Harper house, filled with the glow of several low-burning lamps, was the exception. It was outside one of its glowing side windows, the one marking little Belle's room, that Firestick stood. In the room, closely monitoring the ill child, Kate sat near the window that had been propped open a few inches to allow in some cool, refreshing night air. Hoping for the chance to see her, speak with her before turning in for the night, Firestick had slipped around to the side of the house—knowing he wouldn't be allowed inside—and met with the good fortune of finding her at an opportune moment.

"Okay, I forgive you," Kate said now, in response to his plea. "Although I probably shouldn't. In addition to your poor choice of words, you're undoubtedly breaking the rules of the quarantine by even being here."

"I'm the town marshal. I helped set the rules," Firestick reminded her. "Who has a better right to bend them a little?"

The smooth skin of Kate's brow knitted. "Bend or break—either way, I won't pretend I'm not glad to see you. There certainly wasn't much of a chance before this, not the way everything spun out of control today. First another shoot-out, then the arrival of the Harpers and their sick little girl followed by the diagnosis of her disease . . . it's been a pretty full day, and none of it particularly pleasant."

"I can't say it seems unpleasant right at the moment," said Firestick, his eyes drinking in her beauty and nearness, the way she looked wrapped in soft lamplight.

Kate reached through the narrow opening and laid her hand on his arm. "No, it doesn't. But it's only a moment, and a stolen one at that. There's too much else going on to . . . How is Moosejaw? I heard he was wounded in that shoot-out earlier."

"But not too bad," Firestick told her. "It was a bullet crease across his ribs. The doc patched him up good and tight . . . he's doin' okay. He'll heal in no time." Now his gaze drifted past her, to where Belle lay so still on the bed. "But what about the little girl? And that Davies fella me and Beartooth brought in?"

Kate gave a faint shake of her head. "I don't know much about Davies. They're keeping him in the other room . . . I've been staying here close to Belle. She's holding her own, that's all the doctor will say. We've been able to get her to take some honey and broth, and I sponge her regularly with a cool alcohol solution. If we could only get that doggone fever to break . . ."

"It's a mighty brave thing you're doin', stickin' right close with her and her family at no small risk to yourself," Firestick said. "I'm proud of you for it, but at the same time I won't lie about wishin' you was in a safer place."

"Now you have an idea how I feel about some of the things you involve yourself in," Kate replied.

The wistful smile appeared again, briefly. "But like you always tell me, if it's the right thing to do, then somebody has to do it."

"Yeah, well, now I found out that it sounds better sayin' it than it does hearin' it back." Firestick puffed out his cheeks and released a breath. "But there ain't no changin' it now. All we can do is play out the string. You gotta do everything you can to help pull the little girl—and yourself—through. I'll do everything I can to help pull the rest of the town through."

"How is that going? How are people taking the news about cases of scarlet fever turning up and the town being quarantined?" Kate asked.

"Not too bad so far. But it's still early. There are those who don't even know yet, and for some of the ones who do, I doubt it's had time to sink all the way in. Come mornin', after word spreads across town and the restrictions and frettin' starts to take hold, I expect there'll be some raised hackles." The marshal paused, the corners of his mouth turning down. "You'd think news of something like a scarlet fever outbreak would pull folks together, bring out the best in 'em to concentrate on fightin' what threatens all. But it too seldom works that way. There's usually some who instead show their worst side."

"Maybe this time it will be different," Kate said hopefully.

"Be nice to think so." Firestick placed his hand over hers and held it there for a minute. Then: "Reckon I'd best go catch some shut-eye. You get some rest, too. Mornin' will bring whatever it brings. We'll just have to be ready and do our best."

Chapter 35

After Firestick left, Kate closed the window. The night air was starting to cool the room a little too much.

She went over to the bed and gently laid the back of her hand on Belle's forehead. Still hot, but at least no sign of renewed sweating. Lifting the crisp sheet pulled up under the girl's chin, Kate examined the rash sprinkled over her shoulders and chest. It appeared not to have spread any more and the bright pinkness from earlier seemed to have faded some. Kate thought that might be a good sign, but wasn't sure. Dr. Greaves would have to pass judgment on that.

Turning to the basin on a stand next to the bed, Kate found its contents tepid, not cool enough to suit her. Same for the water and alcohol solution left in the pitcher beside the basin. Smoothing the sheet back over Belle, making sure the child was resting good, Kate took the pitcher and went out into the other room.

Betty Harper was there, in the parlor, sitting on a thinly padded chair beside a table upon which rested a basin and pitcher much like the one in Belle's room.

On the other side of the table, Jack Davies lay on an overstuffed couch draped in more crisp white sheets. He appeared to be asleep.

When Betty looked around at the sound of Kate's carefully soft footsteps, her face was pale and drawn and it was clear she was fighting hard to remain composed. Kate touched a finger to her lips and whispered, "I just came for some fresh ice to cool the solution I'm sponging Belle with. Is there more in the kitchen?"

"Yes," Betty replied in her own hushed tones. "Mr. Moorehouse stopped by to stock some more just a short time ago. It's in a sawdust-lined box by the sink. Here, I'll show you."

Betty got up and after pausing for a moment to make sure Davies appeared undisturbed, she led the way into the kitchen. Once there, the women continued to speak in lowered voices.

"I can't thank you enough for all your help and your attention to Belle," Betty said. "I feel I should be the one in there with her, but Mr. Davies was so distraught when they brought him in that he only seemed to calm down if either I or my husband stayed near. Milo is in the bedroom now, catching a little bit of rest. He'll spell me in a couple hours and then I'll be able to come in and relieve you."

"When will you get some rest?" Kate asked as she chipped some ice off the block with an ice pick. She scooped the small chunks into her pitcher.

Betty shook her head. "I can't sleep anyway. Not soundly. I may doze a little in the chair beside Belle's bed—that will be enough."

"Sooner or later you're going to have to do better than that or you'll be the next one sick," Kate told her.

"I know," Betty said, her voice strained. "But I can't worry about that right now. I can only manage a step at a time, and for the time being, sleep for myself isn't that important. I won't be able to relax until there's some sign that my baby is going to be okay."

Kate managed an encouraging smile. "She will be. She has a great deal of love pouring her way. That, along with care and prayer, will pull her through."

"Yes. I'm clinging to that same belief. My faith is strong," Betty said. "But if God takes my child from me . . ."

"Don't think about that," Kate insisted. "Hold on to your faith and pray hard. It will all work out."

The women left the kitchen and Kate returned to Belle's bedroom. Betty went back to the chair she'd been sitting in earlier. She had barely settled herself when Jack Davies gave her a start by speaking from the couch.

"Mrs. Harper . . ." His voice was hoarse, almost a croak, from the periodic coughing fits he continued to have.

"Yes, Jack. I'm right here."

His eyes remained closed and for a moment she thought he'd fallen back asleep. But then he went on talking. "Mrs. Harper . . . you, Milo, little Belle . . . you're fine people. The best I've been around in a long spell . . . It's an honor and a privilege to have spent time with you. I want you to know that."

"Well, thank you, Jack. You're a fine person, too."

"No. No, I'm not. I don't deserve to be anywhere around folks like you."

"That's certainly not true. If you hadn't shown up when you did and then continued to stick with us, we'd still be wandering lost somewhere back out on the prairie," Betty reminded him. "If our situation is dire now, think how much worse it would have been without you."

"But *I* may be the one who made Belle sick!" Davies said, his voice a tortured moan.

"Don't be ridiculous. There's no need to heap that on yourself. No one can say who or what made either of you sick."

Davies's eyes finally opened and he rolled his head to look at her. "There's more you need to know about me. I want you to hear it . . . I came to Buffalo Peak to kill a man."

"Jack!"

Davies pushed himself up on one elbow in spite of Betty's admonishment to lie still. "No, I want you to hear this. I want somebody to know . . . in case something happens to me. I want the truth to be told."

Betty got out of her chair and went over to the couch, putting her hands on Davies's shoulders. "Alright. I'll listen to your story. But only if you lay back again and keep from agitating yourself too much."

Davies stayed up on his elbow long enough to shudder through a couple of coughs and only then lay back. When he'd caught his breath again, he began talking.

"When I was only two or three years old, my father left home to join a company of men under a Captain Everett Farnham on a huntin' and trappin' expedition high into the mountains. He expected to be gone for months. But the hope and promise was that the men in the company would all earn a big payday from the long, dangerous undertaking. Only it didn't work out that way. Once they got their load of pelts, they were attacked by Indians. Too many to drive off. The company lost all the pelts and many of the men lost their lives. Includin' my father."

"Oh, Jack. I'm sorry."

Davies's eyes had closed again but he continued talking. "At least that was the story told my ma in a letter from Captain Farnham. The *first* story . . . Some years later we heard a different version. The true story . . . You see, my father didn't die at the hands of the Indians. Oh, there was an attack and the pelts got stole, that part was true. And my father was badly wounded in the fighting. Wounded too bad to be moved, else he would've died for sure . . . But the rest of the survivors had to get away from that area, escape before the Indians came back and finished massacring the whole bunch.

"So they drew straws to see who would stay behind with my father, to care for him and protect him until he was healed enough to where he could be taken out, too. It was reckoned that a small handful of men, bein' careful and quiet, would have a chance of stayin' hid from the Indians while the rest of the company made a run for it and drew the red devils off. So that's what they did. The two men who drew the short straws stayed behind with my father and the others fled. And the Injuns followed, just like everybody hoped."

Betty leaned over him, her expression anxious. "So what happened, Jack? Did your father's wounds fail to heal?"

"They never had a chance to heal," Davies said bitterly. "The two men who were supposed to stay with him started to chicken out on their job! They feared for their lives, didn't believe all of the Indians had gone after the rest of the company, that there were some still lurkin' close by . . . So only one night after the others had gone, when one of the men left with my father was asleep, the yellow cur who was on watch dragged my father into a nearby creek and drowned him to put him out of his misery. He threatened to do the same to the other man if he squealed. Then the murderous dogs took off and got safely away themselves. Later, when they joined up with the rest of the company again, they *claimed* my father had died that first night from his wounds. But it was all a dirty lie to cover up their treachery!"

"How did you find out the truth?" Betty said.

Davies had another coughing spell before he could answer. "Some years passed. I was on the brink of becomin' a man," he said, his voice raspier than before. "A fella came by our farm one day. Ma never remarried but she still tried to keep our little farm goin' with just the help of me and my sister. The grind of hard work took its toll. We didn't know it then, but by the time that stranger showed up, she didn't have but a few months left her own self.

"Anyway, the stranger—Arliss Jethro, he introduced himself as—turned out to have been a member of that same expedition my father headed out with years back. He gave his sympathy and all for how things had turned out. And then he revealed how he had been one of the men left to look after my father—the one who was too much of a coward to stand up to the other fella who went ahead and drowned Pa. Jethro was dyin' of a stomach cancer, he claimed, and wanted to clear his guilty conscience before he went to his Maker. He said he didn't know who else to tell because he'd lost track of where the rest of Captain Farnham's company had scattered over the years.

"And then he said he wouldn't blame me and Ma if we was to kill him for his part in the dirty deed and the coverin' up of it for all this time. His eyes kept borin' into mine in a strange way, almost like he was beggin' me to take a gun to him. I woulda done it, too, but Ma wouldn't let me. She said if he really had the cancer in him, like he claimed, then he had sufferin' comin' that would pay him back a whole lot better than a bullet. After that, Arliss Jethro rode away and we never saw nor heard no more about him."

Davies went quiet then. And Betty wasn't sure what to say. Until she remembered how Davies had started out by remarking he had come to Buffalo Peak to kill a man.

She took a step back from the couch. "That's a very sad and tragic tale, Jack. I naturally regret your family's loss and suffering . . . but I'm not sure I follow how any of it relates to our present circumstances or your statement about seeking to kill a man."

Davies opened his eyes and looked at her again. "Don't you see? The man I came here to kill is the second man. The lowdown dog directly responsible for my father's death. The scurvy snake whose hands shoved my poor, helpless father under the icy water of a mountain creek and held him there until he was dead!"

Chapter 36

With the break of a new day, it didn't take long for the raised hackles Firestick anticipated to start revealing themselves. He, along with Beartooth and Moosejaw (after the big deputy completed his ride around to the outlying ranches, notifying them how things stood in town and what to be on the lookout for), had slept at the jail—the marshal on the office couch, the two deputies on cell cots. They woke early and were in the process of finishing a pot of coffee before heading out to make a pass through town, when footfalls on the boardwalk out front sounded in advance of the door opening to allow the entrance of Milt Kruger.

The freight man was cleanly shaven and dressed respectfully in a freshly brushed suit jacket and polished boots. He was on his way to the funeral service and burial of his man Ellis. But the dour expression on his face seemed to have more behind it than just grief for the deceased.

"Marshal . . . deputies," he greeted with a quick bob of his head.

"Mornin', Milt," said Firestick. "Can't hardly say 'good morning,' not with all things considered. I sorta forgot your plan to bury your man so early. Ordinarily, seein's how he was shot here in our town, I'd make it a point to attend. But in this case, I reckon it's best for me and my men to hold off."

Another nod from Kruger. "Yeah, you're right. But that ain't why I'm here."

Firestick pursed his lips. "Okay. I can see you got something stuck in your craw. What is it?"

Kruger's chin jutted out and his lower lip curled up. "It's this damned quarantine we woke up hearing about first thing this morning, that's what! Is it true?"

"I'm afraid it is," Firestick confirmed. "Our town has got a real serious situation on its hands, and we got no choice but to take serious steps to keep it under control."

"So after the burial, me and my men can't leave town—is that what you're saying?"

"That's exactly what I'm sayin'. Nobody leaves . . . nobody comes in. Not until enough time passes with no new signs of the fever and the doctor is able to give an all clear."

"Do you realize what that could do to me? To my business?" Kruger spread his hands in an imploring gesture. "I've got obligations. Contracts to honor. I'm already running a day late on account of not getting those wagons unloaded soon enough, and then the shooting . . . And now you're telling me I not only can't leave to try and make up that lost day, but I have to stay even longer. How much longer?"

"I can't say for sure. Nobody can," Firestick told him. "It all depends on how long it takes for these current cases of the illness to clear up and whether or not any new ones pop up. From what the doc says, we're lookin' at a week or so—at best."

"No! That can't be." Kruger's arms dropped to his sides, both hands balling into tight fists. "That will ruin me."

"If that fever spreads, Mr. Kruger," Beartooth drawled in a flat tone, "the lives of a lot of folks might get ruined in worse ways than your business sufferin'. You might want to stop and think about that."

"Aw, come on. It's not like I don't care about anybody else or don't have sympathy for what kind of widespread damage a thing like this can do," Kruger protested. "I have a young daughter of my own— naturally I have feelings for that sick little girl and her family. But if I lose contracts and money and possibly future hauling jobs, then I have a right to worry about *my* family, too. Especially when including me and my crew in your quarantine is so uncalled for."

"What makes it so uncalled for?" Moosejaw wanted to know. "Why should you and your men deserve different treatment than anybody else?"

Kruger glared defiantly. "Because we didn't come anywhere near that family. We were all in that back lot, dealing with the trouble that led to the shoot-out. Remember? Plus, the way I heard it, that family already had the sickness when they arrived in town. They got it out on the trail somewhere. So how does any of that rope me and my men into having to be held back for possibly carrying a touch of the disease? There's no chance, says I."

"What do you know about how anybody comes down with that fever? How it passes from one person to another?" Firestick challenged. "Some of the best doctors in the country don't know, not for sure. What they do know is that once it shows up in a group of folks—like in a small town—then it spreads among 'em. And anybody leavin' the group runs the risk of takin' a piece of the disease with 'em and spreadin' it wider. Does that sound familiar? Ain't that exactly what we got here?"

"But me and my men aren't part of your group, your town. We're just passing through, in and out after making our delivery. And like I already said, we never came close to coming in contact with that family. That's why I don't see—"

"No, you don't see," Firestick cut him off. "You're only thinkin' what you want to think and believe. You say none of your outfit came in contact? What about Jack Davies, the fella who rode in with the Harper family? He's down with the fever now, too. The second confirmed case. Dr. Greaves discovered that after me and Beartooth fetched Davies so the doc could examine him. And do you know where we found Davies when we went lookin' for him? In the Lone Star Palace Saloon, where he'd been for some time, minglin' amongst other customers who happened to be on hand—includin' half a dozen of your men who I spotted before we got him out of there."

Kruger scowled, his mouth pressed into a tight, straight line. He clearly wanted to say more but couldn't seem to be able to find the right words.

Firestick heaved a sigh. His tone losing some of its edge, he said, "Look, Milt, you and your outfit been makin' deliveries here to Buffalo Peak for a long time. You've always been fair and professional; your men have never caused any serious trouble before. I know this is a tough break for you. I'm sorry. But it's a tough break for everybody. You're gonna have to grit your teeth and make do, that's all I can say. Think how you'd feel if we let you leave and you or one of your men *did* carry the fever out. Maybe to that young daughter of yours. Would you want to live with that?"

Kruger's eyes dropped. It took him another minute before speaking. Then: "No. Of course not."

"Now, go and get your buryin' over with. Try to make your men understand," Firestick told him. "Then find a place to hunker down and ride this out. I'll keep you posted on how things are goin'."

After Kruger departed, the three lawmen stood quietly for several seconds, until Beartooth said, "You think that settled it? Or do you figure we'll be hearin' from him again?"

"Milt Kruger ain't a bad sort," Moosejaw answered. "Naturally he's worried about what a long holdover could do to his business and future work for his freight company. But he's tough and he's a survivor. When that Indian raid killed off all his mules and some of his men a couple years back, he managed to hold things together and stay in business followin' that. I'd bet on him bein' able to weather this, too."

"I agree he'll find a way to weather this," added Firestick. "As far as if we'll hear any more out of him before it's over, that remains to be seen. If this drags on too long and gets very bad, there's apt to be lots of folks wantin' to flee away from here. Holdin' 'em in and keepin' a lid on everything is liable to turn mighty interestin' before we're through."

Moosejaw cocked an eyebrow. "You make that sound like a real good time to look forward to. How many backup deputies you got lined up to help us hold down that lid?"

Firestick reeled off the names. "Sam Duvall, Dan Coswick, Pete Roeback, and Big Thomas from the Mallory House."

"Good men all," Beartooth stated. "But we might want to think of a few more—you know, hole cards to sorta keep ready. *Hombres* who can be counted on to hold the line against their fellow citizens in case a mob gets riled up outta fear and panic."

"Probably a good idea," Firestick allowed. "But first things first—let's take care of the men we've already got. You two go relieve Duvall and Roeback, who've been posted at the opposite ends of Trail Street all night. Tell 'em to go home, grab some grub and then some sleep, in order to be ready for another turn tonight. After I check with the doc and see how things stand at the Harper house and the church, I'll send Coswick and Big Thomas to take over your posts, and we'll meet back here to plan what else we can do to get that lid ready for clampin' on if and when it's needed."

Chapter 37

Betty Harper had fretted for a time over the things Jack Davies had told her. She felt sympathy, of course, for the tragic way his father had died and for what his family had endured as a result. And she shared a loathing for the men responsible. She could even understand Jack *wanting* to exact his own revenge on the only one of the two villains still alive.

But the thought of him actually going through with it . . . that went hard against her personal beliefs in the way justice should be properly meted out. Not to mention the fact that her husband was a lawyer whose driving goal in life—one of their main reasons for coming here to Buffalo Peak—was to try and bring that kind of proper justice to the West.

What she would do, she decided, was to remind Jack of that very thing as soon as he was well enough. Then she would get him to tell his story to her husband and from there Milo could proceed to bring legal charges against the killer and see to it he got punished in accordance to the law. That, rather than seeing Jack resort to settling things with a gun and turning himself into an outlaw on the run.

Once Betty had this resolved in her mind, she was able to put her concerns at least temporarily to rest. Had Jack not fallen back into a deep slumber after sharing his intentions with her, she likely would have tried making her alternative suggestions right then and there. But for the time being, his healing sleep was more important. And since they weren't able to discuss it any further, she felt obliged to keep the matter in confidence until they could. After all, it wasn't like he was going to jump up and do anything rash in his present condition. And it certainly wasn't as if she didn't have plenty else to worry over.

In the ensuing hours, after Milo had relieved her and she in turn had gone into Belle's room to give Kate a break, Betty's focus became very narrow as she sat at her sick child's bedside, holding her hand as she slept, sponging her precious, fever-flushed face. By morning, her concerns for Jack Davies, as far as his plan for revenge, had drifted to a place where they could be visited again, but not with any sense of urgency . . .

"No change. Everybody holding stable."

That was Dr. Greaves's summation of how things stood when Firestick caught up with him at Pastor Bart's church, and that's what the marshal relayed to his two primary deputies when he met with them again back at the jail.

"So what does that mean exactly?" Moosejaw questioned.

Firestick shrugged. "Means what it says. Sickness-wise, those who already got the fever ain't showin' no change one way or the other, and none of the rest quarantined to the church are showin' any sign of comin' down with it. If it stays like that—hopefully with the sick ones pullin' on through, that is—that would be the best that could happen and the quickest way for this to get over with. In the meantime, all we can do is wait and watch."

"And that right there—the waitin'—is what's gonna weigh heavier and heavier on the rest of the folks in town," said Beartooth. "I could feel it buildin' already, just in the time from when we went out to relieve Duvall and Roeback and now as we were comin' back."

"Yeah, I kinda got the same feelin'," Moosejaw agreed. "I stopped by the blacksmith shop for a minute to see Daisy, and she said the same thing. Folks were sorta numb when they first heard the news about the fever and the quarantine and all. But now, as it's startin' to sink in, they're startin' to get scared and more on edge."

"Then it falls on us to try and dull that edge as much as possible," said Firestick. "We need to mosey out, separate-like, and mingle around town during the day. You know they'll be jawin' it up in the saloons and stores and such. We'll need to keep reassurin' folks that everything's under control . . . and all the while hope like hell that nothing changes for the worse. Comes to that, tensions are bound to follow suit."

Moosejaw nodded. "Sounds like the best we can do. But I gotta tell you . . . I'll be able to sound a lot more reassurin' after I get some breakfast in me. Those cups of coffee we had earlier didn't exactly stick to my ribs in any lastin' way. I need me something to eat!"

Beartooth cut a sidelong glance toward Firestick. "If that fever affects a body's appetite, then I reckon we won't have any trouble spottin' early signs in a certain

fella I could name. Although, since not even havin'
his ribs cinched up seems to be slowin' him down,
maybe that won't make any difference, either."

"Hey, it ain't funny," protested Moosejaw. "I'm
hungry, dang it."

Firestick chuckled. "Don't worry. On the way back
here I stopped by the hotel dinin' room and ordered
breakfasts for all of us. Marilu should be sendin' something over any minute now."

"Hallelujah," Moosejaw beamed.

When the meals came, all three lawmen dug in
with equal gusto. As they ate, they talked some more
about keeping the town under control during this
difficult time.

"We got the main road in and out covered at each
end of town," Beartooth said at one point. "But you
know, there ain't a whole lot stoppin' somebody on a
horse—or even with a wagon—from squirtin' out the
sides if they want to hightail it out of here bad enough.
Some dark night when things are quiet and 'most
everybody's asleep . . . Nothing but rollin' prairie
in every direction for miles and miles. They could be
a long way away before anybody even missed 'em."

"That's a fair point," agreed Moosejaw. "The way the
town's spread out, if they stayed quiet and used the dark,
our fellas posted at the ends of Trail Street wouldn't
have much chance to spot 'em. And even if we set up
some kind of roamin' patrol, they could time it and
slip out in between."

Firestick stabbed a pieced of bacon and said,
"You're both right. It's something we need to try and
cover. Any ideas how?"

"Moosejaw's idea about addin' a roamin' patrol, I
guess would be one way," Beartooth replied. "We'd

have to use enough men to make it so's there wasn't enough of a time gap between anywhere they passed for somebody to slip through."

Moosejaw's brow puckered. "That'd take a lot of men."

"How about eliminatin' any horses they could get to?" said Firestick. "If they ain't got a horse to ride or pull a wagon, they ain't likely to *walk* out. And even if they did, we could track 'em and catch up pretty quick."

"Sure, that'd work. But how are you gonna get rid of all the horses in town?" Beartooth wanted to know.

"Wouldn't get rid of 'em," Firestick answered. "We'd *commandeer* 'em—and then corral 'em all at Roeback's livery. Once we had 'em bottled in one place, we could post a couple of guards to keep everybody away."

Moosejaw's eyebrows lifted. "Hey, that might work. Ain't but a couple dozen—maybe thirty at the most— horses around town that ain't already kept at Roeback's to begin with. Wouldn't be much of a chore to round 'em up and herd 'em there."

"You start messin' with men's horses," Beartooth pointed out, "that's a sure way to ruffle some feathers."

"Ain't like we're stealin' 'em. It's part of makin' the whole quarantine work," said Firestick. "Besides, it was your idea in the first place."

"In a roundabout way, maybe," Beartooth admitted somewhat reluctantly. "But it don't matter who thought of what, all I'm sayin' is that messin' with other folks' horses ain't likely to be seen as reassurin' to 'em."

Firestick considered a brief moment, then, setting his jaw determinedly, said, "I can't help it. To keep everybody where they belong, I think it's something we need to do. So, when we leave here, I'll swing by

Roeback's livery and make sure he's got room and feed to take on that many more hayburners. I'm already pretty sure he does. In the meantime, you two, as you move around town, take a tally of who has horses in their own barns or corrals. Then, when we're ready to start our roundup, we'll know where to find 'em . . ."

Chapter 38

The town's building tensions reached a flashpoint sooner than Firestick or his deputies were prepared for. What was more, it flared at a totally unexpected spot.

Figuring that trouble, if it came, was most likely to boil up out of one of the saloons, where belligerent talk fueled by liquor often led to unwise action, the lawmen spent the morning with their attention focused mainly on the downtown area. Strolling around, observing, casually joining in whenever they saw a knot of people engaged in conversation that appeared particularly spirited, their aim was to keep their fingers on the pulse of things and try to prevent an overly dour mood from taking hold.

The plan for rounding up all the spare horses in town and securing them at Roeback's livery—including Milt Kruger's mules—was set to be implemented toward evening, when folks would most likely be at home so they could be advised what was going on as their animals were taken. Pete Roeback himself, and two of his hired men, were on tap to help when the roundup began.

In the meantime, the waiting continued: waiting and hoping for the best; preparing for the worst. Dr. Greaves and Frank Moorehouse passed regularly back and forth between the Harper home and the Baptist church, both somber and haggard looking even as they spoke encouragingly of no worsened conditions or new symptoms.

Until it was Moorehouse alone who came hurrying from the direction of the Harper house, breathing hard, his face flushed and contorted by a deeply agitated expression. He found Firestick and Beartooth standing together in the shade of an overhang on the boardwalk out front of Greeble's store.

"Firestick . . . Beartooth," he puffed urgently from halfway down the block. "You'd better come quick . . . trouble . . . a mob at the Harper place!"

The two lawmen heard all they needed to. They were already in motion as Moorehouse gasped the last words. Not waiting for him to try and keep up, they sprinted out onto the street and then diagonally across—retracing the way Moorehouse had come.

"Find Moosejaw!" Firestick called back over his shoulder.

The two lawmen cut down an alley that ran between two businesses, bootheels digging hard as they burst out the back end and into a residential section of modest houses and cottages with shade trees and grassy backyards. In a matter of minutes, they rounded the corner of a side street and came in sight of the Harper place.

Moorehouse's "mob" was suddenly before them.

At least two dozen people, about a quarter of them women, were crowded together in front of the house that the Harpers had so recently and desperately dragged their belongings and sick child into. A general din of voices, some louder and gruffer than others, emanated from the bunch as the swarm of bodies shifted and shuffled.

Facing the crowd, standing before the house's front door, was Dr. Greaves. He stood holding his medical bag up to his chest as if it were a shield. His hair was once again spilling around his face, and his expression seemed to waver between anger and trepidation.

"Get 'em outta here—send 'em back where they came from!"

"Cut out the poison! That's the thing to do!"

Those were some of the words coming out of the crowd, shouting down the doctor every time he opened his mouth and tried to say something.

Spreading out to a distance of about ten yards apart, Firestick and Beartooth plunged without hesitation into the mob from its back side, shoving bodies roughly aside and out of their way, until they broke through and converged together again out in front. Stepping up beside Greaves, one on either side, they wheeled around and faced the surly, grumbling pack.

With his hand coming to rest meaningfully on the Colt holstered at his hip, Firestick demanded, "What the hell's wrong with you people? What's goin' on here?"

Angry faces glared back at him but for a long, tense moment there was nothing but uncertain silence. Then, all at once, the din started back in again. General murmurings of "Whose side is he on anyway?"

and "Who is it we're paying him to protect?" could be heard. Until finally one man up at the front of the pack—Leo Fanner by name, a burly, gruff-natured carpenter by trade—spoke up louder than the rest. Glaring at Firestick, he said, "We're here to do the only sensible thing, Marshal. We aim to cut through all this quarantine garbage and do what you and that sawbones shoulda done right off, first thing yesterday!"

"I'm supposed to believe something 'sensible' is gonna come out of an angry, snarlin' mob?" Firestick sneered. "Tell me—what should we have done different?"

Fanner thrust out a bulky arm and stabbed a forefinger at the house. "Them inside. Them disease carriers! They need to go, to clear out of our town and take their dirty sickness with 'em. That's what needs to happen!"

"That's the way," shouted a female voice from somewhere farther back in the crowd. "Put the burden of controllin' this plague on them, not on all the rest of us!"

"That's a ridiculous notion," said Greaves. "Running these unfortunate people out of town will in no way lessen the chance of anyone else getting the disease. Not at this point."

"There now! You're admitting there was a point—like when they first showed up—when that *should* have been done," claimed Fanner. "Ain't that what you just said?"

"That wouldn't have necessarily made any difference then, either. There's no way of knowing—"

"If it was a good idea then," Fanner interrupted the

doctor, "then it still has some worth now. Better than keeping them here in our midst, continuing to spew their filthy infection wider and wider."

"You get a poison in yer gut, you puke it out," said a gnarled, gray-whiskered old man standing next to Fanner. Balancing on a crutch thrust up under his right arm, he hoisted the stump of his left leg and, slapping it, declared, "You get a poison in a leg wound, you cut it off afore it spreads and takes all of you! Any infernal idiot knows that much."

"Cut out the poison! Cut it out before it takes us all!" rose up a chant from several members of the crowd.

Greaves shook his head vehemently. "That's not going to happen! Not only would it be incredibly cruel, it would accomplish nothing as far as the potential for more fever to show up, even if they were driven away. These people have every right to stay here and receive the best care I can give them."

"Who are you gonna listen to, Marshal?" said Fanner. "You gonna protect the whole town—*your* town—or are you gonna side with a bunch of diseased strangers?"

Firestick clenched his teeth. "You're gonna talk to me about *my* town? What I'm seein' and hearin' here in front of me right now ain't nobody I recognize—or want to—from the place I call my town. The folks from my town show grit and stand tall and hold out a hand to other folks in a time of need. They don't whimper and huddle together like a bunch of milk-greedy pups willin' to crowd out the runt of the litter so's to practically guarantee he has no chance of makin' it. They pull together, not shove away. That give you a clear enough answer on where I stand and who I'm sidin' with?"

"And in case it *ain't* plain enough," spoke up Beartooth, "let me put it to you another way: Any one of you sorry excuses figure to make a move on the folks in this house or those at the church, you'll have to go through us to do it—and that's a harder push than you and three times your number have it in you to do."

Fanner scowled menacingly. "You and your deputy are barkin' against mighty big odds for just two men, less'n you think that medicine man is gonna pitch in and do you some good."

"You don't count no better than you make sense!" boomed out a voice from behind the crowd. The heads that snapped around to look saw Moosejaw standing out on the edge of the street, brandishing a double-barreled shotgun, its muzzle bores gaping wide and deep. "I make it three barkin' against you," he added, "and I'll let you decide how many more the twin barrels of this gut shredder amount to."

The crowd sucked a collective intake of breath.

The old man on the crutch glared at Firestick and said, "You call it upholdin' the law, threatening your own citizens that way?"

Firestick replied, "We're protectin' *decent* citizens. It's only a pack of lowdown rabble we're threatenin', old man. You better get that straight if you plan to keep your ancient, wrinkled ass planted in front of me much longer."

The crowd seemed to shrink in on itself. Harsh mutterings faded to muted, uncertain whispers. Shoulders sagged and eyes that had been flashing with self-righteous anger only moments ago became abruptly downcast. Some on the outer edges of the pack turned and began to walk away.

Looking past Fanner and the old man up front, Firestick spoke in a somewhat softer, more tolerant tone to those behind them. "Go on home now. Forget you let these wrong intentions get hold of you. Go home and count your blessings that it ain't your house and family that's quarantined." He paused, then added, "Anyway, it probably ain't the smartest thing in the world to be gathering like this around a house where there's such a serious sickness . . ."

That hastened the crowd's dispersal. Pretty soon it was only Fanner and the old man standing there. And then, silently, they also turned and walked away.

Moorehouse had reappeared and moved up to stand beside Moosejaw as the crowd was dispersing. Once everyone was gone, the two of them came the rest of the way forward to join Firestick, Beartooth, and Dr. Greaves at the front of the house.

"Now I feel like I can breathe again," the doctor proclaimed. "I was starting to feel awfully smothered there for a minute!"

"Aw, it wasn't such a big deal," Beartooth said, flashing a reassuring grin and clapping a hand on Greaves's shoulder. "Just a few curious neighbors stoppin' by to see how things was goin' and to let you know they care about the good health of our town."

"Sorry if it sounds selfish, but it wasn't just the town's health I was worried about—concern for my own health certainly crossed my mind during the thick of it," admitted Greaves.

"But you stood your ground all the same," said Firestick. "That speaks well for you, Doc, and I'm sure those under your care are plenty grateful."

"Do you figure we've seen the last of those scoundrels?" Moorehouse asked, scowling after the last of the mob as they drifted away.

"Of that particular bunch, I think," answered Firestick. "But that don't mean that some of 'em might not branch off and try to stir things up elsewhere. Leo Fanner, for one, bears watchin'. He's a loudmouth and a hothead who never seems to know when enough is enough once he's got something stuck in his craw. I can picture him showin' up in one of the saloons—where I expected something like this to flare up in the first place—and try to stir it up all over again."

"Who was that ornery old cuss on the stump leg?" Moosejaw wanted to know. "I don't recall seein' him around before, but he was doin' his share of the stirrin', too."

"Name's Hiram Kolsky," said Moorehouse. "He lives up on the northwest side of town, not far from Fanner. Think he might be some kind of shirttail relative to Fanner's wife. He's practically a hermit these days, since his own wife died a year or so back. Lost his leg in the war . . . has carried a real bitter chip on his shoulder ever since. I think Mrs. Fanner sees to most of his needs; that's why you don't see him out and around very much."

"Saw enough of him today, don't need to see no more," Moosejaw muttered.

Behind Greaves, the front door of the house opened a crack and a slice of Milo Harper's face showed in the gap. "Is everything okay out there?" he asked in a tentative voice.

The doctor turned around and said, "Everything is fine, Mr. Harper. The marshal and his deputies showed up and have dispersed the mob."

"They sounded so . . . so ugly. I have an extremely upset wife in here."

"I can appreciate that, Mr. Harper," Greaves said in a soothing tone. "Just close the door, please. I'll be in in just a minute to check on everyone."

The door closed with a soft click.

Greaves turned back to those gathered about him. "As you heard, I'd better get on inside." His gaze swept across the three lawmen, and very earnestly, he added, "You have my extreme gratitude for your timely intervention, gentlemen. I can't thank you enough—not only for myself, but for those inside as well."

"It's our job," Firestick said tersely, not bothering to remind anyone that he had a deep personal interest in one of "those inside." "We'll be sure to make a regular patrol past here from now on."

Greaves gave a nod and then went on into the house.

Once the doctor was inside, Beartooth cast a long look after the mob members still straggling away and said, "You reckon it might be smart for one or two of us to sorta wander along after that bunch, just to make sure they go their separate ways and some of 'em don't form back into a pack as soon as they're outta sight?"

"Sounds like a good idea," Firestick said.

"I'll go along with you," said Moosejaw.

"How about you, Frank?" the marshal said to Moorehouse. "You goin' in with the doc?"

Moorehouse shook his head. "No, he don't need me. Think I'll head back to the church and see how things are going there."

"I'll walk with you a ways," said Firestick.

The four men were just splitting apart when a voice called out sharply from a corner of the house, "Freeze right there! Nobody take another step and nobody even *think* about reachin' for a gun. I got mine already pulled and I'll burn down the first one who twitches wrong!"

Chapter 39

The positioning of the four men who suddenly found themselves under threat of a gun left them quite exposed and vulnerable. Beartooth and Moose-jaw stood side by side, facing toward the west; Firestick and Moorehouse were similarly posed, facing east. All four were still grouped close together—too close for any reasonable chance to suddenly scatter in hopes one of them might escape an initial sweep of rapid fire. Plus, the alleged gunman was speaking from off to the north, outside the peripheral vision of any he was addressing. Meaning an attempt by any one of them to return fire would involve the time required to spin, draw, and try to lock on the gunman's position— while being shot at—before ever gaining a target to trigger a round at.

Not a good situation.

"Only one man needs to die here today," the voice spoke again. "It's a justice long overdue and something the rest of you shouldn't try to stand in the way of—not only for your own sake but for the sake of what's fitting and right."

"Mighty hard to swallow, hearin' talk of justice and doin' right comin' from a back-shooter," Firestick growled over his shoulder.

"Don't you worry, I aim to do what I'm fixin' to do face on. But before any of you turn my way, you need to shuck your gunbelts. One at a time, startin' with you, Marshal—movin' real slow and usin' just your left hand, unbuckle and let 'em drop."

For a long, tense moment nothing happened. Nobody moved.

His voice sounding strained, the gunman said, "I got six slugs in this wheel. If I have to, I can afford to spend one to make sure you know I mean business."

Moving slowly, grudgingly, his teeth gritted hard, Firestick unbuckled his gunbelt and let his holstered Colt drop to the ground. Beartooth next, then Moose-jaw, followed suit.

"I . . . I'm not armed," Moorehouse said huskily.

"Okay. Still real slow and keepin' close together . . . all of you turn and face me."

Once again, the four men did as instructed. As they came around, they saw Jack Davies standing at one corner of the Harper house with a Colt .45 held at waist level and aimed at them. His face was as red as a ripe tomato and dotted with fat drops of sweat. His chest rose and fell with what appeared to be some-what labored breathing. But the .45 in his fist was steady, unwavering.

"What's this all about?" Moorehouse demanded. "The fever has you out of your head, man!"

"No, don't ever believe that for a minute," Davies replied. "I'm seein' and thinkin' clear as a bell."

At that moment, the house door opened and Dr. Greaves reappeared. "Davies? Jack Davies, are you out here?"

"Don't come another step, Doc!" Davies's words were for Greaves, but his eyes never left the men he was holding his gun on. "Get back inside and tend to little Belle and her ma. Tell Mrs. Harper that I'm sorry I had to do this here and now, but I got to take care of it while . . . while I'm still able."

"Take care of what? Jack, you're a sick man. You need to get back in here and lie down so—"

"Get out of here, Doc! Now!"

Slowly, looking bewildered and perhaps a bit frightened, Greaves eased back inside and closed the door.

Firestick watched this exchange, outwardly motionless while every muscle and nerve in him was raging, writhing with the urge to somehow break into action. And he knew Beartooth and Moosejaw were feeling the same. But neither Davies's eyes nor his gun had wavered in the slightest while trading words with the doctor, providing not a whisker of a chance to make any kind of move.

However, as the door closed, Davies's focus shifted for the first time. Ever so slightly. It seemed to lock specifically on Moosejaw.

"Jim Hendricks," he said, a harder, raspier edge to his voice. "I've been lookin' forward to havin' you in my gunsights for a long time."

A momentary hint of curiosity passed over Moosejaw's face, then his expression went flat and blank.

"You'll have to excuse me," he said, "if I ain't quite as pleased by that as you seem to be."

"No, I don't expect you are."

"Maybe if you explained what all this garbage you're spewin' about overdue justice and doin' the right thing is supposed to mean to me—or any of us— I might appreciate it more."

Davies hesitated a moment, trying to fight back a cough. But even as a pair of harsh eruptions escaped him, his gun remained steady. Then: "I'm going to say a name. That'll tell you all you need to know, you cowardly, murderin' bastard. The name is Nathan Davies . . . *and I'm his son!*"

This time there was no masking the changes that Moosejaw's face went through. First he went chalky white. Then came a flood of raw emotions, each flickering briefly but in stark evidence. Shock; sadness; anger; then confusion and uncertainty.

"I roamed a long time tryin' to track down Jim Hendricks," Davies continued. "I got sidetracked plenty of times along the way, sometimes by bum leads, sometimes by havin' to take time out to survive . . . and you takin' on the alias of Moosejaw fooled me more than a little bit. But then, when I was almost ready to chuck the whole notion, I saw it plain as day in newspapers practically everywhere I looked. Jim 'Moosejaw' Hendricks, the gunslingin', hell-roarin' deputy of Buffalo Peak . . . It was like an omen straight outta heaven . . . or, for one of us, maybe hell."

By the time Davies was done talking, Moosejaw's color had returned and his expression had once again become flat, impassive. "I don't know what you've heard, kid . . . or what you've got in mind . . . but it sounds like you got some things mighty twisted around in your head."

Davies gave a faint shake of his head. "No, not anymore I don't. Not no more. We had 'em twisted around—me and my ma both—based on the pack of lies Captain Farnham sent in his letter. But then Arliss Jethro showed up and set us straight!"

"Arliss Jethro was a back-stabbin', spiteful liar who went plumb out of his head with guilt and syphilis poisonin'! You can't go by nothing he told you!" Moosejaw exclaimed.

"Then why was he the only one to come around and set the record straight for me and my ma? Why would he admit to his own part in what happened to my pa if he was lyin'?"

"I told you! In his later years he was clean out of his mind," Moosejaw insisted. "He went around jabberin' and claimin' all kinds of crazy stuff—until nobody who mattered paid any attention. If he hadn't been sick in the head, I would've killed him for the stuff he said about me. But I couldn't . . . not the way he was."

"Too bad for you that you didn't, Mr. Hendricks," Davies said. "You should've killed him before he got to me. Because I happened to believe him . . . and now, because of what he told me about what you did to my pa, I'm gonna kill *you*!"

"You pull that trigger, kid, you're also gonna be killin' yourself!" Firestick interjected desperately. "No way you can get us all before one of us manages to plug you, too."

Davies fought back another cough. Then, his mouth stretching into a ghastly smile with blood outlining his teeth, he said, "Is that the best you can do, Marshal? Is that supposed to stop me? Can't you see I'm already as good as dead?!"

And then, yes, Firestick saw it all too clearly. Davies was ready to die. There was no stopping him, certainly not with words. Now that he'd stated his case, he was ready to go out in a blaze of what he saw as glory—as long as he could take Moosejaw with him.

That left only one thing to do.

Throw all caution to the wind and go for broke!

Suddenly and simultaneously buckling his knees and folding at the waist, Firestick dropped into a low crouch. Scooping up his gunbelt, he instantly pitched to one side and went into a roll, clawing to pull his Colt free from its holster as he turned over and over in the dust.

Firestick hoped this action would draw fire from Davies, giving Beartooth and Moosejaw a chance to get at their weapons and do some shooting back. Only it didn't work out that way. Davies's gun began roaring a split second after Firestick sank into his brief crouch, but the fact no bullets hit him or came anywhere in his direction made it obvious to the marshal that his attempted diversion hadn't worked. Nevertheless, he *did* sense a flurry of motion from the others who'd been standing with him, so he knew they at least weren't making stationary targets of themselves.

But Davies's gun kept roaring.

Firestick ceased rolling, coming to a stop on his belly. He had his Colt free and was extending it to arm's length, thrusting it at an upward angle through the swirls of dust that he himself had kicked up. Through the dust haze he saw Davies now swinging the .45 in his direction. Moosejaw, Beartooth, and Moorehouse were all sprawled on the ground. Firestick centered the front sight of his Colt on Davies's chest and began pulling the trigger.

Once, twice, three times he fired. Davies jerked and twisted from the impact each time. Before Firestick was done, Beartooth, from where he lay, threw in a pair of rapid-fire shots of his own. Davies got off a final round as he spun wildly, blood arcing out from several bullet holes, before he collapsed heavily against the side of the house. He hung there for a moment and then slid slowly down, staining a recently applied coating of whitewash with a long smear of bright red until he finally crumpled to the ground.

Chapter 40

Moosejaw had taken two bullets, Frank Moorehouse one. Firestick and Beartooth both came out of it unscathed.

Jack Davies died with five slugs in him.

Once the bleeding was brought under control, none of the wounds to Moorehouse or Moosejaw were life threatening. The damage to Moorehouse was most severe, the socket and bones of his left hip busted up pretty badly, some nerves torn; he'd walk with a limp for the rest of his days. Moosejaw took lead to two places on his right arm—at the wrist and up near his shoulder. Broken bone and ripped muscle tissue resulted in each case, but luckily there appeared to be no nerve injury; with the passage of time and some painful, persistent work to make sure it didn't stiffen up, he'd regain nearly a hundred percent usage of the arm.

All treatment and diagnosis was performed in Dr. Greaves's office, where the wounded men were hastily transported as soon as the initial bleeding was brought under control at the scene. Despite their clamoring to come out and assist in the immediate aftermath of the shooting, neither Kate nor the Harpers were allowed to leave the quarantined house. Once everyone had made it to his office, Dr. Greaves—talking as he worked quickly and efficiently on the patients—told what had happened inside the house regarding Davies, including Betty Harper's revelations about what he'd told her the previous night.

It was the distraction by the mob out front that allowed Davies to rise unseen from his couch while everyone else was at the windows, anxiously monitoring what was going on outside. Seizing the gun from his belt and holster that had been removed and hung on a nearby chair when he was initially brought in and bedded down, the fever-riddled man had slipped silently out the back door. His absence went unnoticed until the mob had been dispersed and the doctor came back into the house. In fact, it was the sound of Davies's voice coming from outside, making his opening demands on Moosejaw and the others, that drew full attention to the fact he was gone from his couch.

It was during Davies's exchanges with the men he held at gunpoint that Betty Harper had, in a desperate rush of words, confessed to those in the house what he'd told her about his intentions, what his motives were. She wailed guiltily about not revealing it to anyone sooner, how she hadn't believed it to be an immediate threat and the way she'd hoped to talk him out of pursuing it.

But then all of a sudden the guns were roaring and it was too late.

Once the doctor had relayed all of this, Moosejaw was in a frenzy to set the record straight about the accusations made against him, even though the doctor tried to get him to lay quietly while he was cleaning the big deputy's wounds and preparing to reset the bones in his arms.

"Nothing doin'," Moosejaw said between slugs of whiskey to dull the pain some as the work proceeded. "I won't have a lie like that hang in the air a second longer than it has to. Look at all the damage it's already done by not bein' brought out in the open the first time it got spoke . . . and all because of one other lie right at the beginnin', a long time back. Just a tiny, harmless one meant to ease minds for the better but then growin' into something steadily bigger and uglier, like gangrene spreadin' from a simple scrape."

Firestick and Beartooth stood close by, looking on. Daisy was present, too, watching silently but with an anguished expression as her man was being treated. Propped up as comfortably as possible on a padded bench over against one wall, his wounds already tended and bandaged, Frank Moorehouse also remained in the room. To counter his own pain he gripped a bottle of laudanum in one hand.

"Firestick and Beartooth already know the story. I told 'em the straight of it years ago. But now that it's been dragged out into the open again," Moosejaw continued, "I need to tell the rest of you.

"Everything young Davies told about the expedition under Captain Farnham was true, you see, up as far as the Indian attack and all our furs bein' stole," Moosejaw continued. "I was part of the company and so was Nathan Davies. I was a young pup, barely twenty. It was my first crack at huntin' and trappin' up in the high reaches. It was mostly a good bunch to be part of, especially with Captain Farnham at the head.

He led us smart all winter and we took in one mighty fine haul of prime pelts. Woulda set each of us up with a fat payday.

"But then we found ourselves smack in the middle of a whoppin' big pack of Ute Indians. They must've been trackin' us for weeks, waitin' for the right moment to close in. And when they hit, they hit hard and savage. We was outnumbered and caught by surprise. Men was droppin' like flies. The only thing that saved us from all bein' slaughtered was that we fought back hard and was costin' 'em dear even as they cut us down. Once they had the pelts, they decided that was good enough—leastways for the time bein'—so they withdrew."

Moosejaw stopped talking as the doctor prepared to set his broken shoulder bone. Firestick and Beartooth stepped up to help hold him still. It took Greaves two hard yanks to get the break properly back into alignment. The big man gritted his teeth and let only a loud grunt escape the first time; the second yank brought a yowl he couldn't hold back.

After both men—doctor and patient—had caught their breath, Greaves went back to work and Moosejaw went back to talking.

"Reckonin' that, if we stayed put for very long, the Utes would come back and try to finish us, Captain Farnham made ready to start what was left of our company back as soon as we'd buried our dead. The only problem was Nathan Davies, who was wounded too bad to move. The captain hit on the notion to draw straws, the two short ones bein' men who'd stay behind with Davies and care for him until he was healed enough to travel. The captain reasoned that, number one, the Utes would probably tag after the main body to make sure they left the territory and, number two, only a couple of men stayin' behind would have a good chance of goin' undetected as long as they laid low and played it smart until Davies was ready to move. And by then there was a good chance the big band of Utes would have moved on themselves."

Moosejaw paused for a long pull of the whiskey. "So it was me and Arliss Jethro who pulled the short straws. He started whinin' and wheedlin' right off, tryin' to make a deal with somebody else to take his place. But he got no takers. Jethro was always an odd duck, sayin' and doin' some mighty strange things almost from the start of the expedition. But he was an experienced mountain man, knew his business with a trap line, so everybody mostly ignored his strangeness and put up with him. Later on, back in Fort Collins, we eventually found out he had come down with syphilis before we headed off. But he wouldn't own up to it. So not takin' care of himself and guzzlin' whiskey whenever he got the chance and basically just tryin' to ignore it, the disease had commenced eatin' at his brain, the way a dose will do to a person. That was who and what I was stuck with after the others all took off.

"To make matters worse, Nathan Davies was in fierce pain with his wounds and all we had to help him was a limited amount of whiskey we were tryin' to ration out. Later on, I had a hunch Jethro was probably even nippin' off part of that. Long story short, Davies was in pain worse than he could stand, convinced he was gonna die anyway, so all through that first day and night he kept beggin' us to do for him and save ourselves. But we wasn't havin' any, and I'll give Jethro at least that much credit—he never showed no sign of goin' along with what Davies wanted.

"But sometime toward dawn the next morning, when Jethro and me were both dozin' hard, Davies woke up and dragged hisself out of his bedroll. We was camped in a sort of shallow cave on a hill just above a stream, see. Well, Davies dragged hisself down to the water's edge. Whether he was out of his head or went after a drink of fresh water or flat *meant* to do what he ended up doin', nobody will ever know for sure, but he got too far out into the stream, which was runnin' pretty strong with spring snowmelt, and it pulled him away and drowned him. When me and Jethro woke up, we saw him gone and saw the marks on the ground and . . . well, even if we wasn't sure what was behind him draggin' hisself away, it was pretty clear what had happened."

There was another break in the talking while Dr. Greaves, again with the aid of Firestick and Beartooth to hold the big man still, set the wristbone. Fortunately, it snapped into alignment on the first pull and with a lesser amount of pain. While the doctor then began applying a splint and fashioning a sling, Moosejaw went back to his story.

"That was where the lyin' began," he said bleakly. "Jethro was in a lather right off about how if we rejoined the company and told 'em what had happened, they'd blame us for not payin' closer attention to Davies, practically accuse us of lettin' him die. He was so worked up over it and, like I said, I was still mighty young and green. So I finally agreed we would just say Davies had died in his sleep from his wounds. Keep it simple.

"But I still figured we owed it to the deceased to give him a proper burial. I didn't reckon his body could have floated too far downstream without snaggin' somewhere. So I allowed as to how we should go find it and bury it before headin' back. Well, that sent Jethro into another tizzy. He was convinced there was still Utes in the area and didn't see no sense in riskin' ourselves to be spotted by 'em for the sake of a fella who was already dead. He said Davies was beyond carin' what happened to what was left of him and we needed to start out pronto for rejoinin' the others. Only this time I wouldn't give in. I told him he could do what he wanted, but I meant to do right by Davies's body. I told him to go on ahead and tell the others we got separated on account of havin' to dodge some Indians. Then, when I showed up later, I'd back up that story and also about how Davies passed in his sleep. Jethro didn't like it much, but he finally agreed and we went our different ways."

"And you were able to find Davies's body, right?" Beartooth prompted.

Moosejaw nodded. "I was. Little over a mile downstream, snagged on some branches along the bank, about like I figured. I drug him out, buried him, marked the spot. Then I struck out to rejoin the captain and the others." He took time for another swig of whiskey, his voice taking on an added edge of bitterness when he spoke again. "When I caught up with 'em, that's when I ran into the next lie. The biggest, worst one of all. I don't know to this day why he did it—some part of his brain bein' addled by his sickness, I guess—but Jethro, when he caught up with the others ahead of me, told 'em that story about me drownin' Davies. And then he told 'em I tried to kill him, too, which was why he lit out apart from me, he said, and got to 'em first."

"And the captain and the others believed him?" asked Daisy.

With the bitterness even stronger in his tone, Moosejaw said, "Let's just say they didn't have no choice but to at least give it some consideration. Most of 'em had known Jethro longer than me, and the only thing they knew for sure was that the two of us had showed up with some mighty different stories and Davies was left behind dead. So, until we got back to Fort Collins, where they'd have the chance to sift things a little finer, both of us was kept a close eye on at all times.

"Back at the fort, things started leanin' a little more in my favor. The doctor there told the captain about Jethro's condition, and Jethro himself was actin' stranger and stranger right along. Sayin' and doin' things that didn't make much sense, only made him look more foolish. Finally, Captain Farnham hit on an idea for findin' out the truth of the matter. Some weeks had passed by that point so, figurin' the Utes up in the mountain area we'd pretty much trapped and hunted bare would have moved on by then, he put together a small group of well-armed men, includin' me and Jethro, to return to the cave where the company had left us with Davies. Based on the opposin' stories from me and Jethro, what was found there would give a pretty clear idea who was tellin' the truth. If it was the way Jethro said—that I'd drowned Davies right outside the cave and then took after Jethro, tryin' to kill him, too—then there oughta be some of Davies's remains still right there close. If it was the way I claimed, then I'd be able to take 'em to where I buried the body more than a mile downstream, where it got swept to after Davies caused hisself to be pulled in."

"Which you were able to do—provin' your innocence," said Firestick.

"That's the way it went," Moosejaw affirmed. "At which point, Jethro cut and run. Truth to tell, nobody put much effort into chasin' him. We figured he'd either show up back at the fort eventually . . . or run into some Utes on his own and meet his punishment that way. For a long time after that there was nary a sign of him, so most figured he *did* run afoul of some Injuns. In case his lyin' accusations about me ever cropped up again in any way—knowin' how rumors, no matter how false, can sometimes linger—Captain Farnham wrote a letter statin' how I was cleared of the whole murder business. That satisfied my needs. I carried that letter with me for many, many years.

"Before it was all over, though, Arliss Jethro did pop up again on a few occasions down through the foothills. He'd somehow survived makin' it out of the mountains on his own and further survived carryin' around his sickness for longer than he had any right to. Word got back to me how he was still claimin' I killed Davies, but his overall behavior by that point was so senseless that nobody paid him no attention. Like I said outside the Harper house, I thought more than once about huntin' him down and killin' him for the trouble he'd caused me. But the shape he was in persuaded me not to follow through. If I'd somehow known it would lead to today, all these years later, it was something I now wish I'd gone ahead and done."

"You can hardly fault yourself for showing a measure

of mercy at the time," Dr. Greaves said. "And certainly no man can see into the future."

"Maybe not, Doc," Moosejaw allowed. For a moment his gaze seemed to drift off and look at something far beyond the walls of the treatment room. "But what I do fault myself for, since I was the one there with her husband at the last, was not ever gettin' word to Nathan Davies's widow . . . Not just hollow condolences, but the real truth of what happened and how I buried him with some proper words—leastways the best ones I could think of—said over him. I had my comfort from bein' cleared of his murder. But outside of the captain's letter, nobody thought to contact her and give her any extra comfort. Nobody except lyin', twisted Arliss Jethro. Not that it was exactly comfort he gave her—and certainly not her son—but at least he made contact. If only me or Captain Farnham had thought to do that, to follow up with the whole truth, it would've been a measure of mercy far better than me not killin' Jethro. And it would have gone a long way, I believe, toward preventin' what happened here today."

Chapter 41

As the day passed into afternoon and edged toward evening, something curious began to take place throughout town. The building tension that had gripped Buffalo Peak since the announcement of the quarantine, squeezing tighter and tighter, actually started to ease somewhat. After all the lamentations and the spurt of mob activity that marked the early hours, it was as if the latest shooting—and the condition it left two of the town's better-known and generally well-regarded citizens in—had shoved aside much of the fear and concern over an intangible threat and reminded everyone that the here and now was plenty to focus on and deal with.

Because he would be basically immobile for days and weeks to come, Frank Moorehouse could not be returned home, an apartment behind his barbershop where he lived alone. So he was temporarily moved to the Harper house, where Kate and the Harpers were available to help see to his needs. Due to his previous direct exposure to both Belle and Jack Davies, it hadn't been advisable to house the barber and sometimes doctor with just any caregiver until after the quarantine was lifted. At that point, there would be the choice of two or three boardinghouses in town where he could receive the kind of attention he'd require until he was sufficiently healed.

At Daisy's insistence, Moosejaw went home with her as soon as he was done at the doctor's office. Although the big deputy was capable of getting around on his own, his wife-to-be was bent on pampering him at least in the beginning stages of his recovery, and neither he nor anyone else was up for trying to talk her out of it.

With these matters taken care of and the body of Jack Davies now in the hands of Clem Worden, the local undertaker, Firestick and Beartooth took the opportunity to make a pass through town before returning to the jail. The day's heat had climbed to a scorching level with an unusual degree of humidity in the air. As they walked along, they couldn't help noticing, through the gaps between buildings, that far off on the western horizon a bank of bloated, charcoal gray clouds was thickening and sliding this way.

Yet even with that storm appearing to be gaining strength, the two lawmen could each sense as they walked along how the stormy unrest that had been churning all day in many of their citizens seemed to have leveled off to a large degree. They could *feel* it. There was a general lowering of hackles, almost a calmness, that certainly hadn't been present earlier.

"I don't know what brought it on or how long it will last," Beartooth announced after they were settled in the marshal's office with fresh cups of coffee in hand, "but I'll take it all the same. With this damn quarantine hangin' over everybody's heads and the steady parade of gunfighters that have been marchin' through ever since that attempted bank robbery . . . I'd say a taste of things bein' calm for a while is not only welcome but doggone overdue."

"No argument from me on any of that," replied Firestick. Then, lowering his cup after taking a drink, one side of his mouth quirked up in a wry smile.

"What are you grinnin' at?" Beartooth wanted to know.

"Thinkin' about what you just said."

"Still don't follow you."

"The parade of gunfighters you mentioned," Firestick explained. "Don't you see? Thanks to that Davies kid, in a cockeyed kind of way, whatever else we got ahead of us, dealin' with more gunnies comin' to test Moosejaw ain't gonna be part of it. With his shootin' arm all busted up and not expected to be workin' right for the foreseeable future, word will spread quick enough—and we can be sure to help it along— that there's no longer anything to be proved by comin' 'round to challenge him."

Beartooth's eyebrows lifted. "I'll be dogged. You're right. Moosejaw might not see it as an ideal way for the matter to be put to rest, but that's what it amounts to all the same."

"What's more," Firestick added, "if any trouble-makers come around needin' to be convinced, then neither can the big fella continue to be stubborn about us steppin' in to lend a hand."

Beartooth chuckled. "Oh, he'd still huff and snort probably . . . but, if it came right down to it, even he ain't that foolishly stubborn."

Firestick set his cup down on the desktop and then

slapped his palm down beside it. "You know, by God, I think this is a turn for the better that deserves a snort of something stronger than just coffee."

"You're the marshal, I'm just an obedient deputy," Beartooth said agreeably as he watched Firestick pull out a lower drawer of the desk and withdraw from it a bottle of whiskey. "It seems like we probably oughta have Moosejaw here to take a snort with us, bein's how he's at the center of the whole thing. But come to think of it, he already had plenty of snorts back at the doctor's office."

"Indeed he did. So, with or without him, here's to our friend gettin' a reprieve from the parade of gunfighters." So saying, Firestick tipped the bottle up and guzzled a long pull. Then he handed it to Beartooth, who followed suit, but without any words ahead of doing so.

As Beartooth was lowering the bottle, the front door opened and once again Milt Kruger entered. Accompanying him was Burt Lauson, his head mule skinner. Both men wore sad expressions, and there was a notable slump to their broad shoulders, demeanors far different from the antagonistic one Kruger had been displaying the last time he showed up.

Firestick stood up behind his desk. Feeling the need to explain, he said, "We don't make a habit of fuelin' ourselves with red-eye to get through the day, but sometimes a snort is in order."

"None of my business, Marshal," Kruger replied. "I know you and Deputy Beartooth well enough to know it's not something that gets out of hand. And from everything else I know about your situation in general and the day you've had, it seems perfectly warranted to me."

Beartooth thumbed the cork back into the bottle and handed it to Firestick, who returned it to its drawer.

"As a matter of fact," Kruger continued, "it's your situation that we came to talk to you about. Starting with—speaking first on my own behalf—an apology for my behavior earlier. I was acting like a selfish whiner, something I don't fancy myself as being and certainly not anything I want to come across as."

"This quarantine puts you in a tough position. You had a right to do some grumblin' about it," Firestick allowed.

"Like you told me before, the quarantine and the illness behind it has a lot of folks in a tough position. Life-threatenin' tough, for some of them," Kruger said. "And speakin' of being in a serious condition, though from a different source, how is Deputy Moosejaw? We heard he was in another shoot-out and took some bullets this time."

"He did for a fact. But the slugs he took were to an arm and shoulder. He's gonna pull through okay."

"And there was another fella wounded, too? The barber who also used to do some doctorin' for the town?"

"Frank Moorehouse. Yeah, he took a round to the hip. Again, he'll pull through okay, but the damage is likely to leave him hobbled permanent-like."

"Damn shame. But at least he'll live."

"Both of those fellas," spoke up Lauson, "were mighty important to our crew back when we got hit by those renegade Apaches a couple years back. Moosejaw rode out to warn us and then stayed right there in the thick of it with us, fighting off those red devils. And then, when it was over, Moorehouse showed up and commenced patching and stitching the hurt and wounded. Saved some who weren't likely to have made it otherwise."

"So that's why we're here," said Kruger. "Some of us have been coming to this town long enough now to . . . well, feel like we got friends here. So, despite you saying I've got the right to do some grumbling, I want to do more than that. Do something to help with these problems you've got on your hands, especially now that Moosejaw and Moorehouse are laid up. Me, Lauson here, and several others from our crew if you need 'em are willing to pitch in and help however we can."

"Plus," added Lauson, making a sour face, "I owe an apology, too. For my part in that stupid shoot-out business with Ellis. He was a twerp and a loudmouth who deserved his comeuppance. But I shouldn't've egged him on by stirring up the betting like I did. If I hadn't done that, probably the only thing that would have got shot off was his mouth and he'd still be alive. Most of all, I wouldn't have been no part of putting Moosejaw at risk in the process. Yeah, he won out okay. But there was a chance it could have gone differently. I ain't very proud of that."

"From everything I heard," Beartooth said, "Ellis was the kind who was bound to get hisself shot sooner or later, no matter what. I wouldn't blame yourself too hard for helpin' him get what he was after."

Firestick added, "And as far as the two of you offerin' to pitch in and give us a hand . . . well, with Moosejaw and Moorehouse out of the picture, we could use a couple replacements. Maybe more. We was thinkin' about roundin' up some more fellas anyway."

"You don't have to look no farther," Kruger said. "And there's more of our crew, too, who are willing if needed. We're not gun hands, you understand, but neither are we strangers to shooting irons. And we reckon ourselves rugged enough if we have to be."

"Sounds good enough to me," Firestick said. "But the first job I'd ask you to lend a hand with might stick in your craw some."

"What's that?"

The marshal told them how, toward evening, they planned to round up all the spare horses around town and secure them at Roeback's livery.

"We figure it'll help keep any desperate sorts from takin' a notion to try and bust free from the quarantine," he summed up. Then added, "And we was figurin' to include your mules and horses along with the rest."

"If you're going to do for one, I see where you have to do it for all," Kruger said, though at first not appearing very keen on the idea. But after a moment's consideration, he shrugged. "What the hell, it'd probably be better for our animals than staying hobbled in that open lot for much longer. Especially judging by the look of that storm building off to the west and looking ready to roll in. Not to mention how the graze is going to run out in that lot before much longer."

"Roeback has plenty of feed on hand," Firestick told him.

"Alright. Give us the word whenever you're ready," said Lauson. "We'll get our stock moved in and then help with the rest. That's for starters. Let us know if you want men for anything else. If that storm settles in as big and ugly as it looks like it's going to, those men you got posted out on the street might need spelling more often than you have been up to now."

Beartooth cocked an eyebrow. "You're volunteerin' to stand post in the rain and wind?"

Lauson grinned. "What can I say? We're freighters. We're used to bein' out in the weather, no matter what it is. To tell you the truth, having a roof over my head when it's storming—so all I can do is *hear* the thunder and wind but not be able to see it—that makes me downright nervous."

Chapter 42

After the freighters departed the jail, Firestick and Beartooth got around to realizing that they hadn't had any lunch, and suppertime wasn't far off. First they joked about how, if Moosejaw was present, such an oversight would never have occurred. And then they set about rectifying the problem by making a trip to the Mallory House dining room.

Marilu Rivers, who was overseer of the hotel's kitchen as well as waitstaff, saw to their needs personally, placing before them plates heaped high with meatloaf, mashed potatoes, and greens. Inasmuch as it was well past the standard lunch hour and not yet approaching dinnertime, the dining room was going through its late-afternoon lull. This allowed Marilu time to linger and make conversation as the lawmen ate.

Her round, ebony face etched with genuine concern, she inquired about the conditions of Moosejaw and Frank Moorehouse. And then spent a lot of time asking after Miss Kate, expressing deep pride in her bravery for staying at the quarantine house while at the same time fretting about what she was exposing herself to by being there. The relationship between Kate and Marilu—and also Big Thomas, Marilu's husband—went back several years and was much closer than merely employer/employee. This was never more evident than what Marilu was currently demonstrating by her concern for Kate. Firestick did his best to reassure her that Kate would be fine and, in turn, he promised to get word to Kate that the operation of the Mallory House was in good hands while she was away.

Their meal finished, Beartooth announced his intentions to make another turn around town and in the process check on both Moosejaw and Moorehouse. Firestick allowed as to how that was a good idea and that he would catch up with him after he took care of a matter he'd been interrupted from completing more than a day ago. Namely, the talk he meant to have with Howard Blessingame as a follow-up to the Coffin Bill shoot-out. In view of events that had transpired in the meantime, he had even more reasons for wanting to make contact with the writer.

Overhearing mention of Blessingame, Marilu was quick to offer the information that, although he had been in and out quite a bit this day, she was pretty sure he happened to be up in his room at present.

A handful of minutes later, Firestick was knocking on Blessingame's door.

"Who is it?"

"Marshal McQueen. Like to have a few words with you."

There was a pause, the sound of movement from within, and then the door opened and Blessingame was standing there. Somewhat to Firestick's surprise, given how distraught the man had been the last time he'd seen him, he was clean-shaven and groomed and appeared to be in good spirits. The marshal had been expecting someone conveying more of a rumpled, hiding-from-the-world look.

"Come ahead on in, Marshal. Have a seat. I'm sorry, but I don't have any refreshment to offer except for water."

Firestick declined the water but accepted the seat, settling onto a thinly padded chair just inside the door. The only other chair was at the writing desk where Blessingame lighted. Firestick noted the yellow-lined tablet lying open on the desk, filled with line after line of scribbling from the pencil lying beside it.

Firestick inclined his head toward the tablet. "Appears you been doin' some writin'."

"As of this morning, yes," Blessingame replied. "Through all of yesterday, however, and the balance of the day before—after that dreadful, bloody business with Coffin Bill—it seemed I had, er, lost my muse. Forever, I feared for a time."

"Your will to write, you mean?"

"Yes. That's how it felt."

"Uh-huh. When I tried to talk to you that day out front of the Lone Star Palace, followin' the shoot-out, you seemed pretty shook up," said Firestick. "You were sayin' some things at the time that sounded like you might be ready to give up writin' for good, right then and there."

"In that particular moment, yes, that was exactly how I felt. Certainly for the type of thing I had been writing up to that point."

Firestick's eyes cut briefly to the tablet on the desk. "But now you're back at it again, eh?"

"Oh no," Blessingame was quick to say. "I'm writing again, true—but not material like I was before. The day and a half I spent listless and empty, with no direction evident for me to go with further writing, turned out to be just a mind-clearing experience, an emptying of the past to make way for what I now see as a new way for me to go."

Firestick frowned. "I can tell you're excited about it, but once again, your exact meanin' gets sorta lost in the haze of those forty-dollar words you like to toss around."

"Let me try again," Blessingame said tolerantly. "What I'm trying to say, Marshal, is that I've given up on turning out any more of those gun-blazing, full-tilt action yarns like I've spun so many of up to now. After having witnessed the real thing firsthand, I see there is very little glory and certainly no romance in the actual occurrence of such things. It is only bloody and dreadful and life-ending. To present such as vicarious thrills and entertainment for those who only experience it from the safety of an armchair or to stir the imagination of excitable young boys . . . well, maybe it's harmless enough. But, then again, maybe some restraint in painting it as something glamorous and to be emulated is worth considering, too.

"All I know for sure is that, for me, the latter is the path I intend to take with any future writing. I've decided, you see, that not only is the bloody work of desperadoes and shootists nothing to be held up as grand excitement, but the real heroic deeds of the West—the hard, gritty work carried out by so many yet so seldom heralded—can be found in the day-to-day struggles of the common folks. The folks like the ones right here in Buffalo Peak, pulling bravely and unselfishly together to fight a soulless threat like scarlet fever, isolating themselves to do so for the sake of trying to keep the disease from spreading, even though keeping away outside help might mean keeping away medicine or treatment that would shorten the battle . . .

"At any rate, that's how I see it and *that* is the kind of thing I mean to try and capture with any future writing. How it will be accepted—or even if I can find a publisher for it—I do not know. But it's damned well what I intend to do."

Firestick could scarcely believe his ears. He was grinning broadly by the time Blessingame paused in his spiel.

"What's the matter? Do you find something amusing about my goal?"

"Not a doggone thing, writer man," Firestick assured him. "Matter of fact, it couldn't hardly fit in better with what I came here to talk to you about . . ."

Chapter 43

They got the town's horses—including the animals from Kruger's freighting outfit—rounded up and secured at Roeback's livery just before the storm hit. The first clouds had rolled in dark and low, blotting out the last of the sun and hurrying the gloom of evening. And then the full force came, preceded by whipping gusts of temperature-dropping wind followed soon by slashing sheets of rain. Pitchfork lightning illuminated roiling, purple-black clouds, and peals of thunder pounded the air and caused the ground to tremble.

Firestick and Beartooth stood in the open doorway of the livery barn, gazing out at the torrent lashing down out on the street. Pete Roeback stood with them. All three men were draped in long, shiny wet slickers.

"I gotta tell you," Roeback was saying, "I feel kinda guilty about not takin' my turn at standin' post tonight. On the other hand, I'd be a liar and dang fool if I claimed I ain't glad not to have to be out there in this."

"Don't worry about it," Firestick told him. "With all these extra horses and mules we decided to push your way, you got plenty to keep you busy right here."

"Besides," added Beartooth, "we have it on good authority that Lauson, the fella who's takin' over your watch, don't mind bein' out in crappy weather. In fact, he likes it better than bein' inside where all he can do is hear it howl and not see what's goin' on."

Roeback's forehead puckered. "Well, far be it from me to speak ill of anybody providin' me such a break. So I won't mention that it sounds like this *hombre* might've already stood out in a few too many gully-washers and had some of his smarts washed away."

Firestick removed his hat, poured rain off the brim, then put it back on and snugged it in place. "Well, showin' a lack of smarts when it comes to venturin' out in that frog-strangler ain't strictly the claim of Lauson. Reckon I'll be headin' out into it myself."

"Ain't you gonna wait for it to let up some?" asked Beartooth.

"I ain't so sure it's gonna let up, leastways not any time soon," the marshal answered. "You go ahead and wait a spell here if you want. Me, I'd just as soon make a pass through town, check in the saloons to make sure nobody's upset on account of us takin' those horses, then make my way to the jail and get settled in for the night."

Beartooth frowned. "From what I saw, everybody seemed pretty understandin' about us herdin' the horses all to one place. More so than I expected. You really think something might flare up now?"

"I hope not. But I'd rather double-check on it to make sure. Like you said at the beginnin'," Firestick reminded him, "folks are mighty persnickety about their horses. We caught 'em by surprise, makin' our sweep and gatherin' up the hayburners like we did. If somebody gets to thinkin' and stewin' on it now that the surprise has had some time to wear off, I'm thinkin' they might head for one of the saloons to see if they can find anybody else feelin' the same as them."

"If this storm keeps up this strong for very long," said Roeback, "I'd be surprised if the saloons do much business at all. Anybody with any brains—even if they got a mad on—oughta be inclined to stay home where it's dry and warm."

Firestick nodded. "I hope you're right. The town had just started to come to grips with the threat of scarlet fever and the quarantine. I'd hate to think we stirred things up all over again. But I'll feel better if I make a sweep and confirm nothing new is brewin'." He glanced over at Beartooth and added, "Before I leave the Lone Star Palace, I'll have Gunther build a couple of those extra-thick beef sandwiches they always have the fixin's for in back. Then I'll take 'em to the jail for our supper later on."

"Aw, hell. I'll just come on with you." Beartooth sighed. "You're right, this ain't lookin' like it's gonna let up any time soon. The least I can do is protect my personal interests and make sure one of those sandwiches stays dry."

After flipping up his collar and getting ready to step out into the downpour, Firestick paused to look back at Roeback. "If any fool *does* decide to get pissed off enough over this horse thing to actually try and re-taliate in some way," he said, "I figure it'll be aimed at me. But if I'm wrong and they show up here, since this is where the horses are . . . well, you keep a sharp lookout, you hear?"

Roeback grinned. "Don't worry, Marshal. When it comes to my business and havin' horses in my care, I always keep a sharp lookout."

Liam Scorp started to say something but then, knowing what was certain to follow the flash of lightning that seemed to turn all the world brilliant silver for a moment, he held his tongue long enough for the ensuing blast of shattering thunder to speak first. Once it had, when there was only the wind and relentless hiss of rain to be heard over again, he said, "Remind me again, cousin Jeb, how wonderful this place called Texas is treatin' us."

"On account of this storm, you mean?" Jebediah backhanded a fat drop of rain off the end of his nose. "Come on, Liam, it's just a thunderstorm. Shucks, they got thunderstorms about anywhere you can name. Ain't like Texas has been savin' up this one special just to dump on us."

"All the same, it *is* dumpin' on us and I ain't likin' it one bit," Liam growled. "I'm cold and wet from my ass both ways and I don't see that changin' any time soon, no matter if the sky ever does get around to drainin' itself out."

"If you fellas just hold still and keep blocking the wind and rain a little longer," said Mojave Grimes from deeper in the thicket behind them, "I think I can get a decent fire going here. Once it's burning good, we can feed it with even partly damp wood and we'll have some heat that'll help things considerable."

"You hear that, cousin Liam?" said Jebediah, striving to put a hopeful tone in his voice. "A cracklin' fire and some hot coffee—that'll go a long way toward improvin' things, won't it?"

Liam's face, illuminated by another flash of lightning, was locked in a fierce scowl. "Oh yeah. Everything will be swell then. It'll practically be like dinin' at the governor's mansion—damn it, quit hoggin' all that canvas! Let me have at least a pinch of it!"

The two cousins were hunched close together, jointly holding up over their heads a canvas tarp that was barely big enough for the job. They squatted near the front edge of a dense thicket into which they—along with Grimes and Silas Clapton—had hacked out a burrow of sorts for the sake of squirreling in and seeking shelter from the storm. It had been the quickest thing they could make it to on this stretch of rolling, empty grassland when the sky suddenly broke open above their heads. Their horses were hobbled out in the open, and while Liam and Jebediah temporarily blocked the front opening, Grimes and Clapton were scraping deeper in to make a pocket where they could all huddle out of the worst of the downpour.

"Okay, I got a pretty good clearing dug out back here," Clapton announced, his breathing a little labored. "Hang up that tarp on some of those thorny branches to keep the opening covered the best you can, then crawl farther on back. It's staying fairly dry so far."

"Yeah, and this fire is catching pretty good now,

too," added Grimes. "We got plenty to feed it with, so it ain't going to be too bad."

A long, crooked streak of lightning sliced across the sky, followed by a deep rumble of thunder that made the ground shiver under the four men, as if Mother Nature were responding with a message that she would be the one who decided how good or bad it was going to get.

On their hands and knees, Liam and Jebediah crawled back to where the other two men were. There they situated themselves on another set of tarps that had been spread on the ground until all four were sitting cross-legged close around the fire Grimes had going. He was continuing to feed in small sticks and twigs, and the flames were licking at them hungrily, sending up ribbons of smoke that rose and filtered away up through the higher tangle of thorny branches. This same thick tangle twisted together tightly enough over their heads to serve as a reasonable ceiling that warded off most of the rain, reducing it to a few stubborn, intermittent drips.

"By God," Liam grunted as he held out his hands and rubbed them together close to the fire. "Even though I feel akin to a doggone prairie dog, maybe this ain't gonna be so bad after all."

"It ain't enough of a fire to do no fancy cooking on," said Clapton, "but it's enough to brew a pot of coffee—and *that* will darn sure rate us higher than any old bunch of prairie rats."

As he twisted around and began rummaging for coffee makings in the pack of gear he'd dragged in with him, more thunder crashed outside and some of the bursts of lightning were brilliant enough to penetrate even the dense tangle surrounding them.

"Doggone," Liam lamented. "I sure hate to leave our horses out in the open, the way that blasted storm is carryin' on!"

"There wasn't time to do no different, not as fast as that howler cut loose," Jebediah reminded him. "But they're a sturdy bunch and we hobbled 'em good. Long as none of 'em get hit by lightnin', they'll pull through okay."

"Ain't sayin' they won't pull through," said Liam. "But if it lasts like this for very long, they sure ain't gonna get the rest we need for 'em to get. They did another fine job of eatin' up distance today. Real fine job. We can't expect to get that out of 'em again tomorrow, though, if they ain't rested right."

Jebediah frowned, his broad face still beaded with rainwater. "But we ain't gonna *have* to get another hard day like that out of 'em again, are we? I mean, not the way you been reckonin'. Don't you expect us to reach that town of Buffalo Peak along about the middle of the day tomorrow?"

"That's what I'm expectin' and hopin', yeah," agreed Liam. "But I ain't ever been down this way before in my life. I can't say for double-dog certain I'll be able to march straight to some spot out on that prairie come the middle of the day tomorrow and stamp my foot and say *Here's Buffalo Peak!* It might take a little more time, I might have to do a smidge of course-correctin'. Jesus, Jebediah, to come as far as we have with no bona fide trail laid out or—"

"Don't worry. You're on course just fine," said Grimes matter-of-factly as he continued to poke at the flames of the fire Clapton now had a tall coffeepot perched on.

Liam's eyes darted to the half-breed. "How's that?"

"Our location. You've got us in good shape," Grimes replied. "It's been years, but I've been down this way before. I was very young and we came in a different way—from the west. From where we started this time, to the north, I couldn't have steered us this far any better or even as good as you have. But now that we are near, I'm starting to recognize some of the landmarks."

Liam grinned crookedly. "Why, you redskin rascal. Why didn't you let on?"

Grimes shrugged. "Like I said, there was nothing I could have added to make any difference. But now I can."

"And you agree we're close?"

"Very. Those low mountains we were seeing to the southwest just before the storm rolled in? Those are the Viejas. We'll pass their eastern tip tomorrow morning. We get an early start and cut to a southwest angle as soon as we're below them, we can reach Buffalo Peak by the middle of the day, just like you been saying."

Liam's crooked grin stretched into a wide, full-bore smile. "I'll be damned! You hear that? Middle of the day—I had it nailed all along!"

"Let's hope you got the rest of it nailed as tight," said Clapton. "If you do, then by this time tomorrow night we can be stretched out on crisp bills of bank money instead of soggy wet canvas!"

Grimes gave him a look. "What if this rain keeps up and some of the money we haul out of that bank gets a little damp—you saying you're gonna just throw those bills away?"

"If'n you do, go ahead and throw 'em my way," said Jebediah. "Far as I'm concerned, wet money spends just as good as dry money."

"You better believe it does!" affirmed Liam.

For the next several minutes, the laughter and cheerful hoots that came out of that smoky thicket were almost loud enough to challenge the ongoing roar of the storm.

Chapter 44

Firestick lay on his back on the couch in the marshal's office. His eyes were closed and he was motionless, but he wasn't asleep. He was listening to the storm churn outside while thoughts churned over in his mind. Curiously, however, he felt relaxed for the most part . . . felt a reasonable measure of rest and regeneration seeping into him. He would sleep soon, he knew, and it would be deeper and less troubled than many might expect for a man in his position.

It was a trick he'd learned a long time ago, during his years up in the mountains. When you had the chance to rest, you took it and you made it count. No matter if you were wet or cold or the conditions were otherwise undesirable . . . like maybe a pack of Injuns somewhere close by in the dark, aiming to take your hair if they got a chance . . . you still rested when you could. Your body and brain had to have rest in order to stay sharp, to keep you alive. To survive.

True, there was plenty at hand this night that Firestick could have spent time fretting and worrying over. Two wounded friends; the ongoing threat of the fever spreading and his responsibility for keeping the unpopular quarantine in place; the woman he loved bravely continuing to place herself at increased risk for the sake of helping others in need . . .

Yeah, those were all undesirable conditions. But, on balance, some other things that *had* been problems only a short time ago now were lessened. Moosejaw, as a result of his wounds—or thanks to them, if you looked at it a certain way—no longer stood as a beacon for every twitchy-fingered gun hand who might be inclined to swing this way with the intent of trying to make a name for himself. Blessingame, though previously responsible for helping to promote that kind of thing, was now bent on working to help turn the tide, both via the telegrams he had agreed to send out at the marshal's request, spreading the word on Moosejaw's injuries eliminating him as a fast-draw contender, and also by future writing aimed at no longer glorifying the whole gunfighter mystique.

Furthermore—as once again confirmed by the recent pass Firestick and Beartooth had made through the town and its saloons—the tension that might be justifiable in the good folks of Buffalo Peak under the circumstances remained at a very controlled level. Firestick was impressed and kind of proud. At the same time, he felt a little ashamed of himself for expecting less. But he was happy enough to admit he'd been wrong, and those raised hackles he anticipated and saw signs of early on had mostly smoothed themselves out . . .

Although, he couldn't help thinking, if more cases of the dreaded fever showed up and forced the quarantine to drag on, the mood could very well shift and those hackles could lift again, sharper than ever.

A sudden, intense clap of thunder followed a sizzling lightning flash that filled the whole inside of the jail with blinding whiteness and caused Firestick to give a reflexive, full-body jerk. When he settled back down on the couch again, his mouth was spread wide by a sheepish grin. Maybe he wasn't so calm and relaxed after all, he told himself.

From his cot back in the cell block, Beartooth hollered out, "Jesus! We get another blast like that, the sound you hear next will be me diggin' a hole to crawl in and pull after myself!"

It was after midnight before the storm finally blew itself out and weakened into just a steady, straight-down drizzle. At that point it became a soft, monotonous hiss that was like a soothing whisper lulling the town into peaceful slumber.

Morning brought a brightened sky—pale gray rather than bloated, churning blackness—but the drizzle continued along with gauzy wisps of fog hanging just above the ground in several spots.

"Big change from yesterday's boilin' heat. At least for now," said Beartooth from where he stood gazing out the office window with a cup of coffee in one hand. "Once the rain lets up and the sun finally burns off the last of that fog, though, it'll go right back to bein' hotter than blazes again."

"'Spect so. After all, it's summertime," said Firestick as he turned from the washbasin in one corner, toweling the final streaks of shaving lather off his face.

As he continued to gaze out the window, Beartooth

said, "Folks are already out, even before the rain lets all the way up, clearin' away fallen branches and such."

"Uh-huh. Figurin' to beat the heat that's comin'. Plus, they're probably anxious to see how much other damage last night's wind might have done."

"Yeah, I been wonderin' about that, too. Wonderin' about our own ranch, I mean. Some of our outbuildings, especially, are plunked smack in the open. They likely got knocked around pretty good."

"Luckily, we got Miguel and Jesus on the job. Anything got damaged, you know they'll be lookin' to take care of it first thing," Firestick said. He paused, regarding his friend for an extra beat before adding, "And you know they'll be lookin' after Miss Victoria, too. Not the same as you'd be if you could be there, of course . . . But she'll be fine."

Beartooth reddened a little. "I know that. Besides, Victoria is a big girl; she can take pretty darn good care of herself. It's just that . . . this blasted quarantine and all . . . well, I miss bein' able to see her. That's the long and short of it."

Firestick nodded. "I understand, friend. I got it a little better than you, but I'm also shut off from my Kate. Hell, the last I was able to talk to her, we had to keep a pane of window glass between us."

"I'd settle for that as an improvement, but I can see where it ain't exactly ideal."

Beartooth tipped up his cup, draining it, then turned away from the window. "Before we get to feelin' too sorry for ourselves, I reckon we ought to go out and check on those fellas who stood their post through the storm."

"Their relief should be comin' on about now," Firestick said. "But you're right, it won't hurt to make sure. Then we can make a pass through the rest of town, see about that storm damage."

"You know, a certain amount wouldn't necessarily be a bad thing." Beartooth gave a fatalistic shrug. "Nothing real serious, I don't mean—just enough to keep folks busy doin' cleanup and patch-up, help occupy their minds with stuff other than the quarantine and all."

"Reckon that's one way of lookin' at it," Firestick allowed, his tone somewhat skeptical.

Beartooth spread his hands. "Just sayin'. Havin' something new to fret about sorta pushes an old fret to the back burner for a while."

Reaching for his hat, Firestick said, "Well, let's head out and see if we can't do our part to keep the fret level down on all fronts."

Chapter 45

By late morning, the rain had stopped and only a few wisps of fog still lingered. But the sky remained stubbornly overcast and not without the threat of possibly leaking a bit more before being completely drained.

Standing out back of the First Baptist Church, Dr. Nelson Greaves hung his head and announced in a low voice, "The girl from the Lone Star Palace Saloon—Holly, the dove who was with Jack Davies just before you brought him in—has now come down with a fever." His tone was flat, empty of emotion. "*A fever,* I stress," he continued, finally with some emphasis. "There are no symptoms beyond that. It could be a simple cold. It could be anything at this point. Nevertheless, I don't have to tell you that news of it is bound to be received poorly."

Standing with him were Firestick and Beartooth. Also present, leaning on the rail that ran along one side of the steps leading down from the church's rear door, was Pastor Bart. The holy man, well known for always wearing an expression of comfort and hope, was unable to hide a look of deep concern on this occasion. As for the doctor, in addition to his own display of anxiety, he looked wrung out and exhausted.

"What about the others in the church?" Firestick said. "They must already be aware of this. Right?"

Pastor Bart shook his head. "No, not yet. Unfortunately, you see . . . or perhaps fortunately, as it turns out . . . the others, the families from the houses neighboring the Harper place, have not been very charitable toward Miss Holly. It grieves me to admit it about members of my flock, but because of what she is, where she came from, they have shunned her ever since she arrived here. For that reason, she has kept to herself in a back room of the church with only the regular company of my dear wife."

"How long before you'll know if . . . well, whether or not this is the real thing, another case of actual scarlet fever?" Beartooth asked the doc.

Greaves shook his head. "I can't say. That's just another of the ways this damnable disease can toy with you. With the little Harper girl, she apparently had a bad fever for three or four days out on the trail before the other symptoms showed up. With Jack Davies it only took about a day after he showed his initial fever. So now, when it comes to this girl . . ." He let his words trail off and shook his head again.

Firestick frowned. "The fact she's stayed away from the others here at the church, and her direct contact right before that was only with Davies . . . Any reason to think that might mean, if she *does* have the disease, it could have passed between just them two?"

"Not much of one, I'm afraid," Greaves said. "Even though Holly has been somewhat isolated since she got here, both the pastor and his wife have been in regular contact with her. As have I. And then in turn we've all been in contact with the others. Exactly how much or how little contact it takes for the disease to spread . . . another of its evil mysteries."

"At least, for the time being, something we *can* contain is the news of this. Outside of us and the pastor's wife, nobody else knows. I don't see any hurry for that to change." Firestick sighed. "Like you said, Doc, once word does spread, it's bound to be taken badly."

"Too true," Greaves agreed. "Except for a new wave of fear and unrest, there's nothing to be gained by announcing this latest development at this point."

"So that leaves nothing but more waitin'," Beartooth said sourly. "Waitin' to see if and when this turns into something more, waitin' to see if any more fevers pop up, waitin' to see if that little girl ever comes out of the one she's already burnin' up with . . ."

"If you want to hold out hope for something," Greaves responded, "then there's no better place than right there. The longer Belle Harper hangs on, the better her chances for pulling through. And if one frail little girl can pull through, then by God there will be hope for anyone else who might yet be stricken!"

"Hold it right there, fellas. Sorry, but you can't come no farther."

Sam Duvall rose from the upended wooden crate he'd been sitting on and stepped over to the edge of Trail Street. His dog Shield, an ever-present companion who'd been resting beside his crate, remained in place but his head was raised, alertly watching Duvall for any sign he might be needed.

The four horsemen who'd been about to enter

town, approaching from the east, reined up at Duvall's words. The latter's training as a New York City constable had instilled in him the ability to quickly appraise a man and form an impression that was seldom too far off the mark.

In this case, the impression he arrived at was that the strangers before him weren't the types who brought much in the way of good news wherever they showed up. They weren't from around here, that was certain, and they all had quick, suspicious eyes and scraggly, unkempt looks that suggested they didn't make a habit of lighting too long in any one place.

The bedraggled appearances, Duvall was willing to allow, could be due to coming in fresh off the trail and probably getting caught in last night's storm. But he was pretty sure that wasn't all of it. Sure enough, at any rate, to be glad he had a good reason for turning them away from his town and glad he had a badge on his shirt and a Winchester in his hands to back up the refused entry.

A tall, bushy-bearded specimen—apparently the group's leader—eased up on his reins and edged his horse forward an extra step after initially bringing the animal to a halt. Then he hauled back on the reins once more and peered down at Duvall.

"What's the meanin' of this, friend? We're weary travelers who've ridden far. We have good money to spend, and after endurin' the wrath of that hellacious storm last night, we're badly wantin' the comfort of some hot grub and to top off our supplies with some warm, dry gear to replace that which got water soaked and near ruined."

"I'm sorry for your hardship, mister. I truly am," Duvall replied. "But the fact still remains that I can't

allow you to enter our town. Not you—not anybody."
He inclined his head toward the wooden board that
had been nailed to a nearby post on the edge of the
street. Thick black lettering painted on the board read:
QUARANTINE—NO ENTRY. "As you can see," Duvall
added, "we've got troubles of our own. Troubles, I'm
sure you'll agree, you want no part of, no matter how
bad your other needs."

Liam Scorp scowled fiercely at the sign but it was
quickly apparent he was unable to decipher everything about it. Shifting his scowl back to Duvall, he
growled, "My sorry upbringin' leaves me with another
hardship—I can read simple, but big, fancy words like
the one on that sign stumble me some."

"The word is 'quarantine,' Liam," spoke up Silas
Clapton from where he sat his horse a few feet
behind Liam.

"I still don't know what the hell that means!" Liam
snapped.

"It means Buffalo Creek has an outbreak of a bad
illness. Scarlet fever," Duvall explained calmly. "For
the sake of trying to keep it from spreading, we're not
allowing anyone in and not allowing anybody out."

"Scarlet fever!" snorted Liam. "That's a kid's disease, like mumps or something! It ain't nothing no
grown-ups have to worry about."

Duvall gave a slight shrug of his shoulders. "That's
not exactly true, not according to our town doctor.
Believe me, there are plenty of people here in town
who don't agree with it, either. But as long as the
town council and the marshal do . . . well, the sign's
up and me and another fella on the other end of town
are in place to turn folks away."

"He's right about that there fever, cousin Liam,"

said Jebediah, mounted next to his cousin. "Leastways that was the case for Uncle Festus, if you remember. He was growed up, right enough. Older'n dirt as a matter of fact, yet that's what they said claimed him when—"

"Shut up!" Liam cut him off. "I don't give a damn what happened to Uncle Festus! Besides, he might've been old in years but his brain never amounted to more than a child's. That's what must've made the difference."

"I don't know about all that," Duvall said, still trying to be patient. "But I can tell you for a fact that they planted a fella up on our boot hill just this morning. He was about thirty or so, in years and any other way you could measure . . . yet he had the fever." It wasn't exactly a lie, the old constable just didn't bother to mention the fact it wasn't the fever that had claimed Jack Davies.

His lips peeled back in an ugly grimace, Liam responded, "I'll tell you another fact, and that's this: It's a sorry day for this old world when a whole town refuses succor or pity on four innocent wanderers in a time of need. That kind of coldhearted wretchedness all in one place is nothing short of evil. Maybe this disease that's fallen on your town showed up for a reason, and if Buffalo Peak is wiped off the map it will only be gettin' what it deserves!"

Duvall felt the last of his patience let go. Even Shield, though still remaining over by the wooden crate, emitted a low warning rumble from deep in his chest. His grip tightening on the Winchester, Duvall said, "I think you've said enough, mister. More than enough. Like I told you at the beginning, I'm sorry for your hardship, but you'd best turn those horses and ride on now, or they're apt to get worse."

Holding very rigid in his saddle, Liam glared menacingly down at Duvall for several seconds. Then, wheeling his horse abruptly, he dug spurs hard and surged away, scattering his own men with the suddenness and recklessness of his retreat.

As he watched the four riders fade away, headed back the direction they'd come from, Duvall breathed a sigh of relief. He dropped one hand to his side and Shield was instantly there, head pressed to his master's hip, ready for the scratching behind his ears that was always so welcome.

"Four pieces of trash scattering themselves across the prairie," Duvall muttered. "Let's hope they keep on scattering themselves, well away from here."

Chapter 46

Returning to the jail office after taking lunch together at the Mallory House, Firestick and Beartooth found a surprise waiting for them . . . a pleasant surprise, for a change.

In a straight-backed wooden chair pulled over near the gun rack that hung on one wall, Moosejaw sat with a sawed-off shotgun in his lap. The piece was broken open, held in place by downward pressure from the big deputy's sling-wrapped right arm while, with his free left hand, he was studiously wiping it down and applying a light film of oil. He looked up as the door opened, smiling at the sight of his two old friends.

"Hey, fellas. Figured you ought to be showin' up to do some work around here sooner or later."

Firestick lifted his eyebrows. "Says the *hombre* who ain't been around to do anything for nearly twenty-four hours."

"That's right," chimed in Beartooth. "Reckon he's been away so long he forgot that the 'work' when it

comes to bein' a lawman is out there on the street"—
he jabbed a thumb over his shoulder—"not sittin'
indoors on your duff."

"Oh yeah. It's kinda comin' back to me now,"
said Moosejaw, playing along with the good-natured
ribbing.

Walking over and leaning back against one end of
his desk, Firestick said, "What happened? Did Daisy
run you off for bein' underfoot—or did she threaten
to start turnin' you into a blacksmith?"

"As a matter of fact, I run myself off," Moosejaw answered, his tone turning more serious. "After you
fellas stopped by earlier this mornin' and then moved
on, I got to feelin' guilty for just sittin' around bein' a
shirker. I decided that, yeah, I might be bunged up
a little, but that don't mean I'm helpless."

"But the doc told you it was important to take it
easy with that arm for a few days, especially early on,"
Beartooth reminded him. "Says your best chance for
those bones to heal tight and right is for 'em to start
knittin' proper in the beginnin' stages."

"I know, I know. I heard him, too. But it ain't abusin'
my arm to get out and walk around some, is it? I figure
I can at least make my share of the rounds, maybe man
one of the posts to enforce the quarantine. And in
case of any trouble, I may not be able to shoot accurate with my left hand, but as long as I can pull the
triggers on this street sweeper, I figure the aimin' part
will sort of take care of itself. My fingers on my bad
arm work good enough for pushin' in reloads. Plus,
looky here." Moosejaw's tone shifted again, turned
excited as he took his left hand and slipped it a
ways into the sling wrapping on the underside of his

right wrist. "I even got me a ready-made pouch for carryin' spare shells!"

"Why, hell. You're practically a custom-made shotgun man," said Firestick.

Moosejaw grinned. "Glad you agree. That settles it then. Consider me officially back on duty."

"Now wait a minute. You sure that's a good idea?" said Beartooth. "For the sake of the arm, I mean?"

"My arm can hang in this sling just as good walkin' around doin' something as it can sittin' down doin' nothing," Moosejaw argued.

Firestick said, "We'll let the doc have the final say. Just don't use that scattergun to do your persuadin', Moosejaw. That wouldn't hardly be fair."

"I promise to rely on just my charm and his common sense," Moosejaw replied. "So let's go ahead and figure it's a done deal. That bein' the case, all that's left is fillin' me in on things. Anything new I need to know about?"

Firestick and Beartooth exchanged looks. The lighthearted mood left the office. There wasn't a moment's hesitation about including Moosejaw into the circle of those to know about the most recent development with Holly. But his beloved Daisy, while as honest and trustworthy as the day was long, was so gregarious by nature that when she got to jabbering she sometimes ended up allowing too much to slip out. Therefore, after telling Moosejaw about Holly, it was necessary for Firestick to emphasize, "For right now, that needs to stay within the smallest possible group. I don't need to tell you how it could stir things up in folks who are, for right now, acceptin' things pretty good. If the gal's condition turns worse or more cases show up, we won't have no choice but to be open about it. Comes to that, we'll have our hands full soon enough."

"I understand," Moosejaw said grimly. "This damned disease . . . mighty tough tryin' to fight something you can't grab hold of or put a bullet in."

Using some distance as well as a series of low hills and shallow draws to keep themselves hidden from sight of the town, Liam Scorp and his men had worked their way in a loop around to the north of Buffalo Peak. From behind a fringe of rocks and sparse pine growth, they sat their horses now and gazed at the lumpy smudge of buildings to the south.

As Liam lowered the pair of field glasses he had been holding to his eyes for some time, Jebediah said, "Do you see anything, cousin?"

"Only what we already knew to be there," Liam growled. "Cluster of houses and buildings holdin' the biggest bunch of inhospitable bastards I ever run into in all my days! I've been throwed out of towns before. Plenty of 'em, and better ones than this. But I'm damned if I ever got throwed out before I ever got the chance to go in. It beats all I ever saw."

"The way they see it, they're doing us a favor," pointed out Clapton. "They're meaning to keep us from being exposed to the fever."

"The way I see it," said Liam, "they're keepin' all of us from bein' exposed to the money in their bank and me personally from gettin' revenge for my little brother Hank. Leastways, that's what they're *tryin'* to keep us from. But I ain't havin' any, by damn!"

"There's the talk." Jebediah grinned eagerly. "They'll

find out that us Scorps and any who ride with us don't take easy to being turned away."

"But what about the fever?" Clapton wanted to know. "Ain't you at all concerned about maybe catching something if we go on in there?"

"Way I figure," answered Liam, "robbin' a bank pretty much comes with a guarantee of risks. Maybe stoppin' a bullet while you're in the act, maybe gettin' chased down and hung afterward. So the added risk of catchin' a little kid's disease in this case . . . No, that don't rate too high on my list of worries. How about you, Clapton? You didn't ride all this way just to be turned back by that, did you?"

The muscles at the hinge of Clapton's jaw clenched and unclenched visibly. Then he said, "No, not when you put it that way. I'm all for finishin' what we came here to do."

Jebediah's head bobbed approvingly. "There's more good talk."

Speaking for the first time, in his usual low, steady voice, Mojave Grimes said, "This quarantine thing, if you think on it, could be kind of a favor to us."

Liam gave him a look. "How do you figure?"

"Like I said, just think about it. Stands to reason. With everybody there figurin' nobody's gonna be riding in or out of town, how prepared are they likely to be for a hit on their bank?" The half-breed tossed off a shrug. "More likely they're so tensed up over fear of the disease that they ain't hardly thinking of anything else."

"By God, you're right," Liam said, excitement showing in his eyes. "The disease is practically like another partner ridin' on our side, distractin' the attention of those scaredy-cat fools clean away from what we're up to!"

"It could work that way," Grimes allowed. "I got a good look down that main drag while you was jawing with the deputy who stopped us. It was damn near empty, only just a handful of people straggling about their business."

"Hell yes. Most folks are probably stickin' close to home with their doors locked, hidin' out from the fever." Liam jeered.

Grimes nodded, his dark eyes locked on the far-off town. "When the rain starts up again, there'll be even fewer of 'em wandering around. Be a mighty good time for us to move in and make our play."

Jebediah looked puzzled. "Wait a minute. Rain? That stopped a couple hours ago."

"It'll be back," Grimes told him. "It's just building up in that cloud cover again. Won't be a hard rain, just a steady drizzle that'll blur the sight of us on our approach to town. If we start out now and ride a ways, until we're some closer, then dismount and walk our horses the rest of the way in toward the back side of those houses, the rain will come to cover us while we are walking."

Liam tipped his face up and looked skyward for a long moment. The cloud cover was a flat gray, somewhat darker than before but nothing close to the previous evening. Liam tipped his head back down and looked at Grimes. "You sure about that?"

Grimes just nodded.

"Alright, then. Let's ride a ways closer. Then we'll climb down and walk the rest of the way in . . . to rob ourselves a damn bank in the rain!"

Chapter 47

When Milo Harper stepped out the back door of his house, he was surprised to see that a light rain had begun to fall. It was little more than a heavy mist, actually, but it was still enough to cause him to murmur to himself, "Good Lord, after last night you'd think the heavens would be emptied out for a while."

Luckily, the shingled overhang above the small landing and short set of steps leading down from the rear access was quite adequate to allow Harper to stand there and remain dry. He was glad for that. He held in one hand a freshly packed pipe and was looking forward to a leisurely smoke.

Technically, he supposed he was violating the strict quarantine of the house by stepping even this short distance outside its walls. But other than during last night's raging storm, he had been doing so periodically for the sake of sparing the others confined with him the output of his habit. His wife Betty never objected to his smoking, claiming in fact to enjoy the odor of his tobacco, but he didn't want to impose it unnecessarily on Kate or Frank Moorehouse—and especially not on his gravely ill daughter.

What was more, if he was completely honest with himself, Harper enjoyed these brief moments of being alone and taking in some fresh air almost as much as he did the pipe.

As he held a match to the bowl and gave several rapid puffs to get the tobacco burning, his mouth curved wryly around the stem clenched between his teeth. There was irony for you, he thought—claiming to enjoy a taste of fresh air while at the same time polluting it with intakes of smoke.

In most other aspects, however, Milo Harper was neither a very complicated nor contradictory man. His course through life up to this point had been plotted and closely adhered to from an early age. His goals were simple: He wanted to make it through law school, marry and start a family, then set up practice in a small Western town. The path hadn't always been easy, but it had progressed steadily. He passed the bar, found an understanding and supportive mate in Betty, and then precious Belle had arrived. By the time the child was old enough and strong enough to endure the trek from Louisiana, he'd chosen Buffalo Peak as their destination and had made necessary arrangements through banker Trugood to come and settle there.

But then that evil disease scarlet fever had struck!

The pull of smoke he had just drawn in suddenly turned bitter in Harper's mouth. When he exhaled, he spat it out forcefully. Like he was trying to expel and spit away this whole dreadful business.

If only it were that easy.

He closed his eyes and willed himself to try and

settle down, stay calm. He had to stay strong. For Betty. For Belle. He had to shoulder the weight of this and pull them through it . . . with God's help, of course. Although more than once in the past hours and days, he had caught himself questioning whose side God was on, why he was putting them through the test of such a terrible burden to begin with.

When Harper opened his eyes again, he saw that it was raining harder. Once again just a relatively gentle, straight-down drizzle like early this morning. The neighboring houses and yards looked slick and shiny through the blur of the falling drops.

And then, unexpectedly, Harper saw movement between some of the houses to the north. Off to his left and also off to his right. Shadowy, blurred shapes moving slowly, cautiously forward. Why now? Why out in the rain? he wondered. And who was it out there moving around? Since his house had been identified as containing the only complete cases of scarlet fever— Belle and, for a short time, Jack Davies—all the close neighbors had either been relocated to the church or had elected to pull away on their own. Other than the mob scene the day before, this was the first movement he had seen in or around any of the nearby houses since they'd moved in.

The shapes continued to advance through the rain. Now Harper could make out that they were men cloaked in long, dark rain slickers. Leading horses.

A sudden sense of alarm passed through him. The lawyer ducked quickly back into the house and pressed the door closed except for about a four-inch crack. Trouble was, this made his field of vision too narrow. With the men scattered off to either side, he could no longer see them. But he could still *feel* them out there.

The two he'd been able to make out, and maybe more. And he could feel something else. His sense of alarm was growing stronger.

Whoever those men were, they didn't belong here. Not at all. And certainly not now, not slipping covertly through the murky rain.

Whoever they were, whatever their exact intent . . . Harper was convinced they were up to no good.

"I can't believe the doggone rain has started up again," lamented Beartooth, gazing out the jail office window. "I could've swore we were gonna see sunshine breakin' through before the day was done."

"Maybe we still will," replied Firestick from where he sat behind his desk. "Day ain't over yet, and the sky's bound to run out of water sooner or later."

"Not soon enough to suit me," said Moosejaw. "Talk about a body havin' lousy timin' and stickin' his foot in his mouth as a result. When I offered to go out and relieve Sam Duvall on his post for a while, I wasn't figurin' on doin' it in the rain."

"That's what you get for pesterin' Doc Greaves to allow you to help out," Firestick told him. "He said it'd be okay as long as you took it easy on the arm. And I don't see how you can claim gettin' wet as abusin' your wing."

"Yeah, yeah. I know I can't," grumbled Moosejaw. "But that don't mean gettin' the rest of me soaked, too, is a good idea. What if I catch pneumonia or something?"

"Then it'll take your mind off the arm," said Beartooth, turning around and walking over to where the big deputy was struggling, due to his arm being in a sling, with trying to shrug into a rain slicker. "Here, let me help you with that. The way you're pokin' and floppin' around, it's gonna take you so long you'll have to worry about snow fallin' by the time you make it out there."

"Quarantine be damned!" Kate Mallory declared. "If there are men and horses sneaking around out there in the rain, you're absolutely right they're up to no good. You heard Dr. Greaves tell us about all the horses in town being gathered and secured at Roeback's livery. That means these are obviously men coming in from outside of town and passing through this residential area to avoid the roadblocks at the ends of Trail Street. The marshal needs to be warned!"

"But you know none of us are supposed to leave here," Milo Harper protested. "Dr. Greaves will be coming by again soon. Wouldn't it be better to wait for that? We'll tell him as soon as he gets here and then let him—"

"No. I won't risk waiting." Kate marched to the coat rack that stood near the front door. Without hesitation, she seized a shawl from one of its hooks and swung the garment over her shoulders. She took a step toward the door but then paused to look back at Betty. "I don't mean to be unkind, but you held off telling anyone what you knew about Jack Davies and saw how it turned out. I'm not willing to make that same mistake."

Betty didn't flinch. "I understand. Completely. But what of your own safety? What if those men are still out there, moving about close by . . ."

Kate's pretty mouth pulled into a tight, grim line.

"This is my town. They won't see me if I don't want them to."

And then she was out the door.

After passing undetected, as far as they knew, in a scattered pattern through the residential district on the north side of town, Liam, Jebediah, Grimes, and Clapton were crowded back together in the mouth of an alley diagonally across the street from the West Texas Cattlemen's Association Bank of Buffalo Peak. They were still on foot, their horses tied at the back end of the alley.

Peering through a couple long strings of rainwater running off the brim of his hat, Liam said around a wide, greedy grin, "There she is, boys. Fat and shiny and sittin' there with her thighs open wide like a honeymoon bride. Just a-waitin' to be took by somebody who knows what they're doin'."

Beside him, Jebediah leered above the bottomless black bores of his shotgun. "And that dang sure is us. Ain't it, cousin Liam?"

"I reckon we're about to find out. And I further reckon that's gonna be exactly the case," Liam replied.

"The street's empty, and from what I can see through that big front window, there don't look to be a single customer inside the bank," said Grimes. "I don't see where there's gonna be a better time. What are we waiting for?"

"I'm for that," agreed Clapton. "I'm willing to take my risks in this disease-ridden town, but that don't mean I want to stick around any longer than necessary. Just a straight gun and grab, that's the plan, right, Liam? Plain and simple, meaning there's no fancy last-minute instructions to go over—so let's get to it."

Liam's eyes narrowed. "Gun and grab is right. That's always the best way, and this time even more so. I want plenty of blastin', remember, on account of I want to be sure we bring the law dogs a-runnin'. That's what's gonna give me my crack at gettin' revenge on the stinkin' Texas badge-toter who gunned down my little brother Hank."

"What if there's more than one? How you gonna know which one did your brother?" Clapton wanted to know.

"We mow 'em all down, that'll make sure," Liam grated. "But the one I want personal-like, accordin' to the newspapers, is supposed to be a real big bastard. Save him for me if you can."

"Do my best," Grimes responded. "But anybody with a badge, big or small, starts wavin' a gun in my direction I ain't gonna wait very long to feed him some lead."

"Understood. I got my 'druthers, but as long as I see Hank's killer take his last bite of dust, that's the main thing." Liam glanced over his shoulder. "Clapton, you hang back while us three get across the street. Once we're inside, bring the horses forward. When you hear the shootin' start, haul ass on over."

Liam turned back to face the bank. Pausing only to reach inside his slicker and slip the keeper thong off his Colt, he said, "This is it, boys. Time to go make some money and kill us some law dogs!"

Chapter 48

When Moosejaw pulled open the office's front door, starting out to go relieve Sam Duvall at his post, a sopping-wet Kate Mallory came rushing through the opening and fell against his broad chest.

"Whoa!" exclaimed Moosejaw. Even though she was only about a third his size, the woman's momentum staggered him half a step backward. She also bumped hard against his injured arm, nearly bringing forth an added expletive he barely managed to bite off before it escaped his lips.

Immediately recognizing the intruder, Firestick shot to his feet behind the desk and said, "Kate! What are you doin' here? What's wrong?"

Kate stepped around Moosejaw, pushing back wet tendrils of dark hair that had spilled down over her anxiety-ridden face. "There are men in town, strangers who slipped in through the houses on the north side to avoid the lookouts you have posted. Milo Harper spotted them first, and just now as I was coming over here, I caught sight of them, too. I could see that one of them is carrying a long gun—a rifle or shotgun. I don't know what they're up to, but I'm certain their intentions are bad!"

Moosejaw was quick to say, "When I spoke to Duvall a little while ago and offered to go back and relieve him after a little bit, he mentioned that he'd turned away four men earlier. He said they were strangers, hardcases. Said they gave him some lip but then went ahead and rode off. Could be them comin' back."

"It could be," agreed Kate as she fell into the embrace of Firestick, who had by now hurried around his desk to reach her. "Mr. Harper saw only two, but I could make out at least one more—the one with the long gun."

"And now *I* can see the varmints," Beartooth said from where he'd moved to once again peer out the window. "They're crossin' the street up a ways right now. One of 'em's sure enough shovin' a shotgun out ahead of hisself. Looks like they're headed for the bank."

"Bank robbers!" snarled Firestick, his thick fingers involuntarily digging hard into Kate's upper arms as he pulled her tighter to him. "Makes perfect sense in a dirty, lowdown way—find a town quarantined and crippled by disease, figure that makes enough of a distraction for a robbery to be pulled with hardly any trouble."

Brandishing his sawed-off, Moosejaw said, "I think we can throw a real big kink into that way of figurin'."

Having wheeled around and raced to the gun rack, Beartooth pulled down two Winchesters. Turning back, he kept one in his own grip and tossed the other into the marshal's waiting hands. "I second that notion—how do you want to play it, Firestick?"

Taking time only to tell Kate, "You stay here!"

Firestick broke for the front door with his two pals and deputies close on his heels. There was no time to try and round up anybody else, so once out in the street, he quickly barked his orders for how the three of them should "play it."

"If there's a fourth man," he said, "he's got to be on the side of the street opposite the bank—where the others started across from. Probably holdin' their horses and ready to provide cover for his pals when they come back out of the bank."

"Sounds right to me," Beartooth agreed.

"Then you take him," Firestick replied. "Work your way up behind the buildings on that side and find the alley he's squatted in. You know what to do from there."

Beartooth peeled off and departed in long, smooth strides toward the row of buildings on the left side of the street.

"And me?" said Moosejaw.

"You do the same thing on the right side," Firestick told him. "Come up through that near alley runnin' alongside the bank. Wait there for the robbers to show themselves . . . that'll put you nice and close if you have to go to work with that sawed-off."

"Got it. But what about you?" Moosejaw wanted to know.

"I'm goin' straight up the street," Firestick answered. "I'll stick to the bank side, keep to the shadows along the boardwalk as tight as I can. When those jaspers pop their heads back out, I'll be there to greet 'em, too."

Inside the bank, chief teller Oscar Holman felt like he was reliving a nightmare. Only this time it was even worse than before. Once again he was under the guns of ruthless robbers, but where last time he had merely been pushed around and suffered the indignity of being forced to lie facedown on the floor, now he was on the floor because he had been struck viciously by the butt of a shotgun and knocked there. His head throbbed with agonizing pain and he could feel hot blood running down the side of his face. Through the haze of being knocked nearly unconscious, he was vaguely aware of the rest of the nightmare playing out around him.

The only other teller on duty this afternoon had also been clubbed for no reason and lay sprawled motionless on the floor behind the service counter, just a few feet from Holman. The front lobby was empty. Following the injury to Hefty Shallihan during the last robbery attempt and the subsequent minimal business the bank was doing these days due to the quarantine, bank president Trugood had elected not to hire a new guard until things returned to normal. A decision he was no doubt deeply regretting now because he was currently undergoing his own share of being pushed and slapped around by the three villains who had come barging in with their money demands.

While one of the three held his shotgun—which he had also wielded freely as a club—on Holman and the other teller, his two companions were frantically rifling cash drawers and badgering Trugood to guide them to the largest stashes of money to be found in the safe. The apparent leader of the trio—a tall, wild-eyed specimen with a thick, unruly beard—seemed to be taking particular glee in the task at hand, making curse-laden references such as "this Texas shithole of a town" and "payback for all the blood my family has spilled on this good-for-nothing soil!" The one with the shotgun giggled with delight at his outbursts while the remaining robber, a dark-skinned half-breed, went silently, grimly about his business.

If they meant to kill me, they would have gone ahead and done so right off, wouldn't they? That was what Holman kept telling himself as he squeezed his eyes shut tight and tried to blot out the sounds of the bearded man slapping and cursing Trugood some more. *What sense would it make to club me down only to kill me later? Oh God, I hope they see it that way . . . and please don't let them beat me any more, either . . .*

"You stupid hayburners! Behave there, dammit. Come on, get in line!"

Silas Clapton was having trouble getting the horses to move forward through the narrow, rain-drenched alley with its muddy, sucking bottom and the clutter strewn down its length, recently added to by debris blown in from last night's storm. The building walls too close on either side made the animals nervous, and grinding and bumping against one another only added to their irritability.

And Clapton's growing frustration wasn't helping any. As he tugged frantically on the four sets of reins, he kept glancing over his shoulder at the bank building across the street. Liam and the others had gone in there quite a few minutes ago. Through the wide front window, Clapton caught glimpses of them moving around inside. It looked like everything was going smoothly and at a pretty good clip. Jesus, if they came boiling out and he didn't have these damn horses out on the street and ready, Liam would have a conniption!

"Come on, you hammerheads! A little bit of mud ain't gonna hurt you—get out here!" Digging in his heels and giving a hard yank on the reins, Clapton lost his own purchase in the alley mud. His feet slipped and he nearly landed on his rump. Cursing all the more, he wallowed frantically to pull himself upright again.

It was this scene that Beartooth slipped up on as he reached the back end of the alley. He pressed close to the corner of a building and peeked cautiously around. It was quickly evident what was going on—what the man farther into the alley was trying to do and that the horses were balking at it. But the main part, as far as Beartooth was concerned, was that this provided him one of the robbers not only isolated from the others but distracted enough so that he was practically serving himself up for elimination before the others ever came back into the picture.

The only question was, how best to go about it? With the varmint silhouetted clearly against the mouth of the alley, it would have been easy enough to pick him off right where he stood. Trouble was, shooting a man in cold blood—even a varmint—without giving him any warning or chance didn't set right with Beartooth. The circumstances weren't desperate enough for that. Plus, a shot was bound to be heard by the rest of the bunch across the way, inside the bank, and would give them warning before they came out.

No, this skunk had to be dealt with, but it had to be done quietly. And Beartooth had an idea how.

Leaning his Winchester against the side of the building, he drew his Colt from the holster on his right hip and border-shifted it to his left hand. Then he reached again under his slicker and from the sheath at the small of his back, he pulled the bone-handled Bowie knife that had served him for so many years and had earned him the very name he went by.

Crouching, with the Colt in his left hand and the Bowie in his right, he edged out to the middle of the alley, where he stayed low enough to be hidden behind the shifting, stubbornly stamping horses. When the man holding the reins got squared away again and started pulling once more to try and get the critters to cooperate, Beartooth straightened to his full height and extended his left arm, aiming the Colt.

"Freeze right there, buster!" he commanded sharply. "Drop those reins and raise your hands empty. Then turn and place 'em against the wall. One wrong twitch and—"

He never got any more out. Stupidly, desperately, the man in the alley dropped the reins and made a grab for his gun. He also tried ducking into a crouch, aiming to get out of sight behind the horses. He succeeded at nothing—not pulling his gun free, not dropping out of sight—before Beartooth's right arm snapped forward and the Bowie flashed from his fingers with practiced, lethal accuracy. It *thunked!* hard to the base of the man's throat, just below his Adam's apple, three-quarters of its ten-inch blade sinking out of sight. The man was knocked off his feet as if punched. He landed on his shoulders and skidded a full yard across the sloppy ground before coming to a stop in a motionless heap.

Chapter 49

Inside the bank, Liam was ready to move on. With two bulging canvas bags crammed full of large bills and everything going smoothly, he saw no need to press their luck. His intent to still fit in some personal revenge would take things far enough toward that limit as it was.

"I say we got us a fine haul here, boys, and it's time to go with what we got," he declared as he swung one of the bags up over a shoulder.

"We've cleaned out all but the crumbs anyway," Grimes said agreeably, hoisting the second bag.

Jerking his shotgun toward Holman and the other still-unconscious teller, Jebediah asked, "What about these nancies—do we blast 'em now?"

Liam snorted. "They ain't no more of a threat than a couple mosquitoes. Save your lead for something more important." He started for the lobby but then, as if having second thoughts about it, stopped abruptly and turned back to swing his pistol in a chopping backhand, cracking the barrel one more time across the side of Trugood's head. The bank president, already slumped and battered in a desk chair, pitched the rest of the way off the seat and toppled to the floor.

Returning his attention to Jebediah, Liam next used the pistol to make a jabbing motion toward the wide lobby windows. "You want to use that blaster so bad? Use it on those windows! Time to start makin' some noise so the scum-suckin' law dogs of this town get rousted off their lazy asses and come to see what's goin' on!"

"Yeeehaw!" bellowed Jebediah with obliging delight. A moment later he triggered first one barrel of the gut shredder and then the next, the ten-gauge loads spewing forth and disintegrating the windows, turning them into a thousand tiny shards that flew out and went slicing through the rain.

"Come on out, you gutless sonsabitches," hollered Liam as he rushed around the end of the service counter and headed for the front door. "The Scorp boys are in town and we mean to have your gizzards!"

The bank windows suddenly bursting outward caught Firestick off guard. For a moment he thought it was the result of an explosion. Realizing the truth, his lips peeled back and he bared his teeth in a silent snarl. No matter, explosion or shotgun blast or anything else the robbers had in their bag of tricks, he and his deputies were positioned and ready.

Moosejaw was at the mouth of the alley directly beside the bank, crouched down behind a fat, over-flowing rain barrel. On the opposite side of the street, in the mouth of an alley over there, Beartooth had signaled his success in eliminating the robber who'd been stationed to cover the others when they emerged from the bank. For his own cover, the knife-wielding deputy was clutching the bridle of a tall steel-dust and keeping himself back behind the animal's meaty chest and shoulder. Forming the third point of a shooting triangle set to pour a hell-storm of lead all across the front of the bank, Firestick knelt on one knee in back of a watering trough on the edge of the street just short of Moosejaw's alley.

Three men came barreling out of the bank. Two of them were gripping large canvas money bags in one hand and flashing pistols in the other. A third man had both hands full of a long-barreled ten-gauge shotgun.

"Give 'em another blast, cousin Jeb! Make some noise; let 'em know we're here!" hollered one of the bag holders, a heavily bearded individual who followed his own command by aiming his pistol skyward and contributing to the shotgunner's obedient roar by aimlessly triggering a pair of rounds himself.

While this was going on, the third man was looking wildly about, his dark face bunched with growing concern and his longish black hair whipping back and forth as his head turned this way and that. He made his own kind of noise, saying, "Hey! Where are the damn horses? Where's Clapton?"

The loud merriment of the other two ceased and suddenly their heads were swiveling and they, too, were looking around frantically. Until the fierce glare of the bearded one landed on the steel-dust in the alley across the way. "Clapton, what the hell are you doin'?" he demanded. "Get over here with those horses!"

That's when Firestick took aim with his Winchester and sent a slug tearing through the money bag the bearded man was holding. The bag jerked from the impact, though the robber never lost his grip. The bullet exited in a spurt of shredded currency.

Rising up partway behind the water trough, Firestick instantly jacked home another round and gave the Winchester a menacing thrust as he said, "Freeze right there, you skunks, or the next slug goes into one of you! Your pal Clapton ain't comin' out of that alley across the way—not ever—and you can all meet the same fate as him if you try anything foolish. And anything short of droppin' the money bags and your iron will count as foolish."

The three robbers froze, but only partly as ordered. Their lack of compliance included not releasing anything they'd been told to drop.

"Who the hell do you think you are?" the bearded one wanted to know.

"Far as you're concerned, you can call me End of the Line," the marshal answered. "That can mean right now, permanent-like, or it can mean some time later after you've stood before a judge. Make up your mind quick, or I make it for you."

"Next," sneered the bearded one, "I suppose you're gonna try to tell me you got us surrounded by a whole passel of deputies?"

Firestick gave a slow wag of his head. "Nope. Not a whole passel . . . but plenty to get the job done."

At which point Beartooth and Moosejaw each revealed himself.

If there had ever been a chance for the confrontation to end without gunfire and death, it ceased right at that instant. When Liam's gaze fell on Moosejaw, his maniacal, revenge-crazed mind tore free of what few thin strings of restraint remained. The size and features of the man suddenly looming before him matched so closely to the newspaper accounts he'd pored over that he felt not a heartbeat of doubt as to who he was looking at.

"You!" The words seemed to come out as if rumbled from a deep cave. "Now you pay for my brother, damn you to hell!"

Suddenly the money bag was dropped, forgotten, and Liam's entire focus was on swinging around his Colt and thrusting it toward Moosejaw. But before his arm extended even halfway forward, two Winchesters—in the steady grips of Firestick and Beartooth—simultaneously spat flame and lead and Liam was slammed off his feet by the double impact, never managing to fire a single shot.

Somebody who did get off a shot, though, was Jebediah. Unfortunately for him, and as much so for Mojave Grimes, it came only after Moosejaw beat him to it by stroking both triggers of his sawed-off. The twin twelve-gauge release nearly tore Jebediah in half, and it was as his ripped-apart remains were driven back and sent spinning that his already-dead fingers touched off the remaining load in his own gut shredder. Roaring blindly, the merciless weapon lived up to its nickname—inadvertently cutting down Grimes, Jebediah's own partner, and indeed leaving his middle messily and fatally shredded.

All of this happened within a mere eye-blink of time. The shots came so close together it was like a single crash of thunder that rolled down the street and was swallowed by the steady, ongoing hiss of the rain . . .

Chapter 50

Like blood-drenched bookends, the two attempted bank robberies stood at the beginning and close of one of Buffalo Peak's most violent and troubled chapters.

Within an hour of Liam Scorp and his men meeting their demise in front of the bank, the rain stopped and the cloud cover began breaking apart to allow slices of blue sky and slanting rays of late afternoon sun to appear. Looking back, many would proclaim that an omen. An even greater one, for those who believed in such, came barely an hour later when Dr. Greaves—upon completing his treatment of the bank personnel who had been so seriously battered by the would-be robbers—went to make his regular checkup on Belle Harper only to emerge with the greatly anticipated news that the girl's fever had broken and she appeared to be on the road to recovery!

From there, the momentum and mood of the town only grew brighter. True, the quarantine remained in place and the waiting and watching for any further signs of the dreaded fever continued. But the outlook of most citizens stood firm in new resolve. They believed what Dr. Greaves had been stating all along—that if frail little Belle could pull through, then that had to be seen as strong hope for all.

The only discordant note was struck that first evening, after the bodies of the would-be robbers were hauled away and the bloody street was washed clean by the last of the rain, and most of the town was embracing the news and renewed hope that maybe they'd been through the worst of it.

But a shunned, despondent Holly—the dove from the Lone Star Palace, alone in the back room of the church, fighting her fever and having not been told of Belle's breakthrough—saw fit to end her misery by hanging herself from a high ceiling beam. Pastor Bart and his wife were devastated, and perhaps a twinge of guilt was felt by a few members of the families who'd been part of the quarantined group that so coldly turned their backs on the girl, but otherwise her passing went little noticed.

Five days went by.

The sky remained clear, the days hot and dry.

Identification found on Liam Scorp's body along with newspapers stuffed in his saddlebags—papers folded open to accounts of the earlier bank robbery attempt involving his brother Hank—explained Liam's vengeance-crazed reaction at the sight of Moosejaw. The others, not even Jebediah, were not identifiable other than as men who'd apparently been recruited by Liam to aid him in his quest for revenge and to benefit by way of sharing in the bank loot.

On the sixth day, with Belle Harper continuing

to respond nicely and no additional signs of fever anywhere in evidence, Dr. Greaves and the town council announced a complete lifting of the quarantine. Wires were sent to surrounding towns, notification went out to area ranches, and a celebratory atmosphere swept the settlement.

Beartooth immediately mounted a horse and spurred off to the Double M to be with his Victoria. Firestick and Kate finally got to spend some very private moments without a pane of window glass between them. And Moosejaw and Daisy rode together out to their cabin to, among other things, survey it for any storm damage.

After long anticipating the announcement, Milt Kruger and his crew were fully prepared to hitch up and head out as soon as it was official. Out of gratitude for the assistance Kruger, Lauson, and some of the others had been to him, Firestick made sure he was there to see them off and once again express his appreciation. But when he got there, he was somewhat surprised to find an additional person ready to depart with them.

"Since it will be a while before the stagecoach resumes its run through here, and I am hardly suited to a long trip on horseback," explained Howard Blessingame from where he was perched on one of the wagon seats, "Mr. Kruger's wagon train presented the quickest means for me to return to Presidio. He was kind enough to agree to 'haul' me back."

"For a fee, don't forget," Kruger reminded him. Then, cutting a dubious glance toward Firestick, he added, "After all, the way my freight business is probably wrecked by missing all those contracts I couldn't get back to, I've got to take the opportunity to make a dollar however I can."

"I got a hunch you'll get your business back soon enough," Firestick told him earnestly. "You're too good a freight man for folks to abandon you over a spot of trouble you couldn't avoid."

Kruger sighed. "I hope you're right."

"One thing for sure is that you'll be returnin' here before long. We can count on that, can't we? And no matter what else, something *you* had better count on is makin' it back here in the spring—for Moosejaw's wedding!"

"Yeah, I don't want to miss that," Kruger agreed. Then, a shrewd expression coming over his face, he said, "You really think Daisy is gonna let him wait that long?"

Firestick laughed. "You never know. But I'll be sure to notify you if it gets moved up."

The marshal lifted his eyes to Blessingame. "How about you, writer man? You reckon you'll be comin' back for that shindig? If you want a rootin'-tootin' time to write about, I can pretty much guarantee that's gonna be one."

"I'm supposed to be done with rootin'-tootin' writing, remember?" replied the author. "Besides, I'm surprised you would want me back in your town. For much of my time here, I'm afraid I didn't conduct myself very admirably."

"Mister," Firestick said, continuing to peer up at him, "durin' the stretch of time just past around here, there was lots of us who didn't conduct ourselves in ways we wish we would have or sometimes could have. The thing is, you learn and move on and try to do better goin' forward. The things you told me in your hotel room that time, how you want to change your writin', the things you want to do with it goin' forward . . . That's somebody I'd welcome in my town anytime. That's somebody I'm hopin' is gonna tell the story of my town, and tell it straight."

"Can I quote you on that?" Blessingame said, a corner of his mouth pulling back in an uncertain half smile.

Firestick grinned broadly and said, "You're damn right you can."

Keep reading for an excerpt of the next Johnstone epic!

DIG YOUR OWN GRAVE
A WILL TANNER, U.S. DEPUTY MARSHAL WESTERN
by William W. and J. A. Johnstone

Johnstone Country. Keeping the West Wild.

*U.S. Deputy Marshal Will Tanner is one hell of a
manhunter. But this time, he's chasing six men
across three states with one gun and no backup.
This isn't justice. This is a suicide mission . . .*

DIG YOUR OWN GRAVE
It starts with a prison break in Missouri.
When notorious bank robber Ansel McCoy busts
out, he teams up with five other outlaws. Then he
and his gang rob a bank in Kansas. Now they're
crossing state lines into Oklahoma Indian Territory.
And that's where U.S. Deputy Marshal Will Tanner
steps in. Other marshals from Kansas and Missouri
have already lost the trail. Which means Tanner
has to go it alone. Deep in the wilderness.
Outnumbered and outgunned. One good man
against six blood-crazed killers. Even if he manages
to survive the elements and find McCoy's hideout,
it's not just the end of his search. It's his funeral . . .

*Look for DIG YOUR OWN GRAVE,
on sale now wherever Johnstone's books are sold.*

Chapter 1

Looks like Tom Spotted Horse was right, he thought. He dismounted and dropped Buster's reins to the ground, then preceded on foot to get a better look at the camp by the water's edge. The Chickasaw policeman had told him Ike Skinner had passed through Tishomingo, headed toward Blue River. Will wasn't surprised. He figured Ike was on his way to Texas after a series of train station robberies south along the MKT. So when Dan Stone had sent him to arrest Ike, he had headed down the line to Atoka in hopes of cutting him off before he reached that town. Unfortunately, he was too late by half a day to intercept him in Atoka, but he had an idea that Ike might cut over to Tishomingo. He was sweet on a Chickasaw woman named Lyla Birdsong, who lived there, and that was where Will had arrested him before. Ike was never a man to use good judgment, and it looked like the two years he had spent in prison had done little to teach him any common sense.

Will had also been too late to catch him at Lyla Birdsong's father's cabin in Tishomingo, but he hadn't been hard to track from there. Ike had not waited long to camp for the night, which didn't surprise Will, since he hadn't seen Lyla in two years. *He should have waited at least until he crossed the Red and celebrated their reunion in Texas*, Will thought. He almost felt sorry for him. Ike was not a cruel criminal by any standard. He just wasn't smart enough to make a living from anything but stealing. *Better get my mind back on business*, Will reminded himself, and made his way carefully through the stand of oaks on the banks of the river. Close enough to see the two people seated by the fire clearly now, he took a moment to verify what he had suspected. The other person with Ike was, indeed, Lyla Birdsong. He had hesitated because Lyla had apparently grown some in the two years since Ike was away, not so much up, but out. Will had seen her before on only one brief occasion, and she was a husky woman then. Looking at her now, she looked to be more woman than Ike could handle. He could only assume that she had come with Ike willingly, so he wouldn't have to be charged with abduction on top of the armed robbery charges.

Will moved a few yards closer before suddenly stepping out from behind a tree and calling out a warning. "Don't make a move, Ike, and we'll make this as easy as possible!" As he expected, the warning was wasted as Ike, startled, tried to scramble to his feet. Ready for just such a possibility, Will had his Winchester in position to fire. He placed a shot that kicked up dirt at Ike's feet and stopped him from running. Then he quickly cranked another round into the chamber and placed a second shot in the dirt on the other side of Ike when he started to run in the opposite direction. "I ain't gonna waste any more ammunition in the dirt," Will threatened. "The next one's gonna stop you for good." The warning served its purpose. Ike hesitated a moment, but gave up on the idea of running for cover.

"Will Tanner," Ike moaned plaintively, "I shoulda known it would be you." He stood by the fire, feeling helpless as Will approached, his rifle cocked and still trained on him. "Dadgum it, how'd you find me so quick?"

"You're a creature of habit, Ike," Will replied. "You need to change your old ways, if you're plannin' to be an armed robber the rest of your life. Now, with your left hand, unbuckle that gunbelt and let it drop." While Ike dutifully complied, Will kept an eye on the Chickasaw woman, who had so far shown no reaction to his intrusion. Sitting calmly, her stoic expression registering no sign of alarm, she prompted Will to be extra cautious, lest she might suddenly explode.

"Whaddaya botherin' me for, Tanner?" Ike implored. "I ain't done nothin' to get the law on my tail."

"You held up the train depot in McAlester and again in Atoka," Will answered. "Both stationmasters identified you as the bandit."

"How can they be sure it was me?" Ike blurted. "I was wearin' a bandanna on my face." A pregnant moment of silence followed immediately after he said it. "Uh . . ." he stumbled, an expression of utter frustration cramping his whiskered face. "I mean, he was most likely wearin' a mask, weren't he?"

"Yeah, he was wearin' a red bandanna, like the one you're wearin' around your neck," Will said. "Now, you've rode with me before, so you know I don't give you any trouble as long as you don't cause me any." He turned to the somber woman still sitting there, watching impassively. "How 'bout you, Miss Birdsong? There weren't any reports that Ike had anybody with him when he held up the railroad offices. I'm guessin' Ike just picked you up last night. Is that right?" She looked up to meet his gaze, but did not answer his question. "I'm gonna take that as a *yes*," Will said, "so you're free to go on back home." He watched her carefully while she considered what he had just said. "Ike's gonna be gone for a long spell," he added.

"I go," she spoke finally, and got to her feet. It would have been hard to miss the reluctance in her tone. Will could easily understand why. Lyla had an ugly scar on her nose that testified to her having been marked with a knife for entertaining too many men. Almost certainly, she saw Ike Skinner as her only chance to escape her father's cabin, for no men of her tribe would have anything to do with her. No doubt her father would be disappointed to see her return home just as much as she would be.

When she started toward her horse, Ike pleaded, "Lyla, honey, don't leave me. I came to get you as soon as I got outta prison. We was gonna make it down in Texas."

"You not go to Texas," Lyla said. "You go to jail. I not go to jail with you. I go home."

"I reckon this just ain't your day, Ike," Will said. "She wouldn't have stayed with you for very long, anyway." He pointed to a small tree close by. "You know how this works." Ike knew it was useless to balk, so he walked over and put his arms around the tree. Will clamped his wrists together with his handcuffs, then went to help Lyla saddle her horse and get her things together. When she had packed up her few belongings and ridden away, he saddled Ike's horse, then went to retrieve Buster. In a short time, he rode up from the river, leading Ike and his packhorse behind him. Ike didn't have a packhorse. Will suspected that was Ike's packhorse that Lyla was now riding. The makeshift Indian saddle had led him to believe that to be the case. Her father might not have gotten rid of her, but at least he gained a horse.

Will figured three and a half to four days to make the trip to Fort Smith, barring any interruptions along the way, and he didn't expect much trouble from Ike. When he was working in this part of the Nations, and headed home, he usually camped overnight at Jim Little Eagle's cabin on Muddy Boggy Creek near Atoka. He decided there was enough daylight left to make it to Jim's before dark, and the horses were already rested. Jim, the Choctaw policeman, was a good friend of Will's, and his wife, Mary Light Walker, was always a gracious hostess. With that in mind, he started out with thoughts of maybe a couple of biscuits from Mary's oven for him and his prisoner.

They rode for only about thirty minutes before striking a trail that ran between Atoka and the Arbuckle Mountains, a trail that Will had ridden many times before. Following the familiar trail, they approached a low line of hills and a stream that ran through a shallow pass between them. Will usually paused there to let the horses drink and that was his intention on this day. Sensing the water ahead, Buster quickened his pace in anticipation of a drink. Will leaned forward on the big buckskin's neck to give him a playful pat, instantly hearing the snap of a rifle slug passing directly over his back. It was followed almost at the same time by the report of the rifle that fired it. Acting on instinct, he didn't wait to hear the next shot. Hugging Buster's neck, he shifted to the side as much as possible while giving the buckskin his heels. There was no time to worry about Ike following behind him. His reins were tied to a lead rope behind Will's saddle. His first thought was to find cover, so he drove Buster into the trees beside the stream as a second shot whined through the leaves of the trees. He pulled up only when he felt he had put enough trees between himself and the shooter, who he figured was on the other side of the stream.

That was mighty damn careless of me, he thought as he told Ike to dismount. He had a pretty good idea who the shooter was. "Hug that tree!" he ordered.

"You tryin' to get us both kilt?" Ike complained. "You can't leave me locked to a damn tree with somebody tryin' to shoot us!"

"Hurry up and get down off that horse," Will demanded. "I don't wanna have to shoot you outta that saddle." He waited just a moment to make sure Ike did as he ordered. "I don't think you've got much to worry about. I'm pretty sure I'm the target." Once he was satisfied that Ike was secured to a tall pine tree, he made his way back toward the bank of the stream, where he could scan the other side. There had been no more shots fired after the first two, so all he could do was try to guess where the sniper was hiding. As he shifted his eyes back and forth along the stream, he decided that the best place for the shooter to hide was a narrow ravine that led up the slope. He figured the sniper, having missed the kill shot, might be inclined to depart, so he decided to try to keep that from happening. "You just sit tight," he said to Ike when he came back into the trees and started trotting downstream.

"Where the hell are you goin'?" Ike blurted.

"Just sit tight," Will repeated without turning his head. "I'll be back to get you."

In a matter of seconds, he was lost from Ike's sight, and when he decided he was far enough downstream not to be seen, he crossed over the stream and climbed up the hill on the other side. With his Winchester in hand, he hurried along the top of the hill, back toward the ravine he had spotted. He paused briefly when he suddenly heard a wailing from the trees he had just left across the stream. "Lyla, honey!" Ike's mournful voice called out. "Is that you? Be careful, he's comin' to get you!"

"I shoulda stuffed a rag in his mouth," Will mumbled, and started running along the crest of the hill, thinking he'd have to hurry to catch her before she ran. Then he spotted Lyla's horse still tied behind the hill. More careful now, he slowed down as he approached the top of the ravine, expecting to meet her climbing up out of it. There was no sign of her, however, so with his rifle at the ready, he started making his way down the narrow ravine. He had not gone halfway down when he saw her. She had not run at all, but had remained sitting behind a low shoulder of the ravine, her old Spencer carbine still aimed at the trees across from her.

Taking pains to be as quiet as possible, he inched down the ravine until he was no more than thirty feet from the unsuspecting woman. "Make a move and you're dead," he suddenly announced, causing her to freeze for a few moments, afraid to turn around. "Lyla, forget about it," Will warned when she hesitated, as if trying to decide to act or not. "I'll cut you down before you have a chance to turn around. Now, drop that rifle and raise your hands in the air." She hesitated a few moments more, painfully reluctant to admit defeat, then she finally realized she had no chance and did as he instructed. "Doggone it, Lyla, I let you go before, because you hadn't committed any crime. Now you've gone and tried to shoot me, and all to free that worthless saddle tramp, Ike Skinner. So I'm gonna have to arrest you, and I reckon I oughta warn you, white, Indian, man, or woman, it doesn't matter to me. If you don't do like I tell you, or try to run away, I won't hesitate to shoot you. You understand?" She did not reply, as was her custom, so he asked her again, this time a little more forcefully.

"I understand," she said. "I no run."

"Good," he said. "Now we'll go get your horse. Start climbin' up outta this ravine." He followed her up, carrying her old Spencer as well as his Winchester. Once out of the ravine, they went down the backside of the hill and got her horse. She went along without protest, knowing she had been arrested for trying to kill a U.S. Deputy Marshal and would most likely go to jail for it. She had failed in her attempt to free Ike Skinner, but she had managed to complicate the deputy's job of transporting his prisoner. He didn't want to bother with Lyla, even if she did take a shot at him. *I'll decide what to do with her after I get to Atoka*, he told himself.

Upon approaching the spot where he had left Ike and the horses, Will stopped short and dropped the carbine to free both hands to fire his rifle. He was looking at the tree where he had handcuffed Ike, but Ike was gone. Then he noticed a few broken limbs and branches at the base of the tree. They prompted him to look up to discover Ike about fifteen feet up the trunk, clinging to a limb that was obviously too big to break off. Will was frankly amazed. Ike had climbed up the trunk like a telegraph lineman until reaching the limb that stopped him. As insane as it was, Will had to ask, "What the hell were you tryin' to do? Did you think you could climb right up over the top of the tree?"

Ike didn't answer at once. He had to rethink his failed attempt to escape. Still clinging to the limb fifteen feet up the trunk, he finally replied, "I weren't sure it would work, but I figured I'd give it a try."

Will shook his head and shrugged. "Well, shinny back down. I brought you some company, and I'm plannin' to ride awhile before we stop for the night, so hurry up." He figured he had enough time to make it to Jim Little Eagle's cabin before darkness really set in. He was sure he could count on Jim for some help with his prisoners. Since he had brought only one set of handcuffs with him, he had to tie Lyla's hands with his rope. So he busied himself with getting her in the saddle to the accompaniment of little yelps of pain behind him as Ike descended the rough trunk of the pine. Having arrested the simple man before, Will was inclined not to be surprised by any hare-brained plan Ike came up with. Lyla, on the other hand, could not be taken lightly. She had already proven to be more dangerous.

The Chickasaw woman's attempt to shoot a lawman in order to free her lover was a notable boost to the slow-witted outlaw's confidence. "I knew you'd try to get me back, darlin'," he said when they were both in the saddle. "I'm sorry we wound up in this fix after you waited so long for me."

The stoic woman replied with nothing more than a grunt. It was Will's opinion that Lyla's decision to take a shot at him was not an act of devotion toward Ike. It was more an attempt to avoid growing old in her father's cabin. In view of her past indiscretions and unfortunate physical appearance, she was desperate to go with any male who would have her. In spite of what she had done, he felt sorry for her.

The sun was already about to drop below the far hills west of Atoka when Will and his prisoners entered the clearing on Muddy Boggy Creek where Jim Little Eagle had built his cabin. Will called out and identified himself before approaching the cabin. A moment later, Jim, carrying a lantern and his rifle, walked out of the barn. "That you, Will? I wondered who was coming to call this late in the day. Who's that with you?"

Will rode on in and reined Buster to a halt beside the Choctaw policeman. "I've got a couple of prisoners I'm transportin' to jail. Sorry to be ridin' in on you so late, but if you don't mind, I'll camp here on the creek tonight."

Jim walked back, holding his lantern up to get a better look at the prisoners. When he got to Lyla, he held the lantern up a little longer. Walking back beside Will's horse, he commented, "One of them is a woman. One of our people?"

"Chickasaw," Will replied. "I was thinkin' about turnin' her over to you, her being an Indian. Figured it was more under your jurisdiction. I'll take Ike back to Fort Smith for trial."

"What did she do?" Jim asked, and took a second look at the sullen woman.

"Not much, really," Will said. "Took a shot at me and that's really the only reason I arrested her." He went on then to tell Jim the whole story.

Jim turned his gaze back on Ike then. "So this is the man that stuck a .44 in Sam Barnet's face and rode off with twenty-two dollars."

"That's the man," Will replied. "Twenty-two dollars, huh? Is that all he got?"

They both looked at Ike then, and Jim said, "Yeah, Sam just gave him the little bit in the cash drawer. He said the safe was sitting there with the door open and about twenty-five hundred dollars in it, but your man was in a hurry to run." Ike hung his head, embarrassed upon hearing of his folly. Back to the other issue, Jim said he could put Lyla in jail, since there was no one presently occupying the small building that passed for the Atoka jail. She would be held there until the council could meet to decide her sentence. "Are you charging her with attempted murder?" Jim asked Will.

Lowering his voice to keep Ike and Lyla from hearing, Will said, "I really don't wanna charge her with anything. I'd just like you to keep her till I can get away from here in the mornin' and not worry about her maybe taking another shot at me. Keep her a day, then turn her loose and tell her to go on home."

Jim nodded slowly. "I can do that." He smiled and said, "You're getting a little softhearted. Maybe you've been in this business too long." That reminded him of another subject. "Ed Pine was over here a week ago. He said you were going to get married. Any truth to that?"

"That's a fact," Will answered. "I finally got up the nerve to ask her and damned if she didn't say she would."

"Good for you," Jim said, beaming at Will's sudden blush. "Mary will want to know this. She said you'd never get married. You're gone all the time. Not many women like that." When Will shrugged, Jim went on, "Maybe you hang up your guns and settle down on that ranch you own in Texas."

"Maybe. At least I'm thinkin' about it. I ain't even sure she'd like it there in Texas."

"When's the wedding?" Jim asked.

"To tell you the truth, I don't know. She and her mama are makin' a lotta fuss about planning a big weddin'. Her mama wants to have it around Christmas. I don't care, myself. I'd just as soon jump a broom and be done with it."

"Christmas?" Jim responded. "That's almost five months away."

"Yeah," Will acknowledged with a chuckle. "I think her mama's hopin' Sophie will change her mind before Christmas." He shrugged and said, "I'd best get my prisoners camped and comfortable. I'll bed 'em down in that same spot I used before."

"Who are you talking to out here?" The voice came from the cabin, followed a few seconds later by the appearance of Mary Light Walker. Seeing Will, she answered her own question. "I thought it must be you, Will, so I mixed up some more biscuits. I just put them in the oven. They oughta be ready by the time you set up your camp."

"Howdy, Mary," Will greeted her. "I apologize for

showin' up so late in the evenin'. I didn't expect to bother you with fixin' any food for me and my prisoners."

"You never were a good liar, Will Tanner," Mary replied. "Go ahead and take care of your prisoners. Hurry up, or those biscuits will be cold." As her husband had done, she took a second look at Lyla, but made no comment.

"We can lock the woman up in the smokehouse," Jim volunteered. Will had hoped he would. It would not be the first time they had used the smokehouse this way, and it would make it a lot easier on Will. It was a great deal more trouble to take care of a female prisoner, and even greater trouble to have to tend to a male and female. As they had done before, a blanket and a pallet were placed in the smokehouse for Lyla's comfort, as well as a bucket for her convenience. After she was locked inside the smokehouse, Will made his camp by the creek, secured Ike to a tree, and took care of the horses. Even though Will insisted he would take care of feeding his prisoners, Mary fixed extra ham and biscuits for them. She was happy to do it because, during the time she and Jim had known Will, they had always been the recipients of his generous sharing of any spoils confiscated as a result of arrests and captures.

After everyone had finished supper, Will said good night to his friends and returned to his camp and his prisoner. "I'm damn glad you showed up again," Ike greeted him when he returned. "I gotta get rid of that coffee I drank, and I can't do nothin' with my hands locked around this tree." After that was taken care of, Will sat him down at the tree again, locked his hands, and tied his feet around the tree as well.

When Jim Little Eagle got up the next morning, Will had already gone. He checked on his prisoner in the smokehouse and decided the Chickasaw woman had passed the night peacefully, for she was fast asleep. She was awake when he returned with Mary and her breakfast. "What will you do with me?" Lyla asked.

"Will said he wouldn't make any charges if you promise to go back home and behave yourself," Jim told her. She promptly agreed to do so, but Jim kept her in the smokehouse until afternoon before releasing her.

Chapter 2

As he had figured, it took three days to ride from Atoka to Fort Smith and Will rode straight to the courthouse with his prisoner. Ron Horner, the night jailer, met him at the jail under the courthouse. "Whatcha got there, Will?" Ron greeted him.

"Got another guest for your hotel," Will answered. "This is Mr. Ike Skinner. He's stayed here before. I hope he ain't too late for supper."

"He's just in time," Ron said. "They're just gettin' ready to serve it. I'll go ahead and check him in. What's he in for?"

"Robbery," Will answered. "He won't cause you any trouble. He ain't mean, he just makes some bad decisions." He stood there until Ron led Ike inside and closed the door behind him. He shook his head and sighed. He couldn't help feeling a measure of compassion for the simple soul who was Ike Skinner. *He's probably better off locked up*, he thought. Then he rode down to Vern Tuttle's stable to leave the horses, and he left his saddle and packsaddle there as well.

After a short conversation with Vern, he took his rifle and saddlebags and headed back to the courthouse to see if he could catch his boss before he went home for supper.

"You're just the man I want to see right now," U.S. Marshal Daniel Stone declared when Will walked into his office. "When did you get in?"

"About a half hour ago," Will said. "I brought Ike Skinner in."

"Good," Stone said, then quickly changed the subject, obviously not interested in details of the arrest of Ike. "I might need to send you out again right away, but I won't be sure till I hear something more from the marshal's office in Missouri. How soon can you be ready to ride? I know you just got in and you'd probably like to catch a few days in town."

"Well, I'd like to rest my horse," Will said. "In the mornin', I reckon."

Stone couldn't help but laugh. "That long, huh? Tell you what, come back tomorrow morning and maybe I'll know if we're gonna be called on to help the Missouri office out."

There were a lot of thoughts running through Will's mind as he walked toward Bennett House, as Ruth liked to call her boardinghouse. Most of these thoughts circled around Ruth's daughter, Sophie, and the fact that he never seemed to be in town for any length of time. He had not been around for any of the wedding plans, a fact that made him just as happy, but it seemed to irritate Sophie more and more. He had always thought that planning a wedding was usually the bride's job, with little or no help from the groom. He figured he was like most men, preferring to just have a preacher tie the knot and be done with it.

Walking past the Morning Glory Saloon, he paused and looked at his watch. They would most likely be finished with supper at the boardinghouse by now and probably cleaning up the dishes. If he went home now, he was sure Sophie would insist that he should eat, and he didn't want to cause her the trouble of fixing anything. He hesitated a moment longer, then decided to get something in the Morning Glory.

"Well, howdy, Will," Gus Johnson greeted him from behind the bar. "I see you're back in town."

"You don't miss a trick, do ya, Gus?" Will japed. "You think Mammy might have anything left for supper?"

"She usually does when she knows it's you that's wantin' it," a voice declared over his shoulder.

Recognizing the husky tone of Lucy Tyler, Will turned to say hello. "How you doin', Lucy?"

"I've been better," the prostitute replied. "Ain't seen you in a while. You been outta town, or have you just given up associatin' with the common folk?"

"I've been outta town," he answered.

"Will's wantin' some supper," Gus said, and winked at Lucy. "I'll go see." He walked over to the kitchen door and stood just outside it. "Hey, Mammy, some-body's wantin' some supper. Is it too late to get a plate?" He turned back toward Will and Lucy, a wide grin plastered across his face, and waited for the ex-pected response.

"Hell, yes, it's too damn late!" the scrawny little woman screamed back. "I'm already cleanin' up my kitchen." Gus remained by the door and waited, still grinning. After a long moment, another screech came from the kitchen. "Who is it wantin' to eat?"

"Will Tanner," Gus answered, trying to keep from chuckling. "I'll tell him it's too late." He walked back to the bar.

In a moment, Mammy appeared in the doorway and craned her skinny neck toward them to make sure it was Will. When she saw him, she stuck her lower lip out and blew a thin strand of gray hair from in front of her eyes. "I've still got some soup beans and a chunk of ham. There's a couple of biscuits to go with it. It'll keep you from starvin', I reckon."

"Yes, ma'am," Will said. "I surely would appreciate it."

When Mammy went back inside, Gus shook his head and marveled, "Ain't nobody else in this town Mammy would do that for. Beats all I've ever seen."

"Maybe that's the reason you don't ever wanna go upstairs with me," Lucy joked. "Maybe it ain't that little gal at the boardin'house who's got you buffaloed. Maybe all this time it was Mammy."

"Could be, at that," Will pretended to admit. "Most likely I remind her of her son, if she ever had one." He hesitated to continue with what he started to admit, but decided they would know sooner or later. "You might as well know, I'm supposed to get married around Christmastime."

They were both surprised, Lucy more so than Gus. "Well, I'll be damned . . ." she drew out. "That little gal at the boardin'house, right?" She didn't wait for Will to answer. "I knew that was bound to happen. Did you ask her, or was it her idea?"

"Of course I asked her," Will replied. "At least, I think I did." When confronted with the question, he wasn't sure now.

Lucy continued to stare at him in surprise, finding it hard to believe. She somehow never expected Will Tanner to get married. He seemed to have been bred a loner. Finally, she congratulated him and wished him a long and happy marriage. Then she returned to her teasing. "Christmas, huh? Well, I reckon me and Gus are gonna be invited to the wedding."

"Right now, I ain't sure *I'm* on the invitation list," Will said. The japing was cut short when Mammy came from the kitchen and placed a plate of food on one of the tables. Already sorry he had confessed to his impending trip to the altar, he quickly retreated to eat his supper. It failed to save him further embarrassment, however, for Lucy followed him to the table.

When she saw him place his saddlebags on a chair and prop his rifle against the wall before sitting down, it occurred to her that he was on his way home. It prompted her to ask to be sure. "Are you on your way home?" He nodded. "And you stopped here first?"

"I didn't wanna put her to any trouble," he explained.

"Well, she ain't likely to be very happy if she finds out you stopped at a saloon before you came home to her. I swear, Will, I'm tellin' you as a friend, you'd better eat that food quick and get your ass home. You gonna be in town for a while now?"

"I don't know for sure till I see my boss again in the

mornin'," he answered, choking his food down as fast as he could chew it.

Gus laughed when he heard Will's answer, and Lucy remarked, "Damn! You might be one helluva lawman, but you don't know the first thing about women."

"Well, it ain't like I've got a choice," Will said in his defense.

He paused at the gate in front of the rambling two-story house Ruth Bennett's late husband had built shortly before he died of consumption some twenty years ago. Two of Ruth's longtime borders were sitting on the porch, enjoying their usual after-supper smoke. "How do, Will?" Leonard Dickens greeted him. "Glad to see you got back all right again."

"You were gone for a good while," Ron Sample said. "You'd best hurry inside before the women clean up the kitchen."

"No hurry," Will replied. "I figured I was a little late, so I grabbed a bite at the Mornin' Glory on my way back."

"Just as well," Leonard said. "Margaret fixed her special chicken and dumplin's. I swear, that woman sure ruined a good chicken. She's a pretty good cook with most things, but she don't know a real dumplin' from a lump of clabber dough. My late wife made the best dumplin's I ever et."

Will opened the front door when Ron took his cue from Leonard and began a testimonial on his late grandmother's dumplings. Will found Sophie standing in the parlor, talking to her mother. "Will!" Sophie exclaimed, and moved quickly to greet him. He dropped his saddlebags and rifle when she stepped into his arms, ignoring his embarrassment when her mother witnessed her embrace. When she stepped back, she held him by his shoulders at arm's length as if to examine a wayward child. "No new wounds," she declared. "Thank goodness for that. You must be starving. I wish you could have gotten here when we had supper on the table, but I'll fix you something."

He took a moment to say hello to Ruth before telling Sophie it wasn't necessary. "I knew I was too late for supper, so I got somethin' at the Morning Glory on my way home."

"You stopped at a saloon before you came home?" Sophie responded. He realized then that it would have been best left unsaid. He should have listened to Lucy Tyler's comment. "Gone as long as you were, I would have thought you'd want to come to see me before anything else," Sophie started, then reconsidered. "But never mind, at least you're finally home. For a good while, I hope, because we've got a lot to discuss, a lot of planning for our wedding." She glanced at her mother, and Ruth nodded to confirm it.

That was not particularly good news to him, but he supposed he was going to have to get involved with the wedding plans, so he tried to put on a good face for his bride-to-be. "Let me take a few minutes to clean up a little bit, and we'll talk about it," he said.

"Well, I must say you look a little better," Sophie commented when Will walked into the kitchen to join her. "You were a little scruffy-looking when you came in the door. I wasn't sure that was you under all those whiskers and dirt."

He smiled and rubbed his clean-shaven chin thoughtfully before responding. "I reckon I did, at that, but a man doesn't get a chance to take a bath when he's transportin' a prisoner across Indian Territory." He pulled a chair back and sat down at the table, prompting her to get up and go quickly to get a cup of coffee for him.

"If you had come straight home to supper, instead of stopping at that broken-down saloon, you could have had a piece of apple pie with this coffee," she chided, "but it's all gone now."

"I know," he interrupted, "but I told you I didn't want to cause you any extra work." He had already been scolded for his stop in the saloon before coming home—he didn't need more chiding.

She was about to continue, but Ron Sample came into the kitchen at that moment. "Excuse me for interruptin', Will, but Jimmy Bradley's out there on the porch lookin' for you—says it's important."

Surprised, Will asked, "Did he say what it's about?" Jimmy was Clyde Bradley's son. Clyde was the owner of the Morning Glory Saloon, and Jimmy liked to hang around the saloon doing odd jobs for Gus Johnson. Will had just seen Jimmy sweeping the floor behind the bar when he had stopped in earlier.

"No, he didn't," Ron answered, "just said it was important."

Will looked apologetically at Sophie, who returned the look with one of exasperation. He shrugged as if helpless. "I'll go see what he wants. I'll be right back." He pushed his chair back and followed Ron to the front porch. Sophie sighed and put his saucer on top of his cup to keep the coffee from cooling too fast.

"Jimmy," Will said when he found him waiting by the bottom porch step. "What is it, boy? You lookin' for me?"

"Yes, sir," Jimmy replied, speaking almost in a whisper. "Gus sent me to get you. There's some trouble at the Morning Glory."

"What kinda trouble?" Will asked. Ron and Leonard Dickens, their conversation having stopped, leaned forward, straining to hear Jimmy's message.

"That feller, Maurice, he was there when you came by this evenin'." When this drew a blank expression from Will, Jimmy continued, "He was settin' at a table with Lucy when you came in."

"All right," Will replied. "What about him?"

"He's raisin' hell in the saloon, throwin' glasses at the wall and breakin' chairs and I don't know what all," Jimmy reported, his eyes getting wider by the moment. "He pulled his pistol and shot a hole in the front window."

"Gus sent you here?" Will asked. "Didn't he tell you to go to the sheriff's office?" He was somewhat puzzled. Gus would normally send for the sheriff and one of the sheriff's deputies would handle a rough-neck drunk.

"He said to go get you," Jimmy maintained firmly. "Maurice dragged Lucy upstairs and said he was gonna kill her. He hit her, hard, busted her lip pretty bad, said he was gonna beat her to death. Now he's holed up in her room with her and says he'll shoot anybody who tries to come in."

Will didn't have to be told why Gus sent for him,

then. This type of trouble in the city of Fort Smith was supposed to be handled by the Fort Smith sheriff's office. Sometimes, however, the sheriff, as well as his deputies, was satisfied to let the saloons take care of their altercations themselves. And this time, the life of Lucy Tyler was involved. Gus knew that Lucy was a friend of Will's and Will would come to her aid. "Tell Gus I'm on my way," he said to Jimmy, and went back to the kitchen to tell Sophie.

Reading the look of concern on his face, Sophie asked at once, "What's wrong?"

"There's been some trouble I've gotta take care of," Will answered.

"Right now?" she asked. "Where?"

"In town," he answered. "I hope I won't be long, but it's important. I'll see you when I get back." With no desire to give her any details, he turned then and hurried out the door.

"Will?" she called after him, at first baffled by his behavior. Seconds later, exasperated by the infuriating habit he had of darting in and out of her life, she spat, "Your damn coffee! It's getting cold!" Resisting the urge to throw the cup against the wall, she stood there until she heard his footsteps as he bounded down the back stairs. She ran to the kitchen window in time to see him run past outside. Seriously concerned now, she hurried out to the front porch, where Ron Sample and Leonard Dickens were still sitting. "What was that all about? Where's he going?" she demanded.

"Gone to the Mornin' Glory," Leonard replied. "There's a feller up there gone crazy drunk, threatenin' to shoot the place up. They sent for Will."

"The saloon?" Sophie exclaimed. "He's going to the

saloon to arrest a drunk? That's not Will's job! That's not the job of a U.S. Deputy Marshal."

"I expect that's right," Ron said, "but this is different. This feller has got Lucy Tyler locked up in the room with him, and he says he's gonna kill her."

Sophie was struck speechless. She knew who Lucy Tyler was, a common whore who preyed on the drunken drifters that frequented the Morning Glory Saloon. Gradually at first, but steadily picking up speed, the anger deep inside her began forcing its way to the surface of her emotions until she could no longer contain it. "Damn him!" she cursed. "He just left that hellhole of a saloon and now he's running back to save a whore!" She looked around at the two men in the rocking chairs, staring at her, and realized she had lost her temper, so she spun on her heel and went back in the house.

Ron looked at Leonard, his eyebrows raised, and shrugged. "I don't think she took that too well," he remarked.

"Didn't seem to," Leonard agreed.

Will covered the short distance to the Morning Glory at a trot. In his haste to respond, his rifle was the only weapon he'd taken. As he trotted, he checked to make sure the magazine was fully loaded. He stopped before the two swinging doors that Clyde Bradley had installed at the beginning of summer and peered over them before stepping inside. The barroom was empty of customers, all having fled when the shooting started. Only Gus Johnson remained and he stood behind the bar, his shotgun on the bar by his hand. Will didn't see Lucy or her captor, so he pushed on through the doors. Gus turned when he heard Will come in and came at once to meet him. "I'm sorry as I can be to bother you, Will, but that crazy fool is gonna kill Lucy. I'da sent Jimmy to fetch the sheriff, but he mighta sent one of those two deputies workin' for him, or he might notta sent nobody. I knew you'd come when you heard it was Lucy."

"Where are they?" Will asked. "Up in Lucy's room?"

"Yeah, he's got her up there and the door locked," Gus replied.

"Which room is it?" Will asked.

"I forgot, you ain't ever been up to Lucy's room with her." Remembering then, he said, "That was what she was always complainin' to you about." He paused for a brief moment until he saw Will's look of impatience. "Top of the stairs, first room on the right," he blurted. When Will started toward the stairs, Gus caught his arm to stop him. "There's somethin' else, Will. He said he's gonna kill her, but he said after he done for her, he was gonna kill you." That was a surprise, and Will had to ask why. "Lucy was settin' at the table with Maurice when you came in," Gus said. "When she saw you, she left him settin' there and went to say hello to you, so Maurice thinks he's got to kill you to make sure she don't run to you again."

"Why the hell didn't somebody explain it to him?" Will replied. "Lucy and I are just friends. Somebody coulda told him that."

"You ever try explainin' somethin' like that to a damn drunk?" Gus responded. "Especially when he thinks he's in love and you're standin' between him and his lady."

"I reckon you're right," Will said. "You don't think this fellow's just another loudmouth drunk with his whiskey doin' the talkin'?"

"I don't know for sure." Gus shook his head slowly as he thought about him. "He fetched Lucy a pretty stout fist in the mouth when she told him to go to hell. Then he pulls his handgun and starts shootin' the place up—ran all my customers out and shot a hole in the front window. I tell you, it's a wonder there ain't nobody got shot."

"And now he's locked himself up in Lucy's room," Will declared with a tired sigh. "I'll go upstairs and see if I can talk to him." He started up the steps, not certain what he could do to defuse the situation. If this Maurice fellow refused to open the door, he'd likely have to kick it in, and then he'd have to worry about what would happen to Lucy, once he did. Maurice might be the kind to take it out on Lucy, in the form of a bullet in the head.

When he reached the top of the stairs, he paused a moment to listen for any sounds coming from inside the room. All he could hear was a constant series of guttural mumbling, typical of a rambling drunk running his mouth. He decided that Maurice was in the bragging phase of his drunk, probably telling Lucy what a big man he was. This might be a good time to give him a chance to prove it to her, so he rapped sharply on the bedroom door. "All right, Maurice!" Will bellowed. "Let's see if you've got the guts to back up your big talk!" The rambling voice stopped and Will challenged again. "That's what I thought, all talk!"

In a few seconds, he heard a piece of furniture crash when it hit the floor, and the shuffling of unsteady boots on the other side of the door.

Will heard the bolt slide open on the door and it opened to reveal the unsteady form of Maurice Cowart, a six-gun in hand. He stood there for a fraction of a second, snarling his drunken defiance, before Will planted his fist on the bridge of his nose. Maurice went down like a felled tree, his head slamming against the edge of the bedside table he had knocked over on his way to the door. He was out cold, stopped so suddenly that he had not had the time to pull the trigger in reaction to the blow from Will's fist.

Will kicked the pistol that dropped from Maurice's hand across the floor before looking at Lucy, huddled in the corner of the room. Her mouth and nose were swollen and her clothes were torn from her captor's abusive attempts to conquer her. She didn't get up at once, just gazed at him until slowly, huge tears welled in her eyes. After a moment, she spoke when he walked over and extended his hand to help her up. "I'm glad he didn't get to see me cry," she said, defiantly. Then she looked up at Will. "I thought he was gonna kill me." She put her arms around him and gave him a tight squeeze, like a mother hugs her child. "Thanks, Will, thanks for coming."

He didn't know what to say, so he held her by the shoulders while he took a look at her damaged face. "We might better get Doc Peters to take a look at those bruises," he said. "First, I reckon I'd better take care of ol' Maurice, here, before he takes a notion to wake up."

"I don't know," Lucy said, already beginning to regain some of her confidence. "He went down pretty hard, and he cracked his head on my good side table. I was hopin' he was gonna talk himself to sleep before you came, 'cause he drank almost all of a quart of whiskey."

"I'll haul him outta here," Will said. He grabbed Maurice's boots and dragged him out the door into the hallway. "I swear, he weighs a ton." He dragged him to the top of the stairs and then down several steps before he managed to take his arms and, using the angle of the steps, pulled the limp body over to settle on his shoulder. Gus ran up the steps to help him turn around and steady him as he carried his burden downstairs. "I reckon that's his horse at the rail," Will said. "It was the only one there when I came in."

"Stop just a second," Gus said. "Lemme look in his pockets to see if he's got any money to pay for some of the damage he did."

"Well, hurry up," Will said. "He ain't gettin' any lighter."

He carried the unconscious man outside, and with Gus's help, plopped him across his saddle, just as Deputy Johnny Sikes walked up. Sikes watched silently until the body was resting on the horse. "Will," he said, and nodded. "A feller came in the office and said he thought there was some trouble down here."

"There was," Gus answered. "There ain't now."

"His name's Maurice Cowart," Will said, and told Sikes what had happened, what Maurice had done to Lucy, and the damage he had done to the saloon. "So I reckon you might wanna put him in your jail for a while till he sobers up. Then you might wanna warn him not to come near the Mornin' Glory or Lucy Tyler again."

"I expect so," Johnny replied. "I'll take care of him, and much obliged."

Gus stood with Will for a few moments, watching Johnny untie Maurice's reins from the rail and lead the horse back up the street toward the jail. Then they went back inside to help Lucy. "I'll walk you down to Doc Peters's to let him take a look at you," Will offered when he saw Mammy cleaning the blood from Lucy's face.

"No need for that," Lucy said. "Mammy's took care of me before. This ain't the first time I've been punched by a loudmouth drunk, besides, Doc Peters has already gone home by now."

"Suit yourself," Will said. "You're in pretty good hands with Mammy, especially if she's half as good a doctor as she is a cook," he added, primarily to please Mammy. The only acknowledgment he received from the scrawny little woman was a snort of indifference. "I reckon I'll say good evenin', then." He nodded to Gus, then looked at Lucy again when she called his name.

"Thank you again, Will," she said. "When you come back, I'll owe you a drink, or supper. And anything else you might want," she added wistfully.

"'Preciate it, Lucy, but you don't owe me anything. I'm just glad I could help a friend."

He found Sophie waiting for him in the parlor when he returned and he knew without asking that he was in trouble. The frown she greeted him with seemed to be permanently etched on her face. "Trouble at the

Mornin' Glory," he offered weakly. "I don't know why Gus didn't call the sheriff instead of me." She said nothing, but continued to stare at him with eyes as cold as ice. "Fellow named Maurice," he continued bravely, "shot a hole in the window and mighta killed somebody, if he wasn't stopped. Had to put him in jail—got back as soon as I could."

When he paused, finished with his explanation, she continued to stare icily at him for a long moment before asking, "Is Lucy Tyler all right?"

"What? Oh . . . yeah, she's all right, got roughed up a little, but she's all right." He had hoped Lucy's name wouldn't come up, but evidently Ron or Leonard had told Sophie what they had overheard on the porch. He would have preferred that she not know that he had been summoned primarily because Lucy was in danger, but now that he was facing her cold accusation, he decided it was time to stop acting like he was guilty of something. "Look, Sophie, Lucy Tyler's a friend of mine, that's all. I ain't one of her customers, I never have been. I've also got other friends that are on the wrong side of the law." Oscar Moon came to mind. "But they ain't got nothin' to do with you and me, and I sure as hell ain't had nothin' to do with any woman but you. The sooner you accept that, the sooner you'll keep thoughts like that outta your pretty head."

She continued to look him hard in the eye, until she had to smile. It was the first time he had shown any side of himself other than an innocent confusion in her presence. "All right," she said, "I accept it." She took his hand then and led him to the sofa. "I just hope you're going to be home for a while this time."

"I hope so, too," he said. "I reckon I'll find out

when I report in to Dan in the mornin'." She raised an eyebrow at the remark, but gave him a big smile. The rest of his evening was spent listening to the plans she had for their wedding. When they finally said good night, he was finding it hard to believe it was going to happen to him. He could only imagine the look on Miss Jean Hightower's face when she heard the news. Will could imagine it would seem to her like her son was taking a wife. As for Shorty and the boys at the J-Bar-J in Texas, they wouldn't believe it until he showed up with Sophie on a lead rope.

Connect with Us

Visit us online at
KensingtonBooks.com
to read more from your favorite authors, see books
by series, view reading group guides, and more.

Join us on social media

for sneak peeks, chances to win books and prize packs,
and to share your thoughts with other readers.

facebook.com/kensingtonpublishing
twitter.com/kensingtonbooks

Tell us what you think!

To share your thoughts, submit a review,
or sign up for our eNewsletters, please visit:
KensingtonBooks.com/TellUs.